OPERATION
KING COBRA

Steve Doherty

OPERATION
KING COBRA

STEVE DOHERTY

TATE PUBLISHING
AND ENTERPRISES, LLC

Published by Tate Publishing & Enterprises, LLC
127 E. Trade Center Terrace | Mustang, Oklahoma 73064 USA
1.888.361.9473 | www.tatepublishing.com

Tate Publishing is committed to excellence in the publishing industry. The company reflects the philosophy established by the founders, based on Psalm 68:11,
"The Lord gave the word and great was the company of those who published it."

Book design copyright © 2013 by Tate Publishing, LLC. All rights reserved.
Cover design by Allen Jomoc
Interior design by Mary Jean Archival
Illustration by Rachael Polack

Published in the United States of America
ISBN: 978-1-62746-629-5
1. Fiction / Historical
2. Fiction / War & Military
13.08.13

This book is dedicated to the men and women of the Allied intelligence services who fought in World War Two.

CHAPTER 1

ALGIERS, ALGERIA

The pilot of the Douglas C-47 Skytrain held his feet tightly on the aircraft brakes at the end of the runway. He checked the engine head temperatures and the vacuum pressure on the two engines. Once he was satisfied, he pushed both throttles forward and felt the vibrations move up his leg as the two Pratt & Whitney 1,200-horsepower engines roared to life. When the pilot released the brakes, the aircraft slowly moved down the runway. The C-47 lifted off at ninety knots airspeed. At two hundred feet altitude, the copilot retracted the gear and announced that the flaps were retracted. At five hundred feet, the pilot turned north, headed out over the Mediterranean, and leveled off at two thousand feet. The American Counter Intelligence Corps (CIC) agent was sitting quietly on the jump seat behind the pilots. He was now on his way to Anzio; to find and possibly kill his best friend.

This particular C-47 Skytrain had been specifically made for the British Intelligence Special Operations Executive (SOE). It had a reinforced cargo floor, a large cargo door, and a hoist attachment for lifting cargo on its starboard side. It was a multipurpose C-47 aircraft and could carry cargo, commandos, and even tow a glider. In addition to the glider towing and release mechanism, this particular Skytrain had also been modified with the Model 80 glider pickup system, which included winch, cable, and arrestor hook. Although it wouldn't be used for any snatch and grabs today, it was one of the many capabilities that the SOE had at their disposal in the wartime clandestine business. Nevertheless, the agent silently wished that they would be extracting his best friend.

The Italian Resistance leader, Marcel, sat in one of the canvas fold-down seats in the aft section of the aircraft. *It was going to be an uncomfortable ride*, he thought, *with this parachutes on*. This would be his fifteenth jump from an Allied aircraft since the war started, and he still wasn't comfortable with jumping, especially at night.

After they leveled off, the American agent moved to the aft of the aircraft. But because of the noise, he chose not to talk. It did give him time to think and reflect on the last forty-eight hours.

The agent had spent thirty hours in a B-24 Liberator, flying from Boling Field in Washington, DC, to Algiers, Algeria. At each of the three in between stops at St. John's, Newfoundland; Santa Maria, Azores; and Porto, Portugal, the flight crew took three hours to refuel, get a weather update, stretch their legs, and take care of bodily functions.

The B-24 Liberator was not a pressurized aircraft because of its design. There was an especially large gap between the tail turret and the fuselage that allowed the turret to rotate freely during combat. This gap also let two hundred-knot winds enter the fuselage. Because of this, the pilots flew the B-24 at thirteen thousand feet to avoid having to breathe from the oxygen system during the flight. Even with the waist gunner port windows in place, the temperature in the unpressurized fuselage fell as low as -55°F.

Prior to entering the B-24, the bomber crew had provided him with cold weather flight gear. After he had donned the Shearling leather flight pants, Shearling boots, Shearling leather flight jacket, a leather flight helmet with built-in headphones, flight goggles, throat mike, oxygen mask, Mae West yellow life jacket, parachute, and Shearling leather gunner gloves, he felt and looked like a large stuffed teddy bear. The Shearling clothing was constructed from thick, plush American sheepskin pelts, which provided the required warmth and protection from the extreme temperatures specified by the US Army Air Corps. Despite the cold weather gear, he was still uncomfortably cold throughout the flight. It occurred to him that the Shearling designers probably never flew in the B-24 with the clothes that they designed.

During the approach to Algiers, the CIC agent sat on the jump seat. He watched closely as the Liberator pilot pulled back gently on the yoke, flared the aircraft close to the landing threshold, and pulled the throttles to idle after it touched down on the Army Air Corps airfield.

At the end of the aircraft's touchdown roll, a green army "Follow Me" truck appeared two hundred feet in front of the Liberator. The pilot taxied the aircraft and followed the truck to a parking spot, where an army Air Corps private was standing with two brightly painted orange sticks in his hands. When the aircraft was in the right parking position, he crossed the sticks above his head signaling the pilot to stop and cut engines.

As the engines were shutting down, the crew chief on the ground directed his men to put the wheel chocks in place and open the entry hatch on the underside of the aircraft.

Before the landing, one of the gunners had helped him remove the cold weather flight gear. He was tired and sore from the long trip and in dire need of a pisser, and a good cup of coffee. After he put on his jungle warfare boots, he moved to the exit and stepped backwards down the metal steps. As he placed his feet on the airdrome tarmac, he had to stoop to avoid hitting his head on the aircraft's undercarriage. The American agent was the only person on the tarmac wearing civilian clothes. When he stepped away from the B-24, he arched upwards and stretched his back, reached down and touched his toes, and then stood up. He was a tall, well built, and ruggedly handsome midwesterner named Jonathan Wilson Preston.

Twenty yards from the aircraft, he noticed a parked Willys Jeep with a .30-caliber machine gun poised on its overhead gun mount. The jeep's windshield was folded down, and a very anxious-looking US Army lieutenant was standing beside it.

The lieutenant moved straight toward Jon, stopped four feet away, and saluted. "Sir, I'm Lieutenant Scott Bayless. I'm here to take you to the Office of Strategic Services (OSS) headquarters. And before you ask, sir, Colonel Farrington, our CO, described you and said that you would be the only civilian passenger on the flight." Jon had met Colonel Farrington during his guerilla warfare training in the mountains of Virginia over a year ago.

The lieutenant paused to catch his breath then said, "Let me grab your bags, sir. We can stop and get you some chow before you meet with the colonel."

Jon was impressed with the lieutenant and the courtesy being extended by Colonel Farrington. It probably meant that the colonel wanted something from him.

"Thank you, Lieutenant. That sounds fine. After I eat, can I check into my quarters? I'd like to take a shower and change my clothes before I meet the colonel," Jon stated.

"Yes, sir!" shouted Lieutenant Bayless, struggling to be heard over the engine noise from a taxiing aircraft as he put the last of Jon's three bags in the jeep.

After eating at the Officer's Club, Jon checked into his quarters and took a shower. He pulled a fresh set of khaki pants and a plain white cotton shirt from one of his three suitcases. Nothing he brought looked at all military. In fact, he had all his trousers and shirts specifically tailored so he would look more like a businessman. He deliberately intended not to look military because he planned on returning to Columbus, Ohio, alive and preferably unharmed after the war. In the clandestine business, his instructors told him, "Sometimes it's the little insignificant things that blow your cover." They even had him grow his hair longer before he left the states.

He left his temporary quarters refreshed but tired. Lieutenant Bayless was leaning casually against the Willys Jeep, smoking a cigarette. As soon as he saw Jon exit the building, he put out the cigarette, field stripped the tobacco spilling it on the ground, and stuffed the remaining cigarette paper into his pocket.

This guy, Jon thought, *was the poster soldier's poster soldier. He must be a West Point graduate.*" After ten minutes and a dusty ride across the desert base, they arrived at the OSS headquarters for the North African theater.

The OSS commander, Colonel William Farrington, was built like a tank. He was a thick, barrel-chested man of medium height, a square face with a thick Roman nose, graying black hair, and a commanding presence. Jon estimated that he was somewhere in his late forties. He also noticed that he still wore his West Point ring on his right hand.

The colonel shook Jon's hand and invited him to sit in a wooden chair with arms and seat made of an ugly brown tapestry. He had noticed the same style in his quarters.

"Agent Preston, it's good to see you again, welcome to Algeria. I hate to keep you from your quarters and the rest you need, but I have an urgent request that cannot wait," Colonel Farrington stated.

Jon only nodded, which encouraged the colonel to continue. Colonel Farrington opened a map that had been lying on his desk and turned it so Jon could see it.

The colonel explained that on January 22, the Allies commenced Operation Shingle, the invasion and establishment of a beachhead on the west coast of Italy, forty miles south of Rome. The US Fifth Army Sixth Corps, under the command of General John Lucas, went ashore along a fifteen-mile stretch of Italian beach near a resort town called Anzio.

Ten days before the invasion, the Allies inserted an OSS agent into the area to gather intelligence on the German positions and troop strengths.

"He was supposed to begin transmitting his reports five days before the invasion. However, we didn't hear from him until the evening after the Allied landings," Colonel Farrington said.

By now Jon began to form a picture of what they might be asking him to do. He said nothing and put a puzzled look on his face.

"The reason we are discussing this with you," Colonel Farrington said, "is because we understand that you went to high school and college with the OSS agent in Columbus, Ohio. His name is Sean Patrick O'Brien."

When Jon didn't say anything, the colonel continued. "O'Brien didn't transmit his reports as he was scheduled to do. Therefore, we have to assume that he has been captured by the Germans and is being coerced into transmitting false intelligence reports. We want you to go to Anzio and find out. If he's been captured or killed, we need to know. You're the only one who can identify him."

"Sir, I'm strictly a special mission agent. Any mission I undertake is supposed to be sanctioned by G-2 and the orders delivered to me by one of six colonels that I met before deploying," Jon said.

"I fully understand, Agent Preston. Here is a message we received from the army chief of staff authorizing the deviation from your orders," Colonel Farrington remarked.

Jon read the classified message with the authorization from General George C. Marshal. Jon's only comment was, "Well, Colonel, this is what I'm here for. When do I go in, sir?"

Colonel Farrington turned and shouted for his first sergeant to bring in Mr. Laurent. As he walked through the door, Colonel Farrington said, "Marcel is a member of the Italian Resistance and he'll be going in with you. He's from the Anzio area and knows it extremely well."

"Glad to meet you, Agent Preston," Marcel said, extending his hand.

"Just call me Jon," Agent Preston stated.

"You'll leave with him for Tunis at 2000 hours. At Tunis, you will be briefed by Major Holcombe, the operations officer of the SOE detachment. One of their special aircrafts will be flying you two into a drop zone near Anzio. You will be outfitted with special SOE clothing. Jon, your attire will be returned to my detachment. The SOE folks will answer any further questions you might have. In the mean time, you can study the operational folder and latest reports from Anzio. And since you're headed into the China-Burma-India (CBI) theater, there's a second folder with the latest information on Burma and India and some very interesting intercepts on Japanese troop movements. It will take you several hours to go through the reports. After you finish, Lieutenant Bayless will take you all to dinner and then to Base Operations. Good luck, gentlemen," Colonel Farrington concluded.

Five hours later, Colonel Farrington walked Jon and Marcel through the headquarters office and outside to the waiting Willys Jeep, where Lieutenant Bayless was waiting. Colonel Farrington reminded them that if they needed anything, the lieutenant would take care of it for them. Jon noticed that it was dusk as he moved towards the Jeep.

"I picked up your suitcases and checked you out of your quarters, sir," Lieutenant Bayless said as they got into the jeep. "Tonight is prime rib night at the Officer's Club. It's usually pretty good."

After dinner, Lieutenant Bayless dropped Jon and Marcel off at Base Operations, where they would meet up with the flight crew. An hour and a half later, they were donning much the same cold weather gear that he had in the B-24 Liberator and were climbing into a British Lancaster.

The Lancaster was a four-engine heavy bomber built by Avro for the British Royal Air Force (RAF). In addition to its role as a bomber, it was used quite extensively by the British SOE for ferrying commandos and special mission agents. This Lancaster was currently assigned to the SOE detachment in Tunis.

After takeoff, Jon sat in what quiet he could muster in his mind inside the noisy Lancaster and almost immediately fell asleep. He awoke only when Marcel shook him. By then the Lancaster was already parked, the wheels chocked, and engines were being shut down.

CHAPTER 2

TUNIS, TUNISIA

When they landed in Tunis, it was 2300 hours. *It's too late to do anything tonight*, Jon thought as he worked his way out of the cold weather flight gear. But as he exited the aircraft, he was met by a rather stiff sergeant major of the Royal Marines. The look on the sergeant's face told Jon that the man was definitely on a mission, and it promised to be a long night.

"Agent Preston, Mr. Laurent, if you all would follow me, please," the sergeant major bellowed. "Major Holcombe is waiting to brief you on your mission. We have a change of clothes and your flight gear in the hanger on your left."

It was a good thing I got some sleep on the flight, Jon thought. A guy could get a little worn out with all this urgency.

The sergeant major walked Jon and Marcel into the hangar. A rather large Royal Marine corporal, with a Mark II Sten submachine gun held across his chest, was guarding a door some twenty yards away.

As they approached the door, the guard opened it and stepped aside as the sergeant major, Jon, and Marcel entered. Standing behind a metal desk was a tired-looking British officer. The sergeant major stopped in front of the desk, saluted crisply, and said rather loudly, "Sir, Agent Preston and Mr. Laurent." He then dropped his arm to his side, turned on his left heel, and left the room.

"Agent Preston," the major said extending his hand to Jon and nodding at Marcel, "I'm Major Timothy Holcombe. I'm the SOE detachment operations officer. Our commander is in the infirmary, so I'll be briefing you on your mission later tonight into Anzio."

Jon nodded as he shook the major's hand and said, "Everyone calls me Jon, short for Jonathan."

The major took a deep breath then continued, "Alright, Jon, sorry about the rush, but we are timing your insertion to coincide with a bombing raid early in the morning."

The major gave them a brief situation report. At dawn on January 22, the Allied Sixth Corps landed at Anzio. The British landed on a beach just north of Anzio, and the Americans landed on the beach in town and a beach south of an adjacent town called Nettuno. In all, forty-six thousand Allied combat troops along with three thousand vehicles and supplies and logistics troops occupied the beachhead from six miles north to eight miles south of Anzio. The landing was successful and had apparently caught the Germans totally by surprise. There was hardly any resistance during the initial landings.

"The Sixth Corps headquarters expected to receive reports from Agent O'Brien beginning five days before the landings. However, for whatever reason, O'Brien never started transmitting until the evening after the allies landed. Sixth Corps believes that Agent O'Brien may have been captured and coerced into transmitting false reports. The information that they had received from O'Brien was rather remarkable. It's told us that there were very few German units beyond the beachhead. Our analysts believe the Germans are trying to entice us to move farther inland into a trap," Major Holcombe stated.

Because of bad weather, the major explained, aerial reconnaissance has not been able to provide them with an updated picture of the German strength around Anzio. The last photoreconnaissance was three days before the landings, and it was not conclusive. Although, they did have reliable information that the Germans were sending troops from Rome and from Pescara on the Adriatic Coast.

He further explained that in a little over three hours, two groups of B-24 Liberators from the 324th Bombardment Squadron in Oran would be taking off to conduct raids on both reinforcement columns.

"Our SOE Flight Squadron has a C-47 that we will be using to fly you and Marcel into the insertion area. At the same time the C-47 is inserting you, both bomber groups will be flying slightly south of Anzio at ten thousand feet. After crossing Anzio, one group will head north and the other east to strike the German reinforcement columns. This should provide a big enough distraction for your C-47 to get in and out safely. The C-47 route takes you six miles away from the German anti-aircraft batteries that we've identified. It should provide you all with a safe insertion. Plus, two Italian Resistance fighters have been tasked to meet up with you after you land," Major Holcombe said.

The timing of their arrival was critical because it would be dark when they make their jump. They would be jumping from five hundred feet above the ground into an area two miles southeast of a small town called Valmontone. The area around Valmontone was composed of rolling hills with vineyards and farmland. The latest information from the Italian Resistance indicated that there were no German patrols in the area of their drop zone. However, that might change by the time they reached Valmontone.

O'Brien had been inserted into Valmontone because Highway 6 runs north to south through the town. It's the major highway for reinforcements coming from Rome and from the German southern front. Their insertion point was a small valley to the southeast of their destination.

"The terrain in this area is mostly rolling hills covered with vineyards, farmhouses, and occasional copse of woods. The closer you get to Valmontone, the more woods you will find. Marcel grew up on a farm near Valmontone and will provide you more details as you study the maps of the area," Major Holcombe stated.

"Do you have any intel from local resistance groups that might backup the reports already sent from O'Brien?" Jon asked.

"Sixth Corps put a blackout on all resistance organization communications the day prior to the landing. It wasn't lifted until this morning. And no, we do not have any new information. Our resistance reports prior to the invasion claim that there are two German divisions in the Anzio area. But we have yet to confirm that by aerial reconnaissance," Major Holcombe stated.

After no other questions, the major continued with his briefing. "You will also be taking an SOE miniaturized Paraset wireless radio with you, which both you and Marcel have been trained to use. Once you make contact or determine O'Brien's status, you will need to send us one of four messages in standard Morse code. The messages, derived from your American baseball terms, will be Green Sox, if he is okay; Red Sox, if you determine he has been captured; Black Sox, if he is dead; and Yellow Sox, if he is injured. You will also be carrying a field first aid kit just in case you need it. You will leave the radio with the resistant contacts that will meet you," Major Holcombe said.

The major handed Jon a sheet of paper and continued. "These are the primary and backup frequencies you will be transmitting on. Please memorize them before you leave this room, and familiarize yourself with the map of Anzio and Valmontone. Marcel is a native of Valmontone, and as you, Yanks, like to say, 'knows it like the back of his hand.' He can answer any questions you have," Major Holcombe remarked.

The major walked around his desk, went to the door, opened it, and called for the sergeant major to bring in the sandwiches and coffee for Agent Preston and Mr. Laurent.

Over the next two hours, Jon memorized the radio frequencies and committed the Anzio and Valmontone map to memory. Marcel pointed out the approximate location of the farm they would be heading to and provided further insight to the valleys and ravines they would be traversing on their way to the farmhouse. Once Jon finished with his study, he ate several sandwiches and drank two cups of coffee.

When Major Holcombe reentered the room, Jon stood up. "Major, what is my mission once I find Agent O'Brien?" Jon asked.

"Once you have found O'Brien and transmitted his status, we would like to get you to the closest Allied occupied area called Peter Beach; it's where the British First Division is positioned. Hopefully, this can be done before the Germans begin any major counterattacks. From Peter Beach, you will make your way into Anzio, and contact either the OSS or CIC detachment commander. They will make the arrangements for a boat to take you to a PBY that will be brought in for your flight back to Algiers. Your army chief of staff communicated the urgency to get you to the CBI theater, so we won't delay your stay," Major Holcombe said.

"Should I bring Agent O'Brien and Marcel with me to Peter Beach?" Jon asked.

"That will depend on O'Brien's superiors. If you do find him, he can contact Sixth Corps headquarters and request further orders. Marcel will be staying behind to coordinate the resistance campaign," Major Holcombe remarked.

"What should we do if one of us is injured?" Jon asked.

"If you are injured, Marcel will try to get you back to Allied lines. If Marcel is injured you will help him get back to our lines for medical attention. You will undoubtedly be challenged by the Allied troops when you make contact. When that happens, your only reply to whatever the challenge question might be is April 15, 1912," Major Holcombe remarked.

"The day the *Titanic* sunk?" Jon asked.

"That is correct, Agent Preston. But, no matter what challenge question you are asked the reply is still April 15, 1912. The allied forces that you make initial contact with will probably place you under arrest. Since you will not be carrying any identification, you need to tell them to contact the OSS and CIC detachment commanders for verification of who you are," Major Holcombe said.

Jon thanked the major and continued his study of the maps of Anzio and Valmontone. Marcel pinpointed the location of the farmhouse they would be looking for.

Jon knew from his briefing in Algiers that the Allies had expected major resistance when they landed. But he hoped that the reports that O'Brien had transmitted were the real story. And although Mr. Kilroy was always rising his ugly head when you least expected it, Jon was confident that O'Brien was alive. He was a glass-half-full type and expected to find O'Brien alive and well.

The major asked Jon if he had any other questions, but Jon did not. Eventually, the sergeant major entered the room and nodded to the major.

"It's time to get your jump gear on. The sergeant major will escort you to where the SOE flight team is waiting. Good luck, gentlemen," Major Holcombe concluded.

Jon shook the major's hand, said thanks, and left with the sergeant major and Marcel. The SOE flight team was waiting in another part of the large hangar. When Jon entered the preparation room he was given a pair of black Italian pants, a stained white shirt, and a heavy Italian overcoat to put on. Over the overcoat, he inserted himself into a large black jump suit. Finally, he was given a pair of black lightweight leather gloves, and an old pair of black lace boots. After he finished changing into his new clothes, the crew blackened his face, neck, and hands. The last item of clothing they gave him was a black knit cap.

"Gee, regular commando stuff. Will you be packing and sending my clothes to Algiers?" John asked.

"We'll give them to the sergeant major. He'll see to it that they make it back to Algiers. We have an aircraft that makes the run every day," the flight team leader said.

Next they handed him a loaded Colt .45-caliber automatic pistol with ten extra clips. The Colt .45 was in a black webbed holster and was placed around this waist. The extra clips were secured in his jacket pocket. Then they fitted him with a belly pack with a first aid kit and a very small fold-over commando shovel. Finally, they helped him into his parachute.

As they fitted the parachute on him, the SOE flight team leader said, "Since it will be dark when you jump, sir, you won't need to look up to see if your chute is open. One, it's black as hell, so you won't be able to see it; and two, dropping at twenty feet per second you will only have about sixteen seconds before you hit the ground. And if the chute doesn't open, well, sir, you won't know it until you see St. Peter at the pearly gates."

Jon just smiled and said, "Thanks for the pep talk."

Next, they attached a Sten Mark II submachine gun and a webbed bandolier with long pockets filled with Sten magazines. The Sten was a simple design for an automatic weapon. It was manufactured from stamped metal components that required very little welding, which in turn required only a minimum amount of machining. This made it a more reliable weapon. It had a collapsible stock and a thirty-two round detachable side-mounted magazine filled with nine-millimeter bullets. It was an ideal weapon for insurgency operations; light and compact.

"You wouldn't happen to have a Thompson, would you?" Jon asked. "I would like a little more firepower."

"Next week we'll get a shipment of thirty Thompsons, but we don't have any today," the flight team leader said. Then he mounted the Sten on him so it would be easily accessible and detachable once he landed.

After Jon's parachute had been adjusted, the SOE flight team leader provided a final inspection. He adjusted the harness for an even tighter fit, after which, Jon thought that one of his nuts had been crushed, and pronounced, "Good to go, sir. Your ride is outside the hangar."

Jon and Marcel, in an exaggerated waddle, exited the room together and walked toward the hangar doors, stopping every so often to adjust the straps on either side of their crotch. Outside, a Willys Jeep was waiting with the Royal Marine sergeant major as its driver.

Four minutes later, they pulled up beside a dull black C-47 cargo plane with its starboard engine already started. Jon exited the jeep, saluted the sergeant major, and made his way to the entry hatch. He climbed the portable metal stairs behind Marcel into the waiting aircraft. The jumpmaster pulled the hatch shut and locked it as the pilot started the port engine.

CHAPTER 3

VALMONTONE, ITALY

A heavy jolt of the aircraft, from flying into an air pocket, brought Jon back from his reflections and to the mission at-hand. They were cruising at 160 knots airspeed. It would take the C-47 over three and one half hours to get to their insertion point. Although the straight-line path from Tunis to Anzio was six hundred miles, the aircraft would not fly in a straight line. It would aim thirty miles west and ten miles north of Anzio before turning southeast on its final leg to Valmontone. Because of the parachute, Jon didn't move around the interior of the fuselage, instead, he nestled on his bench seat and tried to relax. Sleep was not an option—he was too keyed up.

They had been flying for three hours. The radio operator came back and gave Jon and Marcel a thirty-minute notice. Jon felt the aircraft start a slow descent and turn to the southeast leveling at one thousand feet above the Mediterranean Sea. Flying at one thousand feet would give the aircraft five hundred feet clearance above the ground for their jump. At ten minutes out, the pilot turned on a single red interior light near the rear portside fuselage door. The jumpmaster then stood up and opened the door. Jon and Marcel stood up and in the dim red light inspected each other's parachute harness. They gave each other a thumbs-up signal, implying everything was good to go.

At five minutes out, the small red interior light started blinking. Marcel attached his static line to a cable that stretched the length of the fuselage to the forward part of the open door frame. Jon stepped behind Marcel and attached his static line to the same cable. When the green light came on, Marcel jumped out the door followed closely by Jon.

It seemed like it happened too quickly for Jon, but he remembered to tuck his knees together and roll when he hit the ground. He immediately jumped up, detached the chute chord mechanism, and eased out of his parachute harness. He then released the Sten submachine gun, extracted one of the magazines from the bandolier, and inserted it into the side-mounted magazine slot. Next, he took off the black jumpsuit, gathered his parachute, dug a hole with his miniature shovel; and buried the chute, harness, and jumpsuit. By the time he stood up, Marcel was at his side indicating it was time to move out.

According to Major Holcombe, the Allied forces had moved inland only seven miles before stopping and digging in to secure their positions. Valmontone was twenty miles from the Anzio beachhead and not yet in the combat zone; but it probably would be, when the German reinforcements arrived. He hoped that the air assault on the German reinforcements would destroy or at least delay them until his mission was complete. He couldn't be more wrong.

The Germans had moved fast in the first two days after the landings. They had created a twelve-mile perimeter around the Anzio area with six airborne divisions totaling to forty thousand troops. The majority of the Germans were six miles west of Valmontone. The three reinforcement divisions were due to arrive later tonight. If they made it through the Allied bombing, it would give the German Fourteenth Army at least seventy thousand troops around Anzio with more on the way, including the Twenty-sixth Panzer Division from the southern front.

Shortly after setting out to Valmontone and the farmhouse, Marcel and Jon were met by two Italian Resistance fighters. One was apparently a good friend of Marcel's and gave him the bad news on the troop strengths that the Germans had achieved. When Marcel translated it into English, Jon was stunned.

"Thank God we have fifty thousand men on the beachhead," Jon said.

A light wind began to blow, adding to the existing chill. One of the resistance fighters guided the group through a mile and a half of ravines and vineyards towards their destination.

The most dangerous times in war, they taught Jon at Fort Ritchie, were dawn and dusk. To Jon, the bushes and grapevines began looking like enemy soldiers hunkered down and ready to spring on him. His imagination could be as dangerous as the Germans, if he were to fall victim to it.

Jon and Marcel spoke quietly as they paused in a shallow ravine a half mile from their destination. Marcel told him that he had grown up on a farm outside of Valmontone. After he finished his schooling, his parents moved to Naples, abandoning the farmhouse, except on holidays, when the family would return and visit relatives. His older brother, who lived in town, worked the vineyard. His parents' farmhouse was the destination where they would hopefully locate O'Brien.

Marcel took the lead for the approach to the farmhouse; he was being extremely careful. There were several barns and a couple small outbuildings that Jon thought he saw the outlines of. Ten minutes later, they had successfully negotiated the vineyard, and they came up behind a four-foot rock wall sixty feet behind the south side of the house.

Farther to the west, Jon heard intermittent sounds and flashes of light from artillery fire. He thought that the Allies might be advancing on Cisterna, which was ten miles to the northeast of Anzio. Hopefully, the allies would break through the German lines and begin their advance toward Rome. He would soon learn that the Germans had begun a major counter-attack.

Marcel told everyone to wait behind the wall while he approached the house. Jon and the two resistant fighters took up defensive positions to cover Marcel as well as their rear. Marcel then crouch-walked the last twenty yards with his head constantly moving to the left and right looking for anything unusual or threatening. He finally skirted around what looked like an outhouse and dashed the last ten yards to the farmhouse.

When Marcel approached one of the rear doors, he cautiously ran his finger around the edges of the screen door. Near the bottom, he found the trip wire he was looking for attached to a packet of plastic explosives. The small canvas pouch contained a quarter-pound of explosives impregnated with ball bearings. It was a particularly nasty device made specifically for the OSS. After he disarmed the charge, he opened the screen and interior doors and entered the house.

The night was gone, and the rising sun was creating a cool fog that hung low to the Italian landscape. It was overcast but still light enough to see Marcel enter one of the two back doors. When it got lighter, Jon saw that the house wasn't just a farmhouse. It was a large two-story Tuscan-Italian villa. Its walls were made with native stone, and there was an outside staircase going to a second story covered patio. The patio was held up by three-arched stone walls.

Jon's only thought was, *I sure hope it survives the war.*

Ten minutes later, Marcel returned and motioned for Jon to come with him. He directed the two resistance fighters to stand guard around the farm. Marcel and Jon walked silently and quickly to the back of the house.

They entered through the same door Marcel had entered initially. Once inside, Marcel took Jon up to the third floor attic. Sitting in a corner tapping out Morse code on an SSTR-1 miniature radio, was his longtime friend and classmate, Sean Patrick O'Brien.

Sean waved at Jon and motioned for him to have a seat in the sparsely furnished attic. After Sean finished his transmission, he took off his headset, stood up, and turned back to Jon.

"Jon, how the hell are you? It's been a while," O'Brien said.

Jon gave him his best smile and eagerly shook his outstretched hand and hugged him.

"It's been a long time, Sean. Good to see you," Jon said

"So, what are you doing in Anzio?" O'Brien asked.

"Sean, the OSS sent me here to find you. They think that you've been captured by the Germans. Since you chose not to carry a sodium cyanide capsule, I have orders to kill you if you've been captured or severely wounded. Why the hell didn't you make your initial transmission at the scheduled time?" Jon asked.

Sean shook his head, expressing frustration, and said, "Damn radio crystals. The one in the radio and the spares were damaged on the insertion when I parachuted into a flooded lowland area south of Anzio. I tried to make my way back to our lines after the Allied landings, but I ran into a skirmish between one of our recon units and a German patrol six miles west of here. After the recon unit retreated and the Germans left, I was able to get a replacement crystal from a dead American radio operator's damaged radio."

Sean paused and took a breath, "By the time I made it back to Valmontone, the damn Germans were already coming down Route Six from Rome. Hell, I nearly got run over by a damn Panzer while trying to cross back over Highway 6. The Krauts now have at least four divisions around Anzio. I can't believe that this farmhouse hasn't been taken over by the Germans yet. But I guess it's not close enough to the beachhead, and it's too exposed to be used as a headquarters. I should be thankful that I've been able to use it," O'Brien finished out of breath.

"So, what's really happening around here, Sean?" Jon asked.

Sean filled Jon and Marcel in on what was happening. O'Brien thought that the Operation Shingle was really screwed up. There were virtually no Germans here when the Allies landed. O'Brien thought that Sixth Corps could have been in Rome by now. But for some reason, General Lucas stopped as soon as he secured the beachhead and moved only six miles inland the first day. That gave the Germans time to organize their scattered units and send in reinforcements, including two separate Panzer units. The Allied forces waited too late to start an offensive. When they finally did, they got stopped cold by the German Tenth Army at the Alban Hills.

"I've picked up several in-the-clear radio transmissions by the Germans yesterday. We also got hammered at Cisterna by the Herman Goering Panzer Division," O'Brien said.

"How bad was it, Sean?" Jon asked.

"It was real bad Jon; real bad," O'Brien said.

Jon just shook his head and wondered how much worse it would get before the Sixth Corps could make a drive for Rome.

Sean relaxed a bit and said, "So, what's up, Jon? Do you have orders for me?"

"Yes, Sean, don't get your ass caught or killed!" Jon remarked. They both laughed.

Jon explained that the OSS had received his reports, but because they suspected that he had been captured and coerced into sending false information, they didn't forward any of his reports to Sixth Army Headquarters.

"Hell, Jon, it appears that the damn pencil pushers are trying to run this battle, while our guys are getting slaughtered out there. One of the Allied transmissions I picked up early this morning said that out of 750 rangers attacking Cisterna, only six survived," Sean remarked.

Jon stood there awestruck and shook his head in disbelief. Then he walked over to O'Brien's SSTS-1 radio, put on the headset, set the correct frequency, adjusted the setting for transmit, and sent the coded message, Green Sox, to OSS headquarters in Algiers. The coded message he received back was brief: Stay put Stop Bombing raid did not succeed Stop Need intel on locations of arriving German divisions End.

When Jon took off the headset and set it down, he looked at O'Brien and Marcel.

"The Allied air strike on the German reinforcement columns headed here failed," Jon said.

"What air strike?" O'Brien asked.

"The 324th Bomb Group was sent this morning to stop the German reinforcement columns coming from Rome and the east coast," Jon remarked.

Jon then told them of the new orders in the message from OSS headquarters. For ten minutes, Sean and Jon discussed the request with Marcel. Marcel talked to the two resistance fighters and decided that they would be sent out after dark to gather intel on the arriving German divisions. Marcel had also given them instruction to capture a German officer.

By now, another cold front had moved in, and rain was falling as well as the temperature. It was perfect weather for intelligence gathering. The enemy would not have the alertness they would normally have if the weather were clear and sunny. German sentries would be more concerned about staying dry and keeping warm than keeping a lookout. The temperature was now in the teens. Plus, the Germans had a tight ring around the beachhead. They wouldn't suspect a fifth element behind their lines gathering intel on them so soon after a landing. It wasn't until shortly after daylight that the two resistance fighters returned with a slightly injured German officer.

"We caught him taking a crap away from his unit. After he pulled his pants up, we attacked and knocked him out. He may have a slight concussion," the leader said.

They brought the German officer into the house. His hands were still bound and he had dried blood on his head and face. They bound his hands and legs to a chair in the kitchen. Since Sean spoke fluent German, without an accent, he began interrogating the prisoner. For two hours, Major Armond Hoffmann only revealed his name, rank, and serial number, in accordance with the Geneva convention. He was not going to cooperate. But because of the urgent need for current intel, Sean pulled out a silenced High Standard .22-caliber pistol and shot the major in his right leg.

Jon had to gag the major until he stopped hollering. O'Brien told the major that he would put a bullet in his knee next if he didn't answer the questions; then he would be crippled for life. The major still stalled. It wasn't until Sean pulled out a pair of pliers and ripped out one of the major's fingernails that he became cooperative. He was told he would be given morphine to kill the pain after he provided information that they needed.

Major Hoffmann told them that he was the senior officer in charge of a divisional communications unit belonging to the Third Panzer Grenadier Division. They had arrived from Rome late last night and stationed two miles south of Valmontone. He provided detailed information on the 114th Light Infantry, the 715th Infantry Division, and the Twenty-Sixth Panzers and Twenty-Ninth Panzer Grenadiers being held in reserve. The major was married and had two daughters and a son living in Konstanz, close to the Swiss border. He was terrified by the brutal interrogation techniques and didn't want to die.

Since it was cold and rainy, Sean asked Marcel to send his two Resistance fighters back out to confirm exactly where the Third Panzer Grenadier Division was located. He wanted grid coordinates so he could send the information to Sixth Corps headquarters. Marcel then got on the wireless and requested assistance from resistant fighters in the Alban Hills and the areas south and east of Anzio. He needed confirmation on the locations of the two other German Panzer Divisions as quickly as possible. If the major's information was correct, there were close to two hundred German tanks. With that much heavy armor, the Germans could stop the Allies from reaching Rome.

Over the next eighteen hours, the information he had obtained from Major Hoffmann was confirmed. In addition to the two Panzer Divisions being held in reserve, he found out that there were two battalions of Panther and Tiger tanks west of the Alban Hills on Route Seven.

By the time Sean had completed transmitting his report to Sixth Army headquarters, it was well after 0600 hours. Sean had been on the wireless for over thirty minutes and was worried about his wireless signals being intercepted by German intercept stations.

Normally, OSS operatives were under standing orders to limit their transmissions to no more than five minutes. Sean had a lot of information that the Allies needed, and he knew that he had stayed on the air far too long. He should have taken his radio into one of the nearby ravines. Transmitting from a ravine would absorb the majority of the radio signals on your left, right, and rear positions and avoid much of the radio intercept capabilities of the Germans.

The German army's field signal intelligence (SIGINT) organization, called the Kommandeur der Nachrichten Aufklaerung or KONA, was organized into nine SIGINT regiments. Captain Chester Eckhart, the commander of KONA-7, needed one more signal capture to be the number one officer in KONA. It would guarantee his promotion to major and if it resulted in the capture or elimination of a resistant operator, he would probably be awarded his fourth Iron Cross. The fourth award was the Grand Iron Cross, which was always presented in Berlin by Hitler himself. He would be the first officer in KONA to receive the award, and he would also be entitled to thirty days vacation. It had been nearly two years since he had seen his wife and two children, who were living on his parents' farm west of Berlin. He was praying for a miracle.

The month of January, however, was always a slow month, and he hadn't had a signal capture that resulted in a resistance takedown since November. Captain Eckhart was standing outside of his KONA-7 unit, on the eastern coast of Italy, smoking a cigarette, when his sergeant interrupted him.

Sergeant Brion Barger had just intercepted a signal from a radio transmitting on a bearing that took it straight through Anzio. It was on the same bearing that he had picked up briefly yesterday, but this time the transmission was lasting longer than five minutes. It was not one of the regular frequencies that the Allies used in their invasion at Anzio.

"Contact KONA-1 and request a bearing on the frequency," Captain Eckhart ordered.

"Yes, Captain," Sergeant Barger replied.

KONA-1, located in Lancut, Poland, replied within minutes with a second bearing. It took Sergeant Barger another two minutes to draw the bearing on his map. It was coming from a location around Valmontone.

"It's probably Italian Resistance fighters. Contact Fourteenth Army Headquarters D/F Team, and give them the position. They have mobile D/F vehicles around Anzio," Captain Eckhart stated anxiously.

Three mobile D/F units were contacted and began searching. Within five minutes, they had pinpointed the position of the radio with their Funkhorchempfanger receivers. Next, they contacted the closest combat unit, the Third Panzer Group. The Third Panzer Group commander thought that this might also be a commando team inserted behind their line to pinpoint his tank group. He did not need Allied cruisers or artillery targeting his tanks. He dispatched a tank and two mobile D/F vehicles with a platoon of infantry to find them.

O'Brien knew that the Germans had fixed monitoring stations that could triangulate on his signal to within two to three kilometers. Once they got their initial triangulation, the mobile D/F vehicles—that used the Nachfeldpeiler P57N direction-finding radio with loop and sense antennas mounted on their roofs—would be sent into the area to get an even more accurate position.

After another ten minutes of reflecting on the situation, O'Brien concluded that evacuation was necessary, and the quicker the better because it would be light soon. He woke Marcel and Jon from their sleep and announced that they had to evacuate to an alternate location. Marcel immediately got up and left the farmhouse. He returned with his two resistance comrades. He told them to take the prisoner and the portable radio and move up the valley two hundred meters north of the house. He and the others would meet up with them there. And if for some reason, he and the others didn't make it; to get rid of the German prisoner and go to their homes.

Jon was slow to wake up. O'Brien was busy packing his radio but stopped and poured Jon a fresh cup of coffee from a pot sitting on a small army issue propane burner.

"Welcome back to the living, Sleeping Beauty," O'Brien said as he handed the cup to Jon. "I have to move up the valley to Labico, blow up some railroad tracks, create some mayhem, and kill some Germans. You've been ordered back to the beach for pickup."

O'Brien rose up from his packing after hearing a soft *wump*. Next, there was a loud explosion that shook the farmhouse. It was followed by several more.

Marcel came running up the stairs, yelling, "Mortars! They know our location. We need to get out now!"

You didn't have to tell Jon twice. He was up and down the stairs and out in the yard with his Sten before the next shell blew the west side of the house off. He and Marcel were knocked to the ground.

"Where's O'Brien?" Jon yelled.

"He's still in the house. He was packing his radio!" Marcel yelled back.

Jon jumped up and ran into the house and up the stairs into the attic. There was a gaping hole in the west side of the attic, and O'Brien was lying on his back with blood spattered on his face and clothing. He was unconscious but still breathing. Jon fired an entire clip from his Sten into the radio equipment that O'Brien had packed and picked up the codebook laying near O'Brien's hand. He then lifted O'Brien onto his left shoulder and carried him down the stairs and out the door as another shell exploded on the north side of the house.

Marcel grabbed Jon by the arm and hurried him past the outhouse through an opening in the rock wall and up the vineyard valley running north. They stopped once they were a hundred yards from the farmhouse. Before they caught their breaths, the two resistant fighters with the German prisoner rejoined them. When Jon laid O'Brien on the wet ground, O'Brien moaned and looked at Jon.

"What happened?" O'Brien asked.

"You nearly got your butt killed. That's what happened. Can you get up? If not, you know the Donovan Directive. I'm going to have to shoot your ass," Jon said, still out of breath.

Suddenly, Marcel turned his head in the direction of a *clink-clink-clink* coming from the south.

"German tank, we need to move to those trees," Marcel said urgently pointing west.

The two resistant fighters with the prisoner in tow led the way. As Jon got O'Brien to his feet, he saw Marcel turn and release four short bursts from his Sten as two Germans moved into the opening between the rows of leafless vines. The two German infantrymen stumbled and fell thirty yards away. Jon had O'Brien twenty yards up the small hill by the time Marcel caught up with them.

"Those are just the lead scouts. With that tank, there's at least a platoon behind them!" Marcel exclaimed.

As they got closer to the tree line, Jon heard firing behind him and then the ricochet of bullets hitting the ground five feet to his left. He moved right to avoid getting hit by another round of fire. One of the resistant fighters had fallen back, and along with Marcel, began giving covering fire to Jon and O'Brien.

From the west, they heard artillery fire and then shells began falling a hundred yards away from the group in the direction of the Germans.

"American artillery, I know the sound," Marcel said.

"Crap, now what! Are our own guys trying to kill us?" Jon questioned, as he and O'Brien stopped to catch their breaths.

"They probably triangulated on the Germans' radio signals. Plus, they don't know we're out here running for our lives," O'Brien stated, as more artillery rounds began exploding; this time even closer to them.

Before they could move toward the trees again, Marcel shoved Jon and O'Brien to the ground as bullets whizzed by where their heads used to be. Marcel knelt and fired six more bursts from his Sten. Several more Germans dropped.

"Thanks," Jon said to Marcel, struggling to get O'Brien on his feet.

"There's at least twenty-five, Jon. Get ready to fight while on the move," Marcel said, as he pulled the empty magazine out of his Sten and replaced it with a full one.

By now O'Brien had his Colt .45 pistol out. Jon turned to O'Brien, "You're hurt," handed him his Sten and took O'Brien's Colt .45 automatic.

"I can shoot two-handed with these, and I'm very, very good," Jon said.

O'Brien nodded and then started firing short bursts from the Sten at the German soldiers he saw coming up through the vineyard. Jon took aim on two other Germans and brought both of them down.

"We need to go now, move!" Marcel said, as he turned and fired four more bursts. "Pierre!" Marcel shouted at the resistant fighter ten yards to his left. "Cover me while I get these two to the tree line."

They continued to move west through the brush thicket and toward a large cluster of trees until Marcel held his hand out indicating stop. Jon looked ahead and noticed the German prisoner and the other resistant fighter crouching near a tree. Marcel then noticed movement in a large copse of trees a hundred yards to the west.

The rain had lowered the visibility down to less than a quarter of a mile. Marcel whispered for Jon and O'Brien to stay put, and he moved cautiously through the thicket in the direction of the movement. Within minutes, he was back whispering to Jon.

"Americans, look at their helmets," Marcel said, indicating the direction with his hand.

Marcel was about to say something else when the left side of his head exploded spraying Jon and O'Brien with a mist of red blood and chunks of brain matter. A second later, Jon heard an *ugh* spill from O'Brien's lips as his left arm was flung back, and he collapsed on the ground.

Jon lifted the now semi-conscious O'Brien to his feet and picked up his Sten. Pierre joined him, and they began dragging O'Brien toward the American soldiers. With one hand, they continued firing at the Germans. As they moved west, all Jon could think was, *God, don't let me be killed by my own troops.*

They approached to within thirty yards of the Americans, and they were joined by the second resistant fighter and the German prisoner. Jon noticed fresh blood flowing down Major Hoffmann's head, where a German bullet had creased his skull. After Jon set O'Brien against a tree away from the firing, he and Pierre began returning fire. Jon fired four bursts from his Sten dropping two German soldiers more before having to change magazines. After he had moved back behind the tree, a clatter of semi-automatic weapon fire erupted and slammed into the tree. Jon then slipped his Sten around the tree and fired a five-second burst, and another two Germans fell.

"This is getting ridiculous," Jon said as he stood behind the tree firing at a half-dozen more Germans moving toward them.

Seeing five people running away from the German gunfire, the American soldiers began directing their fire at the Germans chasing Jon and his group. Jon and Pierre grabbed O'Brien under each arm and moved closer to the Americans.

"We're Americans!" Jon shouted. "One of us is wounded, and we have a German prisoner."

Jon sat O'Brien against another tree, pulled out his knife, and cut through his shirtsleeve to expose O'Brien's wound. He then tore a long strip from the shirt and tied it around O'Brien's bicep to slow the bleeding. He pulled out his first aid pack and extracted a sterilized Carlisle dressing, sprinkled the enclosed packet of sulfanilamide on the wound, and covered the wound with the dressing. Next he broke the seal on a morphine syrette and injected O'Brien with a dose of the painkiller.

Jon looked around for Pierre. Pierre and the other resistance fighter were kneeling in the back of another tree five feet away. Pierre whispered to Jon that he was now in charge of the German prisoner. Then Pierre and the other Italian fighter retreated north further into the woods.

Two American soldiers crept slowly to a position behind a large tree five yards from Jon. One of the soldiers told him he would shoot if any of them reached for the Sten lying on the ground. His buddy moved forward and picked up the Sten. After he removed the automatic weapon, Jon asked him if he would like the pistols he was carrying. The soldier nodded, and Jon slowly pulled out the semiautomatics in his waistband and handed them to the soldier butt first.

"There's a German tank with a platoon of Krauts just over that small rise one hundred yards to the southeast. Can you get us the hell out of here?" Jon asked.

Jon turned abruptly when he heard the *clink–clink–clink* of the German tank topping the hill. Before the soldier could answer Jon, a loud *boom* rang out as the German tank fired on their position. As Jon was shoving O'Brien and his prisoner further into the dirt, he heard an American radio operator five yards from him calling out grid coordinates of the German tank.

The tank's shell exploded ten yards away from the tree that Jon, O'Brien, and the German prisoner were hiding behind. The explosion blew dirt, rock, and body parts all around them. One of the American soldiers that had moved past Jon and O'Brien had not been so lucky. He was within five feet of the exploding shell and was torn apart by the explosion and jagged shrapnel.

Sixty seconds later, American artillery shells began falling around the German tank. The tank was moving slowly down the hill when it took a direct hit from an Allied shell; its turret was blown into the air and landed twenty feet from the blazing vehicle. With their tank destroyed, the fight went out of the remaining German soldiers, and they began retreating back to the southeast.

Jon, O'Brien, and the semi-conscious Major Hoffmann were now surrounded by three more American soldiers with rifles and a sergeant with a Thompson submachine gun; all pointing at Jon, O'Brien, and their prisoner.

"Who the hell are you?" the sergeant asked.

"OSS. This agent and my prisoner need medical attention," Jon answered.

"Nelson, King. Take these two gentlemen, and start heading back toward our lines. Rosenauer, Alvarado. Grab the prisoner. The rest of you cover our rear. We're moving out. And Nelson, don't take your eyes off them. They just might be German spies," the sergeant bellowed.

Jon helped the semi-conscious O'Brien to his feet, and Private Nelson grabbed him under his other arm. Corporal King took the lead as they began moving southwest. The sergeant and remaining Americans spread out and followed.

"What unit are you guys in?" Jon asked.

"Darby's Rangers," Private Wayne Nelson whispered. "Now be quiet until we can get you back to our lines, sir. There are Germans all around us."

The rangers slowly moved the group through the ravines heading west. After an hour, the visibility had increased to a half mile. On several occasions, they had to stop, while Corporal King and another ranger took out several two-man German patrols. After a slow and cautious five-hour trek, they reached a safe Allied location. Corporal King released Jon and O'Brien over to two military policemen. They turned Major Hoffmann over to an OSS captain and sergeant.

After the transfer of the prisoners and their weapons, Corporal Nelson turned to Jon. "You all are lucky it was raining, and the visibility was low. Otherwise, we might not have made it through the German lines to find you all. Where's the third agent?" Corporal King asked.

"Dead," Jon replied.

Without saying anything else, Private Nelson and Corporal Dave King turned and ran to catch up with their fellow rangers heading to their platoon headquarters.

One MP took O'Brien to a field hospital and kept guard over him while he was being treated. The other MP hustled Jon to their field headquarters tent where he waited under guard for over sixty minutes. Eventually, a rugged-looking major with a large cigar in his mouth entered the tent.

"So, you're OSS? For your sake, I hope the hell you can prove it," the major stated.

"I'm Counter Intelligence Corps, the other guy is OSS. Ring up the CIC commander, he's expecting me," Jon said authoritatively.

Thirty minutes later, the CIC commander, assigned to the Sixth Corps, entered the platoon commander's tent.

"I thought I knew all the CIC agents in Six Corps. What's your name, son?" the colonel asked.

"Jonathan Wilson Preston, sir. I'm not with Sixth Corps. I was flown in from Tunis and airdropped in to find Agent O'Brien," Jon replied.

"Yes, I had heard that he might have been captured. Now answer some questions for me, Agent Preston. When did the Brooklyn Dodgers last win the World Series?" the colonel asked.

Jon recalled his instruction from Major Holcombe in Tunis. *No matter what they ask, only tell them what I've told you.*

"April 15, 1912," Jon answered.

"And when did the Boston Red Sox win their last World Series?" asked the Colonel.

"April 15, 1912," Jon answered again.

"It was actually September 11, 1918, but right answer on both questions, Agent Preston. Welcome to Anzio," the colonel stated.

"Can I check on Agent O'Brien, sir?" Jon requested, with a bit of urgency in his voice.

"He's okay, Agent Preston. I looked in on him before I came here. O'Brien and I met before Operation Shingle began," the colonel said.

"So you already knew who I was before you got here?" Jon questioned.

"Yeah, I just wanted to make sure that you remembered what the challenge phrase was and followed your orders. The Red Sox question came from O'Brien; he's a Yankee fan and wanted to humble you," the colonel said.

The colonel then offered a hand to Jon. "Jamie Roberts, glad to meet you, Agent Preston."

CHAPTER 4
CALCUTTA, INDIA

Lieutenant Colonel Michael Patrick MacKenzie was sitting at his desk at the British SOE detachment in Calcutta. Despite the two fans in his office, he was still fighting the discomfort caused by the heat and humidity. He was also dispelling what to do about the hand-delivered orders he had just received assigning three new special mission agents to his detachment. One agent was British, the second was French, and the third was an American.

The code name for the operation was called King Cobra. The purpose of King Cobra was to track down enemy agents, and infiltrate the trio behind Japanese lines in China, Burma, and India to collect intelligence and disrupt supply lines. The more the trio could disrupt the Japanese supply lines, the closer the Allies would be to removing the Japanese from India and Burma.

This was virtually the same strategy that the Americans were using with their fleet of submarines in the Pacific. Allied submarines had already destroyed a significant portion of Japanese merchant vessels that were supplying their Asian and Pacific theaters.

The King Cobra mission also included finding and capturing Japanese spies and double agents. The Americans had also insisted on adding other special missions, which could be tasked on a case-by-case basis. These were missions outside of the

CBI theater, and included Thailand, French Indochina, Malaya, Afghanistan, Pakistan, Iraq, and Iran.

The lethality of the king cobra snake was to be reflected in the lethality of the special missions team. All mission assignments would come from the US Army Intelligence Corps or G-2, as it was commonly called. G-2 was one of the six directorates managed by the US Army's chief of staff.

Operation King Cobra came into being because the vast majority of the Allied resources were being expended in Europe. Although Burma and India were British colonial holdings, Winston Churchill could not afford to take resources away from the protection of the United Kingdom, and the war against Hitler. To fight a separate war in Burma and India was beyond the British resource capabilities. From the lack of resources came Churchill's proposal to involve the United States more in the region. President Roosevelt supported the plan put forward by Churchill, which gave birth to Operation King Cobra. The British SOE was tasked with planning the special missions and had operational control over their execution. The US Army would also provide the needed weapons and aircraft to infiltrate the agents. But General George C. Marshall, the US Army chief of staff, insisted that a US agent lead the King Cobra team; and he had one in mind.

The British SOE was a clandestine organization formed by Winston Churchill in July 1940. It was chartered to conduct secret warfare against their enemies and to provide training and material aid to local resistance movements. The SOE's mission also included sabotage, espionage, intelligence gathering, and counter-intelligence. The British believed that a European agent, because of his color and facial features, could not blend into the local population. Thus, they limited their European SOE operatives to training the native guerillas in the different clandestine activities. The US Army thought differently.

The three agents chosen for King Cobra were selected on their respective combat skills, but more importantly, on their intellectual quickness and acuity. General Marshall asked the SOE for two of their best and brightest operatives. Of the ten names proposed by the SOE, two were chosen. Both had been Royal Marines commandos and had just recently graduated from the SOE training school in Ceylon. General Marshall didn't want an agent tainted with preconceived British notions that would limit their effectiveness. The American that would lead the team was an Army Counter Intelligence Corps agent.

MacKenzie was irate when he read that all tasking for King Cobra would be coming from G-2. *What the hell do the Americans know about covert operations?* MacKenzie asked himself. *The arrogance of these Yanks controlling anything involving the British SOE is absurd.*

The British agent, Miles Parker Murphy, had grown up in London. He obtained his college degree at the University of Oxford and his doctorate at the University of Edinburgh. In 1927, he took a teaching position at Bangkok University and had lived there for the last fifteen years. He spoke Thai and several different native dialects, including Naga and Kachin. He married a French nationalist living in Bangkok in 1932. They had two children; a boy and a girl. Before his assignment to the SOE, he had been a Royal Marine commando and had fought the Japanese on missions in Rangoon, Burma; and Imphal and Kohima, India.

The French agent, Henri Isaac Moreau, grew up in Paris. He moved to the city of Saigon, in French Indochina, in 1915, when his father took the position as vice president of a French lumber company in Southeast Asia. After attending university in Paris, Henri, returned to Saigon in 1932, and was employed by his father's company. He worked his way up the management chain, and in 1939, he was awarded with a general manager position at a lumber mill in Rangoon, Burma. He spoke English, German, Hindi, Vietnamese, and Mandarin Chinese. He married a French-

Thai nationalist in 1937, and had two children; a boy and a girl. He was also a Royal Marine commando and participated in the same campaigns against the Japanese as his English counterpart.

Both agents Murphy and Morreau had been recruited from the ranks of the newly formed British Third Commando Brigade out of Ceylon, which was formed by combining army and Royal Marine Commando Brigades. They had each undergone two months of intense SOE training at the SOE facility at Chatham Camp, Colombo, Ceylon.

They had graduated a month apart in different classes. Their SOE classes included advanced training in close-quarters hand-to-hand combat and small arms. Their specialty weapons included garrote and knife fighting; they received training in demolitions, communications, jungle warfare, and ambushes. They were also trained in safe cracking, espionage, and counter-espionage.

Both agents had also graduated at the top of their respective Royal Marine Commando and SOE training classes. Both agents had been deployed on numerous combat missions as Royal Marine commandos prior to their SOE recruitment. To establish a cover, should they be unfortunate and be captured, Murphy and Morreau were both trained as aircraft gunners on the Lancaster bomber, and the PBY flying boat.

The American, Jonathan Wilson Preston, had no combat experience, and the only foreign language that he spoke fluently was French. He had obtained his college degree from the Ohio State University in Columbus, Ohio, with their highest honors, summa cum laude. According to the information in the MI6 folder, the twenty-four-year-old Yank had achieved the highest score ever recorded on the US Army's intelligence test since the army had started keeping records. He was considered brilliant and possessing an exceptionally productive and creative mind. He was unmarried.

As MacKenzie read on, the report also stated that Agent Preston was an expert in close-quarters combat, rifle, and small arms. And that he had received his point shooting pistol and close-quarters combat training from none other than the famous British Commando trainer, Colonel William E. Fairbairn of the British Royal Marines.

The close-quarters combat training taught by Colonel Fairbairn was among the best combat fighting styles in the world. His Defendu-style fighting was rooted in Kodokan judo, Japanese jujitsu, and several other forms of close-quarters combat that he studied and perfected while living in Asia. His was a kill-or-be-killed win-at-all-costs fighting style.

The report further stated that Agent Preston's nickname was Boomer because of his exceptional ability at hitting home runs in the American sport of baseball.

"Bloody Yanks!" MacKenzie said out loud. "No formality whatsoever. I'll be damned if I'll call this bloody colonist by his nickname. Hell, I can't even make friends with any of these agents. They'll all probably be dead inside of six months anyway. Then what will the Americans do?"

As he stood contemplating the newly assigned Yank agent, he leaned closer to one of the fans and wondered how much hotter it would get in March. In January, it had gotten up to 92°F, and February was already 95°F. March was always worse because of the increased rain and humidity. He exhaled loudly and said, "God, this is going to be impossible. Hell, all Yanks are impossible! This American is too young. It's bad enough to have to put up with a Frog, but a Yank, too! I do not understand why MI6 is doing this to me. We need experienced agents to deal with these damned Japs, not a green Yank kid, and certainly, not a weak, snobby, and opinionated Frog."

He couldn't help but laugh at the terms he had used for the Frenchman and American. His father had told him that Frog was a derogatory name used for a Frenchman because the national emblem of France, the fleur-de-lys, resembled a frog. The term Yank, he learned in school, was what Britons called the people in the New England colonies. It was Lord Horatio Nelson who first used the term in a letter he wrote in the 1780s, shortening the word from Yankee to Yank. Now the term was used to describe all Americans.

CHAPTER 5

CALCUTTA, INDIA

J on had taken a motor launch from Anzio beach to an awaiting
navy PBY Catalina flying boat that took him back to Algiers.
A day later, he was aboard a Lancaster on the first leg of the
five-day 3,700-mile trip from Algiers to New Delhi, India. It
took another day after he landed to catch a flight for the nine
hundred-mile trip to Calcutta. And then he was the last person
called to board the plane.

After landing in Calcutta, Jon took a cab to the American
base and checked into the temporary quarters; a group of army
tents. After six days of constant flying, noise, and dehydration, he
was exhausted. Jon slept for two days before he went and signed
in with the CIC First Base Headquarters Squadron. He wasn't
scheduled to sign in with the SOE for another five days.

Although he was on indefinite loan to the SOE, Jon still
had a CIC mother squadron. The first sergeant at the CIC
Headquarters Squadron directed him to the base motor pool to
obtain his vehicle. He told him to go to the base quartermaster to
get what he needed to set up his camp; meaning his tent and any
other supplies he needed. The area where most American soldiers
were bivouacked was called the American Residential Area. In
reality, it was tent city USA, where over three thousand American
officers and enlisted soldiers occupied tents; with a promise from
Washington of more soldiers and tents to come.

Jon went to the motor pool first and requested a vehicle. Due to the nature of their jobs, CIC personnel were authorized a vehicle. Although Jon wasn't an ordinary CIC agent, his headquarters' squadron was not aware of his special mission operative status. Jon chose a Willys MB Jeep soft-top. He had memorized the specs while at Fort Ritchie; two front bucket seats and a rear bench seat, fifty-four-horsepower four-cylinder engine, floor-mounted three-speed transmission, and four-wheel drive. In the words of his dad, "It was the bee's knees."

With his vehicle secured, he drove to the quartermaster's building, showed his CIC identification to a young private named Tommy Lee Ray, and asked to be rigged up with what he needed for his office and lodging.

Private Ray, who was new to the base and only two weeks into his first assignment, was perplexed by Jon's CIC designation and assumed that Jon was some type of VIP cop; he showed Jon what was available for senior officers. According to the private, the selection was meager. But with Private Ray's recommendation, Jon chose a squad tent for his office and a pyramidal tent for his personal lodging. The private told Jon that it would be ten days or more before he could schedule the delivery and set up of the tents. He also informed Jon that he would leave a note for him at the temporary quarters office with the date and time of the delivery. Before Jon left, Private Ray told him that they were out of fans, but he expected a new shipment tomorrow. He told Jon that he would bring two fans for each tent. Jon thanked the private and left.

With nothing to do, Jon decided to sign in with the British SOE detachment. He parked his Willys at the British American Club in Alipore, and walked down the fifty-foot corridor to the SOE detachment. Alipore was a small suburb located on the southwest corner of Calcutta and adjacent to the large American base. The meeting with the SOE commander, Lieutenant Colonel Michael Patrick MacKenzie, took up the remainder of his afternoon, covering most of the information he had studied in Algiers.

"Agent Preston," the lieutenant colonel said, "you've been permanently assigned to the CIC detachment in Calcutta and are on an indefinite loan to my SOE detachment. As the operational front moves east into Burma, a small support team of seven SOE agents from this office, will also move with the front; as will your CIC detachment," Lieutenant Colonel MacKenzie remarked.

"It's my understanding, Agent Preston, that you will be strictly working special mission assignments with the two new SOE agents being assigned here." Jon didn't say anything but nodded in agreement. "Agent Preston, usually only the very best and most experienced agents are chosen to work special mission assignments. I want you to know, in no uncertain terms, that I totally disagree with this decision. You are simply too young and too inexperienced to be given the responsibility of leading a team of this nature. And you have no combat experience whatsoever. I wonder what dumbass officer in your pentagon decided that a young, inexperienced agent should be working special mission assignments, much less lead my team," Lieutenant Colonel MacKenzie concluded.

"That would be General George C. Marshall, US Army chief of staff, sir," Jon replied, slightly agitated by the lieutenant colonel's remarks.

Lieutenant Colonel MacKenzie flushed with embarrassment and then sneered in anger at Agent Preston as he shook his head.

"You will be introduced to the two SOE agents you'll be working with later in the week. I suggest that you use your free time to get settled into the Yank Residential Area. If you have no further questions, Agent Preston that will end the introduction to your assignment at my SOE detachment. Now get the hell out of my office, Yank, and don't come back until you are summoned," Lieutenant Colonel MacKenzie stated.

Jon got up, grinned at Lieutenant Colonel MacKenzie, and left the room. He declined the first sergeant's offer for a lift to his temporary quarters. He had last eaten an hour before boarding the aircraft in New Delhi, and that was twelve hours ago. He had been too busy getting signed in with the CIC detachment and securing temporary quarters to stop and eat. As he left the SOE offices, he turned right and walked fifty feet down the hallway into the British American Club's main dining room.

While waiting to be seated, Agent Preston thought, *The British American Club was a perfect place for a clandestine office. There were people walking in and out of the club all day and most of the night.* For twenty-five cents, Agent Preston was fed pork medallions in charcuterie sauce, green beans, and oven-roasted potatoes. He wondered if the club served beef. He decided he would ask one of the CIC officers later since most of the waiters were Indians, and he didn't want to insult anyone. After his meal, Jon relaxed and reflected back on Lieutenant Colonel MacKenzie's briefing. All in all, it was adequate, but the lieutenant colonel had failed to mention the entire operational state of the Allied armies in Burma and India.

First, the Japanese success in Burma, and now the threat to India made an Allied offensive extremely unlikely; at least in the near future. Even if General Slim was able to halt the Japanese advance at Kohima, the Allies would be playing defense until they could bring in more divisions of infantry, armor, and aircraft.

Second, the Japanese had four divisions in Burma, which was twice the number that MacKenzie had briefed. Two new divisions had just landed at the Port of Rangoon five days ago.

Third, intelligence recovered from a Japanese intercept, which Jon had read in Algiers, revealed that the Japanese planned to put these two new divisions up the Chindwin River to deny any future Allied offensive into Burma. These divisions were also to be used to spearhead their invasion further into India.

And fourth, the Japanese enjoyed virtually unlimited air superiority, which was hindering Allied aircrafts moving desperately needed supplies into China. It could also hinder some of the plans that G-2 and MI6 had in store for him and his team.

There was a lot to think about, he decided. Number one on the list was how to deal with Lieutenant Colonel MacKenzie. The OSS commander in Algiers, Colonel Farrington, had warned him about Lieutenant Colonel MacKenzie.

"MacKenzie is an excellent staffer; having been an attorney in New Delhi for twenty-one years. But he is extremely bitter about not being assigned as a commander of a combat unit. He is forty-three, slightly chubby, and arrogant as hell. Plus, he does not like us Yanks; which is what the lieutenant colonel calls Americans, and especially a young, inexperienced Yank like you, Jon. He also hates the French because his first wife left him for a French cavalry officer. All in all, Jon, he's a presumptuous jerk. Don't let him get to you because he will surely try. You're smart enough to figure out how to play him into your hands," Colonel Farrington stated.

After the meeting with MacKenzie, Jon concluded that the lieutenant colonel wasn't fit to command a troop of Boy Scouts. Jon had had to grit his teeth to keep from verbally tearing the colonel's head off. His disrespect and lack of military decorum was reprehensible. Colonel Farrington had told him that MacKenzie had been in the Royal Marine Reserves prior to the war. MacKenzie was an intelligence officer and had been frozen in the rank of major for years. When MI6 was forced to expand its forces in India, MacKenzie was promoted to lieutenant colonel and assigned to the newly formed SOE detachment in Alipore, as its commander. All of the officers in his regiment but him had gone to combat positions, and MacKenzie was bitter.

Colonel Farrington told Jon that MacKenzie was smart but exhibited a degree of instability and unpredictability. He did not think that MacKenzie was suited for his assignment as the SOE detachment commander. So Jon had to put MacKenzie's behavior behind him and move on. He would have to come up with a strategy to keep the colonel in check. After a second cup of coffee, Jon got up, paid his bill, and left the dining room.

As he was walking out of the club Jon said to himself, "On a positive note the lieutenant colonel doesn't know about my mission to Anzio yet. That ought to get his dander up."

Jon had intended to spend the next five days exploring the sites of Calcutta. But after Jon left the base and drove into the city, what he found had appalled him. He saw men and women that looked like fleshless skeletons walking in the streets begging for food. Whenever Jon stopped at a Stop sign, he found his Jeep surrounded by small naked children with bloated bellies and sticks for legs, holding up their empty tin cup asking him for food. Calcutta was still reeling from the famine that started in 1943. Over three million Indians had already died.

Instead of sightseeing, Jon stumbled upon a small Catholic mission, six miles from the American base. Over the next two weeks, Jon could be seen helping the priests and nuns feed the starving children they had taken in. Most were too weak to hold a spoon and had to be fed small amounts until their emaciated bodies began to recover. Many of the children died in Jon's arms while he was feeding them. They were too far gone to recover, but some did survive.

After his first day with the Catholic mission, Jon went down to the American docks on the Calcutta wharves. While there, he ran into an army supply captain, who was also from Columbus, Ohio. Jon asked Captain Marty Schottenstein if he had any food that was on the verge of spoiling and not fit for the officers and enlisted messes.

"What do you need it for, Jon?" Captain Schottenstein asked.

"You really don't want to know, do you, Captain?" Jon replied.

Knowing that is was against army regulation to give food to the local population, Captain Schottenstein replied, "Only off the record, Jon."

"It's going to help feed starving children at a Catholic mission," Jon replied.

Captain Schottenstein was well aware of the famine that had struck India. When Jon left the Calcutta docks that day, he had a half of a side of pork, a stalk of bananas, and twelve cases of canned milk for the mission. None of the food was spoiled.

While the famine survivors were recovering, Jon read to them from children's storybooks. The children from Calcutta already knew the rudiments of English, so he focused on them while several of the Sister's, who spoke Hindi, worked with the children that had come in from the country and didn't know any English at all.

Fifteen days after he had visited the quartermaster, he found a note waiting for him. The note said that they would begin setting up his tents in two days and gave him the grid coordinates in the American residential area. Two days later, Private Tommy Lee Ray showed up at the American encampment with two tents, a lot of lumber, and a group of twelve native workers. The workers first built a wooden frame to the dimensions of the squad tent base. Next, they nailed two-by-six boards across the frame to make a sturdy floor that was eighteen inches off the ground. One of the native workers explained to Jon that when the monsoons hit, he would appreciate the raised floor. The squad tent took the twelve men a little over three hours to erect, which included building the frame and the floor. Its dimensions were thirty-two feet long, sixteen feet wide, and twelve feet high. It would shelter sixteen and make a very nice office as well as a place to entertain.

The pyramidal tent, which Jon was going to use for his personal lodging, was slightly smaller and went up much faster. It was sixteen-by-sixteen feet with a twelve-foot-ridge height, and an eight-by-four-foot double-lapped canvas door. Just like the squad tent, it was made from thirteen ounce duck canvas, waxed for waterproofing.

Over both tents, a second canvas was erected, which would serve as primary weather barriers, and keep the occupants dry when the heavy rains began.

Private Ray told Jon that the electricians would come the next day to connect an electrical line to the nearest MEP-003A ten-kilowatt generator fifty yards away. Additionally, the private had sent two standard army cots, along with four sets of sheets, two pillows, four pillowcases, and four standard wool army blankets.

As the crews finished erecting the last tent and installing the furniture, the private approached Jon and informed him that he would bring two fans, two filing cabinets, two desks, and four chairs for the squad tent and two chest of drawers and two fans for the pyramidal tent the following morning. Jon thanked the private and walked into the squad tent admiring its area. He was finally in business and ready to start whatever special missions G-2 would throw his team's way.

The following afternoon, Jon drove back to the quartermaster's depot and looked up Private Ray. Jon thanked him for doing a great job with the tents and presented him with a large package wrapped in brown paper. The private was overjoyed when he opened it and found two bottles of Johnny Walker scotch whiskey. Enlisted men were only entitled to six bottles of beer a week. Only officers received rations of hard liquor.

After a profuse number of thank yous from Private Ray, Jon asked about obtaining a refrigerator. The private smiled at the request and informed Jon that only hospital units were allowed to have a refrigerator; because of the medicines that had to be kept cool the private added.

He did mention that the Third Hospital Battalion had a clinic close to the American Residential Area and that they had just taken delivery of a new eighteen-cubic-foot refrigerator. Private Ray didn't know what they were going to do with the old one. He then told Jon that his tent mate was a supply corporal at the clinic, and he would be glad to ride along and provide any assistance he needed. Jon was thinking silently, *A couple bottles of booze sure do go a long way around here.*

Knowing that he had made a new friend with the whisky donation, Jon invited his new friend to ride with him to the clinic. When they arrived, Private Ray took him directly to his tent mate, Corporal Ed Slater. After Private Ray inquired about the disposition of their old refrigerator, Corporal Slater walked them out one of the clinic's back doors and showed them the refrigerator sitting next to one of the four garbage disposal bins.

Corporal Slater told them that the clinic only had room for one refrigerator. He told Jon that he could have it because his CO had him condemned it on their official paperwork.

Jon immediately asked Private Ray if he could arrange to have the refrigerator delivered to his personal tent. He then turned to the corporal and promised him a special package like the one he gave to Private Ray. Both Private Ray and Corporal Slater were equally joyful. Tonight they would be two of the most popular young enlisted men on the base and no doubt the drunkest.

Before Jon could leave, Corporal Slater asked, "Sir, could you use a real bed?

"What kind?" Jon asked.

"It's a hospital bed," Corporal Slater said.

"Does it come with a mattress?" Jon asked.

"Yes, sir, it does," Corporal Slater replied.

"Can you have it delivered with the refrigerator?" Jon asked looking at Private Ray.

"No problem, sir," Private Ray said.

"Then I'll see you all later," Jon replied as he got in his jeep and left.

The normal army CIC field command structure usually included six officers and forty-nine enlisted personnel. The unit in Calcutta had twelve officers and ninety-two enlisted personnel. Although Jon was indefinitely assigned to the British SOE, none of the one hundred plus CIC personnel in Calcutta had ever come across someone as creative and ballsy as Agent Jonathan Wilson Preston.

After his first two weeks in camp, Jon was the talk of the CIC community. Not only could he get anything he needed from the quartermaster, he somehow came up with copious amounts of booze and beer and was a master at procuring fresh fruits, eggs, pork and poultry. He even had a corporal from the motor pool build him a sixteen-foot barbeque grill out of discarded oil barrels. If someone wanted something, they went to Jon, even the CIC commander. The even stranger part of it was Jon never asked for anything in return.

What people didn't know about Agent Preston was he was a devout Catholic. One of the first things Jon had done after returning from Algiers was to find a church and go to confession. After confession, he then spent an hour with the priest discussing the killings he had done in Italy. Jon thought that he should be more remorseful over killing the German soldiers, even if they were trying to kill him. He was worried about God forgiving him. The priest assured him that any sin, no matter how egregious, was forgivable. When Jon left the church, he wasn't feeling any better than he did before he had walked into the confessional. But at least, he had gone to confession.

The day after his tents had been erected; Jon was instructed to go see the CIC detachment commander, Colonel Ronnie Ray. Thinking he was in trouble for the lavish barbeque he had held for the CIC troops the previous evening, he showed up ready to tell the colonel that he had a direct order from General Marshall to host parties for the troops to boost their morale. However, he wouldn't tell the colonel that General Marshal had given him a discretionary fund of $110,000, part of which was to be used for enhancing the morale of the Allied troops. Jon took this to include the SOE and anyone else that he chose to invite.

Colonel Ray never mentioned the barbeque or the booze. Instead, he informed Jon that he had just had lunch with a Colonel Richard Arvin from G-2. Colonel Arvin was at the SOE detachment office and would like to see him in one hour.

Jon had been expecting this, and he was anxious to receive his next assignment.

Jon exited the CIC offices, went back to his tent to change into fresh clothes, and then drove to the SOE detachment. The first sergeant led him down the hall where a large Royal Marine corporal, with a .9 mm Beretta on his hip, was standing guard outside the door. After Jon entered the room, the MP closed the door and kept a menacing look on his face, to reassure anyone watching, that no one was going to gain admittance without the permission of the senior officer inside.

CHAPTER 6

CALCUTTA, INDIA

"Good to see you again, Jon," Colonel Richard "Buck" Arvin said as he eagerly greeted Jon in his mild southern voice.

"Hello, Colonel," Jon said.

"I read about your excursion into Italy from the report that Colonel Roberts sent to the chief of staff. I'm glad you and O'Brien made it out without too much damage," Colonel Arvin said.

"Not without some help," Jon stated.

"Yes, I guess that Darby's Rangers did help quite a bit. I understand that O'Brien is recovering from his wounds," Colonel Arvin replied.

"Yes, sir. He'll be well enough to fly back to the states in a couple of weeks, but I think he's even more anxious to get back into the war," Jon said.

"With the loss of Marcel, we thought that the Resistance was going to be hurting for a leader. But his brother has stepped up to take his place. And although the Allied offensive has faltering for now, it looks like the Resistance is back in business. We're still waiting for an OSS replacement for O'Brien. All of the OSS agents who can speak fluent German were already assigned and in the field," Colonel Arvin stated.

"So I heard," Jon replied.

"I also briefed General Marshal before I left Washington. He asked me to tell you to keep your cocky Ohio butt out of trouble and to kill more Germans next time," Colonel Arvin said.

"That does sound like the general," Jon stated.

"He also told me that he knew your father at Virginia Military Institute. In 1938, your father took him to a Red Sox game and introduced him to your uncle, who was the general manager of the Boston Red Sox. Your father told him that you had signed with the Red Sox right out of high school and played for their farm team in Columbus. He also told the general that you hit three home runs in your first game," Colonel Arvin stated.

"My dad likes to brag, Colonel," Jon remarked.

"Do you plan on playing professional baseball when you get back, Jon?" Colonel Arvin asked.

"No, I don't. I've got a great career waiting for me back in Columbus and several beautiful girlfriends to choose from, so baseball isn't in my future," Jon said.

"General Marshall is anxious as hell to get things moving over here. He said that he would come over and personally kick some ass if we don't drive the Japs out of Burma by next fall," Colonel Arvin said smiling.

"There's a good chance of that happening, sir. But from what I understand, we need a lot more troops," Jon remarked.

Colonel Buck Arvin was one of six colonels from the G-2 Intelligence Directorate assigned solely to the CBI theater of operations. The six colonels were key players in the army's strategic intelligence strategy for the CBI. They were responsible for delivering special assignments to Jon and his team.

The personal delivery system was the brainchild of General Marshall himself. It was established because of the fear that the Japanese or Germans may have broken the Allies' communication codes. The threat of spies infiltrating into the intelligence organizations in Washington DC was high. No matter how thorough the vetting of employees for top secret positions, these organizations were always vulnerable to people with other loyalties. It didn't matter if it was the United States, Great Britain, Germany, or Japan. Every country's intelligence system was at risk.

Because of those risks and the importance of the special missions, General Marshall had developed a carrier system to communicate directly with the special mission agents in the field. For the CBI region, there would be six colonels that were entrusted with carrying the operational information. Nothing was ever written down. It was always delivered in person by one of the colonels. Ancillary information, which was usually limited to Japanese army troop movement, was carried in a secure pouch, locked and chained to the colonel's wrist. And the colonels always carried a sidearm on their hips as well as a concealed weapon in an ankle holster.

Jon had met all six colonels at a Top Secret meeting in the White House, hosted by President Roosevelt and General George C. Marshall, the United States Army chief of staff and the president's chief military adviser.

The fifty-four special mission agents that Jon had trained with had been boarded on five buses at Camp Ritchie one morning. They weren't told anything except that they were going to Washington DC. When the buses pulled up to the gates at the White House and stopped, they were told to get out and line up in formation.

Expecting to be marched straight down Pennsylvania Avenue to an adjacent government building, they were totally surprised when they were marched through the White House gates and into the east door of the White House. From there, they were escorted by five Secret Service agents into the East Room where rows of folding chairs had been set up.

After the agents were seated, they were even more surprised and struggled to stand, when General Marshall entered the room along with Franklin Delano Roosevelt, the thirty-second president of the United States. With the president's nod, his aides and all but one secret service agent left the room. It was just the president, General Marshal, one Secret Service agent, and fifty-five highly trained special agents. The fifty-fifth agent in the room was General William Donovan, a personal friend of the president, and his director of the Office of Strategic Services (OSS).

After General Marshall told everyone to have a seat, he introduced President Roosevelt. The president spoke not only briefly and frankly, but also with the concern and conviction dictated by his office in times of crisis.

"Gentlemen, you are fifty-four of the best agent combatants that America has trained. You are the elite of the elites from the military services, Secret Service, OSS, and the CIC. You have been chosen to be one of the last lines of defense in this country's fight against the enemies of this nation and the free world. You are to use your skills to be a lethal and positive force for good," President Roosevelt said.

"The orders that you will receive today give you authority over theater commanders, and that includes General Eisenhower. You are authorized to use any and all means that you deem necessary to subdue and defeat the enemy. These orders are designated as 'Eyes Only'; that means these orders are known only to you, General Marshall, and me. You are not to show them to anyone below the rank of lieutenant general; and only then when absolutely necessary. And remember, any special mission orders that you receive from General Marshall you can consider coming directly from me," President Roosevelt remarked.

The president paused before speaking his next thoughts. "It is unfortunate but imperative that we send you into harm's way to accomplish what you've been trained to do. But what you will be doing will significantly impact the outcome of this war, and let's pray that your actions will also shorten it. General Marshal will continue this meeting along with General Donovan and provide you with your written orders, signed by me, before you ship out to your individual assignments. I wish you the very best of luck and Godspeed." With that, the president turned his wheelchair around and exited the room with his Secret Service agent.

That had been an unusually proud and significant moment for Jon, and he expected the other special agents as well. And now he was in the CBI theater and was about to receive his first operational assignment. He silently prayed, *God, let me be up to the challenge.*

"Jon," Colonel Arvin said, "let me introduce you to the two SOE agents you will probably be spending the rest of the war with. To your left is Agent Miles Murphy, and to your right is Agent Henri Morreau. You will be living, eating, and working special mission assignments with these two gentlemen until General Marshall provides you with orders stating otherwise."

Colonel Arvin paused and then continued, "The British SOE and G-2 Directorate are working the CBI theater jointly. However, special mission assignments for this team will come directly through me, or one of the other five colonels that Jon met in Washington before he deployed. All special mission assignments that you receive will have been deemed critically important to the Allies' success in the CBI and coordinated between MI6 in Britain and G-2 in Washington. Jon will be the team leader. Now let's take a look at what we are facing," Colonel Arvin said.

Colonel Arvin proceeded to tell them that when Rangoon fell to the Japanese in March 1942, the defeated British, Indian, and Burmese forces had to abandon the city before the Japanese overwhelmed them. The British had destroyed most of their supplies and munitions. In their haste to exit the city they left behind a tremendous amount of wartime supplies that were in US dockside warehouses on the Rangoon wharves. These materials were part of the lend-lease program and destined for China.

Among the items left behind were twelve hundred trucks, five thousand tires, five hundred cases of M1 carbines, four hundred

M1919 machine guns, five million rounds of M1 cartridges, twenty million rounds of M1919 cartridges, fifty thousand blankets, three hundred electrical generators, rice and food stuff for twenty thousand men, eighty pallets of cigarettes, and three hundred cases of American whiskey.

Most of the stores were located in four warehouses along the Rangoon wharf. The colonel pulled out a large map of Rangoon and laid it on the table. The three agents crowded around to see what the colonel would be showing them.

"The four Allied warehouses are located at the wharves that connect to Eden Street, right here," Colonel Arvin said as he pointed out the location on the map.

"They are exactly three miles past Monkey Point. You'll pass the oil refinery and seven jetties on the right side of the river before coming to the Eden Street jetty. Our primary targets are the rifles, machine guns and ammunition in the warehouse nearest the jetty, and the two middle warehouses that house over eight hundred assembled vehicles with their tanks filled with gas. The fourth warehouse holds the remainder of unassembled trucks and jeeps," Colonel Arvin stated.

Colonel Arvin took a sip of coffee before proceeding, "We've arranged for a British navy PBY to take you all to a location in the Andaman Sea, where you will rendezvous with a fishing boat tomorrow evening at 1700 hours. The fishing boat is well known to the locals and the Japanese in Rangoon. Over the last two years, it has docked at the Eden Street jetty at all hours of the day and night. The boat owner usually sells his catch at a market, which he also owns, two blocks due east of the jetty. After he unloads his fish, he has another crew that takes the boat back out for another catch. The owner is a native of the Andaman Islands. He enlisted in the Indian Army back in 1930 and spent six of his eight years as a Royal Marine commando. All records of his service have been expunged, so he can't be traced back to the British Army," Colonel Arvin said.

The colonel explained that the team would enter the three warehouses through the rotted wood siding at the northwest corner of each warehouse. They would carry their pre-packed explosive charges in crates where the fish were packed in and carried in up the street to the market. Jon would take the first warehouse with the guns and ammunition. There will be fewer charges to set in this one. Miles would take the next warehouse, and Henri would take the third warehouse. He told them that they would be using pencil fuses to detonate the explosives. These fuses were engineered for a three-hour delay. After the agents triggered the fuse, acid would corrode a wire, releasing the striker that would strike a percussion cap and trigger the detonation. That should give them a one-hour window to get back to the boat and begin their return trip to the Andaman Sea and the rendezvous with a PBY for their return to Calcutta.

"Colonel, what do the Jap defenses look like around these warehouses?" Jon asked.

"Our sources in Rangoon are telling us that during the daytime there are three street patrols: 6:00 a.m., 11:00 a.m., and 4:00 p.m. At night, there are two patrols: one at 8:00 p.m. and the other at midnight. After midnight, all but three guards are repositioned around the oil refinery five blocks to the south. The Japanese Thirty-Third Division is occupying Rangoon, and they are short on soldiers because of the casualties incurred in the fight for Rangoon. The Japanese Eighteenth Division just came in by sea ten days ago, but most have already departed to reinforce the Japanese divisions engaging the British at Imphal."

"Sir, what about river patrols?" Henri Morreau asked.

"Henri, the motorboat patrols are on the same schedule as the street patrols. That seems a bit unusual, but everything that the Japs do is unconventional," Colonel Arvin stated.

"Sir, are there any diversions planned prior to our planned entry or exit time?" Agent Murphy asked.

"No Miles, we want this to go as quietly as possible. We want the movement of the boat in and out of the river to be as normal as possible. It's paramount that we protect our asset in Rangoon," Colonel Arvin stated.

Colonel Arvin took another sip of coffee and continued, "We are planning on you all landing at the Eden Street jetty at 0100 hours. You should have all of the charges placed no later than 0300 hours. By the time the charges blow, you should be thirty miles from the jetty."

"Where will we be flying out of?" Jon asked.

"You'll be flying out of the SOE airfield, two miles east of here, tomorrow morning at 0800 hours. The SOE munitions team will deliver the explosives and fuses to the aircraft, but I would get with the explosive boys and make sure you are familiar with how the fuses work. Oh, and we've taken Agent Preston's recommendation from his Anzio operation and will be issuing you all the silenced High Standard HDM .22-caliber semi-automatic pistols with subsonic bullets. When the pistol is fired, the loudest noise will be the click of the bolt. You will have to manually pull the bolt back to chamber another bullet. You will also be taking the newly modified suppressed Thompson submachine gun, which is far from silent. Good luck, and good hunting, gentlemen," Colonel Arvin said.

He shook each agent's hand, and before they left the room, Colonel Arvin said, "Do you all have any further questions? If not, I am available up to the time of your takeoff tomorrow morning."

CHAPTER 7

ON BOARD THE *PEQUOD* ANDAMAN SEA

The following morning, the three agents met at the SOE aircraft hangar number three. The agents had picked up their automatic weapons at the SOE armory shortly after 0600 hours. They each were issued the suppressed Thompson .45-caliber submachine gun. Each agent carried their individual side arms; Jon carried his Colt .45 automatic and Miles and Henri their .9 mm Berettas. In addition, all three were now carrying the suppressed High Standard .22-caliber pistol and two knives; a SOE Fairbairn-Sykes double-edged fighting knife and a slightly heavier OSS smatchet.

While in the hangar, all three agents donned their parachutes and Mae West life vests. For security reasons, they entered the PBY before the large hangar doors were opened. Both the German and Japanese consulates in Calcutta had been a hotbed for clandestine activities since 1936. The Japanese even used their Buddhist religion as a cover for agents because large numbers of monks came from Japan each year to visit the sites and shrines where Buddha had lived, as well as the holy cities of Benares and Gaya.

In fact, over the last week, Jon had uncovered a Japanese agent's upcoming visit to one of the most exclusive hotels in

Chittagong, seventy miles east of Calcutta on the Bay of Bengal coast. He had filed his report with G-2 and was hoping that it would be his team's next mission. Jon decided that there was no need to give Miles or Henri a heads-up on the Japanese spy until their current mission was completed.

At 0940 hours, the pilot had the aircraft towed from the hangar. Once the tow vehicle was clear of the aircraft, the ground crew chief gave the All Clear signal and the copilot started the starboard engine followed by the port engine. After checking the oil and engine temperatures and putting in the current altimeter setting, the aircraft was cleared to taxi. Since the wind was out of the southeast, they were cleared to taxi to Runway 19. At the runway threshold, they ran up both engines and checked all the engine gauges for any discrepancies or red warning lights. When all the checks were completed, they requested clearance for takeoff and were cleared for an immediate departure. The pilot pulled the aircraft onto the active runway, pushed the throttles to 85 percent rpm, and began their takeoff roll. It took a little over one hundred yards to reach the airspeed for liftoff. As the aircraft gained altitude, it turned to a heading of 145 degrees and continued its climb to ten thousand feet.

Twenty minutes after takeoff, they leveled off at ten thousand feet, pulled the throttles back, adjusted the rpm to 55 percent, and began cruising at 125 knots airspeed. The distance to their rendezvous point was eleven hundred miles and it would take a little over eight and one half hours flying time.

Thirty minutes after the aircraft had cleared the mainland, the crew checked for boats or ships within a five-mile radius. Seeing none, the pilot cleared the aircraft gunners for five minutes of live fire practice each. Miles and Henri took turns at the machine guns because they had to fire the guns every ninety days to maintain their currency on the PBY weapon system. Even Jon was allowed to fire to get familiar with the Catalina's .30- and .50-caliber guns.

After eight hours of flying, Jon was awakened from his sleep when he heard the pitch of the engines change and felt the aircraft go into a descent. This meant that they were approximately forty-five minutes from their rendezvous. The aircraft was descending to five hundred feet to avoid radar detection and to enable the pilots and spotters to identify the boat. Due to headwinds, the aircraft wouldn't arrive at the rendezvous location until 1645 hours. Twenty minutes after they leveled off, the pilots picked up the signal from the AN/UPN-1 radar beacon located on the fishing boat. They turned towards the direction that the beacon bearing indicated and descended to two hundred feet. Twenty minutes later, the copilot spotted the fishing boat five degrees off to starboard. The pilot turned the aircraft slightly to the right and waited for a smoke signal from the boat to confirm the direction of the wind. After the confirmation of the wind direction, the pilot positioned the aircraft to land into the wind and gently touched down in the calm Andaman Sea. He then taxied to within fifty feet of the boat's port side and cut the engines to idle.

Before the PBY crewmen had opened the port side sliding hatch, the fishing boat's motorized fifteen foot launch had pulled up to the port hatch and secured a rope to the wing strut. The three agents were helped into the launch followed by seven hundred pounds of RDX plastic explosives. Once the launch cast off, a gunner secured the portside's sliding hatch. The pilot then turned his flying boat back into the wind, pushed up the throttles, and began his takeoff on the glass smooth Andaman Sea. Thirty minutes after touchdown, the PBY was lifting off and heading northeast back to Calcutta.

The three agents helped the captain and four crewmembers secure the explosives and fuses into fishing crates. The crewmen then layered fresh caught fish over the explosives to hide them. After the crates were inspected by the captain and determined that the explosives were well hidden, he told one of his shipmates to haul up the anchor so they could get underway.

Several minutes later, the captain came topside, started the diesel engines, and pointed the boat in the direction of Rangoon. After setting the course, he turned the wheel over to his second mate, came over to where the three agents were sitting, and introduced himself.

"Welcome aboard the *Pequod*. I'm Captain Htaw Ahab."

He told them that he would call them Yank, English, and Frenchy, if it was okay with them. The three agents nodded their heads and smiled. Jon had immediately picked up on the captain's name and the name of his boat's name. He had read and thoroughly enjoyed *Moby Dick* in high school.

"Captain, have you sighted any Japanese ships, patrol planes, or white whales since you've been in the rendezvous area?"

"No, Yank. We haven't sighted any ships, and it is rare to see any Jap aircraft this far out in the Andaman. And the white whales are usually found two hundred miles farther west," Captain Ahab said laughing.

"Have you ever had any trouble with Japanese patrol boats in the Irrawaddy at night?" asked Henri.

"I can't think of a single incident in the last two years, Frenchy, where the Japs have stopped anyone at night. The Japs only have two patrol boats to cover the forty miles of river and the twenty miles of Irrawaddy channel leading to the Andaman. Unless they have been tipped off by Jap intelligence, we shouldn't have a problem. They see my boat every day and every night and haven't bothered me yet; probably because I sell a lot of fresh fish and squid to them. But just in case, keep your weapons handy. I have a M1919 Browning machine gun under the canvas you're leaning on, Yank. If we do have trouble, we'll try to outrun them. And just in case you're wondering, I have two brand new 300-hp diesel engines that are well hidden behind a false bulkhead below deck. I can outrun any boat that the Japs have in Rangoon. If for some reason we can't outrun them, then we will fight," Captain Ahab said.

"Good enough for me," Jon said. Miles and Henri, standing behind him, both nodded in agreement.

"We'll cruise with both engines until we hit the channel then I'll shut one engine down and we'll move up the Irrawaddy just as I always do. It will take us five hours to reach the channel and another hour to reach the Eden Street jetty. I've got Burmese clothing for you all to wear so everything will look normal. There is at least one night guard on duty at the warehouse closest to the jetty," Captain Ahab said.

After Captain Ahab lit a cigarette, he continued, "After we dock, one of my shop workers will approach the guard and offer him tea and sweet biscuits, as she does every night when we dock. Tonight's tea will contain a sedative that will knock him out within five minutes. The Jap guard will no doubt be killed when the warehouses blow, which will also cover our tracks."

"Will we be toting the explosives to the warehouses in our packs or in the fish crates?" Miles asked.

"In the fish crates, English. You can take as many backpacks as you can carry into the warehouse. After we dock, people from my shop will board the boat and begin removing the crates of fish. You all will need to stay out of sight until the guard is knocked out. After all the fish have been offloaded, English and Frenchy will team up with one of my crew and move your individual fish crates to the warehouse assigned to you. English, you will take the second warehouse in from the dock. Frenchy, you will take the third. My men will stand guard while you enter and set your charges. They will hand you the remaining charges after you set the first group. You will each enter the warehouse through the loose wooded panels that my men will show you. After you finish setting all your charges, you all will bring the fish crates back to the boat. The three of you will need to stay in the shadows, and act as armed lookouts until we cast off. If a Japanese patrol boat approaches before we get underway, get into the water, and hide under the jetty pier," Captain Ahab stated.

"Will you be working with me, Captain?" Jon asked.

"I will help carry the last crate to the first warehouse and act as your lookout, Yank. I will hand you the second hundred pounds of explosives when you finish with placing the first," Captain Ahab said.

"Sounds like a good plan, Captain. What happens if a Jap guard or two shows up unexpectedly?" Jon asked.

"Well Yank, I am a trained Royal Marine commando. I'll be carrying a silenced pistol, and I'm very good with a knife," Captain Ahab remarked.

"Okay, Captain. I guess that was a dumb question on my part," Jon stated.

"No problem, Yank. I'd be asking the same questions if I was in your position. Now if you will excuse me, I have some things to prepare before we get to the channel," Captain Ahab concluded.

Jon eased himself to the deck and leaned against the canvas-covered crate hiding the M1919 machine gun. His gut told him that he could trust the captain, which was one thing less to worry about. In fact, it almost sounded too easy; but Jon knew that he had to watch out for Mr. Kilroy, who was always raising his ugly head and causing trouble. Jon had always been very good at thinking on his feet when things went awry. Anzio had proved how quickly he could react in an emergency situation. Nothing like getting shot at to get your adrenaline flowing.

CHAPTER 8

RANGOON, BURMA

Jon woke up when Henri shook his shoulder and told him they were thirty minutes away from the Irrawaddy channel that would take them to Rangoon. They would be docking in another hour and a half.

Jon got out the makeup kit given to him by the folks at the SOE detachment. Each agent would put the brown makeup on his face, arms, neck, and hands. It would take thirty minutes to color their skin, and it would last for twelve hours.

As he was applying his makeup, Miles looked over at Jon and said, "You look rather sexy as a Burmese, mate."

"If I agree with you, English, we'd both be wrong. Make sure you darken that blond hair of yours, otherwise you might glow in the dark," Jon remarked.

"Yeah, English, and make sure you grab a couple bottles of whiskey for the trip home because the ones I grab are for me only," Henri stated.

They all laughed, which relieved some of the tension they were all feeling. Tension was good before an op. It kept your brain and body at a higher state of awareness and could mean the difference in you spotting the enemy before he spotted you.

An hour and a half later, they were approaching the Eden Street jetty. Captain Ahab maneuvered and then turned his boat so the starboard side was against the pier with the front of the boat facing the Irrawaddy.

"Don't worry, I always approach and dock this way. If I didn't do it now, the Japanese would be suspicious," Captain Ahab said.

The jetty and pier extended at least two hundred feet into the four thousand-foot-wide Irrawaddy. Even though the dock looked to be in a state of disrepair, the workers from the captain's fish market hustled down it and were on the boat the minute that the lines were secured to the docking cleats.

After securing the dock lines, Captain Ahab knew something was wrong. There were at least four guards that he could see in the lights of a Japanese troop carrier parked near the last warehouse.

His store workers gave him the bad news when they reached the boat. There would be four guards at the warehouse tonight.

On the captain's order, his workers went into the hold four at a time and began removing the crates of fish onto the pier and moving them to the market. It took the workers three trips to remove all the fish and squid. After the last pair left, the three special crates were removed by two of the crews and set on the deck of the *Pequod*.

Captain Ahab went into the hold where the three agents were waiting. "Gentlemen," Captain Ahab said, "we have a problem. There are four guards at the warehouses tonight. We can abort or continue. It's your call."

"Do we know where the guards are positioned?" Jon asked.

"No, I'll have to check," Captain Ahab said.

"What about giving all of them the spiked tea?" Henri questioned.

"Let me do my reconnaissance. I'll be back in thirty minutes. In the mean time, stay hidden." Captain Ahab told them.

Thirty minutes after he left, Captain Ahab returned to the boat. "There are four guards, two out front of the warehouse closest to the street and two on roving patrol. They increased the number of guards because someone was caught peddling tires today. The

Japs traced it back to the front warehouse and the night guard taking bribes. The guard and thief were executed this afternoon."

"We can still make this work, Captain, as long as there isn't a change in guards during this shift," Jon stated.

"From what my market workers are telling me, there won't be a guard change until 0600 hours," Captain Ahab remarked.

"Tell your worker to take tea and sweets to all four guards. Five minutes after they finish their tea, we'll move on them," Jon said.

Captain Ahab left and went back to his market. He returned thirty minutes later. "The two guards on patrol would not take a break. They're afraid of being shot for dereliction of duty," Captain Ahab told them. "I've instructed two of my men to take them out once they reach the warehouse nearest the river. By then, the two guards out front will be passed out; which should be right about now."

Jon was watching the two Jap guards as they rounded the northeast corner of the warehouse over a hundred feet away. Out of the shadows behind the guards, two of the captain's men appeared. Then both guards were lying motionless on the ground.

As his men were dragging the dead guards into the shadows, Captain Ahab directed his two remaining men on the boat to set the fish crates on the dock.

Miles and Henri each teamed up with a crewmember, picked up a crate containing three hundred pounds of plastic explosives, and moved up the jetty. Jon and the captain picked up the third crate and moved towards the first warehouse.

Miles stopped at the rear of the second warehouse and turned into the alley separating it from the first warehouse. Henri did the same as he got to the third warehouse. They each moved between the warehouses and set their crate down in between the clumps of tall elephant grass. They each moved to where their crewman was indicating the entrance into the warehouse.

It wasn't so much loose panels as it was rotted and termite-eaten wooden boards. They removed the boards and set them down quietly in the grass and vines that clung to the rear walls. They picked up one of the three backpacks in each crate, each with one hundred pounds of explosives, and entered the warehouses. The warehouses were 150 feet wide and six hundred feet long. When they turned on their red filtered flashlights, they immediately saw the rows of heavy trucks. They were parked so close together that Miles and Henri had to side step down the rows.

Miles and Henri began placing two-pound charges beside the gas tanks of every fourth truck. After each placement, they inserted a pencil detonator into the soft clay-like C-4. They crushed the end of the thin copper tube with a pair of sharp-nosed pliers, which crushed the glass vial inside releasing the cupric chloride. When the explosive detonated, it would create enough heat and hot shrapnel to ignite the gas tanks of the trucks around them. After they finished setting all three backpacks of charges, they exited the warehouses and carried the fish crates back to the boat. By that time, the natives had returned their empty crates from the store. Henri was wishing he could stand off a mile away with a bottle of wine and watch the fireworks.

When Jon and Captain Ahab reached the back of their warehouse, the captain began removing the rotten boards. Jon picked up one of the two backpacks loaded with twenty-five four-pound charges and entered the building. When Jon turned on his red filtered flashlight, he began making his way through hundreds of crates stenciled M1 Rifles. It took ten minutes of searching before he found the ammunition stored in the front of the building. He set the first one hundred pounds of explosives throughout the hundreds of pallets of ammunition. On his way to get the second pack of explosives, he discovered where the M1919 Browning machine guns were located. It took him nearly ninety minutes to complete his task.

When Jon exited the building, he and the captain lifted the empty crate and returned to the boat. After the crates were stored below deck, the captain started both diesel engines. When the lines were cast off from the dock, he powered up one engine, moved out into the Irrawaddy, and headed down the river.

A mile after passing Monkey Point, the captain pushed up the throttle on the second engine, and the *Pequod* began cruising at twenty-five knots. After three hours, the acid in the pencil fuse ate through the wire holding back the striker. The striker then flew down the hollow center of the detonator tube and hit the percussion cap. They heard the explosions from thirty miles away and saw the fireballs that reached over a thousand feet into the night sky.

Jon was content that the mission had succeeded, but it had been almost too easy. He knew that eventually it would become more dangerous and sometime in the future they would have to fight for their lives.

An hour later and Rangoon far behind, Henri pulled three bottles of twenty-five-year-old scotch whisky from his backpack and handed one to Jon, one to Miles, and one to Captain Ahab. He then pulled a bottle of French champagne from his backpack for himself.

"I hope you don't mind me keeping the champagne?" Henri asked.

"Not at all," they all replied almost simultaneously.

CHAPTER 9

CALCUTTA, INDIA

Two days after their return from the Rangoon mission, Jon received a coded message from G-2 regarding the enemy agent that he had the OSS investigate while he was gone. Unknown to Miles and Henri, Colonel Arvin had given him a tasking to investigate a suspected Japanese agent here in Asia. Jon had gone through the folder of information, made an appointment with the OSS commander and requested the commander's help in investigating the individual in Saigon.

The message stated that a colonel from the Pentagon would be arriving in three days with the team's tasking order. The term tasking order meant that the president of the United States had to sign off on the assignment using a presidential executive order.

The SOE had received a report from one of its operatives stating that the Rangoon mission was a huge success. In addition to the warehouses with the guns, ammunition, and trucks, the fourth warehouse with the disassembled vehicles and their parts had been destroyed. Also destroyed were the four adjacent warehouses to the north, containing Japanese munitions and hardware. There had been one hundred .75 mm artillery pieces and two hundred heavy trucks loaded with machine guns, rifles, hand grenades, and ammunition that were destined for use in the invasion of India. It had become a bonanza mission for Jon and his team.

OSS Detachment 101 had also passed on a report from one of their agents in the field. The OSS agent had an informant inside Japanese headquarters in Rangoon. The informant's information stated that the Japanese were totally demoralized by the loss of their weapons and that replenishment from Japan would be near impossible due to the war going badly in the Pacific. In the last six months, Allied submarines had decimated Japanese shipping and hardly anything, except small boats, were getting through the South China Sea into the Indian Ocean.

Three days later, Miles and Henri were in Jon's quarters when Corporal Tom Calvert arrived with a message from Lieutenant Colonel MacKenzie. The colonel was requesting their presence at the SOE office for a classified briefing at 1300 hours. The corporal added that Lieutenant Colonel MacKenzie was ordering them to be in their seats fifteen minutes prior to the scheduled briefing time.

At 1258 hours, Jon, Miles, and Henri arrived via jeep at the British-American Club. They entered the SOE offices at precisely 1300 hours. Lieutenant Colonel MacKenzie came storming out of his office.

"Didn't you get my message to be here fifteen minutes early?" Lieutenant Colonel MacKenzie demanded.

"Yes, sir", Jon said, "but we were extremely busy, so I disregarded it."

"That's insubordination, Agent Preston! I'm writing you up for this," Lieutenant Colonel MacKenzie said seething with anger.

Jon approached Lieutenant Colonel MacKenzie and in a low voice said, "And I'll be sure to let Lord Mountbatten know of your behavior at the Jade Gate two weeks ago. Rather unbecoming behavior for a senior officer in Her Majesty's Service, wouldn't you say, MacKenzie."

Jon had accidentally stumbled on the colonel at a Calcutta bar and brothel several blocks from the Catholic mission where he volunteered. The lieutenant colonel, while still in uniform, had gotten into a brawl over being double-charged for drinks. Jon had happened on the scene while driving by the bar on his way to the mission. The bar owner ended up clubbing and knocking out the colonel. He was throwing the colonel into the street as Jon drove by.

Before the bar owner could call the Military Police, Jon intervened, paid the bar owner quite well to keep quiet, and call a cab to take the colonel home. He also told the bar owner not to say anything to the colonel or anyone else about who helped him. In turn, Jon offered him ten bottles of American booze. Jon turned away and left the stunned colonel reeling. *It's always good to have leverage*, Jon thought.

As the trio entered the classified briefing room, Colonel John Renick stood and shook hands with Jon. Jon then introduced Colonel Renick to Agents Murphy and Morreau. After some light talk with coffee, tea, and sweets, Colonel Renick asked to get started.

The colonel started by telling the three agents that eight weeks ago internal security at the Pentagon had plugged a leak in one of the G-2 sections in the Pentagon. During a random exit search, security guards had discovered top secret documents in a G-2 secretary's purse. After FBI agents interrogated the woman, she gave up her boyfriend, who was a supervisor at the French Embassy. Since the embassy worker was an American citizen, FBI agents apprehended him that evening as he left work.

During his interrogation, they discovered that he was spying for his cousin, a high-ranking senior official in the French Vichy Indochina government in Saigon. Seven years ago, at the height of the depression, his cousin had provided him with a sterling recommendation, which enabled him to get a job at the French Embassy, in Washington. He was now paying back his cousin by sending him top secret American intelligence, obtained through his girlfriend and lover. The American secrets were sent through a series of diplomatic carriers until it reached him in Saigon or a location designated by his cousin.

The FBI agents obtained the name of the official in Saigon, Rene Aguillon. They also turned the embassy spy to our side in exchange for commuting his and his lover's death sentences. Mr. Aguillon is the executive director of information for the French Indochina government.

"We also persuaded our turned embassy spy to send several pieces of misinformation to Mr. Aguillon on the planned Allied invasion of Japan. An embassy carrier is scheduled to deliver the diplomatic pouch to Mr. Aguillon next week in Chittagong," Colonel Renick stated.

The colonel continued and went on to say that this information was given to Jon, before their mission to Rangoon, so he could find out when and where Mr. Aguillon was going to be in Chittagong. Jon contacted OSS assets in Saigon and sent CIC agents to Chittagong. They discovered that our Mr. Aguillon has a hotel reservation in the most exclusive hotel in Chittagong, the Circuit House. He would be there in five days.

"We want Mr. Aguillon to take possession of the pouch from the French Embassy courier. We figure that he will deem this information to be so important that he will want to get it into the hands of his contact as quickly as possible. And we want the three of you there when the transfer occurs," Colonel Renick said.

"What is the executive order for?" Jon asked.

"Under Executive Order 44-219, the president and General Marshall want you all to take this spy network down with prejudice," Colonel Renick said.

He then told the three agents to make sure that they have an unfortunate accident. Before the colonel could start another sentence, Jon asked the question that had been on his mind since he had heard about the network.

"Sir, has my identity been compromised?" Jon asked.

"We don't think so, Jon. We interrogated both spies extensively, but no agent names were ever mentioned. Normally, when the G-2 staff sends material to be typed by the Top Secret cleared secretarial pool, it only contains code names. However, we have lost three OSS agents in Indochina in the last thirty days, and we believe they were compromised by the same network of spies," Colonel Renick stated.

Colonel Renick told them that an OSS agent in Saigon investigated Mr. Aguillon. The agent had sent a report stating that this guy was living too well to be just a senior government official. Colonel Renick concluded that the Japanese were paying extremely well and that he was making a small fortune off the secrets he was selling.

"On Thursday, you all will be taking a PBY and rendezvousing with a boat in the Gulf of Bengal, one hundred miles southwest of Chittagong. One of our American OSS agents, Richard Dubois, will be in charge of getting you all into Chittagong. In the folders on the table are your cover identities as French-Indochina opium traders. Memorize the information, and make certain that you leave any identification that you now carry in your locker in this office," Colonel Renick concluded.

The colonel recommended that they go into the officer's club and have an early dinner. It was going to be a long night.

After dinner, they reconvened their meeting and resumed their study. An hour later, Lieutenant Colonel Kenneth Taylor, the operations officer of OSS Detachment 101, entered the room with Colonel Renick. The lieutenant colonel provided them with the latest intelligence he had on Chittagong.

"Chittagong," Lieutenant Colonel Taylor stated, "despite being close to the border of Burma and having been bombed several times by the Japanese, is still a very open city and booming port town. After the invasion of Burma, thousands of Burmese and Eurasian refugees flooded the city. Along with them came a fair number of Japanese spies; the equivalents to our SOE, CIC, and

OSS agents. These people are as dangerous as our own agents, so be very careful who you talk to."

Lieutenant Colonel Taylor went on to state that arrangements had been made for everyone to stay at the same hotel as Mr. Aguillon; that the Circuit House is used exclusively for diplomats, senior government officials, and visiting VIPs. Agents Preston, Murphy, Morreau, and Captain Dubois would have suites one floor down from Mr. Aguillon. He also told them that the OSS had already wired the suite set aside for Mr. Aguillon and that monitoring devises would be set and monitored by the OSS. And just in case Mr. Aguillon suspects anything and requests a different room, we have wired an alternate suite, which because the hotel is full, is the only room the manager can grant him.

He also told them that they would have one of their Japanese speaking OSS agents monitoring the conversations just in case Mr. Aguillon spoke Japanese. There would also be four additional undercover OSS agents in the hotel.

"Your cover as opium traders is well known to the hotel because two of their senior hotel staffers are OSS agents. Your cover as opium traders comes with a rich playboy status, elegant clothes, jewelry, lots of cash, and a 126-foot luxury diesel-powered yacht, called *Miss Anne*. Every Friday night, the hotel hosts a dance. There will be a special charity ball the week that you all arrive. The three of you will be the hotel's guests of honor that evening. We've arranged for the hotel to send out invitations to their key Chittagong VIPs and all visitors to the hotel. Your company has already donated five thousand dollars to the event. We have also made arrangements for ten very beautiful French, Indian, and Thai ladies to be your personal guests. They come from very respectable families in the area. Six of the ladies are trained SOE and OSS operatives," Lieutenant Colonel Taylor said.

Colonel Renick ended the meeting by saying, "To keep your cover as real as possible, there will be five kilos of opium onboard the ship. Each of you will have a kilo in your room. Hand out samples discretely, and you are authorized to tip the waiters and staff in opium. All of the *Miss Anne*'s crewmembers are OSS and they will guard the boat during your stay at the hotel. Your flight will leave at 1600 hours on Thursday. Carry with you only the bare essentials. Everything that you might need will be on the boat, including weapons. You all will have five days onboard the *Miss Anne* to relax and prepare for your mission. Good luck, gentlemen."

CHAPTER 10

ABOARD THE *ANNE MARIE* INDIAN OCEAN

The flight in the PBY was uneventful. But the agents and the flight crew were stricken by the elegance of the yacht as they made their approach to landing. After touchdown, the pilot taxied to within twenty yards of the yacht. The yacht's crew had already launched its twenty-foot motor launch and carefully maneuvered to the starboard side of the PBY to collect the agents.

Once onboard the *Anne Marie*, the three agents were awed even more. She was built with quarter-inch Norwegian steel with lapped plating, secured with speed rivets, which were counter sunk on the outside to create a smoother hull. The decks were built of two-inch teak decking. She had teak panels on the outside and inside and an extravagantly large wheelhouse. Below deck, there were four single and three double staterooms paneled in white oak and trimmed with teak. The doors were made of dark-stained teak, and the hallways and stairs were paneled in teak.

She was the fastest and most stable 126-foot diesel yacht built in Asia in 1926. With her twenty-one-foot beam, eight-and-a-half-foot draft, and a 191-ton displacement, she could cruise at nine knots and had a top speed of fourteen knots. Her usual crew complement consisted of twelve, plus a captain.

The trio were given a double stateroom, two rooms with four beds, two washrooms and heads, and a lavishly stocked bar.

Jon was the first to speak, "I could definitely get used to this."

After an hour of settling into their rooms and helping themselves to the bar, they received a knock on their door. A steward told them that the captain would like to see them in the lounge in thirty minutes. He also suggested that they dress casually in the garments in their closets. If they needed help choosing what to wear, he could assist them.

Jon spoke quickly, "We would like that very much." He turned and winked at Miles and Henri; they were as unaccustomed to what a rich playboy should wear as Jon was.

When they entered the lounge, the steward eagerly greeted them and motioned them to a table near the large mahogany bar. He suggested the 1928 Dom Perignon, which had a unique aroma of both clove and mint that morphed into the more definitive spearmint.

"That is an excellent choice," stated Henri, who turned to John and Miles. "It comes from Espernay, France. My father grew up a mile from the winery and worked there as a teenager. This specific champagne vintage was first produced in 1921 by Moët & Chandon, but they didn't release it until 1936. It is one of the finest champagnes made in France."

"I'll take your word for it, Henri. Serve it up, mate," Miles said smiling and looking directly at the steward.

As the steward finished pouring three flutes of the champagne, the captain walked into the lounge. "I'll have one too, Mitch," Captain Dubois said as he joined the trio at the table.

"Gentlemen, I'm Captain Richard Dubois. I already know your alias names, so let's stick with those. And in case you are wondering, Dubois is my real name. It is a very common name in France, not unlike your Smith surname in America. I assume that your quarters are quite suitable. And may I also assume that you are Mr. Bernard Perrotte," he said looking at Jon; "you are Mr.

Eric Rosier," looking at Miles; "and finally, you're Mr. Christian Thibodeau," he said looking at Henri.

"Don't worry I'm not a mind reader. Mr. Perrotte probably does not remember me, but I was on the Presidential Secret Service detail at the White House when he and fifty of his special mission brothers were entertained by President Roosevelt and General Marshall. I never forget a face, which is good in this profession. I was tapped for this job when they found out I was certified as a ship captain, and spoke fluent French. The other two were quite obvious since Mr. Thibodeau holds his cigarette like a Frenchman."

The captain continued to tell them that Mr. Aguillon's arrival had been delayed two days because of an Allied bombing raid on the railroad yards in Saigon. Therefore they would be cruising our here for seven days, which was ideal because it will allow time for everyone to brush up on their French. With the exception of Mr. Thibodeau, the captain added. "From this point on, only French will be spoken aboard this vessel. Is that clear to everyone?" Captain Dubois asked. All three agents nodded their agreement.

"Good. Tonight we are having a late dinner where you will meet four of my best female agents. They have agreed to act as your escorts during your time in Chittagong. Your room arrangements at the Circuit House have also been changed. Each of us that go ashore will have a separate suite. I will see all of you in the dining room at 2100 hours. Dress in the evening wear that the steward sets out for you."

Jon had understood all of what the Captain had said. He had learned French from his mother and grandmother. They had immigrated to the US after World War I ended. His mother was a war bride. She had married an American pilot flying for the Lafayette Escadrille, an all-American unit that was part of the French Air Service. He brought her and her mother to America in 1918; Jon was born two years later. From as far back as Jon could remember, French and English were spoken in their household. Now it was like moving back into time when all he and his grandmother would speak was French. She used to read the classics to him and he fell in love with the language at an early age.

Now he would be putting his speaking skills on the line. In the morning, he would immerse himself in the language and resurrect those skills. Needless to say, this was going to be an interesting operation. He needed to make the best of the seven days of sailing.

When Jon was training under Colonel Fairbairn, the colonel had discovered Jon's ability to speak French. After that, whenever the colonel flew in to Columbus, he made Jon speak only French. "You will not regret this when you are in the field," Colonel Fairbairn had told him. Now he was thanking the colonel for his forethought.

The cabin steward knocked on their door one hour before dinner. He entered the room and began providing instructions on the dress for the evening. First, he explained dress code etiquette; the when, where, and why certain attire could be worn and by whom. He gave them examples on how to wear the clothing and when to leave a dinner jacket buttoned or unbuttoned. The dress code usually consisted of the traditional dinner jacket, tailcoat, and accompaniments; the black dinner jacket and matching trousers, an optional black formal waistcoat or black cummerbund, a white formal shirt, a black bow tie or alternatively a long black tie, black dress socks, and black formal shoes. However, in this climate, he explained, the white dinner jacket could be substituted with the cummerbund as the preferred covering for the waist. They would be wearing the white dinner jacket this evening.

An hour later, they were dressed and entering the dining room. They were the first to arrive, followed by Captain Dubois. As they had drinks, the captain explained that the boat's power plants consisted of twin 305-horsepower Winton six-cylinder diesel engines. The engines were located sixty-two feet away from the twin forty-eight-inch bronze propellers that were linked by two four-and-one-half-inch-diameter rolled steel shafts. The steering, refrigeration, anchor, lights, and fans throughout the boat were all electric. Passenger comfort had been the driving force behind the state-of-the-art design and construction of the 126-foot twin-engine yacht built in Singapore. The custom furniture and other nondurable goods contributed significantly to the cost of the *Anne Marie*. She was the best in Asia and possibly the world in 1926. She was owned by an American businessman, who had interests in Asia and was on loan to the OSS.

As the captain finished his explanation of the yacht, four of the most beautiful women Jon had ever seen entered the room. The captain seemed exceptionally delighted when they entered, and he moved to them kissing each one on the cheek. "Gentlemen," he said as he turned to the trio, "let me introduce the four loveliest women in all of Asia."

Camille Dupont was the first to be introduced. She was a striking redhead from French Indochina. She was wearing a turquoise taffeta strapless gown with a beaded bodice, arm-length white gloves with a diamond bracelet on her left wrist, diamond necklace, diamond earrings, and turquoise heels. She was to be teamed up with Jon.

Jon was so taken by Camille that he barely heard the captain introduce Jacqueline Lauren, a gorgeous part French and part Thai with short black hair; she was teamed with Miles. And Kathleen Lauren, the twin of Jacqueline, with long, silky black hair; teamed up with Henri. The last lady to be introduced was Desiree Lacroix, a strikingly beautiful French woman with shoulder length blonde hair. She had fled French Indochina with her parents when the Japanese invaded. Desiree would be teamed with Captain Dubois.

The captain sat the men opposite the women at the dining table to insure a continuity of conversation between all the agents. But first, he gave his direction on how he and the girls would support this operation.

"Ladies, Mr. Perrotte is our team leader once we are in port. But, while on this vessel, I am the leader. Our goal over the next seven days is to refresh the French speaking capabilities of these handsome but lethal gentlemen. Speak to them about fashion, drinks, horse riding, and especially, the etiquette of the wealthy, and prepare them for the very rich and influential people that they will meet at the Circuit House. We want them to fit in as wealthy businessmen rather than thug drug lords."

By the time they finished dinner, drinks, and conversation, it was 0200 hours. The captain thanked everyone, reminded them that breakfast was at 0900 hours, and took his leave. After saying thank you to each of the ladies, Jon, Miles, and Henri reluctantly left for their cabin.

CHAPTER II

ABOARD THE *ANNE MARIE*
INDIAN OCEAN

The following morning, Jon was up at 0600 hours seeking out a crewmember that could teach him the French descriptions of the guns and the munitions that were stored onboard the *Anne Marie*. The steward took him to the armory and introduced him to a short Thai-looking crewman with jet-black hair named Brunelle. Jon spent three hours with Brunelle inspecting, learning descriptions, taking apart and putting weapons back together, and learning in detail the French terminology. At 0900 hours he thanked Brunelle, went back to his room, changed clothes, and went to breakfast.

Everyone dressed casual for breakfast. Miles and Henri were already sitting at a table for four in deep conversation with Jacqueline and Kathleen. Jon sat on the empty chair at the table with Camille, Desiree, and Captain Dubois. The captain spoke to Jon as he sat down.

"I understand that you spent some time with Brunelle this morning. Was it of value?"

"Yes, sir, very valuable," Jon replied. "I wanted to make sure that I could disassemble and reassemble our weapons and explain it in French. I want to be able to discuss the value of one weapon over another in French. Being in the drug trade it is sure to come up."

"Very good," the captain replied. "Do you ride horses, Mr. Perrotte?"

"We had a farm in Ohio, and I rode a half Arabian that my dad bought, but I never rode for show. I'd throw a saddle on and ride him around the three-hundred-acre farm. But we only rode on what we call "western saddles." I never rode with those fancy English saddles."

"Good. This morning I want you to spend time with Camille and Desiree. They are both accomplished riders. They both rode on their college equestrian teams in southern California and then the French National Team in the 1936. They will teach you enough general and specific information to get through a conversation with a horse enthusiast. Which, I understand Mr. Aguillon happens to be."

"It will be a pleasure, Captain," Jon said.

After the meal, Jon stayed in the breakfast parlor with Camille and Desiree. Desiree showed black and white photos of her and her horse. They then discussed the kinds of tack; English and dressage saddles; the double-reined bridles, where they used both a bradoon and a curb bit with a smooth curb chain. She also showed Jon photos of the rider clothing. All competition riders wore white breeches with full-seat leather to help them "stick" in the saddle, a belt, and a white shirt and stock tie with a small pin. Most riders wore tall leather boots with spurs. Women riders with long hair usually wore their hair in a bun with a hairnet or show bow.

"It sounds complicated but becomes second nature over time," Desiree stated.

When they got down to discussing competition riding, Desiree showed a film of her riding in jumping competition for the 1936 French National Team. The course, she told him, was 1,200 feet long with twenty jumps that ranged from four to five feet in height. The jumps included one double and three triple combinations and a sixteen-foot water jump.

Camille explained the dressage competition as a test of the ability of rider and horse to precisely execute various gaits and movements. She showed a film of her competing at the University of California Los Angeles (UCLA) in 1936. She explained the piaffe movement, where the horse is performing an elevated trot in place; and the passage movement, where the horse carries an elevated trot. She had to rewind and reshow it to Jon several times to explain extended gaits, which were done at a walk, trot and a canter; and the collected gaits, done at trot, and canter. Jon felt like he was back in college preparing for a competition with his debate team. But Jon was an outstanding student and absorbed everything they taught him.

She next showed him the flying changes or the four-, three-, two-, and one-tempi changes and explained that it often looked as if the horse was skipping when it performed the one-tempi change. The last two movements were the pirouette, where the horse did a 360-degree turn in place, and the half-pass, where the horse goes on a diagonal, moving sideways and forward at the same time.

They broke for lunch at noon, and after a thirty-minute break, they continued with his course on etiquette. They taught him the code of behavior that was expected during social interaction with the people he would be mingling with when they reached the Circuit House. The rules stressed ethical codes but focused mostly on fashion and status.

Camille and Desiree also covered the European sports of cricket and soccer, which Jon found boring but listened just the same. The last subject they discussed was romance.

"The French are a very romantic people, and flirting is always going on at a party," Desiree explained.

Jon learned how to be flirtatious in the right way, what to say, and when to say it, and how to determine when a woman was coming on to him. He also learned when to touch, how to touch, and where to touch. Jon had to admit that he really didn't mind the role-playing that Camille and Desiree put on for him.

Yes, Jon thought, *I could really get used to this kind of clandestine stuff.*

By 2100 hours, they were dressed and back in the dining room for dinner. Tonight, the men were wearing black dinner jackets with the black formal waistcoat. When the ladies arrived, they were all stunningly dressed.

Desiree looked ravishing and seductive. She wore a black faille sleeveless gown with a plunging V-neck that stopped short of her belly button, a gold-sequined belt, black wrap, and black arm-length gloves with a diamond and gold bracelet on her left wrist, a diamond necklace, diamond earrings, and black heels. Even Captain Dubois seemed to be mesmerized by her beauty. The girls seemed to be making a game of it. But whatever they were doing, it was okay with Jon.

After dinner, the men adjourned into the bar, where the captain led them in a discussion and exploration of some of the better liquors and cigars that they would encounter, and how to discuss each. Jon especially liked the 1890 Rémy Martin Louis XIII cognac, and the Argelio Cuban cigar. However, after three hours, he determined that he had explored one too many samples and excused himself from the group.

The next morning the captain dropped by their table and asked the trio to meet him in the ship's lounge after they were finished with breakfast. When they got to the lounge, the captain had a suitcase opened on the bar that was filled with opium. Two crewmen were laying out everything from kilo blocks to small leather bags on two of the tables. For the next three hours the captain and two crewmembers took turns teaching them about opium and a little about the history of the opium trade in colonial Asia.

What interested Jon the most was how opium was a tradable commodity in Asia, like diamonds, jade, oil, rubber, and sugar. The difference between opium and the others was its highly addictive nature. The physical and psychological dependence created by opium created a constant demand for the commodity, which in turn created tremendous economic gain, especially for producers and distributors.

The vast amounts of economic gain even got the Asian nations involved over growing and distribution rights. In the colonial states in Asia, in the nineteenth and early twentieth century, profits from opium created wealth, and wealth created power for the colonial governments. States controlled the opium by licensing agricultural and distribution rights. For every dollar that a state invested in opium, it would get back four. It was seriously big business.

"The three of you have had licensed distribution rights issued by the French Indochina government for the last three years," Captain Dubois said. "When you all walk into the Circuit House, you three are very wealthy and very powerful individuals. And you want to act that way. As you hobnob with the people of Chittagong society, these beautiful women are going to attach themselves to you like a second skin and act very possessive if another woman wants to become part of your inner circle. However, they will allow our other female OSS agents into your circle," Captain Dubois told them.

"What's the downside of this charade?" asked Jon.

"The downside is that there are people out there who want the distribution rights that you all have. So you may be a target for other syndicates. That's why six of the OSS agents that you will meet at the hotel will be acting as your personal bodyguards. Each of you will get two guards that will shadow you wherever you go. They will be visible to everyone and that's what we want. Second, our sources are telling us that the Japanese agent that Mr. Aguillon will be meeting may be a woman. We want you all to be on your toes at all times."

"What happens if one of these other syndicates decides to make a move on us?" Henri asked.

"Between you, the lady with you, and the two bodyguards you should be fine. But just in case, I will have another six agents that will totally be in the shadows."

"Will we carry guns?" Miles asked.

"Yes, the three of you will carry a .32-caliber pistol in a shoulder holster and an ankle holster. Even the girls will be carrying; one in their purse and one on their thigh. If you see anything coming down, don't be shy; or you might end up dead. I don't want to have to answer to General Marshall why one of his special mission agents got killed on my watch."

"When and what time will we be arriving in Chittagong?" Henri asked.

"I've decided to get there when it's light, so we will dock at around 1500 hours on Monday. It's more of a safety factor now than timing. I want to get you all there before Mr. Aguillon, so you can get familiar with the hotel and grounds and the hotel exits. I want you to look for any potential fields of fire and areas were an ambush might take place on the premises; which is quite large."

"I would like to see how each of the girls shoot, and I still need to work on my French etiquette. Will we be working with the girls every day we are out here?" Jon questioned.

"Absolutely," the captain stated, "I want you all to get familiar with having fun with the girls, so it will seem natural when we get to the hotel. So, for the next five nights, there is mandatory dance class on the aft deck. You probably saw the small firing range in the armory. I want you all to work with the girls and make sure they are up to your standards with firearms."

"Great," Jon replied. "Right now I need to go to the armory and run through some extra things with Brunelle. See you all at dinner."

CHAPTER 12

CHITTAGONG, INDIA

The arrival of the *Anne Marie* in Chittagong was treated with a great deal of fanfare. The general manager of the Circuit House had arranged for a small band and the mayor of Chittagong to greet the distinguished passengers of the *Anne Marie* as they docked at the downtown yacht basin.

The OSS didn't want their arrival to go unnoticed but had failed to consult the three agents. Jon became extremely agitated with all the pomp and ceremony. He said to Miles and Henri, "Leave it to the OSS to create a high profile entry for a perfectly planned covert operation. This is unbelievable!"

After the *Anne Marie* was secured, and the engines shut down, Jon approached Captain Dubois steaming mad.

"Before you say anything, Agent Preston, let me explain. It's all part of your cover. We want word to get around that VIPs are visiting the city. The invitations to The Circuit House charity event were sent out three days ago. We wanted to create a buzz in the community. No covert operators would ever do anything like this. We had to think outside the box and play you all up as really important people."

"I wish you would have consulted with us first. Are there any more surprises that I need to be aware of, Captain?" Jon said sarcastically.

"I assure you there are none, Jon. And I promise to consult with you before I do anything else," Captain Dubois said.

"Captain, if I find out that the OSS is doing anything behind my back that might put my team in jeopardy, I will not hesitate to back out. Is that clear?" Jon said.

"Perfectly clear, Agent Preston. I apologize. I should have told you about this beforehand," Captain Dubois said.

Jon spun around and walked back to the foredeck. Still steaming from his conversation with Captain Dubois, he told Miles and Henri to be on the watch for anything stupid that the OSS might be up to; including the girls.

"I won't tolerate these idiots jeopardizing anyone's life on this mission," Jon told them.

As they disembarked, they were told that the hotel's automobile, a 1920 Packard, would take their guests to the establishment. There was only room for four occupants, so Jon told the girls to take the car and send it back in one hour for the three of them and Captain Dubois.

Jon asked Miles and Henri to walk with him back to their room. Jon wanted to make sure that everyone had his shoulder holster and ankle gun. Jon then had Miles and Henri reload their .9 mm pistols with the dum-dum ammunition that Brunelle had prepared for him. Brunelle, knowing that they would also be using .32-caliber weapons, had made the hollow-points for the weapons they would carry on Friday evening in Chittagong.

The dum-dum was a special bullet developed by the British army at the Dum-Dum Arsenal in northwest India in the late 1800s. The dum-dum bullet was designed so its jacketed nose was open and exposed to the bullet's lead core. The aim was to increase the lethality of the round by increasing the bullets expansion upon impact, which created greater internal damage. Although they were outlawed for warfare at the 1899 Hague Convention, Jon felt that the executive order they were operating under would allow their use. Plus, he wanted extra killing power in case they ran into any Japanese operatives or opium syndicates out to take away their supposed opium dealership rights.

"At close range," Jon said, "the recipient of these usually don't get up for a second bullet."

By the time the trio was ready to leave the *Anne Marie*, the car from the hotel had returned to pick them up.

The drive to The Circuit House was a little over a mile and a half. During the ride they became acutely aware of the terrible condition of the people they saw along the side of the road. Many were sleeping in small wooden shacks along the wharf, all looked like they only had flesh covering their bones. Chittagong, it appeared, was still recovering from the aftermath of the famine that had hit India. It was in stark contrast to the luxurious lifestyle they would be entering at The Circuit House.

The crushed shell driveway stretched over a thousand feet before turning into a one way circular drive leading to the fifty-by-thirty-foot covered hotel entrance. The hotel was an imposing E-shaped three-story structure made of white limestone quarried from the twenty-acre lake behind the hotel. The hotel stretched a total length of 225 feet and was 120 feet wide. Although they were not required in this tropical climate, there were fireplace flues running through internal walls, which allowed space for the expansive mullioned windows, which was more typical of Moorish design and very unusual for English architecture. Included in the design were a vast number of carvings of fauna that categorized the local region; included were monkeys, gibbons, tigers, leopards, deer, crocodiles, wolves, and rhinoceros.

As they stepped out of the Packard, they walked up the massive marble steps and entered the hotel lobby. They were stunned by the sheer elegance of the Renaissance décor and gorgeously polished marble flooring. The hotel concierge, dressed in the finery of an English gentleman, greeted the captain and three agents. He told them that they were already checked in and that he would personally escort them to their rooms.

They moved through the lobby and made their way up a grand staircase that must have been twenty feet wide. The staircase was partially carpeted with a plush oriental rug. At the top, they were greeted by more opulence. The hallways were filled with English paintings, and the floors were a polished hardwood that you could almost see your reflection in. There was a ten-foot-wide oriental carpet running down the middle of the corridor. The fifteen-foot-wide hallway was filled with candelabra crystal lighting, not unlike the monstrosity in the lobby, only a hundred times smaller. The room doors were ornately carved in a Georgian style. The rooms were even grander. Jon guessed that this was at least thirty feet square and that didn't include the marble-tiled bathroom that was at twenty-by-fifteen feet. The room contained an extra large bed, two large cedar wardrobes, two large William and Mary settees, two walnut chests, and two writing tables; each with its own chair.

After unpacking his clothes, he went downstairs to take a look at the rest of the hotel. The dining room was huge and able to accompany up to three hundred guests. The lounge was excessively large and paneled in dark oak. It had two standard size billiard tables at the far end. There was also a large reading room. *The ballroom,* Jon thought, *was the nicest of all.* It was large with a high vaulted ceiling and five large crystal chandeliers. There was a stage large enough for a thirty-person orchestra. It could probably hold up to five hundred people.

That evening, Jon, Miles, Henri, and Captain Dubois, along with Camille, Jacqueline, Kathleen, and Desiree had dinner at a table for twelve in the elegant dining room. Afterwards, they broke off into pairs and toured the hotel and walked the grounds. Each agent memorized the layout of the hotel and the grounds. Each agent made notice of blind areas, areas of possible concealment, and areas where a trap could be laid.

For four days, the agents, the girls, and Captain Dubois toured Chittagong and became intimately familiar with the hotel and its grounds. Despite the Japanese bombings, the city was still vibrant with activity and commerce. Ships, fishing boats, junks, and sampans filled the harbor and Karnaphuli River.

Downtown Chittagong was a mixture of high-end and ordinary shopping. Each morning, the girls would go shopping and come back with new dresses, sandals, scarves and hats courtesy of the OSS.

On their second day touring downtown, Jon picked up a tail following him and Camille. Jon took Camille into a bakery and watched their tail walk by. He was a well-dressed Eurasian. That evening at dinner, Jon mentioned it to the group. Everyone had noticed individuals following them, too, none of which were European.

"Time to become extra cautious, gentlemen," Jon stated.

"Shouldn't we capture one and interrogate him?" asked Camille.

"No, that would only tell them that we are on to them," Jon replied.

"What do you suggest, Jon," Desiree asked.

"Tomorrow, when we go back out, everyone carry your Minox Riga camera. Your tail will more than likely be focusing on the men, so it will be up to you girls to get the shot. It would probably work best if you all went into a shop and let us walk several shops down from you. Take the photo through the shop window or through the open door of the shop. Take several photos, but don't let them see you," Jon said.

The third day out, each girl was able to get multiple photos of the men following them. Captain Dubois took the film to the *Anne Marie*, where he had it processed by one of his crewmen. That evening, everyone returned to the *Anne Marie* to view and discuss the photos.

Jon led the onboard discussion. "Everyone memorize the faces in these photos. Girls, if you see them at the hotel, inform everyone by displaying the red book markers provided in the diaries I gave you. From what I've observed, these guys are fairly good, but they're not professional agents. I believe that they may be from one of the drug syndicates. But they are still extremely dangerous."

After everyone had left the *Anne Marie*, Jon and Camille walked the short distance to the shopping district. Despite the late hour, most of the shops still were open. Jon was the first to notice the tail. After fifteen minutes of shopping, he discovered the second man.

"Camille," Jon said quietly as he put his arm around her and pulled her closer, "we've got two guys following us. I think something is getting ready to happen."

Jon walked Camille down a narrow alley to a leather shop they had previously visited. Brunelle had told Jon about his father's shop and had met Jon at the shop the previous day. They talked for an hour over coffee, and Brunelle told Jon that the shop would be a safe place to go if he ran into trouble.

Jon had planned for the trouble, and now their tails were walking into his trap. He and Camille had been browsing through the leather good for five minutes when one entered the shop. The other stayed in the alley. Before either could react, Brunelle and another crewman from the *Anne Marie* had moved from the alley shadows and now held one of the tails with shotguns in his back.

Jon walked up to the man in the shop with his automatic drawn. Jon took a revolver off him and handed it to Camille. He then frisked both men and found a second gun and a knife on each. Brunelle tied their hands behind their backs and pushed them forward with his shotgun. They followed Jon and Camille into the back room.

"Camille, you can wait in the other room if you want, this may get a little bloody," Jon said.

"I'd like to stay, Jon." Camille replied.

When Jon had said bloody, both of the captive's eyes widened. Their hands and feet had been secured to the chairs they now sat in. Brunelle pulled a large, heavy knife from the shelf. Both captive's eyes followed the knife; the younger of the two captive's lips began to tremble.

"Does either of you two speak English or French?" Jon asked.

"I speak both. He speaks only French," said the older one.

Jon switched to French. "Okay, this is how it will go. I'll ask the questions. You will answer the questions. If you don't answer them to my satisfaction, Brunelle will remove one of your fingers. Do you understand?"

Both men nodded their heads. The younger one began trembling even more.

"What are your names?" Jon asked.

"I am Ricard Clairoux. He is Jacob," answered the older one.

"Why are you following me, Ricard?" Jon asked.

"We were paid to," Ricard answered.

"Who are you working for?" Jon asked.

Neither man spoke up. Jon nodded to Brunelle, who slammed the large blade onto the wooden table. Both men jumped. Jon noticed a similarity in both men; same eyes, same nose, same ears, same expression of fear.

"You're related," Jon said.

"We are brothers," Ricard answered.

"Brunelle, remove the little finger from the younger brother's right hand," Jon said.

Brunelle untied Jacob's hand. It took both crewmen to secure it to the table. Brunelle then separated the little finger from the others and grabbed the knife from the table.

"We were hired by an Indochina drug syndicate!" Ricard shouted.

"Go on," Jon stated.

"I run a detective agency in Saigon. We were hired to track your movements. We are not here to hurt you," Ricard explained.

"Why does the syndicate want me tailed?" Jon asked angrily.

"They didn't go into details, but I assume they want to take over your drug business. Your four-year contract expires in six months," Ricard said.

Jon was not aware of this. *Another OSS screw up, or was it planned? Probably planned,* Jon thought.

"What have you reported so far?" Jon asked.

"I will make my first report tomorrow," Ricard said.

"When, where, and who to?" Jon continued.

"One of the syndicate owners, Win Su Yong, will be coming in by boat tomorrow. We will be meeting at a café next to the International Hotel," Ricard stated.

"Let's take a break." Jon said, taking Camille by the arm and moving her into the other room.

"We're you aware of the contract expiring in six months?" Jon asked.

"No," Camille answered.

"I need you to go get Captain Dubois, Henri, and Miles and bring him here. I'll have Carlos escort you," Jon told her.

Camille and Carlos left and returned an hour later with Captain Dubois, Miles, and Henri. Captain Dubois was slightly anxious. He had not given Jon all the information on the drug distribution contract per the orders from General Donovan. Now he would have to endure more anger and distrust from Jon.

Jon met with Captain Dubois alone. "Remember that chat we had about telling me everything that's going on?"

"Jon, I was under direct orders from General Donovan to not mention when the contact expires. I realize now that it was a mistake," Captain Dubois said hesitantly.

"For crying out loud, Captain, if this is the standard way that the OSS operates, it's going to get people killed. Now what else have you held back?" Jon nearly shouted.

"Jon, I swear that's the only thing. I am not withholding any other information," Captain Dubois stated.

"All right, what was the intention of the expiring contract?" Jon asked.

"He wanted to attract the attention of one of the syndicates. Donovan had the details leaked in Saigon. He thought that one of the syndicates would shadow you. It would insure our cover," Captain Dubois answered.

"Sometimes good intentions get people killed," Jon said angrily. "That's why my team isn't associated with the OSS directly. Now let's put our heads together and figure out how to deal with this Saigon detective."

Jon called Miles and Henri into the meeting and updated them of everything. An hour later, they had a plan.

"Ricard, I want you to tell your employer that you overheard me discussing the sale of our contract with my business partners. If you agree, we won't cut your throats and drop your bodies in the river. You also won't have to worry about your getting caught and being interrogated and ruining the reputation of your company. So, what will it be?" Jon questioned.

"I'll do as you suggested," Ricard answered.

"Good," Jon said. "I want the opportunity to meet Mr. Win Su Yong."

Jon had the bindings removed from Ricard and Jacob. He then threw several pages of writing paper and two pencils on the table.

"Write out your report. I want to approve it before you give it to him," Jon told Ricard.

Thirty minutes later, Jon was reading the report that would be given to Win Su Yong.

"After you give this to your employer and he arranges a meeting with us, we will release Jacob unharmed," Jon stated.

"I assure you that I will see that he sends me to arrange your meeting," Ricard said.

CHAPTER 13

CHITTAGONG, INDIA

At breakfast, Jon laid out his plan on how to deal with Win Su Yong. A short time later, Captain Dubois left for the *Anne Marie*. Four hours later, he returned with an answer from OSS headquarters in Washington DC.

"General Donovan agrees with your plan, Jon," Captain Dubois said. "But we need to make sure that this doesn't interfere with our primary mission tomorrow when Mr. Aguillon gets to town."

"Captain, we want to make sure that Mr. Aguillon sees us with Win Su Yong. Chances are that he knows Win Su Yong, and that will work to our advantage. I can't think of a better way to get introduced to Aguillon. Win Su Yong will probably let him know that he is buying out our contract. It will solidify our cover, and we can roam the hotel without suspicion."

"You've really thought this out," Captain Dubois remarked.

"I'm just being creative. I don't want any of our agents getting hurt or killed. Removing suspicion from us can only help achieve that purpose."

Later that evening, Ricard Clairoux entered the hotel and found Jon sitting in the reading room off of the lobby.

"Win Su Yong has agreed to a meeting tomorrow morning. Would you like to have breakfast with him here at the hotel?" Ricard asked.

"That would be perfect, Ricard. I'll reserve a table for 9:00 a.m., and I'll have another table reserved for his bodyguards. Will you be attending?"

"Yes, but for only as long as it takes to introduce you and your partners," Ricard stated.

"Then I'll see you all tomorrow morning."

After Clairoux left, Jon went into the billiards room where Miles and Henri were playing a game. Jon explained the plan then left to find Camille.

Captain Dubois was on the *Anne Marie* putting together the paperwork for the sale of the opium distribution rights. General Donovan had instructed him to insist on payment in gold bullion. After sending an encrypted message to his OSS contacts in Saigon, he received an answer on what Jon should ask for the distribution rights. He thought it was high, but Win Su Yong would probably agree after some discussion. From what he had already learned about Agent Preston, he felt that Jon could probably ask double the price and get Win Su Yong to willingly pay it. Jon was that good.

That evening, the group dined in a private room. Jon explained that only he, Miles, and Henri would attend the meeting. If Win Su Yong agrees to the sale price, they would meet the next day at an attorney's office already picked out by Captain Dubois. Jon also told them that he believed that Win Su Yong had come to Chittagong specifically to purchase the contract and probably would have the gold bullion on his boat. He felt this way because of the large numbers of armed guards around Win Su Yong's boat.

"This guy didn't come to kill anyone," Jon said. "He's a businessman. He wants to do this deal in secret and without any publicity."

That afternoon, Rene Aguillon arrived at the hotel. He entered the hotel with one person, probably an embassy worker assigned to take care of his official needs.

As Captain Dubois had suspected, Aguillon asked for a different room from the one originally assigned. The manager gave him the only remaining room, which was a larger suite, but told Aguillon there would be no extra charge since he was here on embassy business. Aguillon left for his room elated that he would have a great deal more luxury in his accommodations.

Henri was already in the OSS rented suite with the listening devices; he had his headset on. After Jon and Captain Dubois entered the room, each donned a headset, listening to the tapped phone line for any conversation in Aguillon's room. Within ten minutes, Aguillon was making a call. When the phone was answered, he asked for a Mr. Claudette. The female voice told him that Mr. Claudette was out of town. He said thank you and hung up. Jon had been listening to the phone conversation on a second headset.

"That was too quick," Henri said.

"Probably a prearranged signal to let his contact know that he's in town," Jon said.

"Yes, and a female voice at that," Henri stated.

"Okay, looks like it's been set in motion. Captain, notify your agents to standby to tail Aguillon. I assume you are using natives or Eurasians?"

"That's right. No Europeans whatsoever," Captain Dubois answered.

"Henri, it looks like you'll be having dinner in here tonight. Captain, make sure that Henri gets spelled after four hours. I want him fresh for tomorrow," Jon said before he left the room."

Jon and Captain Dubois left the room at the same time. Before the captain walked off, Jon said, "Captain, if there is a female agent involved, we need to be looking for Aguillon to come back to his room with an escort later tonight; one that too obviously looks like a high-end hooker."

"Good thinking," Captain Dubois said. "I'll let everyone know."

"One other thing, Captain," Jon said. "When the OSS vetted our young ladies, are we certain that none of them or their parents, relatives, husbands, or boyfriends had any dealings with the French Vichy Indochina or Japanese governments?" Jon asked.

"You're not thinking that one of our girls is a double agent, are you?" Captain Dubois asked.

"I'm covering all bases, Captain. You need to get on the wire to Washington and to your assets in Saigon and ask that question," Jon stated.

Jon, Miles, and Henri were already seated at their table when Ricard Clairoux and Win Su Yong entered the hotel restaurant. After their introduction, Ricard left. Two of Win Su Yong's bodyguards were sitting two tables away facing Jon's table. Despite their well-tailored suits, Jon could tell they were using twin shoulder holsters. Jon and his teammates were only carrying ankle holster guns.

After they ordered breakfast, Win Su Yong spoke first, "Gentlemen, I am a man of action and few words. I am prepared to pay you £1 million for your contract."

"When the Japanese are eventually defeated and removed from your country, the economy will boom, and opium prices will quadruple," Jon stated.

"Then what do you suggest as a fair price, Mr. Perrotte? Win Su Yong asked.

"Three-and-a-half-million-pounds sterling payable in gold," Jon suggested.

"You are a very shroud man, Mr. Perrotte. I take it that you are well versed in economic principals?" Win Su Yong asked.

"It's mostly common sense, Mr. Yong. You stand to make a fortune after the war. Plus, within six months of our selling, you will recoup your cost," Jon said.

"And what will you do after you sell, Mr. Perrotte?" Win Su Yong asked.

"We plan on moving to America and getting into the oil and lumber business," Jon said.

Taking his time, Win Su Yong drank some of the strong coffee and ate part of the Eggs Benedict he had been served.

"Mr. Perrotte, I don't carry that much gold around. What would you think of one and a half million in gold bullion and one and a half in diamonds and emeralds?" Win Su Yong countered.

Jon looked at Miles and Henri. They both gave him a nod of agreement.

"Mr. Yong, you have a deal," Jon replied. "Our attorney will draw up the sales agreement. If you agree, Mr. Yong, we can sign the agreement in his office on Saturday afternoon at 1:00 p.m.; I will hold the contract until you deliver the gold and diamonds to the *Anne Marie* on Sunday morning. We will need to certify the gold and the gems, of course," Jon said.

"Yes, of course, Mr. Perrotte." Win Su Yong said. "I look forward to our next meeting."

Win Su Yong stood up, shook hands with everyone, and left without finishing his coffee or breakfast.

"Jon, you certainly have the Midas touch," Miles said.

"It's mostly common sense, Miles. We're supposed to be opium distributors, and we need to think like one. Win Su Yong has been sitting on cash, gold, diamonds, and emeralds ever since the Japanese invaded. He knows that I know it, too. What he doesn't grasped is that the colonial French and British states in Asia will be gone within two years of the war's end. If he had known that, he would have paid far less," Jon stated.

"Where do you get these ideas?" Henri asked.

"I was a history major at Ohio State, Henri. There are certain patterns after every major war. This region is already showing those patterns: the civil unrest in India and Burma with the English rule; and the failure of Burma, Thailand, and French Indochina to join the allies. The British and French are the weakest they have been in Asia in a hundred years. These things point to a disintegration of their colonial systems," Jon said.

"I only had one history course at university. Looks like I should have taken more," Henri stated.

"We've got work to do guys," Jon said. "Miles, you check with the OSS agents monitoring Mr. Aguillon. Henri, you go rustle up the girls, and have them meet us at the restaurant at the International Hotel at noon."

Miles and Henri left to do their tasks. Captain Dubois walked in and was about to sit down when Jon stopped him.

"Captain, would you mind riding downtown with me?" Jon asked.

"Not at all, what's on your mind?"

"A hunch," Jon remarked.

Thirty minutes later, Jon and Captain Dubois were having coffee with Ricard and Jacob Clairoux. Jon explained that he wanted to hire them to tail someone. Jon told them that this person was a professional, and they needed to be cautious and better than they were following him. After Jon gave Ricard two thousand in American dollars and a photo, the men left.

"Jon, what made you suspicious?" Captain Dubois asked.

"When we were listening in when Aguillon made that phone call, I noticed a sound in the background. It was the sound that a gramophone record makes at the end of its play before the arm is lifted. I heard that same sound when I was in her room yesterday," Jon said.

"Jon, if you're right this whole operation could be compromised," Captain Dubois said.

"Well, Richard, let's make sure we don't get caught in a trap. I need two of your best female agents in Chittagong; ones that the girls haven't met," Jon Stated.

"We have four more coming to the dance, but they won't be operational," Captain Dubois said.

"How good are they?" Jon asked.

"They've been through the OSS training and I mean the real course at our facility in Ceylon, not the one we give to the Asian agents in the jungle," Dubois said.

"Can you activate your best two on such short notice?" Jon questioned.

"Sure," Dubois answered.

"I'm going to need to meet with them on the *Anne Marie* early this evening before the charity dance," Jon stated.

At noon, Jon met with Captain Dubois and the four newly activated OSS agents at the International Hotel. During lunch, Jon told them to make sure that they kept an eye on Mr. Aguillon during the charity event. "If he leaves the ballroom, let one of us know. If you notice a stranger who is wearing a shoulder holster, let one of us know," Jon told them that since this was their first operation mission; not to charge off and do anything dumb.

At 1800 hours Jon, Miles, Henri, and Captain Dubois met the two newly activated OSS agents onboard the *Anne Marie*.

"Ladies, tonight's mission is potentially very dangerous. I want you to remove the rounds in your automatics, and replace them with these hollow-point dum-dums. They have twice the knockdown power as a regular round," Jon stated.

"At the charity event tonight," Captain Dubois continued, "we want you all to act as if you don't know us. Have the hotel manager introduce you to one of us, and ask that person to dance every twenty to thirty minutes. Be flirtatious but not too overtly. If you order alcohol, order your drink, and preface it with 'Empire', it will be made with one-third the alcohol. After an hour or so, start acting slightly tipsy to insure your cover. None of our other agents know who you are, and it will stay that way. We want you to be just another pretty face in the crowd that is enamored with one of us," Captain Dubois said.

"You'll be our third line of defense. If we need your assistance, one of us will let you know. If it's an emergency, I'll whistle," Jon said as he demonstrated his shrill noise. "When you hear that sound, move to the hotel lobby, and have your gun out and hidden in the folds of your gown. One of us will be there to let you know what to do next," Jon concluded.

"You have a taxi waiting outside and dinner reservation at the hotel dining room; dinner is on me. Enjoy the evening, and please stay sharp," Captain Dubois stated.

CHAPTER 14

CHITTAGONG, INDIA

"Since Aguillon arrived in Chittagong, he has only been at the hotel or the French Embassy. As far as our agents could tell, he hasn't met with anyone while outside the hotel, and no one we know has entered the French Embassy. The taxi drivers that have picked him up have been our men, so we know that he hasn't talked to anyone," Henri briefed, after the two female OSS agents left the boat.

"My gut feeling is that while at the French Embassy, he has had the information he received from the courier photographed and placed on microfilm," Jon said.

"That will certainly make it easier to transfer," Miles said.

"It makes sense if he's meeting a female agent, but I'm not certain that he wouldn't have had it microfilmed, anyway," Jon stated.

"We'll still need to watch everyone he talks to or dances with tonight," Henri said.

"All right, it's most likely that the exchange will be at the dance. It will be noisy and it will be crowded and it will be hard to detect the transfer of microfilm. Captain, inform all of your agents to watch Mr. Aguillon closely. I'll inform our girls before dinner," Jon said.

"I'll brief them," Captain Dubois said.

"Henri, you and Miles, head back to the hotel in the taxi outside. The captain and I have some things to take care of here. We'll meet up with you all at dinner," Jon said.

"Did you get anything from Washington or Saigon?" Jon asked after Miles and Henri left.

"Yes, and it confirms your suspicion," Captain Dubois said.

When Jon and the captain left the *Anne Marie*, they walked down the docks.

"Notice who's still here," Jon said.

"Are you thinking what I'm thinking?" Captain Dubois asked.

"Yes, question is, do we take them down tonight or let the exchange take place and take them tomorrow?" Jon questioned.

"What if we're wrong and she bolts tonight?" Captain Dubois asked.

"This business is all about taking chances, Richard. Since I'm the team leader on the ground, I'll take responsibility," Jon stated.

"You deliberately left Miles and Henri out of the loop. Why?" Captain Dubois asked.

"In case I'm wrong, I don't want to prejudice their judgment towards any conclusion. I want their minds open and alert to everything," Jon said.

"What are you going to tell the girls," Captain Dubois asked.

"Nothing," Jon replied.

The charity event started at 9:00 p.m. The hotel manager and master of ceremony greeted everyone and asked them to give generously. The three hundred people that had arrived between 7:00 p.m. and 9:00 p.m., now filled the ballroom.

"This is going to be tougher that I thought," Jon told Camille.

"Well, before the going gets too tough, you had better dance with me, and make use of the lessons I gave you on the *Anne Marie*," Camille said, leading Jon onto the dance floor.

Halfway through the evening, the hotel manager, with Mr. Aguillon in tow introduced the distinguished government official to Jon, Miles, Henri, and the four girls.

"These three gentlemen are our benefactors for tonight's charity event," the manager said proudly.

"The world could use more people like you," Aguillon said. "Since I do not know anyone here, would you mind if I dance with one or more of these lovely ladies?"

"If it pleases the ladies, go right ahead," Jon remarked.

Aguillon danced with Kathleen. Over the next hour, he came back and danced with Jacqueline and Camille. Towards the end of the dance, he asked Desiree to dance.

"Have you determined which one he's passing the microfilm to yet?" Miles interrupted.

"How did you guess?" Jon asked not taking his eyes off of Desiree.

"You're not the only one with a brain, Jon," Miles remarked.

"Does Henri know?" Jon asked.

"He's the one who figured it out first, mate. By the way, did you notice that Yong's boat is still in the yacht basin?" Miles asked.

Jon didn't say anything. He didn't want Miles distracted.

Henri walked up to Jon while Miles was still standing next to him. "What do you want to do about Aguillon?" Henri asked.

"I've arranged for coffee and dessert for the all of us in the restaurant. Do you two have your dart guns with you?" Jon asked.

"Yes," Miles and Henri replied.

"I've arranged for Kathleen to ask Aguillon to take her out on the veranda for some fresh air. Henri, you cover the veranda, and Miles, you cover the walkway. When they start down the walkway, hit them both with the tranquilizer," Jon stated.

"What about Jacqueline," Henri asked.

"She'll be getting ill in a few minutes. Two of our female OSS agents will be taking her to her room. After she passes out, they will search her," Jon said.

"Covering all bases, aren't you?" Henri said.

"Yes, but when did you learn baseball terms?" Jon asked.

"I've been listening in on your conversations with Captain Dubois," Henri stated.

Miles and Henri were in position by the time Aguillon and Kathleen walked onto the veranda, down the steps, and on the walk toward the lake.

Henri hit Aguillon with a tranquilizer dart from behind, and Miles hit Kathleen in the arm. Aguillon fell over on the grass, but Miles caught Kathleen before she hit the ground. The two agents pulled both of them into the darkness behind a dense hedge.

Two of the newly activated female agents stepped out of the darkness with Jon and began a body and cavity search of Kathleen. Miles and Henri searched Aguillon. Nothing was found on either of them.

"You two get Kathleen up to her room. Here's the key. Stay with her until she comes to. There should be aspirin in her bathroom. Give her two tablets and lots of water when she wakes up," Jon said.

"We've got a hotel car parked in the back," Henri said. "We'll get him bedded down on the *Anne Marie* and meet you in the restaurant."

Jon left and walked back to the ballroom. He took Camille by the hand and walked to the dance floor.

"Is everything okay, Jon? I saw the three of you leave," Desiree said.

"Everything's great, except for figuring out who Aguillon's contact is. Our agents have been shadowing him for two days, but so far, nothing," Jon said.

"I saw Aguillon dancing with four other women beside the four of us. In fact, it was the same four women that were swooning over you, Miles, and Henri. Could it have been one of them?" Desiree questioned.

"They appeared to be too drunk to be enemy agents," Jon said.

"Ladies and gentlemen," the hotel manager said standing at the microphone, "this will be the last dance. Thank you for your generous giving tonight. We raised over twelve thousand pounds."

Camille walked up from behind and pressed tightly against Jon when the band started playing Harold Arlen's "Stormy Weather."

"How about a dance, handsome?" Camille asked Jon.

"Sure."

"I really like you, Jon. Do you think we'll see each other after this mission?" Camille asked.

"Count on it," Jon answered.

The following day, Miles and Henri had a late afternoon lunch with the four girls.

"Captain Dubois and Jon had urgent business on the *Anne Marie*," Miles said. "We'll be meeting him there for dinner."

"It wouldn't have anything to do with the sale of the distribution rights?" Jacqueline questioned.

"In fact, it does, Jackie," Miles answered.

"Then, why can't we be there, too? Desiree asked. "I'd like to see what two million in gold looks like."

"Yes, and Captain Dubois and Jon said we would all share in the diamonds," Kathleen stated.

Jon and Captain Dubois had expected this and had instructed Miles and Henri to bring them to the boat if they asked. In fact, Jon was counting on it.

"Alright, I don't see any harm, do you, Henri?" Miles asked.

"No harm at all, Miles. I'd like to see the gold, too," Henri replied. "I still need to shower, so let's meet back here a 5:00 p.m. and go to the boat.

Miles and Henri were deliberately an hour late getting downstairs. But by 6:00 p.m., the six agents showed up at the *Anne Marie* just as four men were walking off the boat, leaving Win Su Yong with only two bodyguards. As they entered the lounge, they saw a goldsmith inspecting and weighing the bullion and a jeweler appraising the diamonds and emeralds.

When they had all entered the room, Captain Dubois introduced Win Su Yong to Camille, Jacqueline, Kathleen, and

Desiree. He took each girl's hand—with the composure of an English gentleman—and touched his lips gently to their hand.

"I didn't know you had such gorgeous ladies with you, Mr. Perrotte? Otherwise, I would have insisted on meeting them sooner," Win Su Yong said.

"Captain, would you mind if these ladies show me about your boat?" Win Su Yong asked.

"I'll send my first mate along to explain everything. Do you need to take your bodyguards along, Mr. Yong?" Captain Dubois asked.

"No, I trust these young ladies," Win Su Yong said.

Jon had also anticipated Win Su Yong wanting to tour the boat. If there was going to be an exchange it would happen soon.

The tour of the engine room was cramped, but Camille caught the movement of a hand into a pocket as one of the girls pretended to trip and let Win Su Yong stop her fall.

The *Anne Marie*'s first mate had instructions to give his visitor a long and thorough tour. By the time they returned to the lounge, the goldsmith and jeweler were gone. Camille caught Jon's eye and nodded discretely. Miles and Henri saw the exchange, pulled their silenced weapons, and shot the two bodyguards. Win Su Yong reached for his .9 mm but he was clobbered behind the ear by Kathleen.

Desiree was much quicker. She had her automatic out and fired two shots before Jon shot her between the eyes. Henri was hit in the arm, and Jacqueline lay dead on the floor with a bullet through her heart. Kathleen was on the floor next to her sister—sobbing.

Captain Dubois put the crew on full alert and armed all of his crewmen. While the ships engines were being started, Jon dressed in Win Su Yong's clothing, and Miles and Henri dressed in the clothes of his two bodyguards. They left the ship and got in an awaiting cab. It was beginning to get dark.

An hour later, Jon, Miles, and Henri returned to the *Anne Marie* with their suitcases from The Circuit House. A second taxi behind them carried the girls' wardrobes. Thirty minutes later, the *Anne Marie* was backing out of the yacht basin and moving down the Karnaphuli River toward the Bay of Bengal.

CHAPTER 15
ABOARD THE *ANNE MARIE* INDIAN OCEAN

Twenty-four hours after leaving Chittagong, the *Anne Marie* stopped, and the French flag was lowered to half-mast. Once the crew and guests were in formation, the captain called the ship's company to attention. Jon, Miles, Henri, and Camille carried the body of Jacqueline Lauren on a stretcher. Her body had been sewn into sailcloth and weighted with lead in the tradition of a burial at sea. Kathleen walked two paces behind.

Captain Dubois called parade rest, read scripture from the Holy Bible, and said a prayer. He called everyone to attention, and everyone saluted as Jacqueline's flag-covered body was committed to the sea. After Captain Dubois gave a short benediction, he called the formation back to attention and ordered present arms as two crewmen fired three volleys into the air. A third crewman played taps. Afterwards, Jon and Henri folded the French flag; Henri then presented it to Captain Dubois. Up to that point, Kathleen had borne up to the stress of the burial. When Captain Dubois presented her the flag and thanked her for her sacrifice from a grateful nation, she collapsed. Jon and Henri caught her before she hit the deck, and Henri carried her to her cabin where Camille attended to her.

They were still onboard the *Anne Marie* three days later cruising the Bay of Bengal two hundred miles southeast of Calcutta.

Jon was on the aft deck sunning with Camille and Kathleen. Jon was introducing the duo to American baseball. The steward had just brought them iced champagne and was pouring their drinks when Captain Dubois approached.

"Jon, ladies," said the captain, "we have guests arriving in a PBY in one hour. I'll need everyone to meet in the lounge once they are onboard. You'll need to dress in your afternoon casual attire."

After Camille and Kathleen left to go to their cabins, Jon wondered who might be flying out to the boat.

The captain would have let us know if he knew. Maybe it's the debriefing team. Jon thought as he rose to go to his quarters.

When he returned to his room, Miles had just finished showering, and the cabin steward was applying a fresh dressing to Henri's wound. Jon slipped out of his bathing suit and jumped into the shower. Thirty minutes later, all three agents were in the lounge smoking Cuban cigars. Camille and Kathleen joined them ten minutes later.

After they all had been served a glass of chilled mango juice, they heard the roar of an aircraft engine as it buzzed the *Anne Marie*. Everyone exited the lounge onto the aft deck and watched the PBY touchdown and taxi to within twenty yards of the boat.

By the time the aircraft commander shut down the port side engine, the *Anne Marie's* launch was pulling up to the portside sliding bubble to disembark its passengers. The first in the boat was a US Army captain that Jon did not know. The next to enter the boat was Colonel Buck Arvin from G-2.

"This ought to be interesting," Jon said aloud.

"It must be important to bring the colonel out here, mate," Miles responded.

"Hell, there goes our vacation," Henri replied.

"Not yours, Henri, you're grounded for at least three more weeks. If the bullet would have hit the bone, you'd be out for six months at least," Jon stated.

Fifteen minutes after the PBY landed, it was lifting off and heading due north. Colonel Arvin was the first to climb the ladder and reach the aft deck. He saluted Captain Dubois.

"Request permission to come aboard, Captain?" Colonel Arvin stated.

"Granted," replied Captain Dubois as he returned the colonel's salute.

"Captain Dubois, this is Captain Bud Helms," Colonel Arvin said.

"Welcome aboard, Bud," Captain Dubois said.

"Glad to have you aboard, Buck. How's General Marshall these days?"

"He's ornery as ever. You're looking great, Richard. Life on the sea seems to agree with you. Do you miss the Secret Service?" Colonel Arvin asked.

"Not as long as I'm doing this, Buck," Captain Dubois replied.

"How are my three best agents doing?" Colonel Arvin asked.

"They're behaving like good little boys," Captain Dubois said with a smile on his face.

"And how are they dealing with the loss of Jacqueline?" Colonel Arvin asked.

"Mourning her loss, Buck," Captain Dubois said.

"Colonel, would you and the captain like a drink?" Captain Dubois asked.

"That would be terrific, Richard," Colonel Arvin stated.

Captain Dubois ushered everyone into the lounge, where the trio and the two surviving female agents waited. As the steward poured chilled champagne, Colonel Arvin went around speaking and chatted with everyone. Jon observed, from the questions the colonel asked the girls, that he either knew them and their families or had memorized their files. Camille and Kathleen laughed, kissed him on the cheek, and called him Uncle Buck.

After an hour of being entertained by the girls, the colonel gave a quick look to the captain. Captain Dubois then intervened and told everyone that he needed to show the colonel and the captain to their rooms. He mentioned that dinner would be at 2000 hours. Before he left the room, Colonel Arvin went over to where Jon was standing.

"Jon," Colonel Arvin said, "I have a new mission for you all, but we'll discuss it tomorrow morning after breakfast. So, enjoy the evening."

Everyone enjoyed the dinner, which consisted of roasted lobster tail with ginger dipping sauce, grilled wedges of tomato, and snow peas with a slice of lemon. It was served with a fruity, crisp, and un-oaked Puligny-Montrachet Chardonnay. Henri spent at least thirty minutes telling the group about the history of the winery and the vintage. Dessert consisted of a crème caramel served with coffee and black tea.

After finishing dessert, Jon didn't think he could eat anything else until the chef brought out several trays of chocolate-dipped strawberries. Jon stopped the chef as he walked by and politely asked where he had gotten the fresh strawberries.

"There is a small market that sells only fruits a mile east of Chittagong. The owner is my uncle. He makes sure that I get the best fruits," the chef replied.

After he thanked the chef for the excellent dinner, he walked over to where the steward was pouring cognac, and the captain was offering everyone a cigar.

"It looks like our vacation is over," Jon told Miles and Henri. "The colonel will brief us on a new mission tomorrow morning after breakfast."

That evening, both girls went all out to impress Uncle Buck. Camille was striking. She wore an emerald green strapless gown, mid-arm emerald green gloves, and a diamond necklace with a single large emerald drop with matching earrings and bracelet.

After a while, Jon got the feeling that she was trying to impress him instead of the colonel. She sat next to Jon during dinner and hardly paid any attention to anyone else, except Jon. After the strawberries were served, she grabbed Jon's arm and took him to the aft observation deck to watch the full moon rising in the dark eastern sky. It was huge and spectacular. Camille began telling Jon that next month the moon would be even larger. It would be what is known in Asia as a Flower Moon.

"It happens once a year, when the moon's orbit is closest to the Earth. As a result, the Moon appears to be brighter and up to 15 percent larger," Camille said.

"It reminds me of the harvest moon in Ohio," Jon said.

"What is a harvest moon?" Camille asked.

"It's the full moon at the end of September, after what is called the autumn equinox, or the first day of fall in the northern hemisphere. It's called a harvest moon because most of the farmers in the Midwest begin harvesting their crops shortly after the harvest moon," Jon said.

"Were your parents farmers?" Camille asked.

"My grandparents were farmers. I used to go out to their farm on weekends. In the fall, I would help with the harvest," Jon said.

Camille turned away from the moon and looked Jon in the eyes, raised her hand, and touched his face. She pressed her lips to Jon's in one of the longest and most exciting kisses of his life.

"I have only been with one man, Jon. My husband died two years ago when the Japanese invaded Malaya," Camille said. "I know you're going to leave on a new mission. I want to sleep with you tonight. I have a room all to myself. Now let's go to my room."

Jon was speechless. All he could do was nod his head as she took his hand and led him down the two sets of stairs to her room. After they entered, Camille locked the door.

CHAPTER 16

ABOARD THE *ANNE MARIE* INDIAN OCEAN

When they finished breakfast, the three agents moved to the lounge where Colonel Arvin and his team were setting out folders and maps from their briefcases.

The colonel sipped his coffee and finally looked up from what he was reading.

"Good morning, gentlemen. I hope your evening was as enjoyable as mine," Colonel Arvin said.

Jon, Miles, and Henri all nodded their heads in unison.

"Good. This is Captain Crawford Helms. Crawford likes to be called Bud. He will get us started with a little background information," Colonel Arvin said.

The captain went on to explain that in 1942, after the Japanese occupied Thailand and Burma, they decided that they needed a way to supply their bases in northern Burma. The bases in Burma were going to be used for their eventual invasion of India. They ultimately decided to build a railway linking Thailand to Burma.

The captain turned to a wall map of Burma and Thailand that he had pinned to the wall and used the eraser end of a pencil to trace the railroad system he was referring to. The railway ran approximately two 275 miles along the Kwai Noi River. The railway curved north through rugged jungle and granite canyons to connect with an existing railway in Burma. Allied analysts have determined that the Japanese used a labor force of about sixty thousand Allied prisoners of war (POW) and two hundred thousand Asian laborers to build the railway. They also estimated that the death toll of POWs and indentured laborers to be around thirty percent; we're now calling it the Death Railway," Captain Helms stated.

What had the Allies concerned, Captain Helms explained, was the increasing number of rail movements of troops, supplies, and ammunition from Bangkok into Burma. Of particular interest was a trestle bridge in the southwest part of Thailand near a village called Hintok. The Japanese have constructed a railway bridge approximately one hundred yards long. Leading into and away from the bridge, is a viaduct that is built underneath and against a one-mile section of solid granite. There is a narrow gorge where the bridge crosses from the southern to the northern viaduct. In the middle of the gorge, there is a large granite rock that rises sixty feet above the river. That rock serves as the midsection for the bridge. It supports the bridge spans merging from the north and south.

"Does this indicate a further invasion into India?" Jon asked.

"It's possible but not probable, Jon. We think that they are trying to hold on to what they have taken and are desperate for supplies and troops," Captain Helms answered.

Captain Helms told them that the Allies had been trying to bomb the bridge for six months and slow down the number of Japanese reinforcements. No less than nine bombing missions, ranging from four to six B-24 Liberators attacked the bridge and viaduct but were unsuccessful. Allied bombing is largely ineffective because the Tenth Air Force does not have the proper types of aircraft needed to get the job done.

"We've learned that a large munitions train is scheduled to leave Bangkok twelve days from now. We don't want that train to reach its destination, gentlemen. We want the three of you to mount a mission to destroy that train as it crosses the Hintok Bridge," Colonel Arvin stated.

The colonel paused and went back to the table and sat down. "With the help of Lieutenant Colonel MacKenzie, Bud has come up with a name for the operation. Captain, if you would continue."

"Yes, sir. We are going to call it Operation Vulcan Halt. Vulcan is from the Vulcan foundry, where Vulcan locomotives are made in the United Kingdom. From our intelligence reports, there are an estimated 113 locomotives and over nine thousand rail cars available to the Japanese on this railway. At least, sixty are the smaller Vulcan locomotives. The term Vulcan Halt comes from the name of the railway station where Lieutenant Colonel MacKenzie used to get off to visit his grandparents in the town of Warrington, England. It was close to the Vulcan foundry. The lieutenant colonel and I figured a name like this, even if it did become known to the enemy, wouldn't be associated with any particular target; except locomotives in general. Certainly, not bridges," Captain Helms stated.

Colonel Arvin stood and continued, "Over the next three days, we want you all to study the information on the bridge and viaduct and come up with a plan to infiltrate the area and blow it to smithereens. Any and all assets you need from the SOE are available. And, of course, we want you all to get your butts back safely. Whatever plan you all come up with you can execute. Captain Helms has all the target intelligence needed for planning the mission and information on what's available for the insertion and exit. Once you get back to Calcutta, the resident SOE explosive experts can explain how to place the charges to destroy this damn bridge and part of that viaduct," Colonel Arvin said.

"Colonel, won't the Japs just rebuild the bridge after we blow it?" Henri Morreau asked.

"Yes, Henri, they will, and they are very good at rebuilding these bridges and do it quickly. However, with the monsoon season just about upon us, we are hoping that it will take the Japs more than five months. Admiral Mountbatten needs those five months to launch a counteroffensive back into Burma in the fall, and we're going to give it to them. Knocking out this bridge is essential to stopping the Japs from resupplying and reinforcing their troops. The supplies that we stop between now and then will collect in Bangkok. In the mean time, Tenth Air Force will conduct bombing raids on Bangkok and destroy as much of these supplies as possible," Colonel Arvin said.

Over the next few days, Agents Preston, Murphy, and Morreau poured over the information. The OSS had collected a considerable amount of intelligence on the Thailand-Burma railway and the atrocities occurring in the Japanese POW camps along the railway. The State Department had put together a white paper on the Japanese cultural and educational system, which shed light on the Japanese attitudes toward their prisoners.

In the POW camps, there were constant shortages of food and medicine. The POWs were getting only 1,200 calories per day in the eastern Asian camps. However, in Thailand and Burma, the conditions were far worse. The POWs building the Thailand to Burma railway were working up to eighteen hours a day and receiving only two meals a day consisting of a cup of white rice and fish broth. The calorie intake for the manual labor they were performing required over 4,000 calories per day. They were barely getting 1,000 a day.

Over time, the POWs in these camps were reduced to skin and bones, and their resistance to disease was lessened significantly. The OSS report stated that the death rate among Allied POWs was greater than 20 percent. Most of the deaths were due to cholera and malaria and a number other diseases associated with the jungle. But more than a few occurred from beatings from the Japanese and Korean MPs.

The State Department report highlighted the fundamental differences in the Allied and Japanese military systems and the oriental and western cultures. The Japanese educational system and social conditioning instilled a value system, which was diametrically opposite to the fair treatment of prisoners under the Geneva convention guidelines.

The Japanese system taught from middle school upwards that the obligation of the individual was to forgo individual liberty and be willing to die for their emperor. It was also noted that from 1925 onward, uniformed service officers were assigned to all middle and senior level schools, and military training was incorporated into the Japanese school curriculum. This training placed a high emphasis on spirit, sacrifice, obedience, and loyalty.

The Japanese military had also transitioned to autocracy, wielding oppressive powers of the Bushido code of the samurai. The Bushido stressed honor, loyalty, self-sacrifice, and the virtue of suicide over surrender. In fact, many wives of Japanese soldiers had committed suicide, so their husbands could be free to do their military duty.

When Allied soldiers surrendered, rather than fight to the death, the Japanese were appalled that the prisoners were not ashamed of their position of dishonor. It was difficult for the common Japanese soldier to understand how great nations like the US and Great Britain could field armies with such a disgraceful class of soldiers. Thus Japanese soldiers had absolutely no respect for Allied prisoners, and they treated them accordingly. The OSS report on the Thailand to Burma railway captured a Japanese officer's philosophy given to the POWs working on the railway: "You will work for the Japanese until you die."

Information received from Kachin informants around the Hintok area said that the bridge was built using hand tools. The timber for the two-section bridge was cut from the adjacent jungle by POWs and then dragged to the construction site. The bridge was designed following the American Merriman-Wiggin Civil Engineering Standard for Wooden Structures. It had vertical columns that were thirty inches in diameter and weighed as much as two thousand pounds each. The horizontal braces were at least eighteen inches in diameter and were fastened to the columns by nails, bolts, metal spikes, and rope made from jungle vines.

The bridge was located approximately 130 miles northwest of Bangkok. The site of the bridge was a mile northwest of the Hintok Station POW Camp. The Kachin informants had confirmed the two bridge spans together were close to one hundred meters long, sixty to eighty meters high and thirty to fifty meters above the river. It looked to be an almost impossible task to cut through the rock and jungle in this location, but somehow the Allied POWs and indentured natives had accomplished the impossible.

As they studied the maps and photographs, they began to come up with a better picture of the terrain around the bridge. According to the OSS, the Kwai Noi was quite beautiful all along its course. There were occasional rapids and waterfalls, which provide an astonishing contrast to an otherwise smooth and even flow. There were areas where the river was flanked by sandy banks. In other areas, the jungle cover came entirely to the water's edge. Around the Hintok Bridge, granite rock walls rose from the river to over six hundred feet in height, while, on the opposite side, the land rose slowly and was filed with grass planes and bamboo and hardwood forests.

The report even mentioned the bird wildlife, which consisted of grey herons, kingfishers, ground thrushes, hornbills, and Java peafowl. Most of the people of this area made their livelihood from fishing. Because of the monsoons, they had built their villages in the hills overlooking the Kwai Noi. There were also river people who fished the river and lived in their sampans. During the five-month monsoon season, late May through October, the Kwai Noi would be transformed in both size and strength. The river would rise dramatically and the low land areas would be flooded with four to five feet of water.

There were large open grasslands to the west of the river. It would be one of these areas where they would have to parachute into from a C-47. Information from the Kachin informants also revealed that there were very few Japanese patrols at the Hintok Bridge. This meant that the Japanese felt secure with their occupation of Burma. The arrogance of the Japanese could provide a useful advantage to the team.

"Captain Helms, does the SOE explosives experts plan on using dynamite to blow the bridges and viaduct?" Henri asked.

Captain Helms explained why they wouldn't be using dynamite as an explosive. The problem with dynamite, he explained, was its weight. Dynamite comes in the form of sticks that are eight inches long and one and a quarter inches in diameter. Each stick weighs about half a pound. To successfully blow a one hundred-meter-bridge and another hundred meters of viaduct, would require close to six thousand sticks of dynamite, six thousand feet of fuse, and six hundred blasting caps. The weight of the material would weigh close to thirty-one hundred pounds. That much weight would require a team of thirty people just to carry the explosives. Instead, he told them that they would be using a new explosive that they just received from the US Army, Composition C-3.

Composition C-3 was a plastic explosive created in the US. It consisted primarily of RDX or Royal Demolition Explosive, developed by the British. As an explosive, RDX detonated quickly and was extremely powerful and stable when stored under the right conditions. However, it suffered from a relatively limited range of serviceable temperatures. Extreme cold and hot temperatures reduced its stability.

Composition C-3 was almost twice as powerful and one-half the weight as dynamite. C-3 could only explode by using a detonator. Weapons fire would not detonate C-3, which would be good if they encountered enemy fire. What the captain didn't tell them was that tracer bullets would explode C-3, but the Japanese rarely used tracers in Burma.

The amount of C-3 and primacord needed to destroy the bridge and viaduct would weigh around twelve hundred pounds. This was still too much weight for three people to carry, and it meant that they would need to take at least twelve more people to carry the explosives and five additional people to carry supplies.

Captain Helms had already discussed the additional manpower requirement with Lieutenant Colonel MacKenzie. The colonel recommended taking the Kachin rangers assigned to the SOE detachment. They were familiar with the Kwai Noi because they had lived in the southwestern portion of Burma prior to the Japanese invasion, and they had traded up and down the Kwai Noi for generations. The rangers were also in contact with their kinsmen by radio, courtesy of the OSS. Utilizing the Kachin kinsmen could prove to be extremely useful in terms of securing the infiltration and exit locations.

CHAPTER 17

CALCUTTA, INDIA

The Calcutta SOE detachment at Alipore, consisted mostly of British, Burmese, and Kachin rangers. The SOE's primary missions were to train and infiltrate agents behind Japanese lines, supply and aid the Burmese guerrillas, cut communication lines, harass the Japanese, and create as much mayhem against the enemy as possible. The SOE operations required soldiers with knowledge of the areas they infiltrated. To complete its mission, the SOE relied heavily on native Kachin tribesmen.

The Kachin people were combination of several Southeast Asian tribal and ethnic groups. They were renowned for their fierce fighting and jungle survival skills. Jon had heard stories from British officers about the Japanese slaughtering whole Kachin villages that resisted them. After these atrocities, the Kachin decided not to engage the Japanese in head-on battles. Instead, they began a guerrilla war against the Japanese. The Kachin would attack individual or small groups of Japanese. Those killed by the Kachin were found along jungle trails with their throats cut and their ears cut off. Although the Kachin didn't know it, at the time, they had touched a psychological nerve in the Japanese. The majority of Japanese were either Buddhists or Shinto, who believed that the body must go to heaven undefiled. The Japanese believed that after they died, their soul was pulled to heaven by their ears. The mutilation of Japanese soldiers was an abomination that created an unexpected fear in the ordinary soldier and compromised both their morale and psychological spirit.

The Kachin were very effective in employing booby traps in their tactics against the Japanese. They used sharp, pointed bamboo shafts called *panji* sticks that were sharpened and hardened over hot coals. The panji sticks would be stuck in the ground along the side of a constricted trail that the Kachin would chose to ambush the Japanese. The panji stick tips would be coated with feces and then covered with vegetation for camouflage. When a group of Japanese soldiers walked up the trail, the Kachin would fire on them. The Japanese would dive for cover along the side of the trail and impale themselves on the panji sticks. They would either bleed to death or get a deadly infection from the feces.

The Kachin also used hand grenade booby traps. They would hollow out bamboo into cups that the grenade would fit into. They would attach a trip wire, usually made of vine, to the cup and pin it to the ground on the side of the trail. Then they would run the vine across the trail two inches off the ground and tie it to a bush. When a Jap hit the vine, it would yank the cup free of the grenade. The grenade's spring-loaded firing lever would pop off, explode the grenade, and kill more Japanese soldiers. After a while, the Japanese feared the Kachin more than they feared the British.

After meeting with the top ranking Kachin ranger, Captain Li Naw, Jon decided to let him choose sixteen rangers for the mission. Li agreed to do this, but he insisted that he was also going on the mission. When Li introduced the rangers that he had chosen, Jon thought that they looked like young teenagers, but Captain Naw assured them that they were the top fighters of all the fifty Kachin rangers he commanded.

The SOE analysts had already determined that the only way to get safely into the target was by air. The noise made by a C-47 could be heard for several miles, so they couldn't land too close to the bridge. One of the SOE pilots working with Jon suggested a grassland area west of the bridge. He had flown close to the area before and thought that it was far enough from the POW encampment to be safe. But it would mean trekking some fifteen miles to the bridge; a two-day journey in grassland and jungle terrain. They would also need a way to cross the river. Captain Naw said he would take care of those arrangements.

The SOE pilots also decided that they couldn't use the same area for egress that they would use for the infiltration. Another SOE pilot recommended using a clearing only two miles from the bridge. The pilot also recommended landing right at dusk. He could approach the landing site from the west, with the sun at his back, and make it harder for any Japanese at the POW camp to see the C-47 on its approach. He also told Jon that it didn't hurt to fly home under the safety of darkness.

To the trio this made good sense, because they didn't want to remain in the area of the bridge for too long after they destroyed it. Two miles could be easily managed in two hours of hiking. It would probably take the Japanese longer to mobilize any type of patrol and longer yet to get authorization to send a fighter into the area. By then, darkness would shut down any reconnaissance operations and fighter patrols.

Jon's first concerned was being detected by Japanese ground and aerial spotters. Twenty soldiers parachuting from a plane and then walking across a grassland expanse could become a problem during daylight. They would have to do a night drop. Plus, it would be a full moon when they jumped, and they would have the Kachin tribesmen to secure the drop area.

Captain Naw made arrangements with his Kachin kinsmen. They would meet them at the drop zone, guide them to the bridge, and provide boats for the river crossing. The addition of Captain Naw's kinsmen would also provide the necessary manpower to chop their way through the jungle portion of the trek. By using the tribesmen as carriers, the team could also take more food and water. The tribesmen could also serve as lookouts, while the agents and rangers rigged the bridge and viaduct with explosives.

Jon had heard stories about how the Kachin could remain hidden in the jungle forests to anyone walking only four feet away.

They were also noted for taking the heads of their enemy and impaling them on a bamboo pole as a warning. They especially liked taking the heads of Japanese soldiers, whom they now hated.

Yes, Jon thought, *the Kachin rangers will make a great addition to the team, and the Kachin kinsmen would be a welcome early warning system should the Japanese be in the area.*

With the explosives, the entry and egress, the extra manpower requirement, boats, and the security issues all taken care of, all the mission parameters were determined. The trio had also agreed with Captain Naw that the mission could be completed successfully with seventeen rangers. Twelve rangers would be delegated to carry the explosives, primacord, and detonators. Four rangers would carry food and water. The three agents and Captain Naw would act as armed guards carrying Thompsons and extra ammunition. The Kachin kinsmen would act as additional security and guide them to the target. They also agreed that the mission could be accomplished in three days. Two days to hike to the bridge, and one day to set the explosives, blow the train, and egress the area. It could work perfectly if the train was on time.

Before they closed out their planning session, Jon made a suggestion to help with the egress. He asked Captain Helms to arrange for a local OSS agent to set up an AN/UPN-1 portable radar beacon to guide the aircraft to the correct drop zone.

The AN/UPN-1 radar beacon was an ultra portable radar beacon that ground troops could use to guide an aircraft to a fixed location. It worked by using azimuth information being transmitted from the ground radar to the aircraft. It was effective from a range as far as fifty miles. The ground beacon was capable of being interrogated by an airborne radar unit operating on the same beacon frequency. Jon already knew that the SOE C-47 was outfitted with an airborne unit.

Captain Helms thought that it was an excellent recommendation. He would send over his request to the OSS detachment commander this evening.

CHAPTER 18

CALCUTTA, INDIA

The next morning, Jon had gone to the quartermaster's depot, where he had picked up some needed supplies. When he returned to his squad tent, he found Private Albert Fahy waiting for him. The private told him that a classified message had just arrived for him at the SOE detachment and that it was being decoded as he spoke.

The only thing Jon could think to say was, "Thanks, Private. Tell Lieutenant Colonel MacKenzie I'll be over after I put this stuff up." If the colonel was sending someone over to tell him, then it must be coded urgent.

By the time Jon arrived, the encrypted message had been decoded and retyped. The desk sergeant showed him into a private room next to the commander's office, where the ever-present armed MP was standing next to the door. The same procedures that applied to their mission planning also applied to reading classified messages.

Lying on the desk was a light brown folder with the message inside. Both the folder and the message were stamped with Top Secret on the top and bottom of the front and reverse sides, in bold, capitalized letters. The message was short and direct. It informed him that Colonel Ronnie Masek, from G-2, was inbound to his station and due to arrive later today.

It must be something extremely important, Jon thought. *You usually don't plan and get ready for a mission only to have it interrupted.*

At Fort Ritchie, they had briefed him to expect to see one of the six colonels only when they were bringing a new mission. Jon thought that maybe Colonel Masek was coming to review and approve the mission they had just finished planning. But after thinking on it a little longer, he totally disregarded the thought. Jon put the message back in the brown folder, left it on the desk, and exited the room.

Four hours later, Private Fahy returned to his squad tent and informed him that Colonel Masek had landed, and he wanted to see him and Agents Murphy and Morreau in one hour. Lieutenant Colonel MacKenzie was out of the office, the private added. Jon thanked the private and walked three tents down and informed Murphy and Morreau of the meeting. Miles and Henri had moved into the American Residential Area to be closer to Jon. Forty-five minutes later, they were driving together to the British-American Club.

After they entered the SOE offices, the desk sergeant told them to go into the same room he had been in earlier. The same Royal Marine MP was outside the door, opened and closed the door after the trio entered the room. As they walked in, Colonel Ronnie Masek stood up and greeted Jon. Jon then introduced the colonel to Miles and Henri. Before they could take their seats, Sergeant Dunning entered the room and set a tray on the table with three cups of coffee, one cup of tea, and a plate of shortbread cookies.

Colonel Masek continued standing after the sergeant left. "Gentlemen, we have one more aspect of the Vulcan Halt mission to plan; the extraction of a navy commander from the Hintok station POW camp."

The colonel explained that six months ago a navy commander, who was part of General MacArthur's headquarters planning staff, was shot down over the South China Sea when the PBY he was riding in was jumped by a Jap Zero. He was the only survivor after the PBY crash-landed. Within an hour of crashing, he was picked up by a Japanese patrol boat. At the time of his capture, he was dressed as a Navy Aviation Branch Gunner's Mate.

"We are hoping the Japanese don't know who they have," Colonel Masek remarked. He continued to tell them that the commander was privy to much of General McArthur's plans to retake the South Pacific and invade Japan and it is extremely important that they extract him—to keep those plans from getting into enemy hands.

The OSS had obtained the intelligence on his location, three weeks ago, from an American army officer, who managed to escape from the Hintok Station camp. It had taken him two months to get through Thailand and Burma into India. He had had a lot of help from Kachin tribesmen that the OSS was working with along the Kwai Noi River.

From the intelligence that the army lieutenant brought back, the Hintok Station POW Camp still had thirty-eight Allied POWs who were guarded by eighteen Japanese MPs. Tenth Air Force had helped confirm the number of POWs and camp guards through aerial reconnaissance.

"We think it's feasible," Colonel Masek said, "to go in at night, extract the commander before you blow the bridge, and bring him out."

He paused before his next statement. "If you can't extract him, you will need to eliminate him to make sure he doesn't talk," Colonel Masek said.

"You're kidding, right?" Jon asked.

"What we are asking you to do isn't going to be easy. And it isn't going to be pleasant if you have no alternative but to eliminate the commander. However, I hope you understand that it's imperative that we remove him as a potential threat. Do you have any questions?" Colonel Masek asked.

Jon spoke first. "Colonel, I'm going to assume that we can extract him. What do we know about the condition of the commander? Will he be healthy enough to travel to our extraction point?"

"Jon, from what the army lieutenant has told us, Hintok is run by Japanese soldiers only. No Korean guards are assigned to this camp. It is one of the less brutal POW camps along the Kwai Noi River railway. The lieutenant has told us that the commander and the other prisoners are in fair shape health wise, except for the ongoing cases of dysentery and malaria. Whether that will still be the case when you get there is another question," Colonel Masek stated.

"And Jon, since the commander is an American naval officer, we do not expect you to have to carry out his death sentence, if it should come to that. Agents Murphy or Morreau can handle that task," Colonel Masek stated.

"Anymore questions?" Colonel Masek asked.

"One more question, Colonel," Jon said. "Where is the army lieutenant that escaped?"

"He's recuperating in an army hospital here in Calcutta. Why?" Colonel Masek asked.

"We'll need to talk to him and get as much detail on the POW camp as possible," Jon stated.

"I'll see that the sergeant major makes the arrangements for the three of you to visit him in the next couple of hours," Colonel Masek replied.

Jon thanked the colonel and started to leave the room.

"Jon, I'll be around for six more hours. If you have any other questions or special requests, come see me," Colonel Masek added.

Before Jon and the other two agents left the briefing room, Jon had already decided that there was not going to be an execution of an innocent American naval officer. What Jon was thinking now was not within the mission parameters set down by Colonel Masek.

On the way out of the building, they talked to the sergeant major and then drove to the US Army hospital. After a three-hour-visit with US Army Lieutenant Yul Butler, the trio had enough data on the camp for a preliminary plan for the commander's extraction. With the help of Captain Naw, they came up with a plan to use the Kachin tribesmen to scout the camp before they arrived. However, they all agreed that most of the planning would have to be done after they were on-site and scouted the camp themselves.

After the three agents had returned to Jon's tent, Jon looked directly at Miles and Henri. "Guy's, what if we take the entire POW camp? With only eighteen Jap guards, I think it would be possible," Jon said.

"That's not what we've been asked to do, mate!" Miles exclaimed.

"And what if there are more than eighteen guards?" Henri asked.

"Okay. Let's double the number of Japs," Jon said. "I still think it's doable. Look, we're going in with seventeen Kachin rangers. There will probably be at least twenty Kachin tribesmen available to help. I say let's take the damn camp and bring all the POWs out."

Murphy and Morreau were definitely not comfortable with the thought of taking down the entire camp. But it did make sense, if they could extract one POW, then why not all the POWs?

Miles spoke first. "All right, mate, but let's see what the Japs have after we get the bridge rigged to blow. And let's not mention this to anyone, especially Lieutenant Colonel MacKenzie. He'd probably have us put in irons. Okay?"

Jon and Henri nodded in agreement. This would have to be something they did as a spontaneous effort after they had scouted the camp. Jon wondered how difficult it would be to get a second C-47 to carry out thirty-eight POWs. He got a case of beer and left to talk to the two SOE pilots that were flying the mission before he visited the OSS commander.

CHAPTER 19
KANCHANABURI PROVINCE THAILAND

The camouflaged C-47 took off at 1740 hours with seventeen Kachin rangers and Agents Preston, Murphy, and Morreau. Although reluctant, the SOE physician released Henri for combat duty since it had been slightly more than a flesh wound. Flying at two hundred knots airspeed, it would be a seven-and-a-half-hour flight, which would take them from Calcutta southward across the Indian Ocean to North Andaman Island and then due east into Thailand. The SOE's C-47 had been modified with extra fuel tanks that enabled it to make the 3,600-mile round trip with plenty of fuel reserves.

At North Andaman Island, there was an allied coastal spotter, who would turn on his AN/UPN-1 radar beacon thirty minutes prior to their estimated time over his station. Although North Andaman Island was not inhabited by Japanese soldiers, there was still a chance that the Japanese would be monitoring for radio signals. So, for security reasons, the spotter would cycle the beacon at intervals of five minutes "On" followed by five minutes "Off" thirty minutes prior to and after the aircraft's estimated time of arrival.

The radar beacon provided directional navigation information to the pilots. When the beacon locked-on to the ground signal, the pilots would fly the bearing directly to the beacons location. When the directional needle started to swing in the opposite direction, it indicated that the aircraft had passed overhead the ground beacon and they could start their turn east.

The C-47 was cruising at ten thousand feet on a course of 165 degrees when it passed over North Andaman Island. As the aircraft turned east, it began a descent to 1,500 feet. It was a clear night and full moon had risen at 2333 hours. According to Allied intelligence, the Japanese did not have any night fighters stationed at Rangoon or Bangkok, so it should be a safe flight until daylight. For their entry into Thailand, the C-47 flying at 1,500 feet altitude would give them five hundred feet clearance above the highest terrain along their route.

Forty miles out from the drop zone, they locked onto the ground radar beacon. When the C-47 turned toward the bearing indicated by the beacon, the pilots turned on the small red light located on the forward part of the rear hatch. The jumpmaster then stood up and opened the fuselage door. When the door was securely open, the team of agents and rangers rose and began checking each other's parachutes. When the red light began blinking, the team members attached their static lines to the cable that stretched the length of the fuselage and stood in line facing the rear of the aircraft. Five minutes later, the pilot spotted six lit torches indicating the beginning of the drop zone. When the pilot turned on the green light, the team members began jumping out of the plane. After the last man had jumped, the plane reversed direction, and on the signal, the jumpmaster and crew chief began dropping the explosives, ammunition, and rations.

The explosives, extra ammunition, and food had been pre-packed in individual backpacks and placed in eight large canvas drop bags attached to chutes. After hitting the ground, all they would have to do was open the drop bags and extract the backpacks.

Jon was the first to jump out of the aircraft. When he landed, he quickly got out of the parachute harness, detached his Thompson machine gun, and waited for the aircraft to turn around and begin dropping the bags with the explosives.

Naw was the first ranger to land. As soon as he rid himself of the parachute, he called out in Kachin to the tribesmen waiting in the tall elephant grass. Within seconds, the Kachin headman was standing next to Naw telling him that his warriors had set up a defensive perimeter. After the last of the explosives reached the ground, the rangers opened the large black canvas bags and removed the pre-packed backpacks that contained the C-3, detonators and detonator chord. The rangers then gathered all the chute material and stuffed it into the drop bags. The tribesmen would take the chutes and bags back to their village and use some of the material for clothing; the majority would be traded for goats or pigs. No part of the chute would be wasted.

Once everyone was ready, Naw signaled the group to follow the Kachin Headman to the line of trees fifty yards away. The headman took the lead and walked them to a small clearing well inside the forest where they would wait until sunrise. Jon looked at his watch; it would be close to a two hours wait.

After conversing with the headman, Naw informed Jon that there were twenty tribesmen here to help them get to a camp that they would reach later in the evening. At the camp, there would be an additional twenty tribesmen. At the river camp, which was three miles upstream from the bridge, there would be another twenty tribesmen and ten sampans that would ferry the agents, rangers, tribesmen, and explosives across the river.

The Kachin tribesmen had already scouted the target and determined that there were no Japanese patrolling the bridge or the forests on either side of the river. The only Japanese lookout station was four miles downriver. The POW camp still held thirty-eight prisoners and was guarded by eighteen Japanese soldiers and their commander. One of the English speaking tribesmen had talked to an American POW on a work detail outside the camp. The POW, who happened to be the senior ranking American officer, told him that the ammunition train was still due to come through Hintok Station sometime in the next six days; that was two days ago. The tribesmen had done a thorough job, and Jon was impressed with the detail they had provided on the POW camp.

When daybreak came, Jon noticed the wide variety of trees in the forest. There was an amazing combination of hardwood and evergreens. Captain Naw stood next to a large tree.

"Preston, this is the yang tree. It is important to us because of the oil we can take from it. We use the yang oil for lighting our *bashas* and sampans. We can also cook it down into a paste and use it to seal our sampans and make them watertight. It grows to over a hundred feet in height. Our elders tell us that it lives to be five hundred years old," Captain Naw said.

As he continued walking, Naw pointed to another tree, "The *takyas* can grow to 150 feet tall. It is what you Americans call an evergreen. We use it for making dugout boats." He stopped and placed his hand on another tree, pulled off a piece of bark, and handed it to Jon, "This is the sandalwood tree. It is a tree that smells very good. We burn it in our huts for the pleasant smell."

Miles and Henri were intimately familiar with the types of trees in both Thailand and Burma. Before the war, Murphy had lived in Bangkok, where he was a professor of botany at Bangkok University. He and his family had fled to Rangoon and then again to Calcutta to escape the Japanese. Agent Morreau had lived in Rangoon where he was a general manager of a lumber mill. He had spent a lot of time in the Burmese and Thailand forests and knew the tree types as well as the uses of their wood. While he was on a business trip to Calcutta, the Japanese invaded Rangoon. His family was still there in a internment camp. Through a British officer that he knew, who was now commanding one of the commando unit stationed in Ceylon, he had found out that his wife and two children were in a labor camp on the northeast side of Rangoon. Everyone that was European or married to a European was put in the Japanese internment camp.

As soon as it was light enough, the headman said to move out. They traveled quickly, and for the sake of the three agents, they rested every two hours. This gave the agents time to light cigarettes and burn off the leeches that had gotten under their clothing and on their arms, necks, and legs.

It was sweltering hot, and at their second stop, Jon emptied his first canteen of water. If the second canteen ran out before they reached the camp, he would have to fill them from a running stream and drop a chlorine-based halazone water purification tablet into each canteen to kill the lethal germs and organisms that inhabited the jungle streams.

After another hour, the terrain began to change. It was getting steep and becoming more difficult. Nine hours into their trek, the headman guided the group into a densely forested area consisting mostly of tall bamboo and thorny shrubs. Jon was walking in front of Naw as they made their way along what Jon thought was an animal trail, when Jon's right foot stepped on something, which felt like a decayed stick, Naw yelled, "Freeze!" Jon stopped with his right foot heavy on the "stick."

Naw spoke calmly. "Preston, your foot is on the head of a cobra. When I say so, run as fast as you can, and get as far down the trail as possible."

Instead of running, Jon looked down at the position of the snake. He saw the five-foot snake writhing around his feet and legs trying to get free. He could see part of the snake's head sticking out from under his right boot. Jon placed all of his weight on his right foot, and with a quick motion turned his foot sideways and downward. He and Naw heard a soft snap and saw the snake go limp.

Jon's action had broken the neck of the cobra at the base of its skull. It was a trick that he had learned from Colonel Fairbairn during his Defendu-style fighting classes. The colonel told him that not only would he have to defend himself against man, but also wild animals and snakes. His instruction included how to snap a tiger's and leopard's neck if attacked, and several ways to kill a snake if you happened to come up on one or step on one. Until now, it had been an unproven method and almost unbelievable technique. However, Jon was now a believer.

Naw was astonished when Jon picked the cobra up by the tail and showed it to him. The other rangers were mesmerized and began talking to one another in their native Jingpaw, their singsong voices pitched high with excitement.

"Quiet!" Naw called out to the rangers in Jingpaw. "Let's move out."

Naw took the cobra from Jon and cut off its head. He told Jon that he would cook it for supper.

"Cobra makes a very tasty meal," Naw said.

Thirty minutes later, they arrived at the camp. The Kachin headman had established it deep in the bamboo bush where no Japanese would dare to venture. Japs were frightened to death of tigers, and this was tiger country.

Jon was surprised to see several large tents setup, a campfire already going, and food being prepared. There would be no GI cots to sleep on, but Jon was so tired that it didn't matter. The tents were without door flaps and netting, so their only problem would be mosquitoes. They were warned not to bring insect repellant because the smell was so foreign to the jungle that it could be detected downwind from a mile away. The mosquitoes were very thick and bothersome inside the bamboo forest. Jon began wishing that he would have disregarded the warning.

The evening meal consisted of boiled rice, wild deer, and cobra.

"Naw, what kind of deer are we eating?" Jon asked.

Captain Naw proceeded to tell him and the other agents about the barking deer. The adult barking dear was close to thirty-six inches in length and nine inches tall. It weighs around fifty pounds. When it is frightened, it makes a loud barking sound; like a dog.

"And it tastes very good, yes?" Naw asked.

Jon and the other agents nodded in agreement; it tasted very good.

"Now try the cobra, it tastes very good, too," Naw stated.

Each agent ate a piece of cobra and discovered that it was excellent. They each had a second and third piece. Naw got up, left, and came back several minutes later.

"This is the skin and head of the barking deer. This is a male, see the small antlers? And look, their front teeth are fangs. This is their only protection from their enemies," Naw said.

Naw went on to show them the deerskin, which was a light brown color. He then pointed out the unusually long black stripe that ran from the base of the deer's horns down to its eyes. To Jon, it looked like a long black eyebrow. After Naw finished explaining everything about the barking deer, they finished eating and went to their tent. The three agents got to sleep in the large tent, while the headman and Naw took the smaller one. The other tribesmen and rangers made themselves comfortable on the ground around the large fire pit.

It was well past midnight when a large tiger bounded out of the thick underbrush and darkness and grabbed one of the sleeping tribesmen behind his neck. The tribesman's screams aroused the camp. As the other tribesmen and rangers were awakened, they struggled to get out of the way of the tiger, most of them forgetting their weapons, which lay beside them. Naw was quick to get out of his tent and fired his Thompson over the tiger's head hoping it would drop its prey. The tiger, unfazed, turned his head back toward the camp and snarled loudly. He then bounded off into the jungle with the screams of the young tribesman trailing into the darkness.

It would be too dangerous to follow the tiger at night, so no one attempted it. It was impossible for anyone to sleep for several hours. After their nerves had settled, the stunned tribesmen and rangers made a larger fire and sat in pairs, back to back, with their rifles ready to shoot.

"What will happen now?" Jon asked Naw.

"When it gets light, we will follow the blood trail and find what is left of the body. The tiger will not travel very far before stopping to eat its prey," Naw explained.

"Does this happen often?" Miles asked.

"This year has been very dry, and game is scarce. The headman told me earlier that he had heard about several tiger attacks at villages upstream from his. You should try to get some sleep, Preston. Tomorrow will be a long day," Naw remarked.

At daylight, the agents were awakened by Naw. After they burned off the red ground leeches that had attached to them during the night, they had a small breakfast of cooked rice and tea with salt in it, brewed personally by Naw.

After they finished eating, the group gathered and followed the trail of blood for over a mile. They eventually came upon a large pool of blood and a severed arm. The headman looked up into the tree above the pool of blood and found what remained of his tribesman's body, lying across a large branch, twenty feet above the ground. The headman, knowing that the body would be dug up by scavengers if he buried it, told the others to leave it in the tree. He made the sign of the cross and said a prayer for his young tribesman. He then directed the group back to the camp to resume the trek towards the bridge.

After two hours of walking, they reached the next hill, which was much steeper and made of granite.

"If you fall on the trail, you could cut your hands and legs on the sharp pieces of granite. And if you slip and fall into the woods, you might be falling into a deep rocky ravine or taking a deadly plunge over a granite cliff," Naw told them.

The ravines were filled with thick vines, thorn bushes, and fallen trees. Giant rhododendrons grew where sunlight was able to make its way through the thick overhead canopy.

After the group made their way to the top of the sixteen hundred-foot hill, they were led to a dry creek bed that formed a ten-foot path down the backside of the granite hill. At times, they would slip on loose stones and have to crawl over large fallen trees. Other times they had to go around large boulders that had fallen into the creek bed. Jon was relieved that they didn't have to worry about falling off a cliff or into a ravine.

At the bottom of the hill, the team rested. Naw showed the trio a small spring where they could fill their canteens. Ten minutes later, the agents were hearing stories from Naw about some of the tribesmen finding rhino and tiger tracks in the moist creek bed. The entire group became tense and held their weapons tightly in their hands, instead of looped over their shoulders. The term tiger held a new meaning for everyone.

Naw came and squatted next to the three agents. He told them that the last leg of the trip would be traveled on an animal trail at the base of the next hill just inside the forest. They were still three hours from the river, and everyone would need to travel as silently as possible. He also told him that the headman had sent five men ahead as scouts. If the group got to the river before nightfall, they would wait in the forest until dark. Then they would go to the sampans where they would eat and rest for the night. They would make the river crossing before daybreak the next morning.

"Jon, the headman and his warriors think you are good magic. They are calling you Kaubra, which means Cobra in Jingpaw. It is a sign that they really welcome you," Naw stated.

Naw patted Jon on the shoulder, got up, and left. Jon didn't know what to think. As freakish as the incident with the snake had been, he had simply done what he had been trained to do. And he did it without thinking.

Jon had noticed a slower pace since they had left the bottom of the last hill. He was certain it was because the headman wanted to travel more silently and wanted to time his arrival at sunset.

As it happened, Jon was right on both accounts, and they arrived at the river and the sampans right after dusk. To his surprise, the sampans were lighted by yang oil lamps. At the sampan, the agents and rangers were given traditional conical straw hats, which all of the natives wore on the water for protection from the sun.

"The headman," Naw told them, "wanted everyone to look like a native, at least from a distance."

Jon chuckled, thinking that the headman must have taken most of the hats from his village and probably under strong protest. After he had eaten, Jon laid down. Between the comfortable breeze coming down the river and the gentle rocking of the sampan, Jon fell to sleep almost immediately.

CHAPTER 20

HINTOK BRIDGE THAILAND

The next morning, Jon was awakened by a different motion of the boat. They were moving downriver. Twenty minutes later, the sampans were parked on the northeast side of the river. The rangers and a dozen tribesmen began moving the munitions out of the boats and up the banks toward the north side trestle. The headman had already sent a dozen of his men down the river, on the POW camp side, to serve as rear guards. He had another dozen men on the opposite bank doing the same thing.

As daylight approached, Jon saw the viaduct and bridge and was in awe at its construction. To blow it up, all they would need to do is set charges at the base of the bridge, and it would all come tumbling down into the river. However, he wanted to do more than blow it at the columns. He wanted to make splinters of the thirty-inch-diameter columns as well as the smaller sway braces and sills. Colonel Arvin had told them that the Allies needed the repair of the bridge to take the Japs at least five months. Jon wasn't going to leave a single column timber that the Japs could use to rebuild the bridge. If the Allies needed five months to prepare for a successful invasion back into Burma, he was going to give it to them.

Jon laughed out loud and said, "We'll just have to make a hell of a lot of splinters."

Jon broke the team into four groups. Miles would take four rangers and place charges on the first fifty-foot-section on the north side viaduct. Henri would take four rangers and work the fifty-foot-section of the viaduct on the southern side. Jon would take the bridge trestle on the northern side to the solid granite column. The granite rock rising from the river was an ingenious use by the Japanese as the structural column to support the northern and southern bridge spans. Jon didn't have enough explosives or time to destroy the column. Naw would take four rangers and would plant charges on the trestle from the granite column to the southern viaduct.

Jon, Miles, and Henri found it to be difficult work climbing up the long vertical timbers that held the bridge up, so they stayed at the ground level. The rangers were climbing and scurrying like rats across the timbers setting the explosive charges. They broke the sixty-foot-columns into thirds and placed their charges. After finishing each section, they inserted the detonator and ran the primacord to the main contact detonator switch.

If the intention was total destruction of the bridge, they were going to insure it. It took nearly twelve hours to complete all of the work.

The last thing Jon did was connect the primacord to two three-second delay contact fuses. He also connected a three-minute delay contact fuse to the explosives he had placed on the bottom of all the columns and on the riverbank and in the river. These would detonate after the ammunition cars went down the bank or into the river. By the time everyone cleaned up their debris and made it back to the boats, it was dark.

Once in the boats, the three agents and Naw were taken downriver to meet up with the headman. During the day, another group of Kachin tribesmen and the headman kept watch over the POW camp. Jon wanted to infiltrate the camp and talk to the senior American POW and to the navy lieutenant commander. He told the headman to make contact with one of the POWs if he could.

While the agents and rangers were setting the explosives, the Kachin headman had infiltrated the forest and brush near the camp. The headman purposely made contact with the senior POW officer, who again, was out on a work detail. While remaining concealed, the headman explained what the American agents wanted to do tonight. The senior POW gave the headman instructions on where to infiltrate the camp and where to meet.

At 0300 hours, Jon, Naw, and the headman preceded to a location on the perimeter of the POW compound that the American officer had designated. Naw would accompany Jon into the compound and meet with the senior officer. The only weapons they carried were their Fairbairn-Sykes knives, and Colt .45 automatics.

The three agents and Naw decided that the only logical way to take the camp would be to take out all the guards, and capture the Japanese commander. Jon, followed by Naw, squeezed through the loose and rusting wire that enclosed the camp. Six rangers and six tribesmen, along with Miles and Henri did the same at their designated locations. There were no searchlights at the camp. The only light came from a small oil lamp burning on the porch of the camp commander's *basha*, and the light of the moon that was broken up by small groups of clouds. The remaining rangers and tribesmen surrounded the camp, and they would only intervene if something went wrong.

Only two Jap guards were posted during the night. The senior ranking Allied POW had made an agreement that no prisoner would attempt escape as long as they were treated fairly and fed. The senior Allied POW had asked the camp commandant to allow the POWs to trap deer and wild hogs for meat for themselves and their captors. The camp commander had readily agreed.

Jon followed the instructions given to him by the Kachin headman and within five minutes, he was met by Lieutenant Colonel Richard Hobar and Lieutenant Commander Jon Dybik inside of the basha that was reserved for sick POWs. Lieutenant Colonel Hobar was grateful for the rescue and was thankful that they would not be killing the camp commander. He told Jon that he and the camp commander had attended the University of Southern California (USC) at the same time, and they had been in several engineering classes together. He and Major Oshiko played chess in the camp almost every evening. Major Oshiko had told Hobar that he couldn't wait for the war to be over so he could resume work on his doctorate degree at USC.

Within ten minutes, the rangers had taken out the two night guards. By 0400 hours, the rangers and tribesmen had eliminated the remaining guards sleeping in their basha. Jon had awakened Major Oshiko with a knife at his throat. He told the major who he was and what he was doing. If the major resisted, Jon would kill him.

"I will not resist," Major Oshiko responded in perfect American English.

Jon removed the Colt .45 automatic from its holster and had Major Oshiko rise out of his bed and put on his clothes and boots. Lieutenant Colonel Hobar, who had been listening outside, entered the hut and informed Major Oshiko that he was now a prisoner of the US Army. With permission to get his sword, Major Oshiko offered Jon his sword. Jon deferred the honor to Lieutenant Colonel Hobar, who took the sword and accepted his surrender it with a reverent bow.

By 0500 hours, the rangers and part of the tribesmen had roused all of the POWs. One of the rangers brought Jon his wireless radio, which he set up on the camp commander's porch. Jon transmitted an urgent request to the SOE detachment for one additional C-47 and a medical team to pick up thirty-eight repatriated POWs, and one Japanese prisoner of war.

Lieutenant Colonel MacKenzie was in the office when the request came in. His reply wasn't very positive at all. In fact, he was pissed. His message informed Jon he would have him in front of a court-martial for not following orders. Jon's reply was, "Are you sending the damn extra transports or not?"

The next message Jon received was from the Lieutenant Colonel Kenneth Taylor, operations officer of OSS Detachment 101, stating that the extra transports and a medical team would arrive just before sundown at the scheduled pickup location. Lieutenant Colonel MacKenzie's authority had just been usurped by the US Army.

Jon had had it with MacKenzie. He was going to take this all the way to General Marshall if he had too. In the meantime, Jon needed to move fast and evacuate the camp. He instructed Naw to get the tribesmen and rangers to move the American POWs and Major Oshiko to the boats and then to the rendezvous location. He also asked Naw to have his men gather up as many food supplies, from the camp, that was necessary to feed everyone as soon as they got there.

From the information that Lieutenant Colonel Hobar had given Jon, the Japanese ammunition train was due to pass the station sometime after 1500 hours today. Jon wanted everyone at the rendezvous point before the train crossed the bridge.

By 1230 hours, everyone but the three agents, Naw, and the Kachin headman were headed to the rendezvous location. After arriving at the rendezvous location, the Kachin tribesmen set about cutting the elephant grass along a half-mile strip of level grassland. The rangers set up the radio beacon, established a secure perimeter, and began preparing a meal for everyone.

The three agents, Naw, and the headman waited on a large rock hill, a quarter mile from the bridge. Finally, at 1745 hours, they heard the train's engine as it came around a bend a little over a mile from the southernmost portion of the bridge. Jon had set the contact detonators on the far north side of the bridge. As the train came into view Jon could see that it was speeding up to get up the small grade before it reached the bridge. There were two small locomotives in the front, followed by twenty rail and flat cars, a locomotive in the middle, followed by another twenty cars, and two locomotives pushing from the rear. *This was a large ammunition shipment,* Jon thought.

As the train came closer, Jon raised his binoculars and saw Japanese soldiers and civilians crammed inside and on top of all the rail and flat cars. He hadn't expected this; at least not civilians. They were told that it was an ammunition train. But there had to be anywhere from twenty to a hundred people that he could see riding in or on top of each of the cars.

"Good God! They've combined a troop train with the ammunition train. That's why there are so many locomotives and cars," Jon said with anxiety in his voice.

When the two forward locomotives crossed the northern section of the bridge, the contact fuses triggered the detonation. The two front locomotives were blown ten feet into the air before falling into the river. Three hundred feet of trestle, rail cars, and people were blown hundreds of feet into the air. The middle locomotive and several trailing cars plunged down the riverbank into the river. The rear locomotives couldn't stop and the remaining rail cars that had survived the initial blast rushed past the blown viaduct and plunged down the riverbank into the river. By the time all of the cars and the two rear locomotives hit the riverbank and river, the secondary explosion erupted. The ammunition in the rail cars exploded with an unimaginable noise, and the pressure wave knocked the three stunned agents and two Kachin men to the ground.

After Jon got up, he could see the debris falling into the river. It was several minutes before he heard people screaming.

"Oh, my God, what have I done," Jon finally said.

His first thoughts were to go help, but he knew they had to get away as quickly as possible. Sunset was at 2010 hours;

they had three hours to make it to the rendezvous location. He would have to let the Kachin tribesmen deal with the people that were still living as well as the dead ones. *Spoils of war*, Jon thought regretfully.

All the way to the rendezvous point, the only sound Jon heard was the screaming and crying of the wounded or dying. He became ill at his stomach and retched several times during their journey to the rendezvous point. The emotion of remorse he was feeling was natural, but mostly, he felt guilt. If he was unsure whether God would forgive him after Anzio, he was certain that he was bound for hell after this.

Just before sunset, three C-47 transport planes landed on the makeshift runway two miles northwest of what was left of the Hintok Bridge. The first two C-47s landed with medical personnel to take care of the needs of the thirty-eight repatriated servicemen. The third, landed with two American military policemen and a Japanese interpreter. Forty minutes after landing, the first C-47 took off, followed at one minute intervals by the second and third C-47s.

On the return trip, Jon sat alone in the back of the C-47. Much of the time, he spent in prayer and the rest in agony over what he had done. Two hours into the flight, Naw came and squatted next to him.

"Preston," Naw said, "I know you are feeling awful about what you think you are responsible for. But it's not your fault. It's the fault of the Japanese. They are responsible for all those lives, not you. I am a Christian, Preston; my pastor tells me that God will forgive us no matter how many enemy we have to kill to end this war. I know you are very religious, and I also know you teach at a Catholic mission in Calcutta. You do a lot of good that only God knows about. After you talk to your priest, I want you to come to my village and we will talk too." Naw stood up, placed his hand on Jon's shoulder, and whispered quietly into Jon's ear before moving to rejoin his men.

CHAPTER 21

CALCUTTA, INDIA

For two weeks, the trio spent their time finalizing after-action reports. Before they left on the Hintok mission, they hadn't had time to complete their report on the Chittagong mission, which was excruciatingly detailed. Plus, everyone had been distraught from the loss of Katie's twin sister, Jackie. In the evenings, Jon had been spending three or more hours at the Catholic mission helping in any way he could. When Jon had walked into the mission's courtyard on his first day back, a dozen children ran to him and showered him with hugs and kisses. Father Doherty, the mission's senior priest, also embraced him.

"How are you, Jon?" Father Doherty asked.

"In need of a priest, Father," Jon stated.

"Then come, I'll take your confession now," Father Doherty stated.

When Jon left the confessional, it was the same as previous missions—he was in tears. Father Doherty put his arms around his broad shoulders and moved him toward the courtyard.

"Your students have done very well while you were away. In fact, most of them are reading English at the second grade level," Father Doherty said proudly.

Father Doherty's parents had emigrated from Ireland in 1890. He was born in Fargo, North Dakota, in the winter of 1892. Being the eldest son in an Irish Catholic family, he had entered the priesthood at sixteen. At age twenty-five, he was an army chaplain in France, during one of the worst summers of the war.

When they were finally alone, Father Doherty told Jon that it was the same in every war. "Good people die on both sides, Jon. It doesn't seem fair, and it doesn't feel right when you're the one pulling the trigger or throwing the grenade. Friends, loved ones, allies, and enemy will die until there is a final victor. You are very fortunate to be on the side of good. Those Japanese soldiers that died in the explosion and the civilians who were killed are all part of the struggle of good against evil. I thank God every day that we have people like you on the side of good."

The next morning, Jon read a message that had been received during the night. A colonel from G-2 is inbound to your station. Due on March 27, was all it said. Jon showed the message to Miles and Henri. Henri seemed distracted.

The following day at 1300 hours, Jon introduced Colonel Norm Hayward to Miles and Henri. They spent the first twenty minutes giving the colonel a down and dirty synopsis of the Hintok mission and another fifteen minutes telling him about the *Anne Marie*.

Colonel Hayward wasn't one to mince words and got right to the point. "Gentlemen, there's a Japanese coastal spotter post on Great Nicobar Island that we need taken out before a major naval operation kicks off in the Indian Ocean. Operation Cockpit, which commences in two-and-a-half weeks, is an Allied naval bombing raid on a Japanese-occupied port, oil facilities, and the Lho Nga airstrip. These facilities are located on Sabang Island, off the northern tip of Sumatra, and only 175 miles from Great Nicobar Island. Two Allied carriers will be accompanied by a task force of forty warships. For this attack to be a complete surprise, it is imperative that we take this spotter position out. Otherwise, they will report the task force, and we lose all elements of surprise."

"Colonel, will this require any additional SOE assets or just the three of us?" Henri asked.

"We're sending just the three of you, Henri. We don't believe that there are more than a dozen Japanese on the island," Colonel Hayward said.

"Is there anything special we need to take with us, Colonel?" Jon asked.

"Just your personal weapons, fragmentation grenades, and your jungle climbing boots," Colonel Hayward said.

"Where will we be planning the mission?" Jon asked.

"You'll be planning the mission and deploying from China Bay airfield in Trincomalee, Ceylon. At the airfield, you'll be met by Lieutenant Colonel George Linka. He's a US Army liaison officer and G-2 asset with the British SOE headquarters at Fort Frederick. He and the SOE detachment will handle all the preparations, transportation, insertion, and exit," Colonel Hayward said.

Colonel Hayward stood up and continued the briefing. He told the trio that Operation Cockpit would cut off the flow of oil to the Japanese in the Asian region and that they had already put severe pressure on the Japanese supply chain with their Rangoon and Vulcan Halt missions. Colonel Hayward told them that the Allied operation in Burma, called Merchant of Venice, along with the Galahad and Chinese divisions, were causing the Japs to retreat back towards Myitkyina. He told them that the Japs were suffering from serious supply problems and that the Allies were kicking their butts as they retreated. A successful raid on Sabang Island would crush the Japs ability to move supplies and make replenishment of the Jap army in Burma near impossible, which would help the British Fourteenth Army retake Burma.

"I guess we start packing our bags," Jon said.

"No rush," Colonel Hayward stated. "You all will be picked up by a PBY in four days and be flown directly to Trincomalee. We can't take out the spotter post too soon or the Japs will have time to reestablish it before our aircraft carriers and task forces move south of the island towards Sumatra."

160

"In the mean time, you have a couple of days to relax," Colonel Hayward said.

"After all, Jon, we don't want you to miss the birthday party that Miles and Henri have planned for you tomorrow, do we?"

Miles and Henri had visited Father Doherty two days earlier. They told the father about Jon's birthday and that they would provide everything if the mission would prepare it. Father Doherty thought it was a splendid idea.

On the day of Jon's birthday, Miles and Henri blindfolded Jon and told him to relax and let them do the driving. At the mission, Henri removed Jon's blindfold. In the middle of the courtyard were all the children, Father Doherty, Colonel Hayward, Captain Naw and the Kachin rangers, and most of the SOE detachment personnel; even Lieutenant Colonel MacKenzie.

In the middle of one of each of the ten large picnic tables in the courtyard, there was a huge flat sheet birthday cake. The one in the very center of the courtyard had twenty-five lighted candles. After Jon blew out all the candles, the children screamed happy birthday and sat down anxious to get their cake.

While everyone was enjoying the food and cake, Jon's mind was on the next mission. As Jon sat at the picnic table, he began contemplating the logistics of the Nicobar Island mission: three men for a minimum of three days; possibly an insertion involving a submarine or a fishing boat; they would need at least ten gallons of water and thirty K-ration meals. Or they could always find game on the island, and they would have plenty of halazone tablets to purify water.

Jon got up and moved to the edge of the courtyard where Miles and Henri were standing. "Have either of you been to Great Nicobar Island?" Jon asked.

"It's a rather wild and untouched area," Henri said. "My company evaluated the Andaman and Nicobar Islands for lumber but decided it would be too expensive to establish a mill there. Also, the Indian government didn't want to grant lumbering rights because they were worried that it would end up contaminating one of the last primitive tribes on the planet. So we abandoned the effort altogether."

"From the research that our department did at the university, Great Nicobar Island has very rugged terrain and a highly dense jungle canopy. There are lots of saltwater marshes and several waterways that go inland, but they are shallow and filled with saltwater crocodiles," Miles said.

"Then I guess we are going to need a guide. I wonder if Captain Ahab can help," Jon said. "He did say that he had a brother in the Andaman Islands."

CHAPTER 22
FORT FREDERICK CEYLON

The PBY flight from the Calcutta to Ceylon took four hours. Jon spent the time talking with the American flight crew and catching up on what was happening back in the states. The American PBY crew, led by Navy Lieutenant Neil Doten, had only recently arrived in Calcutta. This was their first operational mission in their brand new Navy PBY Catalina. Jon caught up on the news home as well as how the Red Sox were doing.

Trincomalee was a port city on the northeastern shores of Ceylon. It is situated on a large hill at the end of a natural rock formation that overlooked Kottiyar Bay. The bay is approximately four miles wide and five miles in depth. The inner harbor covers about twelve square miles and according to the Royal Navy, is the fifth largest natural harbor in the world. After the fall of Singapore, Trincomalee became the homeport of the Royal Navy's Eastern Fleet and submarines of the Dutch navy, home of the American OSS Asian training detachment, headquarters of the SOE in the CBI theater, and home of the British Third Commando Brigade assigned to the SOE.

Prior to World War II, the British had built the large airfield, RAF China Bay, a few miles north of Trincomalee. The airfield also housed a huge fuel storage and support facility for the Royal Navy. After landing, Agents Preston, Murphy, and Morreau were met by Lieutenant Colonel George Linka and transported by a

British staff car to the SOE headquarters at Fort Frederick five miles away.

At the headquarters, the agents were introduced to Colonel Rodney Mize, the deputy commander of the SOE Headquarters Unit. They were taken to a secure briefing room and served coffee, tea, and sweets. Lieutenant Colonel Linka briefed Colonel Mize on the previous successes of Jon's team and then gave everyone an update on the ongoing Galahad operation in northern Burma, where he had transferred from.

Colonel Mize was one of the last British officers to make it out of Hong Kong before the Japanese invasion. He commanded the British SOE detachment in Hong Kong and helped set up part of the Hong Kong Resistance before the Japanese captured the island. He had stayed until the last minute before being evacuated on a Stinson L-5 Sentinel that flew him to Liuchow, China. He had been running the China Resistance from Ceylon ever since his arrival in Trincomalee.

With the pleasantries over, Colonel Mize closed the door and asked Lieutenant Colonel Linka to start the briefing of the current mission. Lieutenant Colonel Linka stood in front of a wall map of the Indian Ocean and pointed at Sabang Island.

"The Allied naval bombing raid on the Japanese occupied port and oil facilities on Sabang Island will start at dawn on April 19th. Complete surprise is critical to the success of this raid. Interfering with that success is a Japanese coastal spotter position located on Great Nicobar Island. The island is the largest of the Nicobar Island chain and is located 175 miles north of the northern tip of Sumatra. There are hills throughout the island, but the largest of these run in a north to south direction. Mt. Thuillier, which is part of this chain of hills, has the highest elevation of any point in the Nicobar Island chain. It rises to a height of 2,106 feet above sea level," Lieutenant Colonel Linka stated.

The colonel paused before he said his next words, "Agents Preston, Murphy, and Morreau, I understand how dramatically successful your previous missions have been. On Great Nicobar Island, you will be subjected to more heat and humidity than any of your previous missions. The jungle is very dense and hills are very steep, which will only add to the stress of the already high heat and humidity. The only dangerous animals on the island, other than the Japs, are pythons, vipers, wild pigs, and salt-water crocodiles. There is also one of the most primitive tribes in the hemisphere found on the island, the Shompens. But from what we know, they will not pose a danger," Lieutenant Colonel Linka stated.

The colonel stopped, took a sip of coffee, and proceeded. "From the radio transmissions that the Royal Navy has intercepted over the last two months, we've narrowed the location of the spotter's radio equipment. Its most likely position is on the south side of Mt. Thuillier, around the 1,800-foot level," Lieutenant Colonel Linka said.

The lieutenant colonel pulled down a more detailed map of the Great Nicobar Island and used a pencil to point out the position of the spotter location. He briefed them that the RAF has conducted three photoreconnaissance missions across the island in the last six weeks. The SOE photographic interpreters found signs of human inhabitation on the west and south sides of Mt. Thuillier. They also found evidence of caves in the same area, so we could be looking at a well-entrenched Jap outpost," Lieutenant Colonel Linka stated.

Agent Morreau was the first to raise a question, "Colonel, how far is it from the coast to the location of the outpost?"

"Henri, the closest route to Mt. Thuillier is around nine miles. But it is through some densest and most rugged jungle forest that you will encounter in this part of the world," Lieutenant Colonel Linka said.

"Is there any chance of using one of the island natives as a guide?" Agent Murphy asked.

"Not a native of Great Nicobar Island, Miles. But we will be using a native from one of the Andaman Islands, who fishes and traps at Great Nicobar Island throughout the year. We call him Adam. He will rendezvous with you on the northeast side of the island," Lieutenant Colonel Linka said.

"How will we be getting there, Colonel?" asked Jon.

"You'll be taking a PBY from China Bay three days from now. The PBY will rendezvous with the USS *Coho*, a submarine on patrol in the Indian Ocean west of the Andaman Islands. The *Coho* will take you to within five miles of the beach. We don't want to risk taking a PBY to the rendezvous with Adam because it might be heard and spotted. The *Coho* will be surfacing to let you off at dusk. Adam will be off the coast in a 22-foot fishing boat. He will take you to a protected cove, where you all will spend the night. You will set out on your trek to Mt. Thuillier the following morning," Lieutenant Colonel Linka concluded.

With that being said, Colonel Mize recommended that they go to the officer's club and have dinner then come back and finish their study of the island.

Two hours later, the agents were back in the briefing room studying the aerial photographs and the topographical maps provided by the SOE detachment. After an hour of intense study, Jon took a pencil and drew a line from the cove to Mt. Thuillier.

"If we can follow this route, we should be able to avoid climbing these large hills. By following these two hundred-, three hundred-, and four hundred-meter contours, we will eventually end up at the base of Mt. Thuillier. It's going to be a challenging climb. Let's hope we can find some animal trails, and avoid any swampy areas. I would hate to run into one of those crocodiles," Jon said.

Murphy began laughing, and using one of Jon's favorite American terms, said, "For crying out loud, Jon, you're beginning to sound like a 'big woos.' I would think you would be more worried about the vipers and Japs. Instead, you're worried about crocodiles? Hell, the leeches will probably bleed us to death before we even see a crocodile."

Jon had to laugh with Murphy and Morreau. It was rather ridiculous, but he was going to carry his Colt .45 loaded with special hollow-points he had left over from the Chittagong mission.

On Sunday morning, Jon went to Mass at a Catholic church two miles from the base. Later that afternoon, Agents Preston, Murphy, and Morreau were in at the SOE detachment being outfitted with camouflaged khakis and testing and cleaning the weapons they would be carrying. On this mission, Jon would be sure that he and his agents would carry gun cleaning kits. On the Hintok mission, their weapons had developed a small film of rust after the second day. With the environment on Great Nicobar Island, the rust would probably start forming by the end of their first day. He couldn't afford to have a gun jam because of poor maintenance.

All three agents would carry Thompson submachine guns. Agents Murphy and Morreau would carry .9 mm Beretta pistols. Jon would carry his .45 automatic with his special hollow-point shells that Brunelle had made for him on the *Anne Marie*. They all carried their silenced .22-caliber pistols and a Kachin tribal knife called a *maru*. It was a traditional native design with a twenty-five-inch blade and a concave cutout at the end of the knife. Its handle was made of rattan with a brass ferrule at the end of the handle. They had received their knives from the Kachin rangers after they successfully freed the POWs and blew the bridge at Hintok. The scabbard was made of wood with a long strap woven from vines designed to be worn around the neck. It would be great for hacking through the dense jungle.

Jon was also carrying the shrunken head awarded to him by Captain Naw, the commander of the Kachin rangers and tribal headman of his clan. Naw had invited Jon to visit his village after the Vulcan Halt mission for a *Sut ma-nau* celebration—to introduce and welcome a new and good friend to his village.

During the celebration, Jon was made a member of Naw's tribe. He went through a day-long tribal ceremony, where Naw told the story about Jon's bravery as he faced and killed a cobra, without using any weapon; his bravery in facing the Japanese during the rescue of the thirty-eight American POWs; and the destruction of a Jap ammunition and troop train that killed hundreds, if not thousands of Japanese soldiers. Naw had a tendency to exaggerate, Jon found out.

Before the evening meal, Naw dressed Jon in Kachin tribal wear, painted his face like a Kachin tribal warrior, presented him with the shrunken head of a Japanese soldier, and gave him the Kachin warrior name of Kaubra, meaning Cobra. Jon had never seen a shrunken head before, but he wore it proudly around his neck—without question—the entire evening and the next day when he departed the tribal village. He decided not to wear it on base in Calcutta, since it might not go across well with the American and British senior officers.

Now that he was going into the jungle again, he would paint his face like a Kachin warrior and wear the shrunken skull around his neck.

"After all," Jon said to himself, "I am the great Kachin warrior, Kaubra."

Jon chuckled out loud and said, "Hell, I'll probably scare the damn Japs to death before I get a chance to shoot them."

CHAPTER 23

USS *COHO* INDIAN OCEAN

At 1000 hours the following day, the navy PBY took off for its rendezvous with the USS *Coho*. The pilots turned the aircraft to a compass heading of 135 degrees, leveled off at five thousand feet, and adjusted the engine throttles to give them cruise airspeed of 125 knots. The five-hundred-mile-flight would take a little over four hours.

After one hour into the flight, the pilot gave their bow turret gunner and two waist gunners a "Clear for Live Fire" command over their headsets, and the gunners commenced a five-minute live-fire exercise. Just as pilots were required to fly a certain number of hours in a month to maintain their flying proficiency, gunners had to complete a certain number of live-fire exercises to maintain theirs. In this area of the world, the PBY crews saw very little combat, unless they were supporting a task force. And even then, they were doing mostly submarine patrol or aircrew rescue.

The PBY carried three .30-caliber machine guns: two in the nose turret and one located in the floor of the fuselage, just rear of the waist guns; and two .50-caliber machine guns located on each waist blister. After the crew had finished their practice, Miles and Henri put their time in, shot off a couple hundred rounds, and practiced clearing a jammed gun.

After the live-fire exercise, Jon went aft to talk to Henri. Henri had seemed distracted since coming back from the Hintok mission, and Jon was worried about him. The previous evening, Henri had gone to visit the commanding officer of the British Third Commando Brigade. Previously, the commander had provided Henri the initial information he had on his family's internment in one of the Japanese detention centers in Rangoon. But this time, the colonel didn't have any new information about his family. He also told Henri that he didn't know of any future plans to go back into the Japanese occupied city. Henri had left worried and despondent. When he returned to their quarters, Jon and Miles had taken note of Henri's depressed demeanor. Jon was now worried about his ability to perform, and it was his duty to decide if Henri was combat capable.

Henri was sitting on one of the folding down canvas chairs aft of the waist gunner's station reading. Henri had left on a business trip to Calcutta on the second week of January 1943, and had missed his daughter Michelle's tenth birthday party. During the second week, he was in Calcutta when the Japanese invaded and took Rangoon. Henri was familiar with the stories from the civilian detainees that had escaped from Japanese internment camps in Hong Kong and Singapore. They told of the horrendous treatment of the men, women and children, and the lack of adequate medical care and the constant food shortages. Lieutenant Colonel Linka had even confirmed the stories because he was in constant contact with several OSS agents around Rangoon. The situation there was not good, and a lot of the food grown by the detainees was confiscated to feed their captors. This information served only to heighten Henri's stress and fear for his family's welfare. Now he was rereading the last letter he had received from his wife, delivered to him by the Red Cross, over six months ago.

The stay on the *Anne Marie* had also heightened Henri's depression. And even though Henri concealed his fear and depression well, Jon had picked up on several comments made by Henri that didn't seem quite right. Jon should have confronted Henri then, but he was distracted by Camille. He even confided to Camille. She told him that what Henri was going through was natural and that he would pull himself out of it.

The morning of the flight, Jon had gone to the British hospital at Fort Frederick to talk with one of the psychiatrists. After arguing with the charge nurse, who told him he would have to make an appointment, Jon threatened to pull his gun. Within a minute, he was talking to one of the psychiatrists.

Jon told the doctor the story about Henri's family and how depressed Henri had become; that he was at the point of removing Henri from their mission. He needed to know what he could do to pull Henri out of his depressed state because he really needed Henri on this mission. The physician recommended getting Henri to talk about his family and getting him to remember the good times he had with them.

"Get him to speak positive about his family. Ask him what he will do once they are reunited. Give him hope, Agent Preston," the physician said. "You can still pull him off the mission at the last possible moment if you have to."

The doctor also added a warning, "It may not be something you can do in just a couple of hours, Agent Preston. It may take weeks or even months, especially if he's in full-blown depression. If you have any doubts, you should remove him at once and see that he gets treatment."

Jon didn't think Henri needed psychiatric treatment, so on the aircraft he followed the doctor's advice and sat down with Henri and got him to talk about his family. Henri told Jon about his son's last birthday party. Henri had bought him a pony, and his son was totally surprised and absolutely elated with his gift. Every day after school, he would come home, saddle his pony, and ride it on the two-hundred-acre rubber plantation that Henri owned. Henri then talked about his daughter, how beautiful she was, and that one day, he was certain, he would have to chase the boys away with a shotgun. Then Henri talked about his beautiful wife, Mae. He had met her when he first moved to Rangoon. She was a university professor in the forestry department that he was visiting. He told Jon that it was love at first sight for both of them. They dated for almost a year before they were married. Jon and Henri talked a little over three hours before Jon left his side.

Before Jon walked away, Henri grabbed him by his arm and thanked him for cajoling him into talking about his family. Henri revealed to Jon that he had been contemplating removing himself from the mission. Henri then told Jon that he needed to go on the mission because this mission would help shorten the war with Japan and aid in reuniting him with his family. Jon agreed and was relieved that Henri was back and thinking straight.

Jon went forward to talk with Miles who had been standing next to the navigator's table for two hours. The navigator was busy using the sun as a navigation aid to create a sun line of position. He showed Miles how he would compare the sun's line of position with his dead reckoning position and determine the aircraft location on his aeronautical chart. The navigator was also teaching Miles how to use the sextant. He taught Miles how to collimate on the sun using the small bubble inside the sextant eyepiece. He showed Miles how he would take the altitude from the two-minute sextant reading, and using a mathematical sequence on his computation form, convert it into a line of position and plot it on his chart. Miles was fascinated and had taken the last two sextant readings for the navigator before Jon came forward to chat.

"Are you taking Henri off the mission?" Miles asked. Like Jon, Miles was highly intelligent and extremely perceptive. He had also been worried about Henri's state of mind.

"Not now. He finally got his head straightened out. He was just worried about his family. Plus, I don't think being around the girls on the *Anne Marie* and then Jackie's death didn't help him any. Getting him to talk was all he needed. He's good to go," Jon said.

Miles thanked Jon for whatever it was he did to bring Henri back from his doldrums. With a smile, Miles said, "Hell, Jon, I didn't know you were a psychiatrist, too. I'll be sure to make an appointment with you when I need one. Maybe you can help me with my fear of jumping out of perfectly good airplanes."

Now Miles had Jon laughing. Miles was always an upper for everyone who was around him. He reminded Jon of a saying he had read in a book about a sixteenth century navigator named Jacques Carter, "A rising tide raises all ships in the harbor."

Yeah, Jon thought, *Miles is a rising tide kind of guy.*

At 2130 hours, the pilot called for Jon to come to the cockpit. He informed Jon that they were in radio contact with the submarine, and they would be landing in about fifteen minutes. The pilot then began a steep descent and leveled off at five hundred feet. The submarine was first spotted by the gunner in the nose turret and called to the pilot over the interphone, "Submarine fifteen degrees to port two miles, sir." The pilot turned the aircraft fifteen degrees left, pulled the throttles back, slowed the aircraft to ninety knots, lowered the flaps, and began the approach for landing.

After the aircraft had touched down, one of the waist gunners launched a six-man inflatable life raft. Within minutes, the three agents were rowing in the direction of the USS *Coho.* Fifteen minutes later, the raft was tied up to the portside where three submariners were waiting to help the trio climb aboard. Jon was the first onto the sub. Miles passed their backpacks and gun bags to Jon, and then Henri and Miles joined him. By the time the trio climbed to where the Captain was standing, the PBY was lifting off the sea and heading west toward Trincomalee.

On the bridge, the captain of the USS *Coho,* Commander Royce Janca, welcomed the trio. The executive officer (XO), Lieutenant Commander Chad Spivey, helped direct them down into the sub's interior and showed each of them a separate room where they could stow their gear. Over the intercom, the trio heard the announcement, "All ahead full." They felt the movement of the boat and the sounds of the four diesel engines as they came back to life. The XO took the three agents to the mess and asked the cook to serve sandwiches and coffee.

"This is where we hang out when we are off duty," Lieutenant Commander Spivey told them.

The cook apologized to Murphy and Morreau for not having tea. Fifteen minutes later, after the XO relieved the captain on the bridge, he entered the mess and sat across from the three agents.

"This is the first special mission assignment for this boat, so you'll have to excuse my men if they stare. They're not used to visitors," Captain Janca said.

"No problem, Captain. This is our first time in a submarine. How long will it take to get to our rendezvous point?" Jon asked.

"We estimate four hours unless something causes us to have to submerge. On the surface, we'll be running at eighteen knots. If we submerge, we travel at five knots. From the reports we've heard from other PBYs patrolling the area, there are no Japanese surface ships within two hundred miles. And we haven't had any Jap submarine sighting in this area for over two months," Captain Janca said.

"What happens if the fishing boat doesn't show, Captain?" Henri asked.

"Our contingency is to drop you off in a deep water bay on the west side of the island. We'll get you ashore in that inflatable life raft you brought along," Captain Janca said.

"Do you plan on submerging before we get to the rendezvous point or stay on the surface," Miles asked.

"We'll submerge once we get within ten miles of the island. We'll identify the fishing boat through our periscope. If the guy isn't flying the correct flag on his stern mast, it's a signal that something is wrong. The most likely scenario would be a Jap patrol boat in the area. In that case, we'll abort and head to the alternate insertion point," Commander Janca stated.

"Sounds like a good precaution. The SOE didn't brief us on that detail," Jon said.

"We received the alternate instructions four hours ago. I guess this mission is pretty important, we usually only have one option," Captain Janca explained.

"If you all want to relax, you can use the bunks in the quarters that the XO had you store your gear in. If you don't have any more questions, gentlemen, I'll get back to the Conn. The XO will let you know when we are at the rendezvous point," Commander Janca stated.

Three and a half hours later, the radar operator called out, "Surface contact, Captain." The three agents flew out of their bunks when two loud blasts were sounded from the boat's klaxon. *Ahoooga! Ahoooga!* It was followed by the captain's voice blaring over the intercom, "Dive! Dive!"

After slowing down their heart rates, the trio made their way back to the boat's mess for more coffee and sandwiches.

"Green board," yelled the chief of the boat over the intercom. It was followed by, "Pressure in the boat" as the interior lights switched to red. The green board was a submariner's term used to inform the captain and crew that the boat was sealed, water tight, and ready to dive.

"Take her to one-zero-zero feet," Captain Janca commanded. As the *Coho* slipped beneath the surface, they heard the main air induction valves slam shut and the irregular gurgle of water entering into the ballast tanks. The diesel engines stopped, and the boat changed to the battery-powered electric motors for its under-the-water propulsion. Ten minutes later, the diving planesman called out, "Level at one-zero-zero feet, Captain."

"Anything on sonar?" Captain Janca asked.

"Contact, sir, just the screws of a small boat, Captain," the sonar operator called out.

"Bring her up to periscope depth, Helmsman," the Captain ordered.

Like all diesel boats in the Balao class, the *Coho*'s fuel tanks held enough diesel fuel to give them a cruising range of eleven thousand nautical miles. If Japanese patrol boats were loitering around the island, they would move twenty miles west, run on the surface, and recharge their batteries.

Within thirty minutes of submerging, the Captain turned the boat over to his XO and headed down to the lower deck where the three agents were congregated. He told them that he brought the boat back up to periscope depth and identified the fishing boat, but it wasn't flying the agreed upon flag. This told the captain that something was amiss in the area; probably a Japanese patrol boat. Now they were en route to the alternate insertion point. He then told them that part of the alternative plan was for the native guide to bring his fishing boat to the alternate bay. He told Jon that they were to wait no longer than twelve hours for the guide to arrive. If he didn't show by then, they would be on their own.

Jon asked Captain Janca to wait, while he went back to his cabin to retrieve the topographical map of the island. When he returned, he folded the map out on the table and asked the captain to identify the new insertion point. The new insertion point was a medium-sized cove on the west side of the island, five miles from Mt. Thuillier, and five miles east of Ganges Harbor. The closest the USS *Coho* could get the trio to the beach was one mile. The captain explained that the depth of the bay went from fifty to sixteen fathoms in three miles. Sixteen fathoms or 96 feet was the captain's limit.

When the XO returned to the mess and told them that they were approaching the entrance of the bay, the trio had finished planning their new route.

"Battle stations surface," Captain Janca commanded over the intercom. It was followed by the *bong bong bong* of the battle alarm and sailors hurrying to their battle stations.

When the boat surfaced at dusk, the agents felt the pressure change in their ears as the bridge hatch was opened. The captain was the first man onto the bridge followed by two lookouts, two submariners that manned the .50-caliber machine gun, four that manned the 127-millimeter aft deck cannon, and three that manned each of the 20-millimeter automatic cannons on the forward and aft gun decks of the fairwater. The captain wasn't going to be unprepared if a Jap patrol boat happened upon them.

They entered the bay at four knots with the captain requesting depth reports every thirty seconds. Their radar showed that the bay was clear of ships. They traveled two miles into the bay, but when the depth got to seventeen fathoms, the captain ordered, "Left full rudder," and turned the boat so it faced the ocean. Two minutes later, Captain Janca shouted to the helmsman "Rudder amidships, all stop!"

As soon as the boat stopped, four submariners exited through the bridge hatch and removed the six-man inflatable raft that they had stored in an exterior storage compartment, connected a compressed air hose, and inflated the raft. The raft was then lowered over the portside, and one seaman entered the raft waiting for the three agents.

While Agents Preston, Murphy, and Morreau were collecting their gears, the *Coho*'s cook presented them with a canvas bag filled with a selection of canned meats and six extra canteens of water. "Complements of the captain," the cook said.

After the agents entered the raft, the seaman climbed back onto the submarine, released the line, and shoved the life raft away from the boat with his left leg. Miles and Henri began rowing. It took nearly forty minutes to reach the beach. With his Thompson submachine gun loaded and ready, Jon collected their gun bags, jumped out of the raft, moved twenty yards to a large tree that had fallen on the beach, and squatted behind it. Agents Murphy and Morreau secured the oars, picked up the raft with their supplies still in it, and moved quickly to the large tree.

After hiding the raft farther into the vegetation, the trio took turns watching for the fishing boat. After ten hours of waiting, Jon became restless and moved to another location on the beach. It was a full moon and at 0200 hours, Jon noticed the black silhouette of a sailboat entering the bay. Thirty minutes later, the boat touched softly on the beach and a small figure got out of the boat. He came farther onto the beach, cupped his hand over his mouth, and yelled, "Cobra, it's Adam."

From behind the trees, Jon shouted, "What's the name of my favorite baseball team?"

"Boston Red Sox," Adam replied.

With Miles and Henri covering him, Jon moved from his position onto the beach to where Adam was standing. Jon greeted him and asked if his boat could be pulled ashore and hidden.

"With the help of the three of you, we can pull it into the trees, and cover it with fallen tree limbs so no one can see it from the bay. But first, I'll need one of you to help me lower the mast," Adam said.

CHAPTER 24
GREAT NICOBAR ISLAND INDIAN OCEAN

After the four operatives had pulled the boat into the jungle and covered it with tree limbs and brush, they sat down on a fallen tree to rest. It was getting lighter, and they began hearing the calls of a few dozen birds. By sunrise they saw doves, woodpeckers, and kingfishers flying about the trees and many other birds that they could not identify.

Adam told them that he had been fishing in the Andaman Sea waters since he was five years old; that was thirty years ago. At eighteen, he had enlisted in the Indian army and trained as a ranger. He spent the majority of his four-year enlistment stationed in New Delhi. After he resigned from the army, he moved to Rangoon and started his own fishing business. Just before the Japanese invaded Rangoon in 1942, he sold his business to his brother-in-law and brought his family to the Andaman Islands. There, he was contacted by the SOE and had been in their employ ever since.

He told the agents that he had smuggled a small team of British commandos into Rangoon harbor where they blew a tanker full of aviation fuel. Afterwards, he got them safely out of the harbor and rendezvoused with a PBY. He had worked with the British commandos four other times before this mission.

"It's a small world, Adam. I think we met your brother-in-law on a mission a while back. Does he have a forty-foot fishing boat with twin diesel engines behind a hidden bulkhead and go by the name of Captain Ahab?"

Adam nodded and said, "That would be him."

Jon was glad to have Adam. And his family ties to Captain Ahab put Jon more at ease. His ranger training meant another gun if they ran into Japs. Adam told them that he had been stopped by a Japanese patrol boat and boarded the previous day. And he had seen the boat twice more before the scheduled rendezvous with the submarine. Being extremely cautious, he decided not to fly the green pennant given him by the SOE. Instead, he flew the red one indicating something was wrong and to abort the primary rendezvous.

Jon was hoping that the Jap patrol wouldn't mean trouble on their exit from the island. But his worry now was getting to Mt. Thuillier. As Miles and Henri were getting the ammunition, grenades, and explosives unpacked, Jon put the shrunken head around his neck and began applying the Kachin warrior colors to his face. When he noticed Miles and Henri laughing at him, he stopped and said, "Hey, I'm the great Kachin warrior, Kaubra" which only made Miles and Henri laugh that much harder. Jon, slightly agitated, said, "For crying out loud, guys, focus on getting ready. This outfit might just scare the Japs to death."

Jon set his map on the sand and had Adam look at the planned route. With only a few deviations to the plan to avoid walking through the middle of several saltwater marshes, Adam agreed to the route. It would take them around several miles of mangrove forests and up a nine hundred-foot climb through forested valleys and would eventually end up at the base of the Mt. Thuillier. They would still have to avoid the marshes and cross one small stream, but it was the most direct route possible. With Adam in the lead, followed by Jon, Miles, and Henri, they left the beach and headed inland skirting the mangroves and hacking their way through the ten-foot-high elephant grass.

As they got deeper into the mangrove forests, which were a combination of palm, plumbago, hibiscus, holly, and a dozen other varieties of trees and scrubs, the heat and humidity began to worsen. Every hour they stopped to rest and burned the leeches off of each other's body. As they walked the edges of the saltwater marshes; they noticed crabs, turtles, water snakes, and the occasional group of long-tailed macaques; which Adam explained was a small, crab-eating monkey that made a great meal. Jon told Adam he had tried cobra, barking deer, and grubs, so, why not monkey. However, if he ran across a wild pig, he told Adam, he would shoot it with his silenced pistol, and they could have it for supper; after they had taken out the Jap spotter location.

Two hours into their trek, Adam put his hand up and signaled for all to stop. Jon came forward to where Adam was crouching. Adam motioned in the direction of the mangrove, where it made a curve and whispered to Jon.

"Japanese soldier," Adam said.

"How many?" Jon asked.

"Just one," Adam said. "He's probably down here hunting monkey or fishing."

"Let me take the lead," Jon said.

Jon pulled his silenced pistol out of its holster and worked his way forward with Adam close behind. Jon slowly moved from behind the grass and aimed the pistol at the head of the Japanese soldier ten yards away. Still unaware of their presence, the Jap holding a string of fish in his hand finally turned towards Jon and Adam. When the Jap finally noticed Jon's painted face and the shrunken head dangling from his neck, he began screaming. He dropped his string of fish and his rifle and continued screaming as he stepped backward. He was so frightened that he fell backwards into the mangrove swamp. Jon raised his gun to fire, when a large saltwater crocodile grabbed the thrashing and screaming soldier and hauled him under the water. Jon was too stunned to say anything and kept looking at the place where the Jap went under. Miles came up alongside of him shaking his head.

"I have to admire your technique. I swear, mate, I'll never joke about your Kachin warrior getup ever again," Miles said.

Jon looked up at Miles and said, "I told you, we needed to avoid the swamps. Did you see that croc? He must have been fifteen feet long!"

Adam told them they needed to move and keep a sharp lookout for more Japs. Soon they were moving out of the mangroves and climbing the four hundred-foot contours into the dense tropical rain forest. When they stopped to rest, Adam moved up the trail to do some recon. Jon handed Miles and Henri several long sticks of pork jerky to snack on.

"Where did you get this, mate?" Miles asked.

"I had a Kachin Ranger make it for me," Jon said.

"It's quite good. Is it sun dried? Henri questioned.

"No, it's smoked," Jon said.

"Good, I was beginning to wonder if I should be looking for maggots before I ate anymore." Henri replied jokingly.

Adam returned and told the trio that the trail appeared clear, but it would be tougher going for the rest of the climb.

"It's a steep climb. And I still can't see Mt. Thuillier. The canopy is too dense," Adam remarked.

By 1000 hours, they had reached the base of Mt. Thuillier; nine hundred feet above sea level. As the four rested, Jon noticed the outcropping of the igneous rock formed from the cooling and solidification of volcanic lava. Because the rock was so old, it was cracked and loose. The higher they climbed, the harder it became to remain absolutely silent. They had to become even more cautious when the team reached the area where the caves were supposed to be located. By 1600 hours, they had reached the elevation of the spotter location. Cautiously they began moving around to the west and then the south face of Mt. Thuillier. It was there that they found the first cave and signs of human activity. Empty tin cans, rice bags, and sake bottles, had been thrown into the jungle below and littered the side of the mountain. They could even smell the urine and feces where it had seeped downhill.

Moving inch by inch now, it took another thirty minutes before they found the sixty-foot radio antenna and several cables stretching into a large cave. The Japs had cut down the trees that obstructed the view of the ocean.

The view from the cave must be spectacular, Jon thought. Then he saw three Jap soldiers moving in and out of one of the caves.

Before they would take any action, Jon wanted to search for additional caves. They were already aware of four Jap soldiers; one now dead from a croc attack. Jon wanted to know how many more were around. Jon and Adam moved very slowly through the dense forest and found another cave twenty yards further east. They had to stop at a clearing where the Japs had cut down trees to give them a clear view of the Andaman Sea. Jon counted an additional six Japs moving about the cave indicating at least a squad in strength. They would have to play this carefully.

While Adam moved east, Jon went back to where Miles and Henri were waiting. He nearly went past them but Miles stuck a bare hand out and Jon moved to where they were hiding.

Jon told them that they would attack in two-man teams using grenades, Thompsons, and satchel charges if the Japs put up a fight. They would get as close to the caves as possible, and each agent would toss a grenade, followed by continuous machine gun fire. While Henri continued firing the Thompson, Miles would close and toss additional grenades into the cave they covered. Jon told Miles and Henri to wait until his and Adam's grenades went off before they tossed theirs.

It took Jon fifteen minutes to get back into position. Adam had not found any additional caves. When the grenades tossed by Jon and Adam exploded, Miles and Henri tossed theirs. After the first explosion, four Jap soldiers came running out of the large cave covered by Miles and Henri. When Henri and Miles tossed their grenades, they landed at the feet of the Japs. When they exploded, the four Japs were shredded by shrapnel. By the time Henri and Miles started emptying their machine guns into the additional soldiers in the cave, the satchel charge that Jon had tossed into the larger cave exploded; killing six Jap soldiers that were returning Jon's and Adam's fire. Miles, now at the side of the cave opening, tossed his satchel charge as two more Japs stumbled from the dust-filled cave. Henri took them out with Thompson fire before the satchel charge exploded.

The four agents remain hidden for ten minutes before they moved back to the caves. They found that the caves were relatively shallow, and no one had survived the satchel charge explosions. Jon counted ten sleeping mates in the larger cave and six in the small one. *Crap, one got away,* Jon thought. Miles and Henri had killed six at their cave.

"I've got sixteen sleeping mats and only fifteen Japs accounted for. There's one missing," Jon said.

"He was probably hunting," Adam said.

"After all the explosions and gunfire he's probably halfway to the beach," Henri remarked.

"There is probably a cove on the east side where the Jap patrol boat puts in for the night. I can't imagine them going anywhere else with their spotter here," Adam stated.

"If he makes it to their patrol boat, they'll be looking for us tomorrow," Jon stated.

Before they relaxed, Jon had Henri set booby traps fifty yards on either side of the caves. He instructed Adam to stand guard in the forest one hundred feet below the caves. Jon and Miles moved the bodies of the dead soldiers into the smaller cave. When they were through, they searched the bodies and the caves for any usable intelligence that they could take back to Fort Frederick.

After searching through several canvas backpacks and holes in the cave walls, Miles found what appeared to be a Japanese codebook. Miles took photographs of all the pages and replaced the book in the wall nook where he had found it. If the Japs came back, they would be able to inform their superiors that they had recovered the codebook. Hopefully it would leave the Japs feeling secure that their top secret codes were still safe.

By the time they had finished, it was close to dark. When Adam returned, he was carrying a wild pig that he had killed and dressed out while standing guard in the forest. Jon would get his roast pig after all and not have to eat monkey. Adam informed Jon that he had set several bamboo whip traps along a couple highly used trails that he had found on the northern slope, and bamboo cup grenade traps along a trail he found on the east side of the mountain. If any Japs did try to get to the caves during the night, the team would be alerted by either screams of pain or explosions.

Adam had taken the last watch before dawn. By the time the three agents woke, he had cooked the remaining pig over a fire pit, had prepared a large bowl of boiled rice, and a pot of hot tea from what he had salvaged from the Japanese food supplies. Before they left Mt. Thuillier, Jon set up his portable wireless and sent his coded message "Green Light Stop Cobra End", indicating that the team had been successful in taking out the spotter station. He received his acknowledgement and a short message, "PBY Dusk Alternate End."

The team made good time coming down the mountain; returning by the same route that they had taken inland. As they were making their way through the last thicket of mangrove forest fifty yards from where the boat was hidden, Adam held up his hand and squatted in the grass. He had heard the growl of the engines of a motor boat. He motioned for the other to stay as he moved to the beach and peered through a wall of tall grass. The same Japanese patrol boat that had stopped him two days before was slowly making its way toward the beach. The boat was configured with two .30-caliber machine guns; one forward and one aft. And there were at least six Japs on the boat that he could see.

Adam made his way back to the team and told them that the Jap patrol boat was near the beach. If they landed, they would eventually find Adam's boat and start searching for its owner. They would also want to know how he moved it over twenty yards into the jungle. The trio checked the magazines in their submachine guns and pistols. Jon had six Thompson and five .45 magazines and two grenades. Miles, Henri, and Adam had their Thompsons and at least ten extra magazines between them and five extra 9mm magazines each. Each had one grenade left.

The distance from the beach to the trees was only sixty feet, which was well within the range of the Thompson's and their pistols. Jon told them that they needed to position themselves to put the Japs in a crossfire. Jon directed Miles and Henri to the right, while he and Adam would move to the left.

"Get behind a couple of large trees," Jon whispered. "And don't expose yourself to those .30-cals. Wait for me to fire before you engage and then fire at the .30-cal guns first."

As the boat approached it was evident that the shallow draft patrol boat was going to be beached. When it hit the sand, a single Jap sailor jumped from the bow and tied the rope in his hand to a large log that had been washed onto the beach at high tide. Two more soldiers jumped off carrying pots and pans.

"Geez, they're stopping to cook on the beach," Jon said.

The one that had tied up the boat was now searching for small pieces of driftwood to start a fire. Two more soldiers eased off the boat and joined the others. One must have been the boat's captain because he was shouting orders to the others. Only one Jap remained on the boat manning the forward .30-caliber machine gun.

"They don't look like they are searching for anyone. They must have spent the night on another island," Adam said.

Jon labored over taking the Japs out or waiting for them to leave. Adam helped him decide.

"If we don't take them now, they could intercept us later when we head out of the bay to rendezvous with the PBY," Adam stated.

Jon nodded in agreement, raised his Thompson, and fired three bursts into the soldier manning the .30-caliber gun.

Seeing that Jon had knocked out the .30-cal in his first burst, Miles and Henri focused on the five soldiers on the beach. Jon jumped up, ran to the boat, and tossed a grenade into the cabin; just in case anyone was left aboard. It was over in three minutes. Henri climbed into the boat looking for anything of intelligence value. After finding nothing, he opened the engine cowling, dowsed a rag in the fuel tank, and left it for later when he would light it and blow the boat.

By the time that Jon had finished going through the pockets of the dead soldiers, Adam and Miles had cleared the brush and tree limbs from his fishing boat. Jon and Henri joined them to drag the boat to the water.

By 1800 hours, the sail mast had been raised, and everyone but Henri was in Adam's boat. Henri sprinted over to the patrol boat and climbed aboard. He then tied a string around a fragmentation grenade, pulled the pin, and placed it at the top of the diesel-soaked rag, where it entered the fuel tank. He lit the fuel-soaked rag from the bottom where it lay on the transom, jumped off the boat, and sprinted back to Adam's boat.

The rag eventually burned to the grenade and through the string, releasing the striker. When the grenade detonated, it ignited the diesel. Adam's boat was already fifty yards from the Jap patrol boat. The black smoke from the burning diesel would serve as a beacon for the PBY.

CHAPTER 25

PEARL HARBOR HAWAII

When the navy signals analyst in the signal center finished deciphering the Japanese intercept, he looked up at the navy lieutenant standing behind him and said, "This looks extremely important, Lieutenant. It appears to be a life and death situation, sir." The lieutenant took the lengthy decrypted message, read it, and nodded his head in agreement.

"Take this directly to Captain Whitely's office. He'll know what to do with it," the lieutenant said.

Captain Matt Whitely sat at his desk reviewing the latest Japanese intercepts that his signals team had decoded and marked urgent. The captain was tall and lean with the same broad and muscular shoulders from his football days at the Miami University of Ohio. He hated being stuck in an office all day, but that was the job they gave him after being wounded when a Jap Zero jumped the PBY he was flying in. During his internment in the Jap POW camp, he had contracted malaria and occasionally still had to fight the disease. To make up for the time behind a desk, he ran five miles on the beach every morning and evening, pushing himself despite the lingering pain from small shell fragments still in his right shoulder.

Before he could pick up the next decoded message in the stack of hundreds setting in his in-basket, his bright and bubbly secretary, Diane Kolar, entered his office and interrupted him.

"This was just delivered from the vault with Urgent-LAD stamped on it, sir. Do you want me to put it on top of the stack?" Diane asked.

"No, Diane. I'll take it now," Captain Whitely said.

"You look like you need to take a break, Captain. You've been at this since 0600 hours," Diane said. "It's lunch time. Can I get you a sandwich?"

With tiredness in his voice, he said, "No, Diane, but you can bring me a cup of coffee."

Diane left and returned with a cup of black coffee and a ham sandwich. Despite being ten years younger than the captain, she had a crush on him. She knew that he had lost his wife when the Japanese attacked Manila. She knew that he had been wounded and taken prisoner by the Japanese but somehow escaped. The captain was working long hours and she was worried about him. She hoped that he wouldn't crack under the strain of the job and the other stresses she knew he suffered from. At least his two children were all right. They were both attending high school and living with the captain's parents in a small town near Columbus, the capital of Ohio.

Captain Whitely opened the sealed envelope and began reading the rather lengthy message. It was from the Japanese Imperial Army headquarters. It was sent to the Japanese Embassy in New Delhi, instructing them to task someone called Dragon to find and eliminate the team of Allied agents codenamed Cobra. The Cobra team was becoming a thorn in the side of the Japanese army and they wanted the thorn removed, immediately.

Captain Whitely grew alarmed and grabbed a blank message form from the stack on his desk, wrote a lengthy message and addressed it to G-2 at the Pentagon. At the top of the message, he wrote TOP SECRET-LAD, and signed it

CINCPACIN; meaning Commander-in-Chief Pacific Forces, Intelligence Division.

As he slipped the message in a large manila envelope, he called to his civilian secretary.

"Diane, I need you to take this immediately to our communications center," Captain Whitley said.

As Diane entered the captain's office, Captain Whitely handed her the envelope. Before she could take it and leave, the captain said, "Diane, this is extremely important. Make sure they send this as soon as they get it. In fact, don't leave until you have a copy for this office."

"Aye, aye, sir," Diane responded, causing the captain to shake his head.

"You do that just to aggravate me, don't you!" Captain Whitely exclaimed.

"No, sir. I just feel that we need a little more navy decorum in this office," Diane responded smiling.

When Diane returned to the captain's office, Captain Whitely was pacing in front of his window.

"What's wrong, Matt? You look really worried," Diane questioned.

When he finally turned from the window, he told her about the three Allied agents that had rescued him from the POW camp in Thailand. Apparently, the Japanese had found out about the codename that the Kachin tribesmen had given the three agents' team leader and was asking one of their agents in India to find and eliminate them.

"Oh, my God, isn't there anything you can do?" Diane asked.

"Maybe there is something I can do," Captain Whitley said. "Diane, I need you to phone the G-2 at the Pentagon, and ask for Colonel Richard Arvin. I need to speak to him immediately."

Colonel Arvin was one of the people from army intelligence that had debriefed him at the SOE detachment in Alipore. "If anyone can help, I bet he can," Matt said.

Thirty minutes later, Diane entered the captain's office, "Sir, I have Colonel Arvin on the line for you."

The captain picked up the phone. "Buck, this is Matt Whitely, in Honolulu."

"Matt, it's good to hear from you. What's so urgent?"

"I sent you a message about an hour ago concerning a Japanese intercept. I believe it concerns our three friends in Alipore. It's a life and death situation, Buck."

"I'll look into it immediately. By the way Matt, congratulations on the promotion."

"Thanks Buck. Please look after my friends, okay."

"Don't worry, Matt. I'll take care of them."

Matt set the phone into its cradle but still couldn't help but worry. "I hope they get the warning in time," Matt said to himself.

When Colonel Arvin finally got his hands on the message, he was alarmed. The Japanese had probably gotten the name from one of the Kachin natives they had captured and interrogated. He had read the OSS reports that the Japs had rounded up a few Kachin villagers after the Vulcan Halt mission. Most of the villages had been warned, and whole villages of Kachin had disappeared into the jungle or taken their Sampans downriver and disappeared into the delta region.

The entry of a Japanese agent codenamed Dragon, however, was a new addition to the clandestine game. He called to his secretary and asked her to get him on the next flight heading to Algiers with Calcutta as the final destination. He then asked her to schedule an appointment with General Marshall. Thirty minutes later, his secretary called back and told him that General Marshall's 1500-hour-appointment had rescheduled, and the general could see him then.

"Buck, I need you to head to Calcutta, ASAP," General Marshall ordered after reading the Japanese intercept. "These men are too valuable to us. Do we have any other counter-intelligence agents in Calcutta that can find this Dragon character?"

"None as good as Agent Preston, sir," Colonel Arvin responded.

"Do we have anything that will keep them out of Calcutta for a while?"

"Sir, we just sent Colonel Dixon over to put them on the Galahad operation. That should keep them in Burma for at least a month," Colonel Arvin replied.

"That ought to be enough time for the CIC to collect some intelligence on this Dragon character. I want everyone in that Jap Embassy photographed and investigated. It would be my guess that this Jap agent is off the embassy grid. If we don't have this character cornered by the time Agent Preston and his team gets back from the Galahad mission, we can let them run him to ground," General Marshall said.

"I'll put our best CIC agents on the case, General," Colonel Arvin stated.

Before Colonel Arvin left the Pentagon, he had his secretary type up orders for Major Calvin Kurtz. Kurtz was a fictitious army CIC major that Colonel Arvin was going to use to as bait. He would see to it that the fictitious agent's name got used in the restaurants in Calcutta. If Dragon was looking for Cobra, then CIC Special Mission Agent Calvin Kurtz was going to play the part.

Even though Calcutta had over ninety CIC agents, Colonel Arvin believed there was only one group of agents good enough for the job. He would have to pull them into the hunt to get the job done.

CHAPTER 26

CALCUTTA, INDIA

Three weeks after the Great Nicobar Island mission, Agents Preston, Murphy, and Moreau were meeting with Colonel Richard "Rick" Dixon at the SOE Detachment. The colonel had flown in to Calcutta at the request of General Marshall. He needed an assessment of the 5307th Composite Unit, code named Galahad. Galahad was an army long-range penetration special operations infantry unit formed to attack Japanese troops behind their line in northern Burma, and pave the way for the Allies to retake Burma.

"What do you all know about Operation Galahad?" asked Colonel Dixon.

"Isn't that General Merrill's group, the one they call Merrill's Marauders?" Miles asked.

"Yes, it is, Miles."

"I've heard only rumors, sir, but from what I've heard they're giving the Japs a fit in Burma," Miles said.

"Yes, they are," Colonel Dixon stated. "Let me give you all an abbreviated version on Galahad."

The colonel told them about the mission of the Galahad Unit in northern Burma. On February 24th, the unit began an offensive designed to disrupt Japanese offensive operations. Galahad consisted of three battalions totaling 2,750 men. General Stilwell appointed Colonel Frank Merrill to command the unit and promoted him to brigadier general. It was an American war correspondent in General Stillwell's headquarters in Margherita that dubbed the unit Merrill's Marauders.

They began their one-thousand-mile-march from the southern Himalayas in India into the jungles of northern Burma. They maneuvered behind the Japanese lines and engaged the Japanese. They fought three major hit-and-run battles, killing well over a thousand enemy soldiers and disrupting their supply lines.

The Marauders have marched through a thousand miles of Burmese jungle and have trekked over thirty-eight-hundred-foot rainforests where as much as 150 inches of rain falls in three months, Colonel Dixon told them. As much as sixteen inches of rain fell on them in one twenty-four-hour period. The soil in northern Burma was mostly clay covering a weak rock structure that has been cracked and broken by the vast number of earthquakes and tremors in the last one hundred years. When the clay becomes wet, it makes trekking up and down the mountainous terrain extremely hazardous and exhausting.

The Marauder's survived mostly on K-rations, which provided nutrients and calories well below the required daily amount needed for what they are doing. At times, they went as long as three days without food. They were thrown into not only the oppressive heat and humidity of the area, but into a hostile world of leeches and insects that carried a variety of lethal diseases. They had to evacuate their wounded as well as men with dysentery, malaria, and typhus. The unit's doctors were constantly warning General Stillwell's headquarters that the men were both sick and exhausted. Just recently, General Stillwell tasked them to take and hold the airstrip at Myitkyina.

"Despite what he was being told by General Stillwell's staff, General Marshall feels that he is not being told the truth about the Galahad Unit. Because General Stillwell has already tasked them to take and hold the airstrip, the General's afraid that they might not be able to fight another battle, much less hold out for ten days if they do succeed in taking the Myitkyina airstrip," Colonel Dixon stated.

"Where do we fit into this equation?" Jon asked.

"We need you all to meet up with the Marauders before they reach Myitkyina, and document their combat effectiveness. Then we need you all to infiltrate the Japanese positions in and around the village of Myitkyina, and collect as much intelligence as possible. We would like a map showing positions of their infantry and artillery units, and we want you to capture a Japanese officer. When you get back to camp, report to Colonel Chris Spelius; he'll know what to do with the information and the captured officer. He has several Japanese speaking non-commissioned officers who have been trained in interrogation techniques," Colonel Dixon said.

"Where will we be meeting up with him?" Henri asked.

"It looks like you will be jumping from a C-47 over the Marauder's location tomorrow night around 2200 hours. An OSS agent from the Detachment 101 will meet you and take you to the Marauders' camp. He would normally be going along with you all, but the agent and his team of Kachins will be doing reconnaissance elsewhere," Colonel Dixon added.

"What do we do if we determine the unit isn't fit to fight, Colonel?" Jon asked.

"Jon, I'm not sure if anything can be done at this stage of the mission. The Galahad Unit is too close to Myitkyina to be stopped. Keep your finding to yourself, and send them via encrypted message to G-2 after your return to Calcutta," Colonel Dixon remarked.

Jon was about to ask another question but held back. He would talk to Colonel Dixon in private.

"Any other questions?" asked the colonel. "If not, Lieutenant Colonel MacKenzie has your mission parameters. He is setting up everything for tomorrow night," Colonel Dixon concluded.

"Colonel, can I speak to you in private?" Jon asked.

"Certainly, let's step outside and get some fresh air," Colonel Dixon said.

They walked down the corridor of the British-American Club, through the front doors, and into the sunlight.

"What's on your mind, Jon?" Colonel Dixon asked.

"Have you heard anything about a Jap agent in Calcutta named Dragon?"

"No, I haven't. What have you heard?" Colonel Dixon asked.

"The executive officer of our SOE detachment, Lieutenant Tim Holcombe, passed some interesting information to me this morning. He speaks fluent Japanese and overheard two Japanese diplomats talking in a restaurant last night. He heard the name agent Dragon in Calcutta, in their conversation."

"It sounds like they may be creating some disinformation. Their counter-intelligence is very good, Jon." Colonel Dixon said.

"Colonel, this is India, no one here speaks Japanese. Lieutenant Holcombe arrived here two months ago fresh out of officers training. I think he overheard the real thing. Two Japanese diplomats talking; too much sake and two loose tongues."

"It's quite possible, Jon. I'll report this to G-2 and see what they have to say."

The rest of the day and part of the next, the three agents reviewed the latest aerial photos of Myitkyina and studied the layout of the airfield. They would wait to talk to the OSS agent before making any decision on where to infiltrate. Finding the Jap field headquarters would be the toughest job. Jon hoped that the Japanese would be relaxed and over confident and not post guards around their headquarters building. The Japs, like the allies, used safes to keep their maps in at their headquarters. It would be up to Miles to get in, crack the safe, photograph their maps, and leave without a trace. Jon and Henri would have to protect Miles using only their knives and the suppressed pistols. If they were detected, it would turn into a fight, which he didn't think they could win. So stealth and cunning would have to work.

Twelve hours later, Colonel Dixon received a coded message from G-2. It read: "Definite threat Stop Colonel inbound End."

Colonel Dixon showed Jon the message. "Apparently, a G-2 colonel was inbound to task another team. Probably someone in our local CIC group," Jon said.

"That's what I was thinking too, Jon. But if the Japs have had an agent in Calcutta for a while, he must be very good or we would have caught him by now."

"Not necessarily. He could be a special mission type like me. Calcutta is a major Allied logistics port for the CBI. I think we need to hop in my jeep and go check with our CIC group and see if they've had any sabotage activities in town."

Colonel Ronnie Ray greeted Jon and Colonel Dixon and invited them into his office. They accepted coffee and chatted for ten minutes.

"What can I do for you, Colonel?" Colonel Ray asked.

"Ronnie, Jon recently received information about a Japanese agent in Calcutta, code named Dragon. We were wondering if you have any information on him," Colonel Dixon asked.

"That's new to us, Rick. Jon, how did you come by this information?" Colonel Ray asked.

"A Japanese speaking SOE lieutenant overheard two Japanese diplomats last night in a restaurant," Jon remarked.

"What else do you know?" Colonel Ray asked.

Colonel Dixon handed the colonel the message he had received from G-2.

"Well, we have had quite a few sabotage events on the Allied wharves in the last few months. Two explosions killed six American servicemen. Right now, this is the only possible lead we've gotten. It could explain the sabotage and why we haven't solved this case," Colonel Ray said.

"Colonel," Jon said, "if this guy is a special missions type, you probably won't catch him using conventional methods. You'll need to leak disinformation on, let's say, a large ammunition shipment being stored in one of the warehouses. Set a trap and catch him in the act," Jon explained.

"Jon, that's an excellent suggestion. Could we get you to head this up?" Colonel Ray asked.

"Unfortunately, Jon is leaving on a mission, Ronnie. But if there is anything G-2 can do to help, let me know. I'll be here for eight more days," Colonel Dixon stated.

CHAPTER 27

MYITKYINA, BURMA

Colonel Hiro Kobayashi met with his battle staff next to the eight-foot embankment his engineers has created six months ago. Colonel Kobayashi was aware of the Allied army moving his way. The last report placed them one hundred miles to the north, and that had only been a spotter's report of American transports dropping supplies.

"Major Tsukuda, please report our combat status." Colonel Kobayashi asked.

"Colonel, we have 2,380 men that are combat ready, 650 men are in the hospital with dysentery, malaria or dung fever, and 140 are still recovering from combat wounds," Major Tsukuda answered.

"How many do we have covering the airfield?" Colonel Kobayashi asked.

"Sir, there are four companies totaling seven hundred men, which include five machine gun teams, and four mortar teams," Major Tsukuda stated.

"If we are attacked, Major, we will need the men in the hospital put on the line," Colonel Kobayashi stated.

"Colonel, I will make sure that the men are in uniform and have their rifles available," Major Tsukuda said.

"Since our scouts still place the Americans one hundred miles to our north, I will be sleeping at my headquarters on the island tonight. If you hear anything from our scouts that is different, notify me immediately," Colonel Kobayashi ordered.

"Yes, Colonel," Major Tsukuda answered.

"I will tour our fortification before heading to the island," Colonel Kobayashi said.

"Your driver is waiting for you, Colonel," Major Tsukuda said.

It took two hours for the colonel to make the rounds. Occasionally, he would stop and talk with one of his officers. When he reached the island, he went directly to his communications center and read the latest dispatches and scout reports. By the time he reached the large *basha*, where he quarted, his orderlies had his dinner of fresh perch, rice, and sake prepared. After he finished eating, he dismissed the orderlies and went right to bed.

That night a C-47 flew to a homing beacon ten miles northeast of Myitkyina. When the pilot located the flashing white lights of the drop area, he flew directly to them. At the jumpmaster's direction, the three agents, attired in camouflaged khakis, shirts, pants, and skull caps, jumped from the aircraft. The static lines opened their parachutes, and they floated for no more than sixteen seconds before being caught in mid-air by several Kachin natives that were part of OSS detail tasked to meet them.

"Welcome to Burma," said an American in a low voice as he helped Jon out of his parachute harness. "I'm Major Steve Schaefer, OSS."

"Damn it, Major, you nearly scared the crap out of me," Jon stated. "I thought you were a Jap and I was a goner." Jon bent over, put his hands on his knees, and took multiple deep breaths trying to calm his racing heartbeat.

"If these Kachin wanted you dead, your head would have been loped off right before you hit the ground. You wouldn't even have known it. You must be Preston, the American agent," Major Schaefer remarked.

"Yep, but call me Jon," Jon said.

"Okay, Jon. You all fall in behind me. Our Kachin headman will lead us to where the Marauders are camping," Major Schaefer stated.

Twenty minutes later, they entered the Marauders' dark camp with no fire, no lights, and no talk. They made their way to where the commanding officer, Colonel Chris Spelius, was sitting in a small tent with a red filtered flashlight glowing next to the field radio. He was finishing his last C-ration meal and waiting for a radio transmission from General Stillwell's headquarters.

Major Schaefer, still using a low voice, introduced the three special agents. After the initial pleasantries, Jon asked the colonel about the condition of his men. The colonel, although suspicious, answered truthfully.

"Agent Preston, we've just crossed a six thousand-foot mountain range. My men are tired as hell, hungry, thirsty, and half are sick with dysentery, malaria, or both; but they'll damn sure get the job done in Myitkyina. We should arrive at the airstrip tomorrow afternoon. We're sending out two recon units tonight to gather intelligence. We've been told to expect close to six thousand Jap troops. I assume that you all will be going behind the Jap lines also. I sure hope you find a lot less Japs for us," Colonel Spelius stated.

"We'll do our best, Colonel. We've been told to bring back a Japanese officer for you all to interrogate," Jon said.

"That would be great, Agent Preston, but make it quick. We are scheduled to begin our assault tomorrow night," Colonel Spelius said.

The colonel turned back to the radio where his radio operator was decoding a message. Major Schaefer whispered to the three agents, "We need to get moving guys." As they followed the major out of the Marauders' camp, Jon noticed at least twenty Kachin tribesmen had joined them.

After walking for fifteen minutes, the major stopped. He knelt down and turned on a red filtered flashlight. He motioned for the three agents to move closer and shone his light on a map of Myitkyina he had opened up. He pointed out the airstrip, which was two miles west of Myitkyina. The airstrip lay between the village of Singapur, one half mile to the northeast, and Pamati, one mile to the southwest. After discussing probable locations of the Japanese headquarters, Major Schaefer told them that it was probably located in the abandoned village of Zigyun, which was located on a large jungle island in the middle of the Irrawaddy River, one mile south of Myitkyina.

"My groups of Kachins have scouted all over this area, and we have yet to find it. The only place we haven't looked is Zigyun," Major Schaefer said.

The Kachin headman would be their guide to the island. He was the headman of the abandoned Zigyun Village and knew it intimately. The best approach, he told them, would be to travel by canoe on the Irrawaddy to the southern tip of the island. The southern tip was a dense jungle and it would not be guarded. The Kachin headman told the agents to call him Oscar. Oscar told them he had made this trip many times to gather intelligence further up the river.

By 0100 hours, they arrived at a point on the Irrawaddy River one mile west of Pamati. Waiting for them was a fifteen-foot dugout canoe. Before they got in the boat, Oscar instructed the agents on the signaling technique he would use in the village. He told them he would use the croaking sound of a northern Burmese tree frog, which he demonstrated. One croak meant all was okay, two croaks in rapid succession meant trouble, and three croaks in rapid succession meant get out. Jon had to chuckle at the simplicity. He guessed that it probably wasn't much different from what the American Indians must have done in the days of the old west. He just had a hard time bringing himself to believe that he was living it until he reminded himself that this was war, and it was real.

Jon was a little apprehensive about taking the canoe to the island until he stepped inside it. It must have been twenty-five inches in depth and appeared to be very lightweight for a tree that had once been a seventy-inch-diameter log. Oscar had the three agents lay prone while he paddled and steered. Under a partially clouded sky and a half moon, it took only fifty minutes to reach a thick, tight group of brushy trees on the southern tip of the island.

Oscar got into the water and pulled the boat deep into the brush and tied the canoe to a thick branch. He whispered to the agents to exit the boat as silently as possible. He then led them to a small trail that led to the village. It was hidden to all but the people from his village. Since the Japs weren't fond of wandering off into the thick jungle, it would probably remain hidden. The trail ended at a large copse of six-foot-high elephant grass.

Oscar moved aside some of the grass and motioned for Jon to take a look. He pointed to a bamboo and grass hut on stilts. Oscar told the agents that he would cross over to the large clump of elephant grass five yards from the large basha. After he signals them with a frog croak they could cross one at a time, each one waiting for the signal. Jon just hoped that he could tell Oscar's croak from the thousand others he was hearing.

When Oscar gave his soft, deep croak, it was quite distinguishable from the other frogs; Jon crossed first. On the second and third croaks, at least a minute apart, Miles and Henri crossed to the cover of several large clumps of elephant grass. The largest structure, which was their destination, was on the west side of the village along with Oscar's personal basha. The remainder of the villagers' huts were scattered across the three-hundred-yard length of the island. Most Japanese officers and enlisted men, that were on the commander's staff, were staying on the eastern side of the village.

The agents waited while Oscar checked the village. After twenty minutes, he returned and whispered that there were only two guards, and they were having tea in the radio shack over three hundred feet away. They would have to work quickly before the guards resumed their rounds. Oscar led Jon to a position, where he could observe the approach to the large village basha from the northeast. He came back and took Henri to a position so he could observe the approach from the southeast. With Jon and Henri posted as perimeter guards, Oscar returned and took Miles up the steps and into the large village basha. While Miles did his work, Oscar would guard the south and west sides of the building.

Once inside, Miles pulled out a small flashlight with a red filter over the lens. The safe was ancient and small. It measured thirty inches high, twenty-seven inches wide, and eighteen inches deep. It had an unsophisticated, mechanical tumbler mechanism, which Miles opened within three minutes. It took him five minutes to sort through the contents and find a map with the placement of the Japanese machine guns, rifle companies, and 75-millimeter field guns. It helped that the Japanese used pictorial symbols to identify the types of weapons.

The next part would be the most hazardous. Miles had to take the red filter off his flashlight and shine it on the map in order to photograph it. He accomplished this under a desk in the northeast corner and used his body to shield most of the glare from the flashlight. In two minutes he had taken five photographs, returned the map to the safe, and locked it. A minute later, he was safely out the door and crouching in the elephant grass next to Oscar.

Oscar guided Miles back to the trail behind the dense elephant grass, where they started their ingress. Within ten minutes he had retrieved Jon and Henri. Oscar wanted to head to the dugout, but Jon reminded him that they needed to capture a Japanese officer.

Oscar nodded. He knew that a high ranking officer would probably be staying in his personal basha because it was the largest in the village. It was located thirty yards from the village basha but well away from the rest of the village. As headman of his village, he had certain privileges, and one of them was living slightly apart from the other villagers. He needed to be close to the village basha in case he needed to hold a meeting of the village elders and entertain visitors or resolve a dispute. Oscar guided them through the tall grass around the south side of his home until they came to a small dock at the edge of the river. Oscar placed Miles and Henri in strategic positions among the grass and led Jon to his basha. Oscar and his entire village had to desert the island when the Japanese invaded Myitkyina two years ago. Jon hoped that only one officer was living in Oscar's basha, he didn't want to have to take a second officer prisoner.

Jon waited in the shadows, while Oscar slowly crept up the steps and peered into his former home. A single Japanese officer was sleeping soundly with his head turned away from the door. Oscar motioned for Jon to come. When Jon entered the basha, he saw the Jap officer sleeping on a floor mat. Jon silently withdrew his pistol, held the barrel in his hand and clubbed the Japanese officer over the head. He immediately turned the Jap over on his belly, tied his hands behind his back, and bound his feet with the cut pieces of rope he had pulled out of his pants' pockets. He then stuffed a small ball of cloth into the Japs mouth, secured it with a twisted black bandana through the officer's mouth, and tied it securely behind his head. Jon then shouldered the officer and followed Oscar out of the basha into the elephant grass next to the dock.

It took them thirty minutes to reach the dugout. Once everyone was in the boat, Oscar reversed the route they had come by and floated with the current back to their original departure location one mile west of Pamati.

At 0700 hours, they reached the Allied camp and turned their captive over to the Marauders' Japanese speaking interrogators. Minutes later they were standing in front of Colonel Spelius. Miles handed him the camera film, which he immediately transferred to his photo lab technician. Sergeant Dean Valentine was in charge of their new portable photo lab. Both the sergeant and the lab had been flown in on an L-5 the previous day. The SOE planners had thought of everything.

At around 0800 hours, the Marauders began their final stage of deployment to the airstrip. While marching alongside of the troops, Jon had become acutely aware of their physical appearance. They were emaciated, thin, and appeared to be on the brink of physical exhaustion. The fourteen weeks of marching through the Burmese mountains, across hundreds of rivers and streams, and through muddied trails created by torrential rains had taken its toll. Many of the men, who suffered from dysentery, had cut the seats out of their trousers so they could take care of their unannounced body urges without removing their trousers. Others were jaundiced from the effects of malaria. There was no fear at all on the faces of the men. But they all had a distant stare, as if they were animals being led to slaughter. Many of the Marauders were shaking uncontrollably from the effects of the malaria they had contracted. Jon swore that they were moving on will alone.

Jon also noticed that every Marauder's uniform was dotted with dark, stiff patches of dried blood caused by leech bites. Burma was infested with every conceivable size and color leech; black and brown leeches, red leeches, and green leeches were found on the ground, the elephant grass, and on trees and shrubs. They were the most hated insect on the trail. They would attach themselves to your skin and create a lesion without you noticing them. After you removed them with the heat of a lit cigarette, stopping the flow of blood was near impossible because their saliva contained an anticoagulant. The open lesions from the leech bite created another problem, screwworms. Flies would lay eggs in the wounds, which would eventually hatch into screwworms.

Despite the leeches, flies, screwworms, mosquitoes, snakes, the constant downpour of rain, and the struggling on mud trails the Marauders kept moving towards Myitkyina. Jon wondered how an army could possibly fight under these conditions. He didn't have very long to wonder; by sunset they had reached the outskirts of the Myitkyina airstrip.

CHAPTER 28
MYITKYINA, BURMA

Jon was sitting in his tent reading a letter from one of his girlfriends when Colonel Lew Miller walked in and said, "Hey, Jon."

Surprised to see the G-2 colonel, Jon stood up, shook the colonel's hand, and said, "Lew, I didn't expect to see you till sometime in late September. Is something special going on?"

"I heard that you were kicking some Japanese ass in Myitkyina, so I caught a flight over to see if you needed any help," Colonel Miller said.

"Why don't we go have breakfast and catch up on the gossip? Then we can come back here and talk some shop," Jon said.

"That sounds great," Colonel Miller replied.

During breakfast, Jon took Colonel Miller through the Marauders' assault on the airstrip and the Chinese 150th Division's assault on the village.

"It was another command level screw up, Lew. The Marauders took the airfield and the Chinese did a good job assaulting the village, despite meeting heavy resistance. The first twenty C-47s that landed at the airstrip should have carried the remainder of the Chinese 150th Division. They were needed to reinforce the assault on Myitkyina and relieve the Marauders. Instead, some knucklehead at General Stillwell's headquarters decided to send in logistics support troops and aircraft parts. That mistake cost us. With the extra Chinese troops, the 150th could have easily overwhelmed the Japanese garrison," Jon said.

"How much of Myitkyina did the Chinese capture?" Colonel Miller asked.

"They penetrated the western portion of the village but were beat back by Japanese artillery and machine gun fire," Jon stated.

"They must have been pretty well entrenched then," Colonel Miller said.

"The Japs had build an eight-foot-high earthen wall around most of the north and west sides. Their heavy machine guns were deadly," Jon said.

"I take it we didn't have any artillery yet," Colonel Miller said.

"No, that didn't come in for another five days. General Stillwell apparently wanted a fighter unit in here first," Jon said.

He went on to tell Colonel Miller that from the maps that Miles had photographed, they estimated that the Japs had only three thousand troops. The night after the Marauders secured the airfield and the Chinese were beat back, he, Miles, and Henri went behind Jap lines and scouted Jap positions. The only change to the map was the locations of the Jap artillery pieces. The headquarters' screw up had allowed the Japanese to bring in four thousand reinforcements.

"God only knows how long the Japs can hold out now," Jon remarked.

As Lew was about to take a sip of his coffee, a loud *kaboom* thundered outside the mess tent and shook the table. Lew flew out of his chair and onto the earthen tent floor.

The people at the other table chuckled loudly, and Jon heard several mention new-be in their laughter.

"Crap, Jon. Are they still shelling us?" Colonel Miller asked.

"Sorry, sir. I forgot to warn you about that. One of our aircraft must have dropped a bomb on Myitkyina and hit an ammo dump. Our flyers are taking off from the airstrip and within minutes are dropping their bombs on the village two miles away. Their sorties are only lasting about fifteen minutes. Then the munitions troops load them up again and an hour later they do it again. At least the Japs have quit shelling us," Jon stated.

"Did our artillery take theirs out or the flyboys?" Colonel Miller asked.

"When the first fighter aircraft came, they were loaded with five hundred-pound bombs. They had the new intelligence we provided and took out half of the seventy-five's the first day they arrived. The rest have gone silent. We suspect they ran out of shells or are saving them," Jon said.

"Well, someone brought in fresh food for the troops. Where do they get their eggs from?" Colonel Miller asked.

"That will be my doing. During a major enemy engagement, the headquarters doesn't think about sending in fresh food," Jon said.

Jon told Lew his story about how he had been supplying the airstrip with fresh eggs, pork, and alcohol. Fresh eggs were always in short supply, but Jon had a friend at the SOE detachment in Calcutta, who was sending him fifty-four dozens every other day. In turn, Jon provided his friend with ten cases of American beer, which was treated like gold by the British.

Jon told the colonel how he got beer from his friend, Marty Schottenstein. Marty was in charge of one of the Allied depots on the wharves of Calcutta. Jon had met Marty on his first visit to the wharf. When Marty found out that Jon was from his hometown, Columbus, Ohio, they became instant friends. From then on, they exchanged any news from home that was of interest. After that, whatever Jon needed, Jon got. If Marty couldn't get something, Jon got it for him.

Marty liked scotch whisky, and Jon knew that the British had loads of it and gin. In fact, the Brits had barge loads of it. Before the Japanese invasion of Singapore, the British had sent thirty-four barges loaded with the spirits to Rangoon, Akyab, Ceylon, and Calcutta. They couldn't stand the thought of leaving it for the Japanese.

Although it was a closely guarded British secret, one of his SOE friends had told him about the barges. Jon would exchange beer with the Brits for Scotch and gin. Jon exchanged scotch and gin for beer with Marty. The British were happy because they craved beer and couldn't get any from England. Marty and Jon were happy because they had something beside cheap American bourbon. The enlisted men that Jon made friends with were happy because he would exchange whiskey, scotch, and gin for favors when he needed them. And the men of the Twentieth Flying Squadron, SOE, OSS, and CIC were even happier because Jon threw some hellacious parties with lots of free booze. Plus, Jon managed to get most of the nurses, from both the British and American hospitals, to attend. And although Jon hadn't intended on being a matchmaker, he became the best man at six weddings before he left Calcutta for Myitkyina.

Colonel Miller couldn't help but laugh. "Jon," he said, "I think you've found your true calling."

Jon nodded in agreement, "Yeah and it would be a lot more fun if I didn't have to jump out of a perfectly good aircraft and then get shot at."

After another cup of coffee and some more small talk, they made their way back to Jon's tent, where they could have a more private conversation.

"Jon, G-2 was really impressed with your performance. The Hintok Bridge and Chittagong missions were phenomenal. General Marshall wanted me to personally deliver that message to you. In addition to the Purple Heart, he's awarding you the Bronze Star for the Anzio Mission; the Silver Star to you and your team for the Hintok mission, and the Distinguished Service medal to you and your team for the Chittagong mission," Colonel Miller said.

"Hell, Lew, I was just doing what I was taught to do," Jon stated.

"Yes, but you saved O'Brien's life, blew up a critical bridge, rescued thirty-eight American POWs, and captured a significant

Japanese agent and took out his network. And what the general wants he gets," Colonel Miller said.

"If he does that and I have to put on my uniform and be awarded those medals, it could mess up my cover, Lew. Everyone over here thinks I'm some kind of special civilian. I don't want them to know that I'm just a lowly captain. If they find out that I am a junior officer, I couldn't get done what I'm getting done. It would ruin my credibility with the SOE, CIC, and the OSS. I can't accept the awards," Jon said.

"General Marshall said you would probably say something like that. So, they will go into your classified record instead. Plus, you've been promoted to major, so congratulations. And as a thank you, he sent along an extra $100,000 for your discretionary expense account. You'll need it for the next several missions we have planned for you. Do you have a safe place to keep it," Colonel Miller questioned.

"Yes, sir. Lieutenant Colonel MacKenzie gave me a rather large safe at the SOE detachment office. But hell, I've only spent half of the $110,000 you all gave me when I arrived in Calcutta in February," Jon said.

"Well, Jon, you'll just have to use some more of it for boosting the morale of the troops. I assume you are holding parties for them as ordered by General Marshal. Am I right?" Colonel Miller asked.

"Yes, sir, in fact we are having one tonight. Will you care to join us?" Jon asked.

"Damn straight. And I want a bottle of that twenty-five-year-old scotch that I hear you have access to," Colonel Miller stated.

"Great. I was hoping you wouldn't have to leave right away. In fact, Pat O'Brien and Jinx Falkenburg are coming to the party after their USO show. It should be relatively safe since the Japs haven't shelled us in over a week and Colonel Merrill's troops have pretty well cleaned the jungle around us of snipers. Although I've heard rumors that the Japs are short on sake and might try to crash the party," Jon said grinning.

Colonel Miller just shook his head and laughed. "Say, how did you get recruited into the CIC? Can you talk about it?"

Jon eased back onto the military cot he was sitting on and wondered where to begin.

CHAPTER 29

MYITKYINA, BURMA

"Well, it started in 1939, after I hurt my shoulder playing baseball. I left the Boston Rex Sox organization and went to work at the Campus Inn Restaurant on High Street; close to the Ohio State University campus. The owner didn't know anything about business and six months after I started working for him he went bankrupt. I had saved my four hundred dollars signing bonus with the Red Sox, so I went to the bank and offered to buy the business. When they agreed, I borrowed $2,000 from the bank. Of course, my dad had to co-sign with me, but I got the place back on its feet. I added a jukebox and some pinball machines, and hired a couple of gorgeous busty coeds to work the counters. I asked several of my friends on the football team to hang out for free sodas and ice cream and got more and more college kids to come in. Six months after I bought the place, I paid off the bank loan," Jon said.

Jon paused and got a couple bottles of Coca Cola out of his refrigerator, offered one to the colonel, and continued his story.

"In early December, a couple of college professors booked the party room in the back of the restaurant. I thought it was going to be for a Christmas party. Instead, it was a Marxist party meeting. Hell, they had two meetings there in one week. Well, I didn't like what they were discussing one bit. I thought they were being disloyal to the United States. Lew, the bastards were preaching anarchy!"

"After the second meeting, I called the Secret Service and told them everything I knew. Two weeks later, two agents came to the restaurant; one from the FBI, and one from the US Army's criminal investigation division (CID). They asked me to repeat the story I had told the Secret Service. Then they asked if they could set up some recording equipment in the restaurant. Next, he asked me to record what was being said at the next meeting. Before you know it, they were setting up hidden microphones and training me how to work the equipment and change out the tapes. I was told that they would be back in a week to get the tapes. Two weeks later, the CID agent showed up, got the recorded tapes, gave me new ones, and asked me to continue the recordings," Jon stated.

"Did they offer to pay you anything?" Colonel Miller asked.

"No, but I decided to do it for free because I was really against what these Marxists bastards were teaching," Jon said.

"What happened next?" Colonel Miller asked.

"The CID guy came back the following week and switched out the tapes again. He asked me if I had read any of the literature or listened to any of the lectures. I told him I'd only overheard some of what they were saying. Then he asked me to read their literature, act interested in what they were saying, and join the meetings. He wanted me to start writing down names of the professors, students, and any other people attending the meetings. Well, this went on for two more months. Then one afternoon, the CID agent came in, thanked me for my patriotism, picked up all of the equipment, and left," Jon said.

"What happened next?" Colonel Miller asked.

"Towards the end of July 1940, the same CID agent came back and asked if I could meet him the next day over at Fort Hayes, an army facility close to downtown. So I went to Fort Hayes," Jon said.

"What did he talk to you about?" Colonel Miller asked.

"He told me that Washington was preparing for an inevitable war with Germany and asked if I would like to help in the pre-war effort. I said sure. He told me to come to Fort Hayes a week later, and they would start my training," Jon stated.

"So, did he enlist you in the army?" Colonel Miller asked.

"No. He said that they wanted to train me first and that I would be drafted and made an officer when they needed me. He told me not to tell anyone what I was doing because it was all classified. I realize now that they wanted me to be drafted instead of becoming a volunteer. That way I would look like any other American being drafted by the army and not someone special," Jon said.

"So, what kind of training did you go through?" Colonel Miller asked.

"Over the next two years, I was trained in hand-to-hand combat, weapons, military marching drills, and military history stuff. Much of it was the equivalent to US Army officer's training. After the first year, the hand-to-hand combat and weapons training became more specialized. They brought some British colonel in from Washington to train me in a special type of hand-to-hand combat. Apparently, he had developed a specific type of combat technique, which the Brits used to train all their commandos. Lew, I was trained to kill twenty-nine ways with just my bare hands," Jon said.

"Well, I imagine that comes in handy with what you're doing in the field. What kind of weapons?" Colonel Miller said.

"Everything, revolvers, automatic pistols, M1 carbine, and even the Thompson machine gun. They trained me how to shoot accurately from the hip with pistols and rifles. They even trained me on motorcycles," Jon said.

"I hear you're an excellent shot," Colonel Miller remarked.

"Lew, they taught me how to draw my pistol and shoot out the flame of a candle from ten paces shooting from the hip. They told me I was a natural. After that, they taught me how to parachute from a plane. Hell, I was so scared on my first jump that I crapped in my pants," Jon said.

Colonel Miller nearly fell out of his chair laughing. "Sorry, Jon, that was funny. But it had to be embarrassing," Colonel Miller stated.

"God was it, ever. Those instructors never let me live that down. Same thing happened on my first night jump. I really was literally scared shitless," Jon said.

"How was it when you jumped at Anzio?" Colonel Miller asked.

"No problems. But there wasn't much time to think jumping from five hundred feet. Hell, I was on the ground in less than twenty seconds," Jon said.

"What happened after the training at Fort Hayes?" Colonel Miller asked.

"They sent me to Oklahoma to train as a waist gunner on a new bomber that they were testing, the B-24 Liberator. Hell, I thought they were going to put me in the Army Air Corps. After I finished my training and got back to Columbus, I met with the CID agent at Fort Hayes. He told me that being a Liberator waist gunner would be my cover story if I was ever captured by the enemy," Jon said.

"That was still in 1940, Jon. What did you do until 1943?" Colonel Miller asked.

"The army sent me to college at OSU. They paid my tuition and even got me a part-time job with Columbus Coated Fabrics. And it paid great. I sewed cloth for balloons my first year. Then, despite working part-time, I was promoted to a supervisory position. After my second year, they promoted me to the personnel department. Twice a week the CID agent came to the office, took me out of work, and took me to Fort Hayes, where I trained on weapons or hand-to-hand combat. The next year, they made me an instructor at Fort Hayes, training a bunch of new guys they were bringing in from around central Ohio. In the summer of

1943, the CID agent told me that I would be drafted soon. Six weeks later, I was drafted, and they sent me out to Fort Benjamin Harrison, Indiana. The CID agent told me that there would be orders there to send me to some more specialty training. He said that it had to look like I was drafted and went through training just like all the other GIs," Jon stated.

"What about college?" Colonel Miller asked.

"I went to OSU year round and finished in the spring of '43," Jon said.

"Impressive. What happened when you got to Fort Benjamin Harrison?" Colonel Miller asked.

"I did the basic training stuff for a week. One day they had me cleaning the latrines. I was sitting around with a couple other guys after I finished, when the corporal in charge of our barracks walked in and started chewing us out for sitting around. Then, for some reason, he got in my face and started calling me every swear word in the book," Jon exclaimed

"That must have been exciting," Colonel Miller stated.

"Lew, it was humiliating. I had never been called names like that in my entire life. I got so angry that I yelled back at him to apologize to me. This guy must have been 6'4" and 240 pounds. Before I could say anything else, he swore again and took a swing at me," Jon said.

"Geez, Jon, what did you do?" Colonel Miller questioned.

"I side-stepped his punch and hit him in the kidneys several times. When he tried to swing at me again, I hit him in the face and broke his nose and cheekbone. Then I kicked him in the groin and ruptured his balls. The last I saw of him he was crawling out of the barracks on his hands and knees swearing that I would be in Fort Leavenworth before the week was out," Jon exclaimed.

"Damn, Jon, what did they do, throw you in the stockade?" Colonel Miller asked.

"God, Lew, I knew I was going to be in so much trouble. I just sat there on my bunk shaking. Thirty minutes later, two MPs came into the barracks and asked me to come with them to the camp commander's office. I just knew they were going to throw me in prison," Jon said.

"What happened then?" Colonel Miller asked.

"When we got to the commander's building, the MPs had me sit in a chair outside of the commander's office. Both MPs guarded me until the commander yelled out of his office for someone called Peyton. One of the MPs nudged me and told me to get into the office. When I entered the room, one of the MPs stayed and shut the door. The commander kept calling me 'Peyton' and chewing my ass out for hitting a superior. He told me that I'd be lucky to get an assignment cleaning urinals for the remainder of the war after I got out of prison. When I told him that I already knew what my assignment was, he really blew his stack. I tried telling him my name was Preston, but he wouldn't listen. So I yelled, 'My name is Preston; not Peyton.' After that he stopped cold," Jon said.

"Why? What happened?" Colonel Miller asked.

"Apparently, he had a folder on his desk, stamped Top Secret, with my name on it. After he opened the folder and read for a while, his face turned pale. Then he told me that there must have been some kind of mix up and apologized for any inconvenience. He had the MPs take me to the officers quarters where they put me up in a room and told me that dinner was on the colonel at the Officer's Club. The next day, a staff car picked me up and drove me to Fort Thomas, Kentucky, for Cipher School," Jon said.

"Jon, that's the most incredible story I've ever heard. Where did you go after Fort Thomas?" Colonel Miller asked.

"I was sent to Fort Ritchie, where I formed up with fifty-three other guys in what they called a Special Missions Group. It was then that we were told that we were to be part of both CIC and OSS Special Operations. We went through another fourteen weeks of training, including explosives, sabotage and espionage, counter-espionage, and guerilla warfare. After we finished school, we met with General Marshall at the White House. That's where I met you," Jon said.

"Jon, do you think you and your team are ready for another mission?" Colonel Miller asked.

"Lew, that's what we get paid the big bucks to do. What have you got for us?" Jon asked.

"I need you all back in Calcutta before I can get into the mission detail Jon. I need to talk to all three of you in a secure location. G-2 has uncovered some very disturbing information that concerns the welfare of you and your team."

CHAPTER 30

CALCUTTA, INDIA

Colonel Miller stood and pointed at a map on the pedestal next to the desk he was standing behind.

"This is Afghanistan. Officially, it's been neutral in this war, but it's been a hotbed of Soviet and German activities since 1939. A few weeks ago, one of our OSS operatives was found dead in Kabul. He was a captain assigned as a US Army Liaison to the American Embassy. He was suspicious of one of his Afghan OSS agents, Ahmad Khan. He believed that Khan was passing sensitive information to the Germans and Soviets," Colonel Miller said.

"How did he uncover the Afghan?" Jon asked.

"The captain gave him information on a shipment of arms we were sending to an Afghan chieftain that we were working with west of Kabul. He wanted Khan to ride in one of the trucks. During the mission, our trucks were ambushed by Afghan rebels friendly to the Germans. Khan was the only person to escape. When he returned to Kabul he had a flesh wound on his arm. Our embassy physician told us that the wound was either self-inflicted or someone shot him from three inches away. Khan was the only other person in the embassy who knew the date and time of that shipment. Three days after Khan returned our captain was dead. We suspect that he confronted Khan with the results of the physician's examination. His body was found in an alley three miles from the embassy," Colonel Miller replied.

"So, you want us to go in to Kabul and eliminate this double agent?" Jon asked.

"Actually, we have a plan that will keep the US off the hook. It's called family revenge. It's a very real thing in Afghanistan. One of our other local agents has a brother whose son was driving the second vehicle in the convoy. The son was killed in the ambush. If we pass this information to him, his family will want to avenge his death. We want you all to facilitate this. Make it look like a tribal revenge killing, rather than an intelligence community reprisal," Colonel Miller said.

"And if this backfires?" Jon asked.

"Then you can eliminate him, but quietly," Colonel Miller stated.

"Is this sanctioned by the president?" Jon asked.

"Yes, under Executive Order 44-559," Colonel Miller said as he passed the executive order to Jon.

"Do you have any more information on Khan?" Miles asked.

"Khan was recruited by the OSS in 1942. He's the eldest son of an Afghan diplomat serving as an adjunct to the German Embassy for the Afghan government. Khan was recruited after our agents learned that he hated the Germans. We thought we could pick up better intelligence through a family connection. We now believe that his hatred for the Germans was a ruse to get him recruited by the Allies. Apparently, it worked," Colonel Miller stated.

"What kind of local support will we have, Colonel?" Jon questioned.

"We have a very reliable Afghan agent that is the nephew of a tribal chieftain we are working with. He is unknown to the double agent. He will be your guide and bodyguard while you are in Kabul. You will leave as soon as there is a break in this rain. In the meantime, you can study up on the information compiled by our late agent. Also, one of the SOE personnel here, Sergeant Major James O'Dell, was stationed at the British Embassy in Kabul for nine years. He will be your Pashtu language tutor until we leave. As an added security measure, he will accompany you to Kabul. So, in effect, you'll have two bodyguards," Colonel Miller concluded.

The monsoon weather didn't break for six days. This gave the trio extra time to delve deeper into conversational Pashtu. And since all the three agents had one hundred percent recall, they absorbed a lot of Afghan in six days and could understand a great deal of Afghan conversation. Jon decided that he would use this to his advantage and informed Sergeant O'Dell that they would play dumb in Kabul and use only the rudiments of greetings and salutations. It would serve as another security measure.

At their next meeting with Colonel Miller, Henri asked, "Is Khan still working for the OSS or has he gone into hiding?"

"Khan is still providing intelligence reports every two weeks, but some of the information is bogus. The information he's provided on the Soviets air dropping guns to Afghan chieftains is incorrect; he lied. It was actually the Germans. Our counter-intelligence team has been giving the OSS commander at the embassy information to divulge to Khan in their one-on-one meetings. The same information has been leaked in the United Kingdom to make it more convincing. General Marshall wants to send additional OSS agents into Kabul, but not before we do something about Khan."

"What about the *Abwehr* operative running Khan. Do we know who he is?"

"Yes, he's a German army major at the German Embassy."

"Do we take him out, too?" Jon asked.

"That was discussed, but we are not quite sure how to accomplish it without reprisals from the Afghan government," Colonel Miller said.

"Let us give it a shot, Colonel? We'll come up with something, but we'll have to plan it after we get to Kabul," Jon stated.

"Alright, you can plan it there, and send me the details in a diplomatic pouch. I'll be in Calcutta until your mission is completed," Colonel Miller said.

"When do we leave for Kabul?" Miles asked.

"You'll leave Saturday. That will give you four days to study up on both Afghanistan and Kabul and read the intelligence report that I brought. There is also a European working with the Soviets. His name is Lawrence Dugan. He's a British colonial from New Delhi that was accused of murder. He fled to Afghanistan, prior to the war. We believe that he may have helped the Afghan's rebels attack the arms convoy. Since Dugan's a hired thug, we don't anticipate any government reprisal if he is eliminated. He will be your team's primary tasking," Colonel Miller stated.

"Why not let the OSS do the job?" Miles asked.

"We don't' want any OSS involvement in either of these guy's deaths. We can't afford having the Afghan government demanding their removal from our embassy. The OSS mission in Afghanistan is too important. They are trying to undermine Soviets' involvement here as well as the Germans," Colonel Miller said.

"Has Dugan been trained as an agent by the Soviets?" Henri asked.

"His habits and behavior lead us to believe that he's not trained. He constantly hangs out at the same two restaurants and has been seen falling down drunk on more than one occasion. There are a dossier and a photo of him in one of the folders," Colonel Miller replied.

"What kind of weapons do you want us to carry?" Jon asked.

"On this trip, you'll carry your stiletto, a double shoulder holster and two .32-caliber automatic pistols, and your silenced pistol. Plus, we have some special equipment that might come in handy. You will need to practice with it at the armory," Colonel Miller said.

After lunch and four hours of reading the intelligence on Afghanistan, the trio went to the armory to take a look at the special equipment that the colonel had told them about. It was a highly specialized spring-loaded retractable spike, which was mounted on a forearm scabbard. It was triggered by wrist action. Jon was ready to discount the whole idea until he saw it demonstrated on a goat that the SOE detachment was going to roast at a picnic the following day.

The SOE weapons expert demonstrated how to walk up behind someone, either standing or sitting, place your hand innocently on their upper back, flip your wrist upward, and release the seven-inch spike into the back of their brain. The spike was released and automatically retracted in a fraction of a second. It was so fast that the eyes could not detect it and there was only a small speck of blood on the back of the head of the goat. Each agent was allowed to practice enough to become proficient with the weapon.

Jon was impressed. He could visualize entering a café in Kabul, acting like a friend and placing his hand on the back of the double agent, flicking his wrist to release the thin spike, steadying the dead man on his seat, and then walking out of the café. He wanted one.

For three days, Jon and his team studied the information on Kabul and memorized the military map of the city. Each agent knew that it was only partially accurate. They would have to walk the streets in order to get the actual layout and distances to do their mission planning. They would have to be doubly careful while tracking the Abwehr agent. The team would be in greater danger because they didn't know the other Afghan languages, and they would have to rely on a local Afghan OSS agent for help. Jon knew that they would have to be constantly on alert. It would be more mental than physical strain, and it would be twice as dangerous as infiltrating behind Japanese lines. In Kabul, they couldn't meld back into a jungle and hide.

On Saturday morning, the trio went into the armory to pick up their special weapon. They were met by Colonel Miller.

"Gentlemen, our mission is delayed until a dispute is settled between the US and Afghanistan over the amount of agricultural products that the Afghans can export to the US in 1945; specifically, wool, pistachio nuts, and almonds. The Afghans are not letting any US aircraft land until the dispute is settled," Colonel Miller stated.

"Colonel, you know as well as I do that anything that the state or agricultural departments are involved in is not resolved quickly. It could take weeks or months," Jon remarked.

"The War Department is already putting pressure on them to resolve this before they get the president involved. If the president has to intervene, some heads are going to roll," Colonel Miller said.

"It's more than likely that India is the problem in the negotiations," Miles said. "They're afraid of lost profits. India will want the US to compensate them for the Afghans selling direct to the US instead of buying the Afghan products from India."

"I've sent a message to the American Embassy in Kabul requesting permission for one diplomatic mission aircraft to land with five additional negotiators. The embassy should have a response from the Afghan government by this evening. If the government grants us permission, we'll leave tomorrow or the next day," Colonel Miller stated.

"What do you mean by 'we,' Colonel," Jon asked.

"I've been directed by the chief of staff to be part of this diplomatic mission to Kabul; your names and Sergeant O'Dell's are also included as negotiators. Our diplomatic papers are being prepared at the American Embassy in New Delhi, and will be flown in tomorrow. So keep your bags packed," Colonel Miller stated.

"Does that mean we will be rooming in the embassy compound?" Henri asked.

"Indeed, it does, Henri. Indeed, it does," Colonel Miller said.

"Thank God. I've heard only bad things about Afghan hotels. They're not heated and their swarming with bed bugs," Henri said cringing just thinking about the bed bugs.

"Oh, for crying out loud Henri," Jon stated, "the damn leeches in Burma are ten times worse than bed bugs. All you have to do is put a half a cup of diesel in your bath to kill them."

"I didn't know that," Henri said.

"Or you could drink a half a cup of diesel," Miles said laughing, "and chase it with a glass of gin."

"Screw you, Miles. That rot gut gin you limey's get would probably kill me before the diesel," Henri stated.

Jon was glad that his teammates were kidding each other. It meant that they had a solid friendship, and neither would let each other down in a time of crisis.

CHAPTER 31

KABUL, AFGHANISTAN

The 1,335-mile flight to Kabul, took over nine hours in the Curtis C-46A. It was the heaviest and largest Army Air Corps twin-engine aircraft to see operational use in the Asian region. It was originally designed as a commercial airliner, however, in 1942, the design caught the attention of the War Department, and it soon became a heavy military transport.

The C-46A ordered by the War Department had a strengthened cargo floor that allowed heavier cargo loads. With the upgraded engines, it had a service ceiling of twenty-seven thousand feet and could easily fly over the Himalayan mountain range.

As the aircraft's engines were shut down, two tan sedans pulled up and stopped ten yards from the plane. When the portable metal stairs were moved to the aircraft door, a young embassy worker left the lead car and moved to the bottom of the metal stairs. When Colonel Miller ascended the steps and stepped on the aerodrome tarmac, the embassy worker said a few welcoming words, took the colonel's bag, and walked to the car. Jon, Miles, Henri, and O'Dell followed and stuffed their bags in the trunk of the second car.

The American Embassy compound took up at least five acres on the east side of Kabul. As the car pulled up to the compound, an army MP opened the ten-foot-high steel gate and let them drive through.

For two days, Sergeant O'Dell led the trio through the streets of Kabul, visiting the restaurants, shops, and getting the layout of the city. On their third, they met the Afghan OSS agent, Dilip Shah, at a small restaurant called Khosha.

Colonel Miller had told Shah that morning that Khan was responsible for his nephew's death. He also told him that he wanted his family to take care of Khan. However, Dilip would not be able to participate. But Jon was suspicious of Dilip; he knew that a person bent on revenge could also be careless. He would have to keep Dilip at his side the entire mission.

"That's Ahmad Khan sitting three tables away," Shah said.

"Who's that sitting with him?" Henri asked.

"That's the German Embassy's agricultural attaché," Shah said. "Khan and his family have been exporting pistachios and almonds from this region for a hundred years. My clan competes with his in the same market. They are always looking for ways to make more money," Shah said.

"Maybe we can use that to our advantage. Guys, it looks like we are going into agricultural exports," Jon said.

"Well, we do have the right credentials," Miles said.

After discussing their plan with Colonel Miller, he told them that it looked like a solid way to get into Khan's confidence.

"You can tell them you are commodity brokers, but not farmers. You are here to evaluate the agreement being negotiated purely from a commodity perspective and counseling the negotiating team what the US market can handle in 1945," Colonel Miller stated.

"We'll need to see the agreement," Jon said.

An hour later, the trio was reading a single copy delivered by one of the negotiators. He told them he would come by in two hours to answer any questions.

For all intents and purposes it was a simple agreement; only twenty-two pages long. It was written at the sixth-grade English level; specifically for the Afghans. Apparently, the negotiations were stuck on the Afghan wool exports. The Afghan wool was too coarse for clothing and fit only for use in making carpet. The US, of course, would purchase some, but not the eighty thousand tons the Afghans wanted. The US, no doubt, would sell the Afghan wool to India at a steep discount. After discussing the agreement with the negotiator, the team was ready to talk to Ahmad Khan. The Afghans had only negotiated twenty-five thousand tons of pistachios and thirty thousand tons of almonds. The US negotiators were willing to accept double the tonnage.

When Khan came to the American Embassy for his meeting with the OSS commander, he was introduced to Jon, Miles, and Henri. The commander told him they were part of the US team negotiating the agricultural contract. Jon let slip that he expected the Afghan government to demand more almonds and pistachios for export. The US market, he told Khan, could handle twice what his government was asking. That got Khan's attention.

"Mr. Preston, my family exports almonds and pistachios. I would be privileged if you and your cohorts would meet with me and discuss what exactly you do in the US export business," Khan said.

"My partners and I have tomorrow afternoon off. I've been dying to eat at the Attock restaurant. I hear their lamb is the best in town. Could you meet us tomorrow at 3:00 p.m.?" Jon asked.

"That would be perfect. I know the restaurant well," Khan said.

Jon had picked the Attock because of its remote location on the west side of town. The restaurant seated twenty people downstairs and twenty people upstairs. But at 3:00 p.m., the place would be virtually deserted. Dilip's brother would be at the restaurant, too.

When Kahn entered the front door of the Attock, Jon, Miles, Henri, and O'Dell were sitting at a corner table near the front door windows. Khan was wearing a *salwar kameez* (dress), a *chapan* (coat), and a *keffiyeh* wrapped around his head. As Kahn joined them, Jon noticed two people sitting in the car that Kahn had driven to the restaurant. When Jon looked again, a few minutes later, only one remained in the car. He would have to keep a sharp eye out for the missing man.

After a lengthy discussion on pistachios and almonds and several cups of very strong coffee, Khan excused himself to go to the bathroom. As he reentered the restaurant, through the back door, Dilip's brother Amit made his move. Amit Shah was squatting low to the floor behind a solid partition. As Khan drew even with Amit he threw Khan's *salwar kameez* up over his head. He then grabbed Khan's testicles and cock, and in one swift motion with his right hand cut them off. It happened so fast that Miles and Henri missed it. Khan was screaming and writhing on the floor and bleeding profusely. Jon had his silenced pistol out by the time the Afghan from the car entered the back door with his gun drawn. Jon didn't hesitate and placed a single shot through his right eye socket with his silenced pistol. As the second man from the car entered the front door, he heard Amit Shah screaming over Khan, "For my son's death!" as he slit his throat. The second man seeing the carnage, left before he became a victim. The team had a witness to the revenge killing.

A day later, Sergeant O'Dell took the team to a restaurant where Lawrence Dugan usually hung out. O'Dell had met Dugan when he worked for the embassy. They weren't good friends, but Dugan would remember O'Dell.

"How do we want to do this?" Jon asked.

"Since he's a British subject, I think Miles should take him," Henri stated.

Thirty minutes had passed before Dugan entered the restaurant. He was staggering slightly and sat at the only open table in the room. O'Dell got up and went to the table where Dugan was sitting.

"Larry, how the hell are you," O'Dell said.

"John, what are you doing back in this hellhole?" Dugan replied.

"Back at the embassy for another tour," O'Dell said.

Before Dugan could ask O'Dell another question, Miles bumped his chair. "Oops, sorry old chap. Just trying to get through to the loo," Miles said as he placed his hand at the base of Dugan's neck and flicked his wrist. Dugan went limp and nearly fell out of the chair, but O'Dell caught and steadied him until he was secured and sitting slightly crunched in the chair. Miles continued to move towards the bathroom.

"Larry, it was good talking to you. Try not to drink so much," O'Dell said as he moved away.

A few minutes later, Miles came back from the outdoor bathroom and joined his teammates.

"That was slick a hell. I didn't even see the spike," Henri stated.

"We had better finish our lunch and leave before one of the waiters discovers their latest heart attack victim," Jon replied.

Four hours later, Colonel Miller entered the embassy planning room where the agents were reading. "We're leaving Kabul in one hour. Your bags are already on the way to the airport and there's a car in the compound waiting to take us there," Colonel Miller stated.

"Why, what's happening?" Jon asked.

"The Soviets and the Abwehr is what's happening. The Soviets think the Abwehr killed Dugan and they've started shooting. Three German agents have already been taken down and two Soviets are dead," Colonel Miller stated.

"Colonel, this isn't exactly what we wanted, but it sure takes the heat off of us. Plus, it's taken care of what the US wanted to accomplish in Afghanistan. If this little war moves to the other provinces, there will be fewer Germans and Soviets to deal with. Hell, they might just abandon Afghanistan altogether," Jon said.

"You're absolutely right, Jon. But we need to go, anyway, there's a colonel inbound to Calcutta, with a new mission for you all," Colonel Miller stated.

"How soon before we deploy on the new mission, Colonel?" Miles asked.

"Around fifteen days, Miles. The message was sketchy, but I was working on a new mission with Colonel Jim Sage before I left the Pentagon. There's a lot of planning to be put in place involving some friendly guerillas and OSS agents in the field. They will need tons of supplies dropped to them, and the OSS agents will need time to pull the guerillas together. Until then, you all will be officially on vacation and can go anywhere you want."

CHAPTER 32

ABOARD THE *ANNE MARIE* INDIAN OCEAN

After the trio returned from Kabul, Miles took a train to New Delhi to be with his family. Henri caught a hop to Fort Frederick to check with his commando friends to see if there was any new information on the situation in the detention center in Rangoon. Jon hopped a navy PBY taking supplies to the *Anne Marie*, still cruising in the Indian Ocean.

Aboard the Anne Marie, Captain Dubois entered the dining room where Jon and Camille were finishing their lunch.

"We've got visitors arriving in thirty minutes," Captain Dubois said.

"Do you know who is coming?" Jon asked.

"The message didn't say, Jon," Captain Dubois said.

"I guess G-2 thinks it's time that I go back to work," Jon stated.

The PBY Catalina flew over the *Anne Marie*, banked, turned into the wind, and touched down one hundred yards from the 126-foot luxury yacht. By the time the PBY had turned to taxi back towards the yacht, the *Anne Marie* had sent its twenty-foot motor launch to retrieve its visitors. Twenty minutes later, Colonel John Renick climbed the ladder and stepped on the aft deck of the *Anne Marie*.

"Request permission for my party and me to come aboard, Captain?" Colonel Renick asked.

"Granted, Colonel, welcome to the *Anne Marie*," Captain Dubois said.

As the remaining visitors climbed the ladder and stepped onto the deck, they were greeted by the captain.

"Miles, Henri, glad to have you back onboard," Captain Dubois said.

Jon stepped forward as Lieutenant Colonel Steve Schaefer stepped on the deck. "Captain Dubois, may I introduce Lieutenant Colonel Steve Schaefer. This is the guy that nearly scared the pants off of me when I parachuted into Myitkyina last month. Congratulations on your promotion, Steve."

"It's a pleasure to meet you, Colonel," Captain Dubois said.

"You have a beautiful boat, Captain," Lieutenant Colonel Schaefer responded.

"Gentlemen, you're just in time for an afternoon cocktail. If you would follow me into the lounge," Captain Dubois said.

Jon remained behind with Miles and Henri. "Good to see you all. Have you been briefed on any of this yet?"

"Not a thing, Jon," Miles said.

"We were only notified to get packed yesterday afternoon," Henri stated.

"Must be something big to bring the OSS out," Miles said.

"Probably joint mission involving their agents," Jon said.

In the ship's lounge, Captain Dubois introduced Camille Dupont, Kathleen Lauren, and his two new female agents; Monique Basil, and Brigitte Prefontaine. His newest OSS agents were both French Malayans. They had been living with their parents in Ceylon, when they were recruited by the OSS.

After an hour of socializing and having mango juice cocktails and sandwiches, Colonel Renick told the captain that he would like to get started.

"Ladies, if you would please excuse us, the colonel needs to talk to these gentlemen in private," Captain Dubois said.

"It's alright, Captain," Colonel Renick said, "the ladies can stay. They will be involved in some of the missions coming up that relate to this mission. Everyone, please have a seat."

Colonel Renick took a second to gain his composure then proceeded. "As you know already, the Allies have a firm foothold in the Pacific, and the Japanese are being beaten back from Burma into Thailand and Indochina. But we are here because of the recent information we've received on Japanese biological and chemical warfare experiments. We've know, since the war began, that the Japanese have been conducting biological and chemical warfare experiments in northern China. Only recently, however, did we receive evidence that they are conducting experiments in southern China and French Indochina, which is now called Vietnam. Our latest reports are telling us that the Japanese are now conducting experiments using American POWs. The biological and chemical agents have us very concerned, and the medical experiments, to say the least, are atrocities against mankind. Colonel Schaefer will fill you in some of the details."

Lieutenant Colonel Schaefer outlined the story of Japanese Unit 731's use of biological and chemical weapons and human experiments that began in 1933 in northern China and that now extended into Thailand, French Indochina, Malaya, and southern China. He ended with the stories that OSS agents had been told about the atrocities in medical experimentation conducted by the Japanese at a POW camp in French Indochina. After investigating the abandoned POW site, OSS agents were told by natives in the area that Japanese doctors were experimenting on American POWs. After the doctors had completed their experiments, the bodies of mutilated servicemen were burned.

"After the Japanese abandoned the camp, Vietnamese natives, along with one of our OSS operatives, found the dog tags of twelve American servicemen. OSS operatives have identified six potential camps where we think the medical experiments are now taking place. We want to send you all to a camp fifty miles east of Hanoi to capture the physicians conducting these experiments and bring any surviving POWs out. The camp is located on Kao-Lan Island," Lieutenant Colonel Schaefer stated.

"Henri," Colonel Renick said, "we understand that you have some knowledge of this area from your time in the lumber industry."

"Yes, sir. I'm very familiar with the area. We used to log on Kar-Ba Island, twenty miles west of Kao-Lan. I even went to Kao-Lan several times to check on its suitability for logging. It's the largest island among the hundred or so islands around it," Henri remarked.

"We also know that both you and Miles speak fluent Vietnamese," Colonel Renick said.

"Yes, sir," Henri and Miles said in unison.

"How had you planned on getting us in, Colonel," Jon asked.

"Through China," Lieutenant Colonel Schaefer said. "After you fly out of here, you'll take a transport from Calcutta to Ledo; from Ledo, you'll fly to Kunming; and from Kunming, you'll be flown and airdropped west of Hanoi. You'll be met by an OSS team led by a Captain Tan Tong. We also have an OSS agent that will be going with you. You all met him at Fort Frederick, Ceylon. Lieutenant Colonel George Linka, he's the US Army liaison to the British Third Commando Brigade. He was an American missionary in Japan before the war and speaks fluent Japanese,"

"How many Japs can we expect at Kao-Lan, Colonel?" Henri asked.

"No more than twenty Japanese, plus a captain that is the camp commander," Lieutenant Colonel Schaefer said.

"What kind of support will we get once we get to our drop zone?" Jon asked.

"You'll have a native OSS officer and ten Vietnamese guerillas that will get you down river and onto the island," Lieutenant Colonel Schaefer said.

"That's a lot of people to be moving downriver colonel," Miles said.

"They will be using four different sampans to move everyone. The river traffic from Hanoi to Haiphong is too much for the Japanese to monitor. In fact, they don't even bother with it. They've had to send most of their troops into Cambodia to reinforce units fighting the guerillas aligned with us," Lieutenant Colonel Schaefer added.

"Colonel, what kind of hazards do we need to be concerned about at the camp?" Jon asked.

"We know for certain that the Japanese are experimenting with anthrax, bubonic plague, cholera, diphtheria, glanders, encephalitis, and smallpox. Most of these you've been vaccinated for. You'll receive a vaccination for Japanese encephalitis and anthrax when you get back to Calcutta. But we just don't know what the Japs may be experimenting with. However, our more immediate concern is the chemical experiments, not the biological pathogens. Chemical agents can be mass produced much easier than biological agents," Lieutenant Colonel Schaefer said.

"What's glanders?" Henri asked.

"It's a disease that primarily effects horses, mules, and donkeys but can be transmitted to humans. There is no vaccine for it, and it is fatal to humans," Lieutenant Colonel Schaefer stated.

"What do we do if we find infected POWs?" Jon asked.

"Contact us on your Paraset wireless radio, and we'll arrange for a navy medical team to be flown in. It will take too long to use army transports, so we'll use PBYs from the USS *Saratoga*," Lieutenant Colonel Schaefer said.

"And what if we capture the Japanese medical personnel?" Jon asked.

"They'll be flown out with you and debriefed by an army biological intelligence team," Lieutenant Colonel Schaefer said.

"So, we'll be flying back to the *Saratoga*, too," Jon remarked.

"Yes," Colonel Renick said. "A colonel from G-2 will be there to give you details about your next mission."

"Another Unit 731 camp?" Jon asked.

"I don't know, Jon. I was only privy to this mission. I was told to tell you that a G-2 colonel would be on the *Saratoga*," Colonel Renick stated.

CHAPTER 33
KAO-LAN ISLAND FRENCH INDOCHINA

Agent Jon Preston was lying on his belly next to his Vietnamese guerilla guide, Captain Tan Tong. His field glasses were focused on a structure, where three men in white coats had just entered. It was one of five large bamboo huts with elephant grass thatched roofs. The Japanese compound was approximately thirty yards square and surrounded by a ten-foot-tall barbed wire fence. There was one entrance, which was large enough for the four-ton Japanese truck parked under a bamboo lean-to to pass through.

Agents Miles Murphy, Henri Morreau, and Lieutenant Colonel George Linka were scouting the opposite ends of the compound. This was where the quarters of the Japanese soldiers, medical staff, and the camp commander were located. The quarters were separated from the larger compound and surrounded by its own fence. Miles counted ten soldiers, but there were probably four or five from the night shift who were still sleeping. Henri crawled through the elephant grass that had grown up against the fence. When he tested the strength of the lowest row of barbed wire, it broke. It was probably wasn't over three years old, but it had become rusted and brittle from the constant wet and humid coastal climate. Getting in and out would be easy. Getting in and out safely was another question.

After four hours of observation, the Allied agents met back at their jungle encampment. They would rest the remainder of the day and go back at dusk to observe the night shift.

"What did you find?" Jon asked.

"We counted eleven guards, three cooks, the camp commander, and four medical staff in white lab coats," Miles stated.

"That's what I counted, too," Jon said.

"The barbed wire fence is so brittle that it broke when I touched it. The soldiers' barracks and camp commander's office was only fifteen yards from our location. It should be easy for both of us to get to the barracks and toss our satchel charges through the windows," Henri said.

Do you want to take the commander alive?" Miles asked.

"Our priorities are the Allied POWs, medical staff, and camp commander in that order. Once we secure the camp, we'll radio the USS *Saratoga*. The closest area for a potential landing strip is only two miles away, but there's no road to it. It looks like the navy will have to fly in several PBYs," Jon remarked.

As Jon finished speaking, two groups of Vietnamese guerillas entered the camp from different directions. Both groups converged on their leader. The first group told Captain Tong that a Japanese supply boat had landed on the beach. The second told him that the Japanese truck had left the compound headed north on the road to the beach.

"Alright, let's get back in position and see what's going on," Jon ordered.

Within an hour, Jon's team had moved to their observation locations. The Jap sailors unloaded the supplies on the beach. It had taken two trips to get the supplies to the camp. At the compound, the Japanese soldiers brought out ten POWs to do the unloading. Only six were European looking. But all ten were undernourished and emaciated. Two POWs that struggled to lift the boxes were beaten by the guards. When the camp commander heard the screams, he came out of his quarters, admonished the soldiers, and returned to his office. The two prisoners that were beaten were returned to their hut, and two additional prisoners were sent out to take their place.

Jon was angered by the beatings the Allied POWs suffered. He decided then that he would not give mercy to any of the Jap guards. Two hours after dark, they returned to their camp with enough information to plan their assault.

"We'll assault the compound just before daybreak. That will give us time to take out all the guards while it's still dark. Jon explained. "Captain Tong, I'll need five of your best men to take out the guards. Have them strip the guards, and put on their uniforms. They can take their places until we set off the satchel charges. Miles and Henri will assault the guard barracks. You and I will take the medical personnel. I'll need two of your men to capture the commander and two to back them up."

At 0300 hours, Jon was awakened by Captain Tong. An hour later, everyone was in position outside the compound. At 0500 hours, five of Captain Tong's best guerillas infiltrated the compound and took out the five guards. At daybreak, Miles and Henri slipped through the wire closest to the barracks; Jon and Captain Tong entered closest to the hut, where the medical team slept; and four of Captain Tong's guerillas entered the compound and crouched on the west side of the commander's quarters.

Miles and Henri triggered their satchel charges and eased them through the open windows on the north and south sides of the barracks. Both agents then ran behind the cooking hut and waited behind the rock oven.

When the satchel charges exploded demolishing the guard huts, Jon and Captain Tong rushed into the medical hut, where the medical team was sleeping and captured four men. At the same time, four Vietnamese guerillas entered the camp commander's hut and had him bound and gagged before he could get out of bed. The five guerillas that had taken out the Japanese guards shed the Japanese uniforms and were now standing guard in front of the five structures in the large compound.

Jon and Captain Tong pulled the four medical team personnel out onto the ground in front of their hut. Lieutenant Colonel George Linka, who spoke fluent Japanese, then strode up to them and began asking questions. No one spoke until Jon pulled his .22-caliber suppressed automatic and shot one of the Japanese medical personnel in the thigh.

"I learned that interrogation technique from my buddy Sean O'Brien in Valmontone, Italy, six months ago," Jon said to Lieutenant Colonel Linka.

The other three began speaking almost simultaneously. Lieutenant Colonel George Linka had to shut everyone up before he could restart his interrogation.

"Very effective," Lieutenant Colonel Linka said.

Lieutenant Colonel Linka separated the four Japs and began his interrogations. After two hours, he had a complete picture of what the Japanese were doing here. Linka spoke to the three agents and informed them that the Japanese were conducting human experiments with chemicals agents that they considered promising for chemical weapons. Five prisoners would be injected with the chemical agent, and two medical officers and their assistants would euthanize one of the infected prisoners at hours four, eight, twelve, twenty-four, and forty-eight. Then they would perform an autopsy to determine the effects of the agent. They documented their finding in a journal and sent a duplicate journal to Unit 731 headquarters every month.

Lieutenant Colonel Linka told them that the bodies of the last five victims had been burned already and that they were waiting for a shipment of new chemical agents before they began their next experiments.

"It's alright to open the huts and release the POWs," Lieutenant Colonel Linka said.

"I told them that if they lied, we would inject them with the chemicals in their laboratory and perform a vivisection on them."

"Captain Tong, you and your men take the Jap prisoners outside the perimeter fence. In case they are lying, we don't want any of you being contaminated; you too, Linka. The three of us will open the POW huts. George, after you free the prisoners and get a head count, you can set up the radio and contact headquarters and tell them how many need extraction," Jon stated.

One by one, the huts were opened and the Allied prisoners freed. A total of ten prisoners walked outside; the two that were beaten by the guards had to be carried out on their cots.

One POW walked up to Jon, "Thanks for coming to our rescue, Agent Preston," Lieutenant Neil Doten said.

"Holy cow, Neil, I had no idea you had been taken prisoner. What happened?" Jon said.

"We were shot down by a Jap Zero flying near Malaya. A Jap patrol boat picked us up and then we ended up here," Lieutenant Doten said.

"Lieutenant Doten, meet Agents Miles, Murphy, and Henri Morreau. They're with the British Special Operations Executive," Jon said.

"Aren't you that chap with the new PBY that took us to Trincomalee, last April?" Miles asked.

"Yes sir. Thanks for rescuing us, but don't you all know you're deep in Japanese territory?" Lieutenant Doten asked.

"Not anymore. The Japs are slowly being kicked out of Burma, Thailand, and Indochina. The Allies have control of the air and can hit anywhere they please without being bothered by Jap fighters. We should have a couple of PBY Catalina's here shortly with a medical team. Hopefully, we'll have you out of here before nightfall," Jon said.

Lieutenant Colonel Linka sent his wireless report to the SOE and waited for a reply before walking over to where Jon was standing.

"Lieutenant Doten, meet Lieutenant Colonel Linka. He's with the OSS," Jon said.

"Call me George, Lieutenant."

"And you can call me Neil, sir."

"Jon, the *Saratoga* is sending four PBYs with a fighter escort," Lieutenant Colonel Linka said.

"Great. Captain Tong, do you think your men could get the stoves going, and prepare some food for everyone," Jon asked.

"We'll take care of it, Jon," Captain Tong stated.

CHAPTER 34

USS *SARATOGA*
SOUTH CHINA SEA

Aday after landing on the *Saratoga*, Jon's team was greeted by Colonel Norm Hayward in one of the ship's classified briefing room.

"Jon, Miles, Henri, how are you?" Colonel Hayward asked.

"We're still trying to get our sea legs. Sir, let me introduce Lieutenant Colonel George Linka. George is the US Army Liaison to the British Third Commando Brigade in Ceylon. He was with us on Kao-Lan Island," Jon said.

"George was one of the OSS instructors in a class that I sat in on last year. It's good to have you on the team, George," Colonel Hayward said.

"When do we leave for our next mission, Colonel?" Jon asked.

"In ten days. Let's sit down and discuss the details," Colonel Hayward said. "Henri, I understand that you speak Cantonese."

"Yes sir. I learned it while working near Canton early in my lumber career," Henri said.

"Well, we're going to need your Cantonese skills on this mission. We're sending you all to Hong Kong to finish off the last agent in the Japanese spy ring that you took down in Chittagong. Our interrogation experts extracted the name and location of the last agent from Win Su Yong, the Japanese spy you captured in

Chittagong. Apparently, this network is all a bunch of relatives. The last agent is Win Su Yong's brother-in-law. His name is Nicolas Fournier; he's Eurasian. He and his wife are staying at the Claremont Hotel; it's one of the better hotels in Hong Kong. It's located right on the beach," Colonel Hayward said.

"How will we be getting to Hong Kong, sir?" Miles asked.

"You'll be rendezvousing with the USS *Coho* west of Luzon in two days. After that the *Saratoga* is joining a battle group and will be providing fighter coverage while the remaining carriers launch airstrikes against Japan. From the USS *Coho*, you'll be rendezvousing with a Chinese junk a hundred miles east of Hong Kong. The Junk will get you into Hong Kong," Colonel Hayward stated.

Two days later, a launch from the *Saratoga* took them to the USS *Coho* that had stopped 200 yards from the carrier. After boarding, they were greeted by Commander Royce Janca, and his executive officer Lieutenant Commander Chad Spivey. Commander Spivey showed the four operatives to their berths while Commander Janca readied the boat to dive.

When the captain ordered dive, the chief of the boat (COB) sounded two blasts on the boat's klaxon. *Ahoooga! Ahoooga!* It was followed by the captain's voice blaring over the intercom, "Dive! Dive!"

"I'll need to join the captain on the Conn. You think you can still find your way to the galley? The cook's got sandwiches and coffee for you," Lieutenant Commander Spivey said.

"No problem. We'll see you later," Jon said.

"Green board!" yelled the chief of the boat over the intercom. It was followed by "Pressure in the boat" as the interior lights switched to red. A green board was the submariner's term used to inform the captain and crew that the boat was sealed, watertight, and ready to dive.

"Take her to one-zero-zero feet," Captain Janca ordered. As the *Coho* prepared to slip beneath the surface, the diesel engines stopped, and the boat changed to its battery-powered electric motors for its underwater propulsion. The main air induction valves slammed shut, and the irregular gurgle of water entering into the ballast tanks could be heard throughout the boat.

Fifteen minutes later, the diving planesman called out, "Level at one-zero-zero feet, Captain."

"Come to heading 320 degrees," Captain Janca ordered.

"Heading 320 degrees, Captain," the planesman stated.

Twenty minutes after submerging, Captain Janca turned the boat over to his XO. He then headed down to the lower deck where the four agents were having coffee and eating sandwiches.

"Gentlemen," Captain Janca said, "we're thirty hours from your rendezvous. We'll be running submerged because the Jap aerial activity is heavy in this area. We'll surface after sunset, which is approximately five hours from now. Jon, I see you brought someone new onboard."

"Captain Janca, meet Lieutenant Colonel George Linka," Jon said.

"Make yourself at home, George. These guys know their way around the boat. If you need anything, ask me or the XO. You'll be able to go up on deck once we surface," Captain Janca said before he left.

Once the sun went down, the boat surfaced, and the four agents took turns going up on deck. The water was choppy, and it was raining, so they didn't stay long.

At 2200 hours the next evening, the radar operator called out, "Contact, Captain! Bearing 290 degrees."

"Sonar?" Captain Janca questioned.

"No screws, Captain," the Sonar operator stated.

"XO, check what's out there," Captain Janca ordered over the intercom.

"Morse code, Captain," the XO called out over the deck intercom, "Romeo-Juliet-Tango-Golf-Romeo-Alpha-Oscar."

"That's a good code, XO. Send the response code," Captain Janca ordered.

"Aye, Captain. Sending Mike-Alpha-November-Delta-Oscar-Oscar-Sierra," Lieutenant Commander Spivey responded.

"Have they acknowledged yet?" Captain Janca asked.

"I have acknowledgment, Captain," the XO stated.

"COB," Captain Janca said, "go get our visitors. XO, prepare the six-man life raft."

Thirty minutes later, the four agents were climbing aboard the Chinese junk. They were greeted by the junk's captain, Lee Yi.

"Welcome aboard. If you will follow me, I have your change of clothes and war kits in my cabin," Captain Lee Yi stated.

An hour and a half later, the four agents stepped out of the captain's cabin. All were wearing clothing from the Hong Kong market, and all had used the items in the war kit to darken their skin and color their hair jet-black. Since they were going into enemy territory, they needed to look as much like Eurasians as possible.

That evening before sunset, the junk docked at one of the typhoon shelters located on the north side of the island.

CHAPTER 35
HONG KONG, CHINA

There were at least two hundred other vessels at anchor in the typhoon shelter. After dropping anchor, Captain Lee and the agents were rowed to the docks. On shore, four bicycle taxis were waiting as prearranged by Captain Lee. The taxis departed in different directions. Jon and George were heading to a physician's office, five blocks south of Victoria Hospital. The traffic was a mixture of automobiles and electric trolleys. The taxi drivers were hurrying to get the agents to the office before dark. It would take nearly thirty minutes to get there.

Miles and Henri were taken to a fish market east of the North Point electric power station. Their journey would take only ten minutes. Henri had been to Hong Kong in 1938. Except for the light traffic, it resembled any other large city in Asia. Henri noticed only a few Japanese soldiers and military vehicles during his ride, but none of the soldiers seemed to pay any attention to the taxi and its rider. What were missing, however, were the Europeans. The Europeans that were stranded in Hong Kong, after the Japanese invaded the city, were being held in a large detention center on the south side of the island. The Eurasians and Chinese were free to carry on business, but the lack of marketable products had shut many businesses down. When Henri arrived at the fish market, he was taken down an alley to a side entrance.

When he entered through the side door, Miles was sitting and being served tea by the shop owner.

Jon and Colonel Linka arrived at their destination at the same time. Jon got out of the taxi slightly ahead and entered the doctor's office first. As they walk in, Jon noticed that the office was empty, except for a small Chinese woman standing behind the counter.

"I'm here to see Dr. Mei Li Zou," Jon said.

"I'm Dr. Zou, how may I help you?"

"I'm Jon, and this is George. Captain Lee said that you were expecting us," Jon stated.

Dr. Zou came out from behind the counter, locked the outside door, and turned off the office lights. She said, "Follow me, please."

She took them down a hallway and into a separate section of the building. It was obvious to Jon and George that this was her home.

"You will be spending the night here. Tomorrow you will go to another house," Dr. Zou said.

"We are grateful for your hospitality, Dr. Zou. Will there be someone to guide us through Hong Kong?" Jon asked.

"First, you eat, and then we will talk," Dr. Zou stated.

Over the next hour, she fixed then served them steamed rice and stir-fried vegetables and hot tea. While they ate, she told them that her husband and son had been killed by the Japanese when they invaded Hong Kong, in December 1941. Her mother had died of influenza the following September. She had been working with the Chinese underground, specifically, the East River Column since the summer of 1942, and had helped over forty British, Australian, and Indian soldiers and civilians escape into China.

"The gentleman you will stay with tomorrow is my husband's first cousin, Feng Zou. He has the information you are seeking for your mission," Dr. Zou told them.

Because they had not been able to get much sleep on the submarine or the Chinese Junk, they awoke late the next morning.

A short time later, Dr. Zou came back to her living quarters, and fixed them lunch of rice and smoked fish. They had just finished their lunch when Feng Zou knocked on the back door and entered the house.

"We must leave quickly. The Japanese are searching the hospitals and physician offices for a wounded American flyer that was shot down early this morning while strafing Japanese cargo ships in Victoria Harbor," Feng Zou said.

As they stepped out the back door, two bicycle taxis awaited them. Feng Zou would stay with his cousin until the Japanese soldiers had finished searching her office and house.

It took over forty-five minutes for the taxis to get Jon and George to a house near the eastside docks. The house was only four blocks from the Royal Hong Kong Yacht Club. Most of the luxury yachts had escaped before the Japanese invasion, but a few were still berthed there. The Claremont Hotel was next door to the yacht club. It was one of the nicest hotels in Hong Kong and had a spectacular view of Victoria Harbor. There was a two hundred-foot strip of sandy beach out its back door and one of the best outdoor cafes in town. Nicolas Fournier had breakfast there every morning promptly at 0600 hours for the last two years. Except for an occasional early morning riser, Nicolas was usually the only patron at the outdoor restaurant. After finishing breakfast, he would sit and read the newspaper and drink tea until 0800 hours. Then he would take a taxi to his job at the Japanese Consulate where he worked for Japanese intelligence. Japanese intelligence had taken over part of the consulate building shortly after the invasion.

"When will we meet up with our other two agents?" Jon asked Bao-Zhi Lin, the owner of the house who greeted them.

"They will arrive at the house next door at noon. There is an underground access between our houses, and they will use it to come here," Bao-Zhi Lin said.

"Will they have the information on our mission target?" George asked.

"Yes, my brother, who owns the market, has already passed the information to them," Bao-Zhi Lin said.

"We appreciate your help, Mr. Lin," Jon said.

"We hate the Japanese as much as you do. Whatever we can do to help you shorten the war, benefits us as well. My younger brother was caught selling products on the black market. He was only fourteen, but he was still beaten to death by the Japanese," Bao-Zhi Lin said.

Miles and Henri arrived shortly after noon and joined Jon and George for lunch.

"Your brother sent this package of fish with us," Miles said. "I'm amazed that there are not more Jap soldiers in downtown Hong Kong."

"Most of the soldiers have been sent into China to fight the Nationalist Armies. The majority of the remaining soldiers are busy with the detention center or working with the Japanese Secret Police, the *Kempei Tai*, chasing down escapees and spies," Bao-Zhi Lin said.

"The less soldiers, the better for us," Henri said.

"It's the Kempei Tai that you need to worry about," Bao-Zhi Lin said.

"What do you have for us, Henri," Jon asked.

"Nicolas Fournier is still staying at the Claremont Hotel," Miles stated.

Miles proceeded to tell Jon and George the details about Fournier's daily routine and his workplace. Between the four agents, they worked out a plan to take Fournier down.

The following morning, Jon and George were having breakfast at the Claremont Hotel patio restaurant. They were sitting at the closest table to the kitchen thirty feet away. Despite being 65°F, Nicolas Fournier was sitting where he did every day when it wasn't raining, overcast, or too cold; the closest table to the steel rail surrounding the outdoor restaurant. Today, the sky was clear and the view breathtaking.

Henri was sitting on a park bench near the yacht club entrance, ten yards from the hotel pretending to read a newspaper. When the waiter finally served Fournier's breakfast, Henri got up and walked towards the entrance to the café. Over his suit, Henri was wearing a black three-fourths length cloak around his shoulders. So Fournier wouldn't notice Henri walking up behind him, and to serve as a distraction, Jon and George got up and walked in the opposite direction when Henri was ten feet from Fournier's table. When Henri was five feet away from Fournier, he whipped the cape off his shoulders and threw it over Fournier's head. Then with one swift motion, he pulled Fournier's head backwards and slit his throat. Henri picked up the cloth napkin lying on the table, wiped the blood off the knife, and walked away.

CHAPTER 36
CLARK FIELD LUZON ISLAND

C olonel Ronnie Masek stood in front of a map of China. A red circle marked the city of Canton. From his briefcase, he pulled a packet of maps labeled Air Target Maps and Photos, China Coast, CINCPAC-CINCPOA, October 15, 1943.

"Gentlemen, your next mission is going to be a Japanese POW camp that is experimenting in germ warfare. The POW camp is located six miles east of the city of Canton and a mile west of the Canton University airfield. The camp houses approximately forty POWs and twenty medical personnel and guards. Our agents in Canton are telling us that they are experimenting with anthrax and tetanus. In 1944, we thought this camp was a lumber mill because the information we initially received was about a project codenamed *Maruta*, meaning 'log' in Japanese. However, we later found out that the Japanese were referring to the prisoners that they were experimenting on as *logs* in order to fool the local authorities into thinking it was a lumber mill," Colonel Masek stated.

"Colonel, how contagious is anthrax?" Jon asked.

"Anthrax does not usually spread from an infected person to a noninfected person. However, it is lethal if you contract the disease. Death from anthrax is usually sudden and is characterized by dark, non-clotting blood that oozes from the body orifices. So you'll need to absolutely avoid contact with any contaminated POWs and the body fluids of any victims. We also learned that the infected POWs are being subjected to vivisection before they are dead and without the benefit of anesthesia. We believe the Japanese do this while the POW is alive because they fear that the decomposition process would affect their test results. We've also learned that the Japanese have vivisected women, children, and pregnant mothers," Colonel Masek said.

"What about tetanus?" Miles asked.

"Tetanus usually occurs through wound contamination. The incubation period is around eight days. The symptoms usually start in the jaw muscles, which is why it's often referred to as a 'lockjaw.' As the disease progresses, the spasms can affect the chest, neck, back, and abdominal muscles. We think that they are experimenting with infected meat that is fed to the POWs. In addition to biological testing; we also have evidence that the Japs are testing weapons. The OSS has reported that several natives saw flamethrowers being tested on prisoners and human targets being used to test hand grenades. There's another report stating that prisoners were tied to stakes and used as targets so the Japs could test germ-releasing bombs. But that was at another site farther north," Colonel Masek stated.

"Colonel, it makes me sick to think about what they are doing to our POWs. It makes my blood run cold. Can we just kill the bastards this time?" Henri asked.

"Since we won't be able to fly transports in to bring any POWs out, that would be my recommendation, Henri. However, we do need at least one of the physicians brought back alive, if possible," Colonel Masek said.

"How will we get to Canton, Colonel?" Jon asked.

"You'll be flown from Clark Field to the USS *Coho* at 0800 hours tomorrow morning. The USS *Coho* is patrolling a hundred miles northeast of here. The *Coho* will rendezvous with a Chinese

Junk one hundred miles southeast of the Canton River Estuary at approximately 1900 hours four days from now. The Junk will take you as far as the Chuenpi Channel, where you'll transfer to a Sampan. The Sampan will take you to a small cove on the Canton River, four miles south of the university airfield. You should arrive at the cove around 0900 hours on the 18th. You'll be met by an OSS agent, who will get you to the POW camp. The details are in the folder. Please memorize the names of the Junk and Sampan captains, the OSS agent, and the map of Canton area," Colonel Masek stated.

"How do we get out, Colonel," Miles asked.

"The POW camp is a mile from the university airfield. A B-25 will land there at exactly 1730 hours on 21 March. That will give you one whole day to reconnoiter the camp and plan your infiltration. There are several regiments of soldiers around Canton guarding Japanese bomber bases, so be aware if anything goes wrong, they will probably be called on. You'll need to plan the capture of the physician on the afternoon of the 21st as close to 1830 hours as possible. You can steal one of their trucks, and drive to the airfield. Don't miss your flight home, gentlemen," Colonel Masek said.

"And if something happens and we do miss the flight?" Jon asked.

"You're OSS guide will have to walk you out to a Chinese-friendly area. There's a Nationalist Chinese-held airfield in Nan-hsiung, approximately 150 miles northeast of Canton. If you make it there, we can insert a B-25 and get you to the Philippines," Colonel Masek said.

"Will we need to take a radio with us or will the OSS agent have one already?"

"You'll be carrying a Paraset wireless radio, Jon. Before you get on the aircraft, leave it with the OSS agent," Colonel Masek said.

CHAPTER 37

CANTON RIVER CHINA

The sampan was making only five knots against the flow of the Canton River. In the last twelve hours, they had passed no less than ten Japanese patrol boats, none of which paid them any attention. Miles and Henri had already put on another application of skin color from the war kit; the skin coloring only lasted twenty-four hours. Jon and George were just now beginning their second application. However, they were eight hours behind schedule. Jon hoped the OSS agent would wait for them.

The owner of the sampan said something to Henri in Cantonese. Henri turned to the other and said, "The cove is two miles ahead."

"Thank God," Jon said.

When the Sampan entered the cove, the owner moved the boat into a large group of bamboo trees near the water. It was early afternoon, but the OSS agent was there to greet them. As the foursome jumped off the boat, they were greeted by the Chinese American agent.

"I'm First Lieutenant Randy Chang. I have a camp set up a thousand yards north in a large bamboo forest. If you like, we'll spend the night there and move out before daybreak."

"I'm Jon, Lieutenant Chang. This is Miles and Henri. Are there any Japanese patrols we need to worry about?" Jon asked.

"None until we reach the POW camp. The rain will help keep the visibility down, and the morning fog is heavy. We shouldn't have a problem taking them out if we need to. Please call me Randy," Lieutenant Chang said.

"Randy, we need to check out the camp before nightfall. Is that possible?" Jon asked.

"Not a problem, Jon. I'll have my men break camp and move to a location closer to the POW camp," Lieutenant Chang said.

"All right, Randy, let's head out," Jon stated.

Randy carried the Paraset wireless radio. The trio picked up their Thompson submachine guns and backpacks of extra munitions and explosives and followed Randy to a wooded knoll overlooking the POW camp two hundred yards away.

It wasn't as large as Jon expected. When he viewed the compound through his binoculars, he saw two block buildings, one small and one large, and four large bamboo huts. Lieutenant Chang told them that the large block building housed the guards and mess hall, the small block building was the medical laboratory and the bamboo huts housed the POWs.

It had to be rough on the POWs, especially when it got colder, Jon thought.

From another vantage point farther north, the group counted five perimeter guards and ten medical personnel going in and out of the smaller block building. Lieutenant Chang pointed out the road leading to the university airfield. At the entrance, they noticed a car and a single driver entering the compound.

"That will be one of the physicians. He must have forgotten something or had to come back and check on an experiment. They have a Type 98 passenger car. The guards are transported in a heavy truck," Lieutenant Chang said.

"Do you know the doctors' schedule? When they arrive and leave the camp?" Jon asked.

"Yes, they arrive every morning at 0700 hours and leave every evening at 1645 hours," Lieutenant Chang stated.

"Is it possible to take them after they leave the compound?" Jon asked.

"It's possible. Like most Japanese, they are fairly rigid with their schedules." Lieutenant Chang said. "Or we can take them when we take the compound."

"Because of our B-25 schedule, we'll have to do it during daylight and no more than an hour before our 1730 hours departure time. Anything earlier we risk the rest of the Jap neighborhood finding out. And I don't want to have to fight the Jap army," Jon said.

"I have a way of doing it, if you'd like to go over it now," Lieutenant Chang said.

"Let's get back to your camp and discuss it," Jon said.

They arrived at the camp as it was getting dark. There were four men waiting. The bamboo and elephant grass lean-to that Randy's men had erected was just large enough for ten men.

"Is this all of your men, Randy?" Jon asked.

"No, I have half a dozen more men stationed throughout the jungle. They have formed a defensive perimeter around us for the night. If anything happens, we will head east and away from here," Lieutenant Chang said.

"Do the Japs control this whole province?" Jon asked.

"No, the Jap controls a one hundred-mile radius around Canton. There's a large contingent of Chinese infantry 150 miles east of here. Most of the fighting in Canton is done by the four anti-aircraft regiments during Allied bombing raids. There are two Jap bomber bases ten miles to the northwest," Lieutenant Chang remarked.

"What all does your group do?" Miles asked.

"We mostly gather intelligence these days. We've attempted to infiltrate and sabotage the bomber bases, but the security is so high that it's impossible to get inside the perimeter. There are two rings of barbed wire fences. The outer ring is mined, and the inner ring has roving dog patrols. Inside the inner ring, the fence is constantly patrolled by armed vehicles," Lieutenant Chang said.

"What about the POW camp, is it guarded heavily?" Henri asked.

"The Japs seem to want to keep the camp low profile, so there are only a total of ten guards. There are at least ten medical personnel; several have left; probably reassigned to another facility. Right now, there are only ten Allied POWs here. Twenty were moved a week ago," Lieutenant Chang said.

"Have you found the best way into the camp yet?" Jon asked.

"I think I've come up with a way to get in. But it's going to take some pretty big gonads to pull it off," Lieutenant Chang stated.

"I think we have plenty of those, Randy," Jon said.

CHAPTER 38

CANTON POW CAMP
CANTON, CHINA

Jon, George, and Lieutenant Chang moved through the jungle to the north side of the POW camp. Miles, Henri, and the ten OSS guerillas stayed on the eastern side. At 1630 hours, Miles and Henri and two guerillas infiltrated through the rusted barbed wire and under one of the bamboo huts. Fifteen minutes later, after the guards had move around the compound again, Miles and Henri made it to the bamboo hut closest to the guard barracks.

As two guards were making another round of the compound, Miles and Henri jumped out from behind and waste bin and knifed the guards. They then dragged the bodies and hid them under one of the bamboo huts.

After Lieutenant Chang had entered the compound, he moved quickly behind the laboratory building and hid behind a large utility truck parked next to it. When one of the three remaining guards rounded the corner, there was a soft report of his silenced pistol.

Jon and George waited behind the farthest bamboo hut for the last two guards. The two guards were talking loudly and when they rounded the corner of the building they were silenced by another two muffled shots from silenced weapons.

After all the dead guards had been hidden, Miles and Henri moved to the guard barracks. When Miles opened the door, Henri tossed a satchel charge into the guard quarters and slammed the door shut. The cinder block and the closed door muffled the loud *whump* as the charge exploded. The satchel that Henri had tossed was small, but packed with six pounds of ball bearings. When the charge exploded, it killed anyone in the building.

As the team moved toward the front door of the laboratory, a young technician came out the door. Jon shot him with his silenced pistol and moved his body around the back of the building.

When George and Lieutenant Chang entered the laboratory, they came face to face with one of the physicians. George reacted quickly, swung his pistol and hit the doctor behind his right ear, rendering him unconscious. When Jon entered, the pair were about to open one of the laboratory doors, but Jon stopped them.

"Let them come to us. We don't want to go into any contaminated areas," Jon said.

It didn't take long before two more medical personnel came out. George and Lieutenant Chang grabbed them and placed knives to their throats. George interrogated each man. Both were physicians.

"Ask them which one is the senior physician," Jon stated.

When the older Jap doctor raised his hand, Jon knocked the other physician unconscious.

"Ask him how many more medical personnel are in the lab and if there are any more physicians," Jon stated.

"There are six technicians still in the lab; no more physicians," George said.

Jon pointed to the other man lying unconscious. "Ask him what this guy does," Jon said to George.

"He's a microbiologist; PhD," George stated.

"Now ask him what kind of experiments they are performing now, and how many infected POWs are in there," Jon stated.

"Anthrax and five POWs," George said.

"We wait here until 1715 hours. George, ask the doctor if the infected POWs will survive the anthrax?" Jon asked.

George shook his head and said, "No. They died early this morning.

"Now ask him how many POWs are left in the huts," Jon stated.

"Four," George replied.

"Ask him where they keep the keys to the vehicle outside."

"In the truck," George answered.

"Randy, will you drive us to the airfield?" Jon asked as he turned toward Lieutenant Chang.

"Sure, no problem," Lieutenant Chang answered.

"Great, can you check to see if the keys are in the truck and then check on the remaining prisoners?" Jon questioned.

"On it," Lieutenant Chang said as he turned and went out the front door.

"What have you got in mind, Jon?" Miles asked.

"We're going to take the four POWs, the doctor, and microbiologist with us. Then we're going to blow the building," Jon said.

Captain Chang pulled up in front of the laboratory in the Model 94A utility truck and parked it with the motor running. The Model 94A was equipped with a six-cylinder diesel engine and had a top speed of fifty miles per hour. Its bed was equipped with three-foot-high solid steel railings welded to the frame, and it had a canvas top.

Hearing the familiar clatter of the diesel truck as it pulled up, Jon said, "It's time to get the POWs loaded in the truck. Randy, you drive. The four of us will get in the back with the POWs and our two prisoners."

Miles and Henri supervised the loading of the POWs. One POW, an airman, had an infected wound. His B-24 had been shot down on one of the raids against the Ten Ho and White Cloud bomber bases. He had only been in the camp for one week. Miles and Henri helped the airman up onto the truck bed.

As Jon was moving to get the Japanese microbiologist, now sitting in the outer office. The microbiologist jumped up and ran to his desk. Jon was startled that the doctor could move so fast. Before Jon reached him, the doctor had activated an alarm.

"Crap!" Jon yelled as he knocked the physician out with a fist to the side of his head. "He's activated some sort of alarm."

"That probably goes to the Ten Ho Airfield, three miles to the southwest," Lieutenant Chang stated.

"Tell your men to get out of here. It'll be crawling with Japs in fifteen minutes. Let's get him in the truck and haul ass," Jon said.

After they loaded the physician in the truck, Jon jumped in the back, and Lieutenant Chang got in the cab and put the truck in motion. As he exited the gate, he saw a cloud of dust in the direction of the airbase. The Japanese were already on the move.

By the time he got the truck a quarter of a mile down the road, Lieutenant Chang could see a Japanese truck in his rear view mirror. The truck he noticed was similar to the one he was driving. He hoped it was a four-cylinder model that he could outrun. If it were a six- or eight-cylinder, they would be in trouble.

Jon had noticed the vehicle also. It appeared to be gaining on them. He told everyone to lay flat on the bed. The tailgate was also made of steel and it would give them protection from bullets. No sooner than he had sat down and looked back, a dozen bullets from a Japanese .32-caliber machine gun began hitting the tailgate. The truck was only a quarter mile away and gaining.

Jon shouted at the other three agents, "Get your Thompsons ready! When they get in range, let them have it."

As they topped a small knoll, Lieutenant Chang noticed a B-25 on final approach to the university airfield. This was going to be close. If he stayed with the truck after he got everyone aboard, he would be a dead man. Jon must have been reading his thoughts.

Jon yelled through the open rear window, "Randy, you're getting on the aircraft with us."

Randy nodded. The truck was now a hundred yards behind them and still firing. He could see in his mirror that there were two men in the truck bed manning the machine gun.

Jon edged his Thompson over the tailgate and fired his entire clip. While Jon reloaded, Henri fired his Thompson. Randy was checking his mirror and noticed that one of the men on the machine gun had been hit. The driver was crouching low behind the steering wheel, and the truck was still gaining on them.

As they rounded the last curve and began moving downhill to the grass landing strip, the B-25 had landed and was turning around to get into takeoff position.

The agents in the back were still firing their Thompsons as they pulled up parallel to the aircraft's rear door. The aircraft's waist gunner was now firing at the oncoming truck. The gunner's .50-caliber fire took its toll on the truck's engine, and it came to a stop fifty yards away. The machine gun was still firing, and it began riddling the side of the truck and aircraft with .32-caliber fire.

Jon jumped over the side of the truck and took aim on the Japanese soldier firing the machine gun. After four bursts, the gunner went down. George, Henri, and Miles were getting the POWs and two prisoners aboard the aircraft when another Japanese truck came over the knoll and began firing. The waist gunner went into action with this .50-caliber but was hit by Japanese fire and went down. Henri ran to the gun and began firing at the Japs.

Jon opened the passenger door and pulled Randy from the truck. He had been hit several times when the truck had pulled up to the aircraft. Miles pulled Randy into the fuselage as the aircraft's engine came to full power. Jon jumped up and grabbed George's hand as the aircraft started its takeoff roll. George finally pulled him into the fuselage halfway down the runway.

The Japs were still firing as the B-25 lifted off the ground. It was soon lost in the evening sky.

CHAPTER 39
CALCUTTA, INDIA

The agents took a five-day off after returning from Canton. Jon spent his time off working at the small Catholic mission. This time he came out of the confessional spiritually refreshed. He now saw the deaths that he had caused as a necessity to rid the evil that had gripped the world and was trampling mankind. The hours he spent teaching the brown-eyed Indian children was refreshing. By the end of his five-day vacation, he was ready to go back to work.

On Friday, one of the newly promoted SOE enlisted men, Corporal Tom Riehle, entered his tent.

"What is it, Corporal?" Jon asked.

"There's an American Colonel at the SOE Detachment that wishes to see you and Agents Murphy and Morreau, sir," the Corporal replied.

"Tell him we'll be there in thirty minutes," Jon said.

Twenty-six minutes later, Jon drove the two miles to the British-American Club with Miles and Henri in tow. As they entered the club and made their way down the hall to the SOE Detachment, they ran into Colonel Kenneth Dale going the opposite direction.

"Hey, Jon, give me ten minutes to grab a sandwich, and I'll meet you in the briefing room," Colonel Dale said.

Colonel Kenneth Dale was a tall Texan, West Point graduate, and veteran of the North African campaign. After being severely wounded and awarded the Congressional Medal of Honor, he was taken in by General Marshall to be on the G-2 staff and promoted to his present rank. When Jon met the colonel at the White House, he took an immediate liking to the always grinning cowboy. Colonel Dale had grown up on a ranch in West Texas, and Jon envisioned him as the perfect Texas Ranger right out of the Old West.

Although this was Colonel Dale's first trip to India, he was intimately familiar with Jon's, Miles's, and Henri's record of accomplishments. When he returned to the briefing room, he commented, "Well, boys, are ya'll ready to kick some more Jap butt?"

"Yes, sir," the trio replied in unison.

Colonel Dale was a straight shooter and didn't like to beat around the bush. "We're sending ya'll back to Rangoon."

"More armor and munitions for us to blow up, sir?" Miles asked.

"Yes, Miles, something like that. And there's something that Henri will be extremely interested in, too," Colonel Dale stated.

"What would that be, sir?" Henri said, leaning forward.

"We've been kicking the hell out of the Japs in Burma for the last three months. Their supply lines have been severed, and they are retreating back into southeast Burma and Thailand. Rangoon is secured with only one division of Japanese, totaling around three thousand men. The British 14th Army is moving south toward Rangoon using the 4th and 15th Corps. However, the monsoon has stalled their advance sixty miles north of Rangoon," Colonel Dale said.

The colonel paused a moment and took a bite of the sandwich he had picked up in the club. After he swallowed he continued.

"You all will be involved in Operation Softball, an airborne and amphibious assault on Rangoon. The British 3rd Commando Brigade from Ceylon and the 20th Gurkha Rifles out of Alhilal, in the Himalayan foothills north of the Punjab, will lead the airborne assault of the city," Colonel Dale said.

"How do we fit in, Colonel," asked Henri.

"The three of you will go into Rangoon ten days prior to the invasion and work with our SOE and OSS agents to take out the Jap command and logistics structure. Cut the head off of the snake and the rest might fall. Without a command structure the Japs will be confused and ineffective and make the ground invasion of Rangoon a little easier," Colonel Dale stated.

"How are the 3rd Commando and 20th Gurkha Rifles getting to Rangoon," asked Jon.

"The seven hundred and fifty commandos will be air dropped over the Rangoon airport at 0600 hours on August 5, thirty minutes before an artillery barrage on Japanese defenses commences. Shortly before that, a SOE agent and three hundred Kachin guerrillas will take out the airport perimeter guards, capture the airport power plant, and secure the airfield. From what the SOE agents have told us, there are no more than two hundred Japs assigned to guard the airport," Colonel Dale said.

"What about the Gurkha Rifles?" Miles asked.

"Once the airport is secure, three regiments of the 20th Gurkha Rifles consisting of nearly two thousand men will land at the airport," Colonel Schaefer said.

"I didn't know we had that many transports in India," Jon stated.

"We're flying thirty C-47 transports in from Africa to fly in the commando's and fifty C-46 transports to fly in the Gurkha Rifles. We have another twenty-five transports that will airdrop supplies two hours after the Gurkha Rifles land," Colonel Dale said.

"What about the Japanese radars? Won't they be alerted to our aircraft?" Jon asked.

"The two remaining Japanese radar sites in Burma, one at Pyinmana and the other at Pegu, will be taken out at 2300 hours on August 4," Colonel Dale said. "Most of the Japs in Rangoon are bivouacked in their fortifications on the north and northeast sides of the city. The Japs consider the Irrawaddy a defensive position and are hardly guarding it. We estimate that 300 to 400 soldiers are quartered near the Jap headquarters. When you take out the headquarters there will be a lot of chaos, so we want you to take out the Jap barracks too."

"When will the main bodies of troops arrive?" Miles asked.

"The 4th Corps are already moving south from Mandalay and should arrive within twenty-four hours of the airborne assault. Fifteenth Corps will be leaving Akyab on the HMS *Ocean* tonight. They will transition to LSTs (Landing Ship, Tank), LCUs (Landing Craft, Utility), and Higgins boats and land at the Rangoon wharfs 0630 hours. The three Jap shore batteries around Monkey Point will be taken out by three OSS teams. Another OSS team will take out the patrol boats. At least six assault craft with Kachin Ranger's will secure the wharfs prior to the ships entering the Irrawaddy channel. And another two thousand Shin guerrillas will probe Japanese defenses at the perimeter of the city to tie the Jap troops down. By morning we should have at least eight thousand troops engaging the Japanese in and around Rangoon," Colonel Dale stated.

"What about the Japanese internment camp housing the civilians? They'll be in peril when the attack begins. Who's assigned to take the camp?" Henri asked.

"Well, Henri, we thought that you would like that honor. There will be another OSS agent with two hundred Shin guerrillas to help you," Colonel Dale remarked.

"Will we be split up, sir," Miles asked.

"Yes, you will, Miles. Jon will lead the SOE group that will sabotage the command headquarters and troop barracks. You will lead the group that will blow up the supply depot and be in charge of the operatives that capture the fuel depot. With fuel being in short supply, we don't want to destroy the fuel tank farm," Colonel Dale stated.

"When do we go, sir?" Jon asked.

"In three days, if you all can be ready by then," Colonel Dale stated.

"I think we can just make it," Jon said, smiling.

"Henri, since your family is in the Japanese internment camp, is this going to be too emotional for you attempt?" Colonel Dale asked.

"I've been waiting three years for this, Colonel. I wouldn't miss it for the world," Henri replied.

"I thought you'd say something to that effect," Colonel Dale said, smiling. "You all will be flying out of Ceylon in a PBY and rendezvous with a fishing boat that I think is already familiar to y'all. The rendezvous with Captain Ahab will occur eleven nights before the invasion. Captain Ahab will get you to the dock in Rangoon where you'll be met by one of our SOE agents—a Captain Jim Ballangy. Captain Ballangy will take you all to a safe house in Rangoon. He has all the information on the Japanese headquarters and troop barracks, supply depot, and the detention center. He'll introduce Miles and Henri to the two OSS agents they will be working with, and you all will disperse from there."

"What will we need to take with us?" asked Jon.

"Just your usual compliment of armament: Thompson's, handguns, and grenades. The SOE will supply you with enough C-3 explosives to get the job done," Colonel Dale replied.

Henri walked up to Colonel Dale, extended his hand, and said, "Thanks for including us, Colonel. We won't let you down."

"Henri, the thought never crossed my mind."

CHAPTER 40

RANGOON, BURMA

Captain Ahab maneuvered his boat alongside the Eden Street pier just like he had done every night for three years.

On the way to Rangoon, the captain told the agents that the secondary explosions from the Japanese warehouse had sent incendiaries into his fish market and partially destroyed his business. The captain was happy that this had happened because it removed all suspicion from him. The explosion, however, had killed three of his workers.

Before they reached the Irrawaddy Channel, the trio had darkened their skin with Jon's war kit, and Captain Ahab had given them native Shin clothing to wear. The clothing consisted of a dirty dark brown shirt, baggy white trousers, and a headdress. For this mission, Miles had dyed his hair jet-black, but he wore the headdress just the same.

They were met at the pier by the SOE agent, Captain Jim Ballangy. He got them to a building that was a half mile from the Japanese barracks and headquarters. Miles and Henri were immediately introduced to their OSS partners and left for their safe houses.

After a few hours of sleep, Jon and Captain Ballangy began planning the reconnaissance of their targets.

"Jim, have you come up with a place for us to observe the headquarters and barracks? Jon asked.

"There is a vegetable shop directly across from the headquarters. It is run by one of my native agents. The barracks are two blocks to the north of the headquarters. There is a brothel across the street from the two barracks. The proprietor is also one of my agents," Captain Ballangy stated.

"What about movement between the two locations?" Jon questioned.

"There is a narrow alley that you can take. It's dark as hell at night, and because of the thugs and thieves, hardly anyone uses it after dark," Captain Ballangy said.

Captain Ballangy also told Jon about the houses and observation areas that Miles and Henri would be using. Their reconnaissance would begin tomorrow.

Captain Ballangy then told Jon that the city had been preparing for four weeks for the inevitable Allied invasion. Most of the garrison's soldiers had been deployed to the outer ring of defenses. Only a small contingent of one hundred soldiers was left to protect the headquarters and even less to protect the logistics depot.

For four days and nights, Jon and one of the native Shin agents had been observing the Japanese headquarters. They were watching the patterns and habits of the Japanese staff and guards looking for weaknesses.

During each night shift, the two Japanese guards patrolling the grounds took a ten-minute break; one at 2300 hours and one at 0300 hours. Each morning during reveille, a color guard would raise the flag and then fire an 1800s-era six-pounder field cannon. The Japanese commander and his staff would all stand at attention on grounds in front of the porch. Even more interesting was the cannon, twenty yards away, faced the headquarters building head-on. At night, the flagpole and cannon were cast in a shadow from both floodlights shining on the front of the headquarters building instead of the grounds. Jon saw a serious flaw in their morning ritual and formulated a plan to exploit it. But first, he would discuss it with Captain Ballangy.

The constant movement of couriers and field commanders, in and out of the headquarters, revealed how anxious the Japanese really were. They knew that the Allies were coming and they did not have the manpower or supplies to sustain a protracted engagement. One of the captain's female SOE agents worked at the headquarters building. She had reported that the Japanese commander's orders were to fight to the last man. The SOE agent also reported the commander's plan to abandon the Rangoon headquarters, and let his troops fight it out in a delaying action. Jon would try to interrupt his escape plans.

An Allied diversion at Pyinmana, two hundred and fifty miles to the north of Rangoon, gave the Japanese a feeling that they were stalling the Allied Fourteenth Army. To add to the diversion, Allied counter-intelligence agents had been planted as aviators in bars around Calcutta. They came across as drunken flyboys and began talking about a major Allied air offensive that would send bombers into China in the next ten days. When this was reported back to Japanese intelligence, the Japs were confident that an offensive on Rangoon would not begin anytime soon. And if they did, it would be without air support.

Jon's team knew that the Japanese did not expect the Allied invasion to begin for another thirty days. The Allied invasion would actually commence in five days. This gave Jon and his team just enough time to put together a plan to hit the headquarters building. He would still have to plant explosives around the building; not just inside the building.

On the eastern side of the city, Miles and his team of one OSS agent and six Shin operatives had discovered numerous weaknesses in the Japanese defenses around their logistics depot. The Japanese had been using most of their manpower to prepare their vehicles for moving replenishment supplies to the Japanese perimeter once the battle started. Their fleet of trucks was loaded and ready to move once the Allied offensive began. Over three hundred vehicles, which included a mixture of Type 94 six-wheeled trucks and Type 97 four-wheeled trucks, Type 95 mini trucks, and an assortment of jeeps and personnel carriers had been fueled and loaded with ammunition and supplies. In the early morning hours, between 0200 hours and 0400 hours, there was hardly a Jap visible in the depot. Miles saw an opportunity and began probing inside the Japanese depot.

Henri and his team had been planning the capture of the Japanese detention center on the northeast side of the city. Because of the increase in readiness in the Japanese fortifications, many of the military police, assigned to the detention center, had been transferred to the combat units. This left only two dozen Jap MPs to guard a detention center with twelve hundred civilian detainees; twelve during each shift. Henri was planning to take out half of the guards with his Shin operative using only knives. The remaining guards, posted in their twenty-foot bamboo towers, would have to be taken with Thompsons. They couldn't use hand grenades because they could send shrapnel into the bamboo huts and wound or kill civilians. The dozen guards in the barracks would be taken with satchel charges because their barracks were a hundred yards from the compound. The Shin operatives, Henri knew, were masters of stealth. If for some reason things went awry with the initial assault, he would still have close to two hundred Shin guerillas deployed around the detention center. However, Henri was meticulous in his planning and thought of everything, but he still had his doubts. "Damn it, Preston, you and your Mr. Kilroy. I wish I'd never heard of him," Henri said out loud.

The morning of the raid, all three teams were in place. Jon waited until the Japanese guards took their 0300-hour break and then made his move.

Jon dressed in black clothing and his war makeup on, moved from the vegetable stand and eased up to the cannon. He placed a cartridge of gunpowder and twelve pounds of ball bearing packed in burlap down the gun. Jon then used the rammer to push the charge into the back of the chamber. At the same time, two Shin agents slipped silently to the east and west sides of the headquarters building and planted forty pounds of C-3 plastic explosives in the two maintenance accesses beneath the building. Two more Shin operatives also moved and place forty-pound charges on the side of the communications building and behind the bushes surrounding the two smaller building on either side of the headquarters. Their explosive charges were set to go off at 0615 hours, to inflict even more damage when troops would rush to scene of the devastation caused by the grapeshot charge and exploding headquarters building. Ten minutes after they had started, Jon and the Shin operatives were moving to their next objective; the Japanese barracks.

They moved into an alley and headed two blocks north where they collected more satchels of explosives. After another two blocks, they began placing C-3 charges around the Japanese barracks and under the front steps. As one of the Shin agents was placing his charge, a Japanese sentry came around the corner of the building. Jon was watching the scene unfold from twenty-five yards away. There was nothing he could do but pray. The Shin agent was too far away to use his knife, so he charged the sentry head on. Before the sentry could react with his rifle, the Shin was upon him and slamming his head into the sentry's solar plexus. With the sentry out of wind, the Shin wrapped his right arm around the sentry's neck and snapped it with his left. He dragged the sentry into the alley, placed him behind some wooden crates, and covered him with trash strewn about the alley. He then walked across the street and headed back to the safe house.

Jon was astonished at the quickness and efficiency that the Shin had reacted and killed the Jap sentry. The OSS had certainly trained the agent well. *I couldn't have done it any better*, Jon thought.

At 0555 hours, five Japanese soldiers were standing in formation next to the cannon. A lieutenant, in charge of the color guard, ordered his sergeant, the chief of the cannon, to proceed. The sergeant then ordered a cannoneer to swab the bore, and ram the load. He ordered a second cannoneer to prime the cannon. Once everyone was back in formation, he ordered a third cannoneer to stand by to fire the piece.

At precisely 0600 hours, with the headquarters staff assembled on the porch, the bugler played reveille. One of the flag bearers raised the Japanese flag. When it reached the apex of the pole, the sergeant gave the order to fire, and his cannoneer pulled the lanyard.

A half second later, the commander and fifteen officers and enlisted staff were lying dead or wounded on the headquarter porch; their bodies shredded by the ball bearings. It took several seconds for the excess smoke to clear before the cannon crew could fully see the mayhem. The lieutenant in charge of the cannon shouted the alarm, and a klaxon began to sound.

As Japanese soldiers responded to the klaxon, the three barracks disintegrated into balls of fire. Japanese soldiers that had gotten out of the building and down the street were knocked to the ground. Others that had just exited the barracks were killed by the shock wave that ruptured every organ in their body.

Jon watched as Japanese fire brigades hastened into the chaos. Within ten minutes over a hundred Japanese soldiers had descended on the headquarters building helping those that were still alive. At 0615 hours, the last charges exploded killing most of the soldiers in the vicinity. The head of the dragon had been severed.

After the last charges went off, Jon and the Shin operatives began slipping down an alley towards their safe house. After they had moved a block, they were jumped by three Jap soldiers. The Shin operative had seen the Japs first. He pulled his weapon, fired, and killed two of the Japs. When Jon raised his .45 automatic, he was shot in his left shoulder by the third Japanese soldier. As Jon was falling to the ground, he fired his automatic and killed the Jap. When he hit the ground, he passed out.

As the mayhem was playing out downtown, the airport came under siege. Two hundred Kachin guerrillas penetrated the airport defenses, killed all but a few Japanese soldiers who ran away in the darkness, and captured the power plant. At 0630 hours, the first of the thirty C-47 transports began dropping the British Third Commando Brigade. An hour later, all seven hundred and fifty commandos were dug in around the Rangoon airport waiting on the Gurkha Rifles to arrive.

On the other side of town, Miles and three teams of operatives entered through the rusted supply depot perimeter fence and planted their explosives among the fueled trucks using sixty-minute pencil fuse. A fourth team entered and planted explosives at the communications building.

Miles's fifth team of twenty Shin guerillas, led by a native OSS lieutenant, penetrated the massive fuel storage depot south of the Eden Street jetty. By the time the teams had finished, fifteen Japanese soldiers were dead. They exited the fuel depot at 0555 hours. At 0605 hours, explosions rocked the wharf five blocks north of the fuel depot as one of the two Jap patrol boats exploded, while it was being fueled. Two Shin agents had penetrated the wharf defenses using the Irrawaddy. They used a satchel charge to blow the boat. The other Jap patrol boat was still on patrol.

The three Jap shore batteries around Monkey Point were quickly dispatched by an OSS team but not before one of the batteries discovered the six Higgins assault craft with Kachin rangers. The third battery took out the lead boat with twenty-five rangers.

In the Andaman Sea, Fifteenth Corps had already been transitioned to the LSTs and LCUs and were now being led up the channel by Captain Ahab in the *Pequod*. As the flotilla reached Monkey Point, the remaining Japanese patrol boats came out the Karnaphuli River and sprayed the *Pequod* with machine gun fire. Five Shin operatives died from .30-caliber fire before Captain Ahab's M1919 machine gun responded and ended its attack.

When all hell broke loose downtown, Henri's team attacked the four machine gun positions at the internment camp. A sudden burst of fire from a Japanese .30-caliber machine gun caught Henri by surprise sending lead in his direction. Henri rolled sideways but not before one of the .30-caliber bullets has grazed his leg.

A Japanese soldier trying to lob a grenade at his attackers took a round in his chest. His grenade flew through the door of one of the huts and landed under the cot of a sleeping child. When it exploded, shrapnel exited his abdomen taking most of his internal organs with it. Blood and body parts had been scattered all over the room.

After the fight ended, Henri entered the hut where the grenade had exploded. A young girl was on her knees next to the dead boy. When she saw Henri, she jumped up and wrapped her arms around Henri's waist crying. "Why did my brother have to die?" she asked. Henri picked the girl up in his arms and held her tightly, feeling the pain of her loss. It could have easily been his son or daughter. With tears streaming down his face, he handed the young girl to a European woman standing next to him. When he left, he began calling for his wife, Mae. It was a large compound, and it took him thirty minutes to find her and his children.

When Mae saw Henri, she ran to him. She grabbed him and began crying uncontrollably. After finally letting go of Mae, Henri kneeled down and hugged his two children. Now everyone was crying.

CHAPTER 41

ABOARD THE *ANNE MARIE* INDIAN OCEAN

When Jon woke up, he was in a small room. Sitting in a chair next to his bed was Camille. She stroked his black hair gently when she noticed that he was awake.

"It's good to have you back," Camille said.

"Where am I?" Jon asked still groggy from his last morphine injection.

"You're on the *Anne Marie*, Jon. We are headed out to sea."

"Miles, Henri, how are they?"

"They're doing fine, Jon. They're in separate cabins. You're in my cabin."

"Did anyone else get hurt?"

"Henri was grazed in his leg by a bullet. But he's doing great. It only took six stitches to close the wound. His family is with him."

Before Jon could ask another question, Captain Dubois knocked on the door and entered the cabin.

"Well, it's about time you came around. How are you feeling, Jon?" Captain Dubois asked.

"I'm alive, that's what's important. And I couldn't have a better nurse. How long will I be out of action?"

"Well, according to the doc who patched you up, at least three months to heal and another month to get your strength back," Captain Dubois said.

"Are you taking me back to Calcutta?"

"No, Jon, it looks like you're stuck on the *Anne Marie* for at least a week or two then we'll take you to Trincomalee. But we've got an army nurse on board and Camille to take care of you until then. Your only job right now is to heal."

"How did I rate this good treatment?"

"The orders came from General Marshall himself. Of course, if you want to question his judgment, I can send him a message," Captain Dubois said.

"I'll defer to the general's good judgment. Can I get something to eat?" Jon asked.

"I thought you'd never ask. How about some poached eggs on toast with juice and coffee?" Captain Dubois said.

Jon lay in bed for another day before the restlessness caught up with him.

"Can I get up and try walking?" Jon asked the nurse standing next to the bed.

"Absolutely, let me get Camille to help you. We've got a break in the weather. You can probably go out on the aft deck and get some sun," Lieutenant Janella Garner said.

When they arrived on deck, Henri and Miles were there. Miles was sunning, and Henri was playing with his children. It made Jon's heart warm to see Henri with his family. Henri was all smiles.

"Welcome back to the living, mate," Miles said as he walked over to Jon.

"How well did the mission go?" Jon asked Miles.

"One hundred percent successful; that job you did on the headquarters was a masterpiece," Miles stated.

"Did we lose any Shin operatives?" Jon asked.

"We lost half a dozen on the assault of the detention center. Ten Kachin rangers were lost in one of the Higgins's boats and fifteen wounded, and we lost five Shin operatives on Captain Ahab's boat," Miles said.

"What about Rangoon, is it in Allied hands?" Jon asked.

"It took four days to dislodge all of the Japanese, but it's secure now. Most of the general staff that survived your attack fled to Thailand," Miles said.

"Do you think they'll keep us together or break us up when we return to Calcutta?" Jon asked.

"Are you kidding? We've got a Jap agent in Calcutta looking for us. He's our next mission," Miles said.

"While you're healing, we are going to be busy in Ceylon going over all the intelligence being collected by your CIC on this guy. So don't go soft on us," Henri said as he walked away.

"I should be well enough by December," Jon said.

"And you should be playing professional baseball by this time next year," Captain Dubois said as he walked out onto the deck.

Jon was about to say something else when the sound of an aircraft caught his ear. He turned and looked north and saw a PBY on final approach for landing.

"That will be Colonel Sage. He's bringing us the latest intelligence on Dragon as well as your team's Silver Star citations and Purple Hearts," Captain Dubois said.

Jon stood up and whispered something into Camille's ears. When he finished, she nodded her head and kissed him.

"Just one other question, Captain," Jon said grinning. "Will you marry Camille and me?"

"It would be my honor, Jon," Captain Dubois said.

Jon looked at Miles and Henri who were already grinning from ear to ear. "Will the two of you serve as my best men?"

CHAPTER 42

CALCUTTA, INDIA

It had taken Japanese intelligence weeks of searching the countryside around Hintok Bridge to find anyone associated with the Allied team that had destroyed the bridge and ammunition train and rescued the Allied POWs. Their only lead was an old Kachin tribesman, who had heard of an American that the Kachin people were calling Cobra. The American they called Cobra, he told them, had stepped on and killed a king cobra with only his boot.

Unlike the intelligence team at the Japanese Embassy, Akemi Nakada did not dismiss the Kachin story as fantasy. Someone who could kill a cobra with just his foot must be highly trained in martial arts. This had been the only lead on the allied agent until they had gone back and researched all the intelligence reports over the past year.

There were three reports from the Burma and India regions where an exceptional agent or team of agents had penetrated Japanese defenses and kidnapped a high-ranking officer. Another had blown up a munitions warehouse. There was one rather spectacular report about one of their top espionage teams that had gone missing in Chittagong. The report stated that as many as four American agents were involved, and they were possibly being transported in a luxury yacht named *Anne Marie*. This was the only solid lead that they could use.

Upon direction from Akemi, the Japanese Embassy sent a message to their field agents to find the *Anne Marie*. Two weeks went by before a message was received from Ceylon. The *Anne Marie* had been seen in Trincomalee, in September, but it was no longer there. Akemi drafted a message to the agent in Ceylon to look for any Americans at Fort Frederick and China Bay.

Akemi received a reply a week later. Two Americans had been seen at the SOE headquarters. One was recovering from a wound. Akemi's next message was to get photographs and forward to the embassy in Calcutta.

"You may finally have a solid lead, Akemi," Akiko said.

"We could have had this information months ago, Akiko, if we had not been sent on the mission to Saigon," Akemi remarked.

"You're right, Akemi, but we'll corner and kill this American agent. It is our destiny, as the lightning and fire dragons, to become the greatest of all Japanese agents," Akiko stated.

"Your ego is too big, sister. If you do not control it, it may get us killed," Akemi said sternly.

"Do not mistake ego for confidence, Akemi. We are the brightest and smartest of all the Japanese agents. Master Hotaka said so himself," Akiko replied.

Akemi had to reflect; she and Akiko were outstanding agents, but Akiko was reckless at times. Akemi had always been the stabilizing factor in their training and on their missions. Twice in the last two years, Akiko had nearly been killed when she under estimated her opponents. Had it not been for Akemi, Akiko would have died.

Now they were going after an American agent that was stronger and possibly more cunning than they were. Master Hotaka had also trained her and her sister to kill snakes with their feet. *This agent*, thought Akemi, *was not the typical American cowboy; he was a highly trained and dangerous adversary.*

Akemi didn't think that the Americans had the time to train their agents in the martial arts; that took years. But she made a mental note to check with their embassy in Washington and find out just what kind of training the American agents were receiving. Akemi did not believe in leaving anything to chance. She would dig deeper.

It took four weeks before they received photographs from Trincomalee. One of the American's was in his late forties and walked with a cane. The second American was young and had an arm in a sling. A second photograph of the young American was a close-up and showed his eyes. *Yes*, Akemi thought, *these eyes are alert and reflect intelligence.*

Akemi showed the photographs to her sister who looked at them with abeyance.

"This could be anyone, Akemi. Just because he's at Fort Frederick doesn't mean he's an agent," Akiko said.

"That is true, sister, but I am following the leads. Look, Akiko," Akemi said, "Hintok Bridge, Chittagong, Great Nicobar Island, and Rangoon. All were missions carried out by the Allies without a trace as to who did it. All carried out by an individual or a team of highly trained and effective agents."

"Yes, there seems to be a pattern," Akiko said.

"In the report on the raid at Rangoon, most of the headquarters' staff and General Takahashi were killed using a field cannon that their color guard fired every morning at reveille. The person who planned these raids and the person who is responsible for uncovering our agents in Chittagong is brilliant," Akemi said.

"We know that there are American OSS and CIC and British SOE squadrons in Calcutta. We need to go through all the photos that our agents have taken of the Americans and British. If we find his photo, then maybe he is stationed out of Calcutta," Akiko remarked.

Akiko was right for once. Akemi thought, scolding herself as she wrote a note to their intelligence chief. *I should have thought of that a week ago.*

Within an hour, over a thousand photographs were brought into their secure planning room. It took nearly two days to find the multiple photos of the American with the alert eyes. Oddly enough, he was photographed with the same two men in more than a half a dozen shots.

After reading through a new group of intelligence reports, Akemi found another clue. It was reported that one American was wounded in the Rangoon raid in August. Four Americans boarded the *Anne Marie* and one of them was on a stretcher. However, no photos were taken, and there were no descriptions of the people who boarded.

Not quite a dead end, but a small hint, Akemi thought, *maybe, just maybe another piece to this complicated puzzle.*

Akemi wrote another note for the embassy intelligence chief to provide photos of the American to all their agents in Calcutta. She included a request to keep an eye out for the *Anne Marie* at the Port of Calcutta.

Two months went by without a trace of the American.

CHAPTER 43

FORT FREDERICK, CEYLON

Jon's shoulder wound had healed much faster than his army doctors had anticipated. The bullet that hit him had passed clean through without hitting any bone. Despite the constant ache in his shoulder, he began a moderate exercise program of running and lifting. Though still in pain, Jon quickly brought himself physically back to his old self. He divided his time between the SOE headquarters at Fort Frederick and a beach house on the northeast end of the military reservation.

Henri and his wife and children had also taken a cottage on the Fort Frederick beach a quarter mile away from Jon. Henri's wound would have healed in a month's time, but he got an infection and had to go through a painful process of scraping the infection out of the wound and stitching it up again. In late September, Henri's children began attending school at Fort Frederick, and his wife, Mae, had procured a teaching position at the base's middle school.

By the end of October, the Allied Fourteenth Army had built up their forces, and now they were pounding the Japanese. The Japanese were losing major battles and were retreating south and east. The Japanese forces that did fight the Allied Army often fought to the last man.

Jon finally passed his medical exam and received his doctor's approval to return to combat status. Although Jon still had a week's leave due for his official honeymoon, he was anxious to get back into the field. Camille used her best seductive voice to sway him into using every day of his leave. But Jon was adamant about getting back to work.

Camille had been temporarily assigned to the SOE headquarters at Fort Frederick. She served as an OSS liaison to assist Jon's team in going through the hundreds of intelligence reports that might lead to uncovering the Japanese agent called Dragon. Since the discovery of Dragon, the US Army CIC agents had been working overtime to locate the Japanese agent.

From April to October, CIC agents had been looking for a male Japanese agent. It was Miles who picked up on the strategy to look for a woman.

"What in hell's name makes you think the Japs would use a woman to track us down?" Henri asked.

"For the simple reason that we haven't been able to find any clue to a male agent," Miles replied. "And because most dragons in Japanese folklore are females."

"And exactly why wouldn't the Japanese use a female agent, Henri," Camille asked.

"It just doesn't make any sense," Henri said. "There's no way a female agent could take the three of us down."

"Maybe they don't know about the three of you. Maybe they only know about the guy the Kachin call Cobra," Camille stated.

"Miles might be on to something, Henri," Jon remarked.

"If you look at the last report on the message evaluated by the signals folks in Hawaii, the Japs used a word in that message that's usually has a feminine connotation. That could be our first clue. The Japanese aren't infallible when it comes to mistakes," Jon said.

"And what if it's all Jap counter-intelligence and misinforma-tion?" Henri asked.

"Well, Henri, we'll have to wait for another Japanese message to be intercepted. If it was a mistake, I would imagine the

Japanese will try to cover their tracks by emphasizing a masculine phrase more than once in their messages. If they do, I think we can assume that Dragon might be a woman," Jon stated.

"I think we need to ask the CIC to send photos of all the females taken at the Japanese consulate and of all the female contacts of the Japanese male employees," Camille suggested.

"That's a good idea, Camille. Can you draft a message and send it out? Maybe we can get the photos sent on the next ferry flight," Miles said.

"Is your arm too sore to write, Jon," Camille said with concern in her voice.

"Only a little bit. I spent thirty minutes on the range this morning firing my Colt. I still need to build up more strength in my firing arm," Jon said.

Several days later, a large package arrived for Jon's team. When Miles opened it, there were at least five hundred photographs of Asian, European, Eurasian, and Indian women.

"Great, we're looking for a needle in a haystack," Henri said.

"We always were, Henri," Jon replied.

"So we're starting all over then," Henri remarked.

"Looks like it, mate," Miles said.

"Ok, let's go through the stack and narrow the group down to twenty," Jon said.

"Using what criteria?" Henri asked.

Jon thought a moment then said, "Look at their eyes. Find the ones with the most alert-looking eyes."

After two days, the group had the number of photos narrowed down to twelve women. They sent the photos back to Calcutta and asked the CIC to investigate. Twenty-four agents were assigned to watch, photograph, and follow the twelve women. After ten days, the CIC narrowed down the number to five, who did not exhibit redundant daily patterns or bad habits that you would readily notice.

The CIC had done great work. They discovered two Soviet agents, and one MI6 operative that the CIC and OSS was not aware of. The two remaining women became the subject of intense CIC study. Both had strong Japanese features but with European eyes. And except for how their hair was cut, they looked remarkably alike.

When Jon received the photographs, he thought he was looking at the same woman. As he studied the photos closer, he began to pick out subtle differences. One had a small mole on her left cheek, the other a mole on her chin. *They're twins*, John thought.

"Guys, look at these photos, and tell me what you see," Jon said.

"They're the same woman, mate," Miles said.

"I agree," Henri stated.

"Look again, closer this time," Jon said.

Miles and Henri looked at the details.

"Oh, my God," Miles said.

"They're twins," Henry stated. "Look at the moles and the subtle difference in their chins"

"Yes. You've got double trouble," Camille remarked.

"I think it's time to move back to Calcutta and get on with the hunt guys," Jon said. "We should leave for Calcutta the day after tomorrow."

"Jon, can't this wait until after Christmas?" Camille asked.

Jon knew why Camille wanted to postpone the move. She was thinking about Henri and his family. Plus, this was their first Christmas together.

"I should have realized that," Jon said. "On second thought, tomorrow's Christmas eve. Let's wait until the twenty-seventh before we head back. Miles, you can head home. You can probably catch a flight this afternoon, and meet us in Alipore, on the twenty-eighth."

"I'd love that, Jon. Thanks for thinking about me," Miles said.

"It's been nearly four months since we've seen MacKenzie. You think he's still a jerk?" Henri asked.

"One can only hope," Jon said.

"Leopards don't change their spots, mate," Miles replied.

"Why don't we head back to the bungalow, and you can tell me all about MacKenzie," Camille said.

"Why do I get the impression that we won't be talking that much?" Jon whispered in her ear.

CHAPTER 44

CALCUTTA, INDIA

"MacKenzie will be gone until January 10," Jon told Miles and Henri.

"Aw, and I wanted to hug him and wish him a Merry Christmas," Miles said.

"And I wanted to give him a stocking full of leeches," Henri added.

"I think you will discover a new and refreshed MacKenzie when he returns," Jon said.

"Yeah, right," Henri said.

"Here's the latest stack of photos and CIC reports. Let's go through these and see if there's anything new," Jon said.

The CIC reports were comprehensive, but the CIC agents had lost track of the women they were tailing, and one CIC agent had gone missing. There were several reports of Asians taking photographs close to the OSS and SOE detachments and on the docks. One was apprehended, but he immediately took a sodium cyanide pill and died within minutes.

"There is some serious spying going on around here, Jon," Miles said.

"Yes. I suspect that they know who we are or at least who I am," Jon remarked.

"Here's a report of a photographer caught at Fort Frederick yesterday after we left for Calcutta. The spy had a photograph of Jon on him," Henri said.

"Looks like you're right, Jon, they know who you are," Miles said.

"I think we need to assume that they know all of us. I suspect that they did what we would have done and went back and reviewed all their intelligence reports from the last year and found clues. They probably had a report of the *Anne Marie* leaving Rangoon with three Europeans and another being carried aboard on a stretcher. From there it would be simple to track the whereabouts of the *Anne Marie*. That's what led them to Fort Frederick. If I were Dragon, Calcutta would be the next place I would check. We're dealing with some seriously clever Japanese agents," Jon stated.

"Jon, as soon as they find us here, they're going to act," Miles said calmly.

"Then we need to write the next act and set the stage," Jon said.

"Like Chittagong?" Henri asked.

"Yes, but we must be more clever and more careful. Chittagong cost us lives," Jon remarked.

"What do you suggest?" Miles asked.

"We need to alert the CIC, OSS, and SOE to the presence of these twins, and we need a SOE team to shadow us. They won't make a move with the extra protection. We also need the *Anne Marie* in Calcutta," Jon said.

"I like where you're taking this," Miles said.

On the 5th of January, the *Anne Marie* docked at a yacht basin in the Port of Calcutta. Jon met Captain Dubois on the yacht and explained his strategy. After their meeting, Camille walked into the dining room. Jon was absolutely shocked to see her. Captain Dubois noticed Jon's surprise.

"Jon, Camille was ordered back into my service after you left for Calcutta. I also have two new agents I'd like you to meet," Captain Dubois said.

"Captain, I do not think that this is a good idea. Camille's presence could distract me, and that could prove to be fateful to my team," Jon said.

"Or, it could heighten your awareness and prove to be an asset. With me around, you might not be as reckless as you were in Chittagong," Camille countered.

Jon thought a minute before he spoke. "You're right, Camille, my eagerness to catch the spies caused me to be reckless and put you and the other girls in danger. It cost Jacqueline her life. But I don't want a repeat performance of Chittagong," Jon stated.

"Jon, we understand. We can take precautions to limit the girls' exposure. I believe we can use them to our advantage," Captain Dubois said.

"Jon, these twin dragons are very dangerous. You said so yourself. When they see four women aboard the *Anne Marie*, we want them to think that we are there for pleasure, especially when we act like ditsy blondes. And believe me, we can act this up," Camille stated.

"I think I see where you are taking this. Four young women in bathing suits having cocktails on the aft deck, shopping sprees in downtown Calcutta, and lunches at the Polo Club or the Ambassador Hotel. This could work to our advantage," Jon said.

"Of course, it will. It was my idea, Jon," Camille said.

"Camille, it could also backfire. What if the twin dragons decide to kidnap one of you and torture you for information," Jon said.

"Jon, I will have two male agents and a driver taking them wherever they go. Plus, they will always be carrying an automatic in their purse and on their thighs," Captain Dubois said.

"And a stiletto," Camille added.

"I don't like it, but I'll have to live with it, won't I, Camille?" Jon asked.

"That's right, Jon. I'd never let you live it down if you excluded me. You'll just have to visit me here," Camille said in her most sultry voice.

"All right," Jon said, "but I can't have you seen with me until this is over. We can't afford to give them any kind of leverage whatsoever."

CHAPTER 45

CALCUTTA, INDIA

When Jon met with Colonel Ronnie Ray at the CIC detachment, the news was not good. Their missing agent had been found with his throat cut in an alley in downtown Calcutta. The two women had gone underground.

"We lost them last week, Jon," Colonel Ray said.

"They're on to us, Ronnie. Probably were all along. These women could be the best agents in Asia. Did you research what I requested last week?" Jon asked.

"Yes, we did, and it's disturbing. Two consular personnel admitted to having a relationship with the women over a twelve-month period. Five American and British officers have gone missing in the last six months. We interviewed all their friends and discovered that each of the officers had been with these women," Colonel Ray stated.

"Spying 101 for women, Colonel," Jon said. "Seduce your enemy and get information. Were any of the officers in intelligence?" Jon asked.

"A lieutenant from the CIC," Colonel Ray answered. "The rest were in logistics and transportation."

"Any sabotage on the wharves or convoys?" Jon asked.

"Yes, quite a few. Two ammunition barges headed to Cox's Bazar; one in July and one in August. Three supply convoys going overland to Myitkyina were ambushed by Burmese rebels, one in May, and two in June." Colonel Ray said.

"You said transportation; air or ground?" Jon asked.

"One from each," Colonel Ray said.

"Has there been any unusual Japanese air activity?" Jon asked.

"I'm sure you heard about General Wingate's plane being shot down last March," Colonel Ray stated.

"Yes, that was a highly classified mission he was on, too. Did anyone in the American Embassy know about his flight?"

"Yes, several, and both had been with one of the twins," Colonel Ray answered.

"Anything else?" Jon questioned.

"We had several bombing missions intercepted by Japanese fighters where there hasn't been any previous Jap air cover," Colonel Ray said.

"What about OSS teams in the field? Have any been reported missing or killed?" Jon asked.

"Around Saigon, we have lost six OSS and two SOE agents. Do you really think that these two women had anything to do with those agents going missing, too?" Colonel Ray asked.

"It's not out of the question, Colonel. These two women are probably like my team. They work only special missions, and they're lethal as hell," Jon remarked.

"How are you going to stop them, Jon?" Colonel Ray asked.

"I'm not sure yet. We'll come up with something. Are there any special convoys or munitions barges being moved anytime soon or VIPs inbound?" Jon asked.

"Lord Mountbatten, General Kenneth Wolfe, General Claire Chennault, and Ralph Block, the representative of the Office of War Information in India, are meeting here in two weeks. The War Department is hosting a dinner and dance for them at the Ambassador Hotel. Do you think that they will be in danger? If so, I can try to get them to move it to New Delhi," Colonel Ray stated.

"This has probably been planned for a while. They'd never go for that. I've met General Wolfe and General Chennault; they're fearless and stubborn. But it does give us an opportunity to set a trap, Colonel," Jon said.

"Whatever you need in support, Jon, just ask," Colonel Ray said.

"Colonel, I do need to know if any of your men have restaurant or serving experience," Jon said.

"I don't know, but I'll find out and get back with you. Can we meet in two days?" Colonel Ray asked.

"Yes, and find out how many waiters, bus boys, bartenders, and wine stewards they will be using for this banquet," Jon said.

It took Colonel Ray three days to accumulate the information Jon wanted. After their meeting, Jon began to formulate a plan.

On January 10, Lieutenant Colonel MacKenzie was back in his office asking questions about what Jon and his team were up to. Jon was very open with MacKenzie and explained about the Japanese agents called Dragon.

"Yes, I remember Colonel Arvin showing me the intercept when he came back from Myitkyina, in July. Do you really think you can spring a trap on these two agents?" Lieutenant Colonel MacKenzie asked.

"I certainly do, Colonel. And I'm going to need your help." Jon said.

"Anything you need, Jon," Lieutenant Colonel MacKenzie said.

"I need you to contact the War Department in New Delhi, and make sure that they invite the French Indochina delegation to this event." Jon said.

"What are you planning, Jon?" Lieutenant Colonel MacKenzie asked.

"I believe that the twins will be at the banquet, possibly as the guests of two of the delegations' intelligence officers," Jon stated.

"Jon, do you think that Ralph Block and Lord Mountbatten will allow you to conduct a mission at this banquet?" Colonel Ray asked.

"With two of the most dangerous Japanese agents in Asia possibly coming to it, I don't see how they can refuse. But I'll get permission from the chief of staff and an executive order from the president just in case," Jon stated.

"Anything else I can do for you, Jon?" Lieutenant Colonel MacKenzie asked.

"If I can think of anything else, I'll bring it up in two days," Jon said.

After MacKenzie left, Miles and Henri looked at Jon with bewilderment in their eyes.

"What?" Jon asked.

"What the heck is going on with MacKenzie, mate," Miles asked.

"I told you he would be a new person after his vacation, didn't I?" Jon stated.

CHAPTER 46
CALCUTTA, INDIA

Jon waited until the afternoon of the banquet to meet with the War Department representative, Ralph Block. Jon explained the situation and showed him the orders from the army chief of staff and the president, however, Block was not pleased. Jon did not give him any detail about the Japanese agents.

"Agent Preston, I will comply with the orders, but I am not happy about it. Can you guarantee the safety of Lord Mountbatten, General Wolfe, and General Chennault?" Ralph Block asked.

"No, sir, I cannot. But I can guarantee that they will be in greater danger if my team is not there," Jon said adamantly.

"Can you tell me what you have planned?" Ralph Block asked.

"I'm sorry, sir, but that would compromise our security protocols," Jon stated.

Block shook his head and said, "God help us if any of these people are killed."

When the French Indochina delegation arrived at the Ambassador Hotel, Akemi was being escorted by an assistant to the Indochina Consular. Akiko was not present.

Jon and Captain Dubois were sitting two tables away from the French Indochina delegation, facing Akemi. Camille and Kathleen were sitting with their backs to the delegation. Jon noticed a brief smile on Akemi's face when their eyes met; Jon nodded his head slightly.

In the kitchen, a native worker was opening the back door to the alley and taking out a large basket of vegetable debris. As she lifted the basket into a larger trash bin, an arm grabbed her from behind and snapped her neck. Akiko dragged her body across the alley and placed her under a stack of broken down cardboard boxes. Akiko then entered the kitchen and closed the door. She was dressed as a server.

Henri was working as a wine steward and Miles as a bartender. When the servers came from the kitchen carrying large bowls, they watched carefully as the twenty servers began placing salad on the guests' plates. The servers returned to the kitchen to retrieve more salad and came back out. Henri noticed something familiar in one of the servers. Finally, it hit him. *The chin, it's the same chin in the photo only the face is darker*, Henri said to himself.

When the servers passed Henri on the way back to the kitchen, Henri caught the eye of one of the SOE agents acting as a server. Henri gave him the alert signal and followed him into the kitchen.

Henri's actions did not go unnoticed. Both Camille and Kathleen saw Henri's signal. Kathleen excused herself and left the table. She headed for one of the restrooms just off of the kitchen but slipped through the open double doors into the kitchen. She entered just as an OSS agent was approaching one of the female servers.

Akiko had noticed the male server approaching her with his hand behind his back. When he was within four feet, she turned and stabbed him in the stomach with a slender stiletto. Henri was closing on her when she drew a pistol. Before Akiko could fire, Kathleen fired her silenced Beretta. Akiko was hit in the throat. When she fell to the floor, Henri kicked the weapon away from her hand.

"That's for my sister, bitch," Kathleen said as she stuffed the .32 caliber pistol in her handbag and headed to the bathroom.

Akiko was stunned and dying. Her only thoughts before she slipped into unconsciousness were, *How could this happen? I'm too good for this to happen.*

By the time Kathleen returned to her table, the servers were returning with the entre. Both Jon and Captain Dubois noticed that she had been crying.

"Is she dead?" Camille whispered.

"Yes," Kathleen answered.

"You?" Camille asked.

"Yes," Kathleen said.

Camille had guessed that Kathleen had shot the Japanese agent because she smelled the faint trace of gunpowder that was lingering in Kathleen's purse.

"Anyone hurt?" Camille asked.

"Yes, one of our OSS agents was stabbed," Kathleen answered.

Camille put her arms around Kathleen and hugged her. *One down, one to go,* Camille thought.

Jon and Captain Dubois didn't know what was going on, but he knew something had caused Kathleen to cry. When Jon looked around and didn't see Henri, he became aware that something had happened. As the wine stewards began serving more wine, Jon eased out of his chair and headed toward the kitchen. Henri was heading out the door as Jon entered the kitchen.

"What happened?" Jon asked.

"One of the Japanese twins was a server. She stabbed an OSS agent. Kathleen saved my life, Jon. She killed the bitch before she could shoot me," Henri replied.

"Where is she?" Jon asked.

"One of the OSS agents dragged her body into the alley," Henri replied.

"How is our agent?" Jon asked.

"He's in serious condition—stabbed in the stomach. Another agent is getting him a medical team, and then they'll take him to the army hospital."

"All right, make sure they take the Japs body away. We don't want this to go public," Jon said as he turned to leave.

Akemi Nakada was on her way to the restroom and was standing twenty feet away when her sister was shot. It took all her strength and will to not react when Akiko fell to the floor. She knew Akiko was dead.

"The Americans must pay. I will kill Lord Mountbatten, and the American agents will be blamed," Akemi said to herself. She was about to head to the restroom when one of the American agents came out the double doors.

Henri nodded his head at Jon and went to attend to the wounded OSS agent and check on the medical team. When Jon came through the double door, Akemi was standing in the hallway with tears streaming down her cheeks. She was pointing a silenced pistol directly at Jon's head.

"You killed my sister, didn't you," Akemi said.

"An occupational hazard in our business," Jon replied.

"We tracked you from Chittagong to Fort Frederick. We figured you would be here. You are very clever Agent...?" Akemi said.

"Preston," Jon answered.

"Well, Agent Preston—"

Before Akemi could finish her sentence, Jon activated the derringer attached to his forearm and fired twice. One shot hit her in the lung, the other near her heart. As Akemi fell to the floor, she raised her gun and fired. The bullet grazed Jon's head.

Jon knelt beside her and propped her against the hallway wall; blood was flowing down his face from the wound.

"I guess it's only fitting that my two sisters and me die together. We are Samurai," Akemi said struggling to breathe as blood bubbled between her lips.

Jon held her hand as she breathed her last breath. He continued staring at the beautiful Japanese agent until Henri and another

OSS agent walked up behind him. Jon let go of her hand and stood up.

"We heard the shots," Henri said.

"She had the drop on me. She should have killed me, but I think she wanted me to kill her instead. Oh, crap, she said two sisters," Jon said.

Jon jumped up and sprinted towards the large dining room. Before they could get through the hallway, they heard a scream and then a shot fired in the dining room. As they entered the dining room, Camille was leaning over the body of a server. When she got up, she had blood on her hands and dress.

"A server stabbed Kathleen and was about to shoot Lord Mountbatten. I killed her," Camille said with no emotion in her voice.

Jon rushed to the table where they had been sitting. Camille and Henri followed. Captain Dubois was sitting on the floor with Kathleen's head on his lap. She was bleeding badly and had already lost a lot of blood and was having trouble breathing, but she was still alive.

"A metal brace in the fabric-covered chair deflected the knife away from her heart and punctured a lung," Captain Dubois said.

A few minutes later, an army ambulance team on standby outside the hotel entered the banquet room hotel. After stabilizing Kathleen, they rushed her to the American Army hospital. Captain Dubois rode with her.

Thirty minutes later, Jon, Henri, Miles, and Camille were standing in the hotel manager's office. Lord Mountbatten was standing beside Ralph Block.

"It looks like you and your team saved my life, Agent Preston, and especially, this young lady," Lord Mountbatten said.

"Just doing what we are trained to do, sir," Jon replied.

"How is the young lady who was stabbed?" Lord Mountbatten asked.

"The knife punctured her lung. If they get her to the hospital in time, she will probably recover," Camille said.

"I understand that there were three Japanese agents," Lord Mountbatten said.

"Yes, sir, triplets. We only knew about two of them, though," Jon said.

"Well, I am very grateful. You will be hearing from me in the near future," Lord Mountbatten said as he shook the four agents' hands.

Under protest, Camille drove Jon to the American Army hospital. Henri and Miles stayed behind and supervised the removal of the bodies. The French Indochina delegation was ejected from the premises.

A week later, Jon and Camille were aboard the *Anne Marie* sailing down the Ganges toward the Indian Ocean. Jon's head was still bandaged, and Camille was doting after him like a mother hen.

"Jon, you've got to let me clean the wound and change your bandage," Camille said sternly.

Jon grabbed her around the waist. He gazed into her eyes, kissed her, and held her tight as they fell into bed.

"Now, about that honeymoon," Jon said.